Praise for Maya Linnell and

'Two big thumbs up for an authentic Aussie story.' Mercedes Maguire, *Daily Telegraph*

'Loved this book . . . such a delight from beginning to end.' Emma Babbington, *New Idea*

'Charming and enjoyable . . . fans of Maya's first novel will keenly enjoy this latest outing.' *Canberra Weekly*

'Pure escapism, with a plot twist you won't see coming.' *Lifestyle1 Magazine*

'A natural warmth oozes from the pages . . . a truly heart-warming read.' *Western District Farmer News*

'Engaging and distinctly Australian. A great country read.' Rick Whittle, ABC Wide Bay

'*Bottlebrush Creek* will keep you turning pages into the early hours of the next morning.' Bestselling author Tabitha Bird

'Everything you want in a rural romance: relatable characters, farm life, the sound of the ocean . . . and the perfect fixer-upper.' Bestselling author Fiona Lowe

'*Bottlebrush Creek* is a lovely reading experience.' Bestselling author Cassie Hamer

'Maya's deep understanding of living in country Australia and down-to-earth good humour give her story great authenticity. *Bottlebrush Creek* is a ripping good read.' *Australian Country*

'A beautiful story that illustrates the loves and lives of rural Australia.' Tanya Nellestein, *Hearts Talk* Magazine

'Heart-warming, funny and poignant, *Bottlebrush Creek* will capture your heart and imagination. An absolutely delightful and enjoyable read.' Blue Wolf Reviews

'A stellar follow-up . . . an incredibly modern and relatable tale.' 6PR Perth Tonight Book Club

Praise for Maya Linnell and *Wildflower Ridge*

Shortlisted for Favourite Australian Romance Author, Favourite Debut Romance Author and Favourite Small Town Romance in the Australian Romance Readers Awards 2019

'A sparkling entry into the rural romance arena.' *Canberra Weekly*

'You'll devour this rural read in one go.' *New Idea*

'Very authentic rural flavour, a surprise fast-paced ending, shows you can't deny what's in your heart.' Australian Romance Readers Association

'My favourite romance of 2019. A masterful and moving tale . . . her writing is flawless and very believable. Can't wait to see what's next!' SHE Society

'Idyllic . . . Maya Linnell tells a good yarn.' *Ruth* magazine— Queensland CWA

'Beautifully written with strong characters and a true depiction of life on a farm with all its trials, tribulations . . . love, family and laughter. I loved this book and didn't want it to end.' Beauty & Lace

'Five stars—a great addition to the rural family fiction with a dash of romance, a sophisticated plot, very convincing characters . . . a book you can't pass up.' Happy Valley Books

'What a fabulous debut. Moving and heartfelt . . . this one was a page turner. Five stars.' Helen, Family Saga Blogspot

'Familiar, comforting and warm—perfect for a winter's day read in front of the fire.' Blue Wolf Reviews

Bestselling rural fiction author Maya Linnell gathers inspiration from her rural upbringing and the small communities she has always lived in and loved. *Bottlebrush Creek* is her second novel, following *Wildflower Ridge*. Her new novel, *Magpie's Bend*, will be released in June 2021. A former country journalist and radio host, Maya also blogs for Romance Writers Australia, loves baking up a storm, tending to her rambling garden and raising three young bookworms. She writes to a soundtrack of magpies and chickens on a small property in country Victoria, where she lives with her family, their menagerie of farm animals and the odd tiger snake or two. For a regular slice of country living, follow Maya on social media or sign up to her monthly newsletter at mayalinnell.com.

MAYA LINNELL

Bottlebrush Creek

ALLEN&UNWIN
SYDNEY • MELBOURNE • AUCKLAND • LONDON

Allen & Unwin
83 Alexander Street
Crows Nest NSW 2065
Australia
Phone: (61 2) 8425 0100
Email: info@allenandunwin.com
Web: www.allenandunwin.com

 A catalogue record for this
book is available from the
National Library of Australia

ISBN 978 1 76087 960 0

Set in Sabon LT Pro by Bookhouse, Sydney
Printed and bound in Australia by Pegasus Media & Logistics

10 9 8

 The paper in this book is FSC® certified.
FSC® promotes environmentally responsible,
socially beneficial and economically viable
management of the world's forests.

To Jason, my owner–builder fella.

For building a life, a family and a house with me, and
helping me build my author dream, one chapter at a time.

One

Angie McIntyre dusted her hands on the polka-dotted apron, opened the oven and groaned. Instead of a gush of hot air that normally sent her curls into ringlets, it was cold in the dark and silent cavity. *Not again.* She twisted the temperamental temperature dial left and right, but no matter how hard she willed it to work, the oven didn't so much as hum.

Angie slammed the door shut and surveyed the mess in front of her. Clearing the bench full of ingredients would be easy enough but the cake would be ruined if she didn't get it into a hot oven soon.

The sound of her mobile ringtone cut through the quiet kitchen. As she hunted for it on the benchtop, a pile of magazines slipped to the ground. The glossy pics of grand kitchens and elaborate bathrooms fanned out across the floor, mocking the cramped space.

A cold breeze followed Angie down the corridor as she went in search of her phone. No amount of gap-filler had yet fixed the endless draughts in the sixties brick veneer, and pigs would fly before the landlord would make good on his promises to bring their Eden Creek rental into the twenty-first century.

Two little feet poked out from beneath the king-sized bed. Angie could hear snatches of conversation.

'Claudia Isobel Jones. Do you have Mummy's phone?'

Claudia's pink socks retreated, quickly replaced by a shock of blonde curls and the cheekiest grin this side of the South Australian border. Angie raised her eyebrows. The little girl handed over the phone, adding a handful of fluff-covered sultanas into Angie's outstretched palm for good measure, then ran down the hallway in a blur of sequins to escape a scolding.

'Rob?'

'Hey Ange, wondered how long it'd be till you realised she'd pinched your phone.'

'She gets that from you, sassy thing.'

'Fat chance of cheekiness being allowed in the Jones family. Must be the McIntyre in her,' he laughed. 'So, fancy a drive this arvo?'

'A drive? You'll have been travelling since 4 a.m. What happened to our quiet night in when you get home?' Angie frowned. Her chances of pulling off this impromptu birthday party were getting slimmer by the minute.

Rob laughed again. 'Thought you'd like a surprise, so get the ... ready ... home ...' His voice faded in and out before the reception failed altogether.

'Rob? Hello ... ?' Angie stared at the beeping phone. *I'm the one planning the surprise around here ...*

Back in the kitchen, she twisted the oven dial one last time. Still nothing. She hated the idea of letting Rob's birthday pass without a homemade cake and racked her brain for a Plan B.

'C'mon, Claud. Let's go next door and ask if we can borrow their oven again. Then it's tidying up time.' With the brimming cake tin in one hand, and Claudia's little fingers in the other, she glanced around the cramped rental. It was barely big enough for a couple, let alone a family, but if she gave the place a quick tidy while the cake baked and popped a few candles on, they'd have everything they needed to celebrate Rob's birthday.

The landscape of western Victoria whipped past the windscreen in a green blur. Freshly shorn sheep dotted the paddocks, their bright white wool catching the sunlight like coconut on a lamington, but Angie couldn't drag her eyes away from Rob Jones.

Rob's height was always more pronounced in her little hatchback. His dark hair almost touched the car roof and his legs were cramped underneath the steering wheel.

He'd barely stopped to take a breath since he'd pulled into the driveway, dumped his backpack on the porch, whisked them outside and pointed the car towards the coast.

'There's enough land to crop and run cattle. The bones of the place are sound. Owners upgraded the wiring a few years ago, so it's not a death trap like all the other houses we've looked at,' said Rob, his animated gaze switching between the road and her. 'Deadset winner!'

Angie couldn't help laughing. 'You've said that about every old place we've seen. Remember last time you were home? That dive in Macarthur? The real estate guy had to catch the front door when it fell off its hinges. And the floorboards in that "renovator's delight" in Allansford had more termites than timber.'

Angie smoothed the newspaper clipping in her lap. Rob had waved it around like a winning lottery ticket when he'd arrived home. With four bedrooms, two living areas and acreage, there'd be ample room, but by the look of the photograph, there was a lot of hard yakka required.

'They've used the phrase "fixer-upper" twice. That's code for downright awful.'

Rob took his large hand off the steering wheel to squeeze her knee. 'Wouldn't stay that way for long with the two of *us* on site.'

Small country towns blurred into one another as Rob took them down unfamiliar back roads and single-lane tracks. The ocean glimmered in the distance, and after two hour's driving they finally arrived in front of the weatherboard cottage.

'Perfect, or what?'

Angie felt a surge of excitement as she studied the building. It was even more derelict in the bright spring sunshine than the photograph had suggested, but the ornate latticework and wide verandah offered an air of elegance. Even in its state of disrepair, she could see the cottage had once been someone's pride and joy.

She looked back at the advertisement, feeling the need to balance Rob's excitement. *She* was normally the one who rushed into things, yet Rob looked like he was about to whip out his wallet and lay down a deposit as soon as she gave the nod.

'Better than the others we've seen,' she said cautiously. 'Probably miles outside our price range, though.'

Rob tapped his nose as he unbuckled Claudia from the back seat. 'Motivated seller, apparently.'

He grabbed Angie's hand, almost dragging her down the driveway. The smell of wisteria and jasmine wafted up from the neglected garden. Overgrown rose tendrils snagged Angie's jeans as she followed the path to the house. The newspaper photograph must have been taken years before, or strategically cropped so that the wild garden beds and piles of rubbish at the side of the yard were out of shot. The lawns had been given free rein, growing knee-high and creeping up onto the path around the cottage. Even so, just as she'd been drawn to the black-and-white photo in the ad, Angie found herself gravitating towards the old building.

'Here's the agent now,' said Rob.

Angie stuck out her hand but the agent leaned in to kiss her on the cheek before slapping Rob on the back. 'Good to see you, Jonesy! And Angie, I've heard so much about you and this little cutie.' He tweaked Claudia's nose. 'What a great opportunity, hey?'

Angie lifted an eyebrow as the man shoved a key into the front door. Friendliest real estate agent she'd ever met. Rob took her hand and they slipped inside.

They went from room to room. The high ceilings and generous windows made the cottage feel spacious, and even with furniture, there'd be oodles of room for hide-and-seek, plus enough floor space for those oversized jigsaw puzzles Claudia loved and maybe two sofas, instead of the two-seater they'd made do with in Eden Creek. Sunshine streamed in through dirty windows and dust motes danced. Angie swooned when she saw the ornate ceiling roses in the lounge room, and more in the smaller bedroom, which would be perfect for Claudia.

The real estate agent noticed Rob admiring the open fireplace and launched into his sales pitch. 'Winters snuggled up in front of the wood-fire, summers at the beach down the end of the lane. What more could you want? There's even a creek at the back of the property, if you fancy some eel trapping,' he said.

Angie almost caught herself nodding, and strode out of the room. *The floral carpets in the bedrooms would need to go, and most of the bathroom fittings and cabinetry.*

Angie tried to remain impartial, willing herself to find fault with the pressed-tin kitchen ceiling, cracked foot-high skirting boards and worn floorboards. But after half an hour inside, the cottage had an undeniable hold on her. The features she loved steadily outweighed the cons. She could picture them here as a family. It felt like they'd found their new home.

Angie buckled a tired Claudia into the car seat, watching her daughter's eyelids flutter close. She joined Rob and the real estate agent in a surreal conversation about timelines and deposit options, unable to believe that they may have finally found their dream cottage. Enough land to run a few cattle. Close to the ocean. With a little orchard. Room to plant a weeping cherry tree in memory of her mum, Annabel. The perfect place to turn Claudia into a little green thumb, and, maybe one day, expand their little family.

'Cooooeee.'

Angie swivelled towards the familiar voice. *No, it can't be . . .*

'Yoo hoo. Is that the birthday boy and his beautiful girls?'

It wasn't until Angie spotted Rosa Jones striding across the paddock that she noticed the black-and-white Friesian cows, and the thick bottlebrush hedges that camouflaged the neighbouring property. She flashed Rob a look of disbelief and sucked in a sharp breath. *What is his mother doing here?*

Angie barely had time to comprehend the situation before she was squeezed in a vice-like hug, complete with back pats, murmurs of delight and the scent of roses.

'Oh Angie, isn't this great? I've barely slept a wink.'

Okay, how did Rosa know about this before me?

The real estate agent drove off with a toot and a wave. Rob strode over to his mum, his tall frame dwarfing Rosa as she gave him a tight squeeze. They shared the same black wavy hair and olive skin, but Rob had definitely inherited his father's height.

'What did you think? And where's my beautiful granddaughter?'

'Mum, she's aslee—'

Rosa yanked the back door open. A sharp cry escaped from the car. Angie and Rob both grimaced.

'Oops, Granny woke you up. Let's get you out of that seat, poppet.' Rosa fumbled with the five-point harness. 'I've got some beautiful new calves to show you.'

Claudia shook her head mutinously. Angie knew exactly how she felt.

'Here, Mum, let me.' Rob squeezed in and lifted Claudia out.

Rosa stepped in closer. 'Granny's missed you, poppet. And haven't you grown tall!'

Standing on tiptoe, Angie whispered to Rob. 'It's within walking distance of the dairy? How could you not mention that?'

'Would you've come?'

Angie groaned, now spying the Jones's dairy and farmhouse further down the road. Of all the fixer-uppers in the country, had she just fallen in love with the one right next door to his folks?

Two

Rob watched Angie's face for a sign, hoping she wasn't going to discard the entire prospect on the basis of the neighbours.

'Don't write it off yet,' he whispered, landing a kiss on Angie's cheek. Keeping their arrival time a secret from his mother and driving in the back way clearly hadn't helped one bit; Rosa had probably been watching Enderby Lane all afternoon.

'I couldn't help hearing voices while I was out pruning my David Austins. You're coming round for dinner, aren't you?' Rosa said.

Rob waited for Angie's response. He'd thrashed the pants off her in enough games of strip poker to know she was wearing her polite smile, not her 'What a fabulous idea!' smile.

'When Rob said the property was by the coast, I didn't realise it was quite so close to your house. I've made . . . Well, we've got plans tonight, that's all,' said Angie, apologetically.

Rob put an arm around Rosa's tiny shoulders to soften the blow, but her face still plummeted. 'Oh . . . right, of course . . . I'll just pop your present in the post then. Chickens will be happy with a bit of sponge cake tomorrow.'

Rob shot Angie an appeasing look. She knew as well as he did that their visits were few and far between, even though they only lived 200 kilometres away. Didn't seem to worry his father, but barely a week passed without his mum inviting them around or reminding him she was free to babysit whenever they needed. Making excuses was always easier over the phone, or when he was working 4000 kilometres away at the mine.

'Maybe a quick piece of cake before we hit the road, Ange? Our quiet night can handle a little delay, right?'

He knew the cake, as much as the occasion, tipped the scales in his favour: Angie couldn't bear to see food going to waste, especially something that had been baked with love.

'A cuppa would be lovely, Rosa,' said Angie.

Less than two minutes later, they were standing in his parents' kitchen. As always, the garden was in immaculate condition, from the golf club–quality lawns to the hot-pink roses lining the dairy walls, Rosa's nod to aesthetics in an otherwise industrial part of the property.

Rosa nestled a cosy over the teapot and wiped her hands on her neatly pressed slacks. 'So what do you think?' Her voice was hopeful. 'Might be hard to imagine, Angie, but that cottage used to be the prettiest little thing. Yellow weatherboards instead of that faded mess, a snazzy burgundy roof without a hint of rust, and heritage-green latticework. Ivan and Ida took such great pride in it.'

'It's certainly something to think about,' said Angie, taking another forkful of sponge cake. 'Needs a lot of work, but it's got—' She paused as Rosa's voice cut in over the top.

'Good bones, hasn't it? Wouldn't take much to bring it up to scratch,' said Rosa.

Angie speared Rob with another look. He didn't need words to know what she was thinking. *Here for five minutes and your mum's already finishing my sentences.*

Angie's earlier excitement had waned significantly since Rosa's appearance. Now Rob felt his own enthusiasm droop as a familiar maroon farm ute pulled into the driveway, metallic paint gleaming like it had just been washed.

John Jones unclipped his dogs from the ute tray before pulling a comb from his back pocket, running it through his thin grey hair and walking into the house.

Rob returned his father's brief nod. His father's nods and handshakes were the opposite of his mother's bone-crunching embraces.

Rosa crossed the room and pecked her husband's clean-shaven cheek. 'Look how big this little sweetheart is,' she said, patting Claudia's shoulder.

John raised a heavy eyebrow. 'Now, which one are you again? Cathleen? Kym?' He made it sound like he had dozens of grandchildren instead of one.

Claudia stuck out her little chin and fixed John with an indignant look. 'I'm *Claudia*.'

John's lips twitched. 'Really? You any good at feeding calves?'

Claudia pondered the question, polished off her biscuit and climbed down from her stool. She reached for Rob's hand, pulling him towards the back door. 'C'mon, Daddy.'

Rob hesitated. 'You go with Pop, Claud. I'll be there in a minute, okay?'

To his surprise, Claudia slipped her tiny hand into her grandfather's.

John turned to his wife. 'Almost time to get the girls in too, Rosa. Can't spend all afternoon chinwagging when there's cows to milk.'

'They'll keep a few more minutes,' said Rosa, putting a cup of tea into Angie's hands and pushing a present towards Rob.

Rob glanced at the framed family portrait on the sideboard as he unwrapped his gift. In the photograph, Rosa's smile was extra wide, as if to compensate for her twin sons and reserved husband. Rob and Max had both been a head taller than Rosa by that stage, with a smattering of teenage acne and the bulge of braces behind closed lips. Rosa had bemoaned their grim expressions when she'd collected the enlargement from the photographer, even though she couldn't have known it would be the last picture they'd all willingly pose for together. Rob wondered if Max was unwrapping a hand-knitted jumper at this very moment too, or if anyone had baked him a cake today. *Not that I care*, he thought.

Rosa's voice jerked Rob back to the present. 'We hope you buy the cottage. We'd sure love to have you closer, wouldn't we, John?' Rosa said, calling out the door as John helped Claudia into a pair of old gumboots.

Rob looked away. He didn't need a visual of his father's hesitation as well.

'Be a good buy for the right person. A house isn't like those motorbikes you've got cluttering up the hay shed, mind you, Rob. Can't just stop and start as you please. It'll be fine for someone who's prepared to put in the hard yards.'

'Unlike me, right?' The words were out of Rob's mouth in a flash.

'Enough,' commanded Rosa, heaping a huge slice of cake into a takeaway container and sliding it towards Angie. Not another word was shared between the two men, but a seed of determination sprouted as, through the window, Rob watched Claudia and his father walk to the calf sheds. *I'll show you, Dad. This might be the perfect opportunity to finally prove myself.*

⁂

Angie's mind chopped and changed with every kilometre between the coast and Eden Creek.

How can I even consider living so close to his parents? But how could we let that cottage slip through our fingers?

Rob interjected occasionally, but she batted his questions right back at him, still miffed.

'It's quite the fixer-upper, isn't it? Just a stone's throw from the beach,' said Rob.

'And spitting distance from your parents. How long were you planning to wait until you delivered that bombshell?'

Angie closed her eyes, picturing the wonky bullnose verandah, the pitched roof and the old bubbled glass. New verandah posts, fresh tin and double-glazed windows were an easier fix than the issues they'd face if they moved next door to the Joneses.

'What would we do for work? You've only got one shift left until the mine scales back its operations.'

'My retrenchment payout from the mine should cover the deposit and I've looked into renewing my building licence, working as a sole trader. You've talked about selling the beauty salon for ages, maybe now's the time to put it on the market? If it sells, you could be home with Claud, like you wanted. There's enough work at the cottage to keep you busy.'

Angie huffed. *Why does he have such good comebacks?* 'That cypress hedge would have to come out.' She knew she was clutching at straws now.

'Yeah, it blocks a fair bit of sunlight, although it is handy shelter against a howling south-easterly. But if that's what it takes, I'll sharpen my chainsaw tomorrow.'

Her mind whirled. She thought of the brick path that led to the backyard, and her joy at discovering a mulberry tree in the middle of the overgrown lawn. It had dozens of gnarled branches forking off its wide trunk, with hundreds of white flowers adorning the smaller limbs, reminding her of childhood mulberry wars at McIntyre Park. It had been the stuff of dreams—and the stuff of parents' nightmares when they'd arrived home covered in sticky purple mulberry juice.

'And what will Claudia do while we're busy building? I don't want her to suffer if we embark on this crazy journey.'

'She'll be there with us, Ange, learning to count with boxes of screws and tubes of silicone. As well as fussing with dolls and Duplo blocks, she'll be playing with set squares and hammering nails into timber offcuts. It'll be good for her, I promise. And good for us.'

Claudia's soft snores filtered in from the back seat.

Maybe a project like that was exactly what they needed to bring them together? They'd been like ships passing in the night for most of their relationship. Angie had worked throughout her pregnancy, and returned to running the Eden Creek Beauty Salon when Claudia was six months old, while Rob worked fly-in fly-out. It hadn't been her dream scenario, but the salon and her clients had been the one constant throughout her adult life. *Maybe this cottage could be a catalyst for change? A chance to turn us into a real family, one that pitches in to get the job done. A family like the one I grew up in.*

She reached across the gearstick and took Rob's hand, ignoring the voice in her mind that questioned her sanity. 'You know I'm not a builder, right?'

Rob raised an eyebrow and waited. She could have sworn he was holding his breath.

'If it wasn't for the location, it'd be perfect. Let me think about it for a few days.'

Three

Rosa Jones sat the phone back down, mentally counting off the days since she'd last spoken to Rob. Two? Three? She pumped the bottle of Spray n' Wipe forcefully and polished her benchtop until it shone.

'Pass the phone book, John. I'll try Angie's number. She's the one who needs convincing anyway. Rob looked ready to sign the papers there and then.'

John looked up from the *Port Fairview Gazette*. 'You're wasting your time. Rob's too busy for a chinwag, let alone a project like that cottage. Be a different story if Max was considering it.' John tapped the newspaper back into perfect alignment, folded it neatly and walked across the kitchen. He leaned his chin on the top of Rosa's head and wrapped his arms around her, engulfing her in his fresh outdoorsy scent.

'Don't start that.' Rosa twisted in his arms and looked up at her husband of thirty-five years, resisting the urge to grab a pair of nail scissors and trim the wiry hairs protruding from his ears. 'You could've sounded a bit more enthusiastic.'

'Rob's an adult. He doesn't need me pumping up his tyres. You fawn over him enough for the both of us.'

A flash of movement caught Rosa's eye and she turned to see a white farm ute belting down Enderby Lane. Her heart jumped. For a second she let herself imagine it was their other son, Max, until the dust cleared and her heart reminded her both boys were too busy living their lives to visit regularly.

She wandered to the fridge and picked up a postcard from a tropical island off the coast of Sumatra. 'Wonder which continent Max's in now?'

'God knows.' John stirred sugar into both their mugs.

Rosa accepted the cup, letting the black tea burn her lips as penance for her failings as a mother. 'I'm virtually a stranger to Claudia. As the child's only grandmother, you'd think Angie would be a bit more interested in fostering a relationship . . . The craft girls were full of stories about their grandies last night, running themselves ragged with all the weekend babysitting,' she said. She pressed her lips together to prevent a wistful tone from creeping in.

'Not in my job description. I've done my fair share of raising children.' John sat down with his tea and snapped the newspaper open again.

And look how well that worked out, thought Rosa, her heart flooding with regret. She took another sip of scalding tea and smiled as a plan formed. Even though they didn't know it, her boys still needed her help. And she sure as heck wasn't going to miss her opportunity a second time.

Red clouds of Western District dust floated behind Angie's hatchback as she pulled into the McIntyre Park Merino Stud driveway. Angie had grown up with the Grampians on the horizon, but it wasn't until after she moved out that she'd come to appreciate the majestic mountain range on visits home.

The jolts as they crossed the corrugated cattle grid shook Claudia awake in the back seat. 'Perfect timing, little pumpkin. We're at Grandpa's house,' said Angie. A trio of kelpies raced towards them, and escorted the car the final hundred metres to the farmhouse.

She parked between a battered Subaru Forester and an immaculately clean white four-wheel drive. The condition of the vehicles perfectly reflected their drivers: her sisters Lara and Diana.

The sheepdogs greeted Angie as she climbed out of the car and into the dappled sunshine. The family farm was only half an hour's drive from Eden Creek, and Angie knew she'd miss McIntyre Park when they moved to Port Fairview.

There would be many perks of living on the tail end of Victoria's Great Ocean Road, with its beautiful beaches and mild weather, but the proximity to Rob's family, and the extended distance from hers, put a slight damper on things.

Claudia scrambled up the verandah steps as Angie pulled a salad and overnight bags from the back seat. The aroma of roast lamb tantalised her all the way across the gravel driveway, overpowering the fragrance of the thick lavender hedges. She swung the screen door open, slipped off Claudia's boots one-handed, and then removed her own. Familiarity washed over her at the sight of her sisters sitting around the battered pine dining table.

Angie threw her arms around her closest sister, inhaling the perfume Penny always wore. 'Look at your tiny bump, Pen.'

'I know, isn't it great!' Penny rested a hand on her softly rounded belly.

'She makes pregnancy look effortless, the cow,' groaned Lara. Not so long ago, an exchange like this between the two middle McIntyre sisters would have started World War Three. Thankfully, the rift between them had been mended not long after Penny returned to the farm, and insults had been replaced with gentle teasing.

'Great to have you home, Angie. And, Penny, by the time you've had four like me, you'll be popping out at the six-week mark. You're only early days yet, still five *long* months to go,' said Diana, taking the salad from Angie and pulling her into a warm hug.

'Where is everyone?' said Angie.

'The boys are all out the back with Dad. Pete and Tim were supposed to be knocking off that rowdy rooster but they've been sidetracked.' All four sisters glanced out the window. A red Aussie Rules football soared back and forth between Diana's four sons, while Diana's husband Pete leaned against a long-handled spade. He laughed with Penny's husband Tim, their task evidently forgotten.

'I think they were looking for an excuse to bail on the pregnancy talk. And Evie's already commandeered Claudia as a customer for her nail salon on the deck,' said Lara. 'She's hoping you'll have a baby girl, Penny, to lift the female cousin ratio against Diana's all-blue crew.'

'And then *you* need to have another baby, Angie-bee— another girl—and we'll almost have even numbers,' said Penny.

Angie held up her hands. 'God, I'm not quite ready for that. I still haven't lost the baby weight from Claudia,' she said, pulling her T-shirt so it didn't cling quite so tightly to her stomach. 'But guess what surprise I *do* have?' Angie smiled as her three curious sisters clustered in around her. 'The beauty salon sold this week *and* the vendor accepted our offer on the Enderby Lane cottage.'

Her sisters' responses came all at once, tumbling on top of each other.

'How fantastic! Congrats.'

'I hope you didn't get ripped off?'

'Are you going to manage living so close to your in-laws?'

Angie laughed. The questions reflected the personalities of each sister: sunny Penny, cautious Lara and their astute oldest sister, Diana.

'Thanks, Penny. Who would've thought the salon would sell so quickly? And the cottage was a bargain. We went in low, preparing to haggle, but they accepted it off the bat.'

'You know, there's a lot of work involved in a project like this, Angie,' said Lara, setting the table.

'It's not like the patchwork quilting classes you joined because I was doing them, and all those half-finished craft projects upstairs in our old bedroom. This is a huge commitment,' said Diana.

Angie huffed indignantly, recalling the comment Rob's dad had made.

'Of course I know that,' she said, shredding a paper napkin into her lap. 'You make me sound like a slacker.'

'We didn't mean it like that,' said Lara. 'It's just that you're a bit of a pushover. Are you sure this is what you both want, or is Rob leading the charge? And why the change of heart for him? Last I heard, all the tea in China wasn't enough to make him visit his parents.'

'He's always been close to his mum. She has him on speed dial, I'm sure of it. Things with his dad have never been perfect, but John's always busy with the dairy, so they won't cross paths much. And of course I want to do it! Ten years in the beauty industry is enough for anyone.' Angie pushed aside her worries about Rob and his father. *No family's perfect.*

Penny shot Lara and Diana a reproachful look. 'Look at the way they managed a surprise pregnancy just months after they met. I'm sure they can manage a little house renovation,' she said. 'Perfect bonding opportunity.'

Angie gave Penny a grateful smile. 'That's exactly what I thought. Nothing like a bit of hammering and painting to get the romance going, right? And there's a paddock between us and the Jones's. It's not like we'll be in each other's pockets.'

Lara threw back her head and roared with laughter. 'Are we talking about the same Rosa Jones? If it were me, I'd be getting a high-voltage electric fence installed. A leopard doesn't change her spots.'

'Maybe I overreacted last time. It was so long ago I can barely remember what all the fuss was about,' lied Angie.

Carolling magpies practised their morning chorus at McIntyre Park. Angus McIntyre brushed the crumbs from his work shirt and gestured to Angie with his glass of water. 'Scones were delicious, love. Come home and bake any time you like.'

Angie finished her scone and relaxed into her chair too. There was something extra special about early mornings on the farm with her dad, watching the sun sneak over the paddocks and bring out the blue in the mountain range.

'Bit doughy. I think I've lost my knack. There's always too much to do at home and now this renovation will probably take over our lives. Tell me I'm not crazy, Dad.'

Angus's tanned face crinkled into a smile as he slathered butter onto a third scone. 'Bit late for cold feet now, isn't it? Didn't you already sign on the dotted line?'

Angie nodded, annoyed with herself for letting yesterday's friendly banter cast a shadow over her good news. She'd dreamed about the cottage last night: Claudia blanketed in afternoon sun, piecing together puzzles. Rob flipping bacon and eggs in the open-plan kitchen. The images were so clear in her mind, so affirming, that she'd been surprised to wake up in her old bedroom and find it had just been a dream.

'There's so much potential, so much room for us to grow, so many memories to be made there.'

'You'll be fine, love. Change is as good as a holiday, right?'

Angie nodded. The novelty of running a beauty salon had lost its shine after Claudia's arrival, but at least she knew what she was doing with potions and lotions, waxes and pedicures . . . unlike the whirlwind of motherhood.

Her father pointed to a cluster of new lambs frolicking in the paddock under the watchful eye of the nearby ewes.

'Be good for little Claud to be with you every day, instead of picking up more bad habits at that childcare centre,' he said. 'And don't forget, we're only two hours away. Your sisters will be down to help, I'm sure. And they'll set Tim and Pete to work the second you ask. Plus Rob's folks. They'll be on the other side of the fence whenever you need a lift or an extra set of hands.'

Angie groaned. Angus grinned.

'Didn't they welcome you with open arms? How about that fancy pram and cot they bought the second they found out you were up the duff?'

Angie nodded. 'Well, yes . . .' She didn't point out Rosa's top-of-the-line gifts required an engineering degree to operate. Three years on, she still longed for the fuss-free stroller she'd been considering before Rosa's gifts arrived.

'And, like us, didn't they love Claudia from the minute they met her?' said Angus.

Angie closed her eyes for a beat. Rosa had been so delighted with her first grandchild that she'd insisted on staying in the spare bedroom for the month after Rob's paternity leave finished. 'They sure did,' she said, reaching for another scone and heaping cream on top.

'From what you tell me, Rosa's always offering to babysit. You should let her. Your mum can't offer you the same luxury, I'm afraid,' Angus said.

A flock of corellas settled on the gum trees beside the shearing shed, laughing raucously. Maybe it was the sight of her mum's weeping cherry tree in the far corner of the garden, but above the sound of her father's voice, the birds and the frogs croaking in the dam, Angie could hear her mother's voice.

'You're stronger than you'll ever know, Angie-bee.'

The hairs on Angie's pale arms were raised as the memory of Annabel McIntyre's unwavering belief gave her the soft push she needed.

Rob and I can do this. We will do this.

Four

Happy squeals echoed as Angie entered the Eden Creek daycare centre. She followed an artwork-lined hallway to the under-threes room and was greeted by a new staff member.

'Hi. I'm here for Claudia Jones. Blonde, about yay high?' Angie held a hand about mid-thigh. 'Also known as the resident vampire?'

The new daycare lady laughed, then lowered her voice. 'She only bit one little boy today, on the hand. But seriously, we'd all love to sink our teeth into that kid, so don't lose any sleep over it.'

Angie cringed, scanning the room for bite marks on other children but finding none. A bite on the hand was a relief compared to the Claudia-shaped teeth marks she'd spotted on a little girl's cheek last week.

Claudia—little blobs of dried paint on her face—greeted her with a hug. Angie bustled her out the door before they could be lumbered with any more finger-painted masterpieces.

The receptionist waved as they signed out. 'Oh, Angie, have you finished the grant application yet?'

Angie glanced at the centre's worn playground, the one they'd been fundraising to replace. The one she'd suggested would be the perfect candidate for the next round of council grant funding. The one she'd clean forgotten about. *Me and my big ideas.*

'Yes. No. I mean, I haven't finished the application yet.' *Or gotten any further than printing out the application criteria, and then burying it under piles of clean washing.* 'I'll get onto it next week before we leave.'

'You're the best, Angie.'

Angie's smile slipped from her face as she burst through the double doors and gulped in mouthfuls of fresh air. The Eden Creek mums-and-bubs fundraisers, daycare parents' committee, show society and the senior citizens' pamper sessions had been great to start off with, but . . .

She tugged at her neckline. She wasn't quite sure how she'd managed to get herself so deeply entrenched in this community—the warm fuzzies she'd initially felt at all the commitments now felt like a noose around her neck. *This is the perfect time to be leaving town.*

A fresh start in Port Fairview was sounding more appealing by the day. Some breathing space while they renovated and then she'd carefully choose her volunteer roles, instead of agreeing to them all. Angie wrestled her salon uniform back into place so it skimmed her curves instead of clinging to the bumpy bits.

A new town, a new me, she thought. *Maybe I'll finally find time to get back into shape.* The thought brightened her up as she drove through the quiet town.

Rosa wiped down the farmhouse fridge before affixing Claudia's drawings to the door. She smoothed the artwork with her hand. The black-and-white blob surrounded by blue was apparently a dairy cow in the middle of the ocean, and although the likeness was debatable, it pleased her to know Claudia was already thinking of her new home. There'd soon be enough colourful creations to wallpaper the entire house.

Angie's invitation to babysit in Eden Creek next week had been the icing on the cake. Driving two hours north, and then two hours back to the coast the following day didn't worry her in the least. It would be wonderful to have Claudia all to herself—listening to the joyous sound of a child's laughter, the whoops of delight when she sang her granddaughter's favourite nursery rhyme. Rosa backtracked, realising she didn't yet know Claudia's likes and dislikes. *Mere details.*

This was what had been missing from her life, and if things went to plan, there'd be plenty more babysitting opportunities. Angie couldn't shut her out when she lived so close.

Rosa smiled again at the idea of future family gatherings and shared meals. *Maybe we could start a tradition of Sunday-night roasts. Wouldn't that be nice?*

Rosa startled as she heard John's ute turn into their driveway, and spritzed some more cleaning spray around the kitchen. She wouldn't mention today's little errand.

Not yet.

They'd been good neighbours to Ivan, and nobody else needed to know about the cheque she'd taken him today. Ivan would keep his word and stay quiet about the sweetener, and that oaf of a real estate agent was so happy with his commission he'd never question why the vendor had accepted such a low offer. But what if it somehow slipped out? She banished the thought quickly, as if thinking it would bring it about. *As long as I keep quiet, nobody will find out. John never checks the bank accounts anyway, and if he does, I'll explain it's just an early wedding present instead of waiting around for the day Rob and Angie decide to tie the knot. It's a win–win,* she reminded herself. *Everything's coming together perfectly.*

Five

Rob paused at the mine office doorway, the bright Western Australian sunlight dazzling him one last time. Noise tumbled out from the television room. The men he'd worked with for the last two years were watching Australia smash the All Blacks in rugby, but he'd averted his eyes as he passed. He'd already said his goodbyes before doing one last sweep through his room and packing his belongings.

Rob took a deep breath. Except for the pay-cheque, there was nothing he'd miss about this place, or the fly-in fly-out lifestyle.

Be happy. Be excited. New beginnings ahead. The girls. Our own place. He'd started a notebook to scribble down ideas for their upcoming project, and as he hopped aboard the transfer to Perth airport, and then the plane to Melbourne, he almost filled it. In no time at all, he was striding through Tullamarine arrivals hall, resisting the urge to kiss the Victorian ground. His phone vibrated with an incoming call.

'Hey, Brett?'

'Bugger me dead, Jonesy. Bumped into your mum today, and she said you were moving back home. I told her she was stark-raving mad, because the Jonesy I knew was hell-bent on flogging his guts out at a mine.'

Rob located the luggage carousel for his flight and leaned back in his boots.

His high-school friend continued incredulously. 'Also told her there was no way Rob Jones, lead wicket taker, sharpshooter and all-round wonder child, would dare return to the region without consulting his oldest friend. Tell me she's wrong, Jonesy. Tell me that after all those years covering your arse every time we got into trouble, you wouldn't forget to mention something like that.'

'Didn't want to spoil the surprise, mate.'

Like the luggage carousel's lazy circles, this move back to his hometown after so many years away would bring him full circle. He couldn't decide whether it was a good thing or not.

'You're finally doing up the old cottage, then? I thought you'd thrown the baby out with the bathwater when your brother left? Hope you're not outsourcing the lot, or anything like that. You want it done right, you're better off doing it yourself.'

'Pfft, Max was going to do a lot of things, wasn't he? Ange and I will give it a red-hot crack. She's just sold her salon in Eden Creek, so it's good timing.'

'Tessa will be pleased there's a new hairdresser in town. I can't believe you haven't brought her down to meet us yet. And your little tacker too, what's she now? Almost one?'

Rob wedged the phone between his shoulder and ear, and stepped forwards to grab his backpack.

'Ange's a beautician, not a hairdresser, but I've seen what she can do with a rosebush—she'd probably make a darn good hairdresser too. Claudia's two and a half.'

'Reckon her and Tessa will get along. Our little Scarlett is the same age. So, I know a good plumber in town, he might lend you a hand with these renos.'

'Hoped you'd say that, mate. We're down soon to collect the keys. Don't want to drag this project out for years,' said Rob, weaving through the airport terminal.

Brett's laugh echoed down the phone. 'There's a new one. Double your timeline, triple your budget and you'll be about right. I'll drop around with a few cold ones, see what you've got yourself into.'

Rob took the shuttle to Southern Cross Station and spent the next three westward hours reassuring himself he hadn't bitten off more than he could chew.

Angie reached for the daycare sign-out sheet, puzzled to see Rosa's signature already beside Claudia's name. Angie glanced at the clock hanging above the double doors, and back down at the logbook.

Rosa Jones, 1 p.m.

Rosa signed Claudia out three hours ago? She must have driven up from Port Fairview as soon as the morning milking was finished. The daycare worker hurried over, her face creased with confusion.

'Sorry, I thought you knew? Rob's mum said you were heading away for the weekend, which was what you'd told me this morning. Said she wanted to maximise her time with Claudia and save you a few extra minutes. I couldn't reach you, but I got an okay from Rob,' she said. 'Is she a bit of a monster-in-law?'

'No, no, Rosa's fine. She's just a little'—Angie paused to think of the right word—'enthusiastic, that's all.'

Enthusiasm was a Rosa Jones specialty. She'd been enthusiastic about a christening for Claudia, although Angie wasn't the least bit religious. Enthusiastic about cloth nappies, even though she wasn't the one soaking, washing and trying to dry the darn things in the depths of a wet winter. Enthusiastic with her advice on controlled crying, the pros of breastfeeding and the cons of co-sleeping. Angie had almost cried with relief, and guilt, when a full-time place opened up at the Eden Creek daycare centre.

'It's the first time I've asked her to babysit Claudia for the night, and she's driven up from Port Fairview just for the occasion. I guess we got our wires crossed.'

'My folks said they're moving to Queensland when I have kids. Apparently their retirement's going to be full of golf tournaments and leisurely lunches, not changing dirty nappies and wiping snotty noses. You're lucky.'

Angie gave the staff member a nervous smile as she left.

Give her an inch, and she'll take a mile. Weren't those her sisters' exact words when she'd mentioned Rosa was babysitting in Eden Creek this weekend so she and Rob could visit their new property at Port Fairview?

Angie sped through town, regretting their decision to turn the key collection into a mini-break, just the two of them. It was too soon. As much as she wanted to trust Rosa not to intefere, this early daycare collection was a wildly waving red flag.

֍

Angie could smell something baking as soon as she opened the front door. Ginger, cinnamon and honey by the smell of it. Rosa had already made herself at home, obviously. *How did she get the oven working?*

'Rosa? Claudia?' Angie tossed her shoes into the wicker basket. She forced herself to calm down at the front door, taking a moment to guess what was baking instead of rushing

in straightaway to confront Rob's mother. *Ginger fluff?*
Gingerbread men? Knowing Rosa, it was probably both.

Angie exhaled slowly as she walked into the kitchen. Claudia
looked up from a lump of dough, delight all over her flour-
dusted face.

'Don't look so worried, Angie. You don't have to eat it
all at once. It's just a few meals and snacks to keep us going
while you're away, and a couple of freezer fillers so you don't
have to cook while you're packing,' beamed Rosa, leaving the
stovetop to wrap her in an exuberant hug.

Angie's eyes widened as she noticed their dining table. It
was laden with baking trays, cooling racks and a commercial
quantity of plastic takeaway containers, each brimming with
homemade delicacies.

Rosa held Angie at arm's length, her sharp brown eyes
uncomfortably appraising. Angie shoved her hands into the
front pockets of her beautician's uniform, hiding her figure. She
could almost see the cogs turning in Rosa's mind, wondering
if the tight uniform was covering a baby bump, or just too
many frozen pizzas and bakery lunches. *She'll be disappointed
when she discovers it's only the latter.*

'Thanks for coming up for the weekend, Rosa. Sorry the
house is a mess. It's been so hectic recently, I've barely had
time to scratch myself with all this packing.' Angie gestured
to the couch, surprised to discover the piles of washing had
disappeared. The tidal wave of toys was nowhere to be seen,
either. 'Oh! You don't waste any time, do you?'

*Who is this Wonder Woman, and why didn't I invite her
into my life sooner?*

'I remember how busy it is with little ones. And it'll be
good for you to get away for the weekend. The oven was a

bit dicky, but I got it running again. Amazing what a whack with a rolling pin and a bit of string can do,' said Rosa.

Angie gaped. Sure enough, the oven door was tied shut with a length of twine. She'd assumed Rob had inherited his knack for improvising from his father, but maybe it was from Rosa?

She walked over to Claudia's stool and gave her a kiss. 'Aren't you a lucky girl, getting home early to bake with Granny?' said Angie, flashing a look towards the oven. *Mention it. Start as you mean to go on.* 'You know, I . . .'

Rosa looked up, a broad smile matching her enthusiasm.

Angie took a breath and tried again. 'Er . . . I wasn't expecting you until later.'

'I wanted to make the most of our time together, and I had a hankering to bake with this little one. You don't mind, do you?'

Rosa sat Claudia on a stool next to the oven as Angie gazed around the house. Everywhere she looked there was evidence of Rosa's helpfulness. Angie felt guilty for seething on the drive home. She forced her shoulders down and adopted a breezy smile.

'Who could complain about this?' She looked around the room again. *Had Rosa even dusted the pot-plant leaves?*

'Oh, this is nothing. When you move down, I'll be able to babysit all the time.' Rosa waved her off as she turned back to the pot of soup on the stovetop. 'Now, you go pack for your naughty weekend away. Everything's under control here. Isn't it, Claudia?'

Claudia nodded, slipping another ball of dough into her mouth.

Angie walked to the bedroom, willing herself to feel okay about leaving Claudia for the weekend. *It'd be different if Mum was still alive,* she told herself. She tossed clothes into the overnight bag, running her finger down the to-do list she'd written in the wee hours of the morning in an attempt to get back to sleep. *Pillow. Phone charger. Book. New nighty. New lingerie.*

Angie groaned as she realised the carrier bag containing her dusky-pink lingerie was still in the salon, stashed under the front counter after yesterday's lunchtime shopping spree. *Darn it. Still, I'm sure we'll find other ways to celebrate . . .*

A quick rifle through her chest of drawers revealed one matching set of bra and briefs in the mountain of grey, black and beige cotton granny-undies. She held them up to the light, frowning at the slightly stretched and faded fabric, before stuffing them into the bag. *When did the state of my underwear slip so far beneath the radar?*

Angie shrugged out of her beauty salon uniform, took her hair down from the high bun and let her curls cascade over her shoulders the way Rob loved.

She caught a glimpse of her reflection as she swung the wardrobe door open. Cruel schoolyard jibes ran through her mind. *Chunky monkey. No staying power, that Angie McIntyre. She'll be lucky to find a fella with her lard arse and those ugly freckles. Who wants someone who changes her mind as often as she changes her knickers?*

No matter how hard Angie had worked to erase those taunts from her memory, they still had bite. Narrowing her eyes at the mirror, she set her hands on her hips. *Are you really going to let those old insecurities ruin your night away?*

She spun away from the mirror and pulled on a pair of opaque tights, slipped a grey dress over her T-shirt and topped off the outfit with a woollen cardigan, a quick spritz of perfume and a slash of lipstick before slamming the wardrobe door shut.

She checked her watch. In two hours they'd be collecting the keys to their new home. Her nerves about leaving Claudia with Rosa evaporated into excitement. Suddenly she couldn't wait to collect Rob from the train station and head to the coast.

Rosa hugged Claudia closer as Angie's little red car disappeared from sight.

'You and I are going to have so much fun this weekend, Claud,' she said, stroking her granddaughter's curls. Despite many offers to babysit, and invitations for Claudia to have a sleepover at the farm, this was the first time Rosa had had her alone overnight.

It didn't matter that she'd had to drive 200 kilometres to their house. She would have driven to Mars if it meant more time with her only grandchild. The fuss from years ago would be water under the bridge by the time Rob and Angie moved home, she was sure of it.

'Baby steps, love. Whatever makes them happy,' she'd told John, when he'd complained about the impractical arrangements.

'They're coming down to Port Fairview. It would make sense to bring Claudia and stay in the spare room, instead of you trekking 120 miles north and them wasting money on a riverfront apartment,' John had said, his head still buried in the newspaper. He had flicked the page over, and she knew his focus was split between the new cattle export regulations and her excited chatter.

'It's no trouble, John. Whatever makes them happy. And my little granddaughter makes me happy, so everyone's a winner,' she had said.

'Cooking, Granny?' said Claudia, bringing Rosa back to the present.

She kissed her granddaughter's forehead and lingered on the driveway. 'We're all done for tonight, poppet. Tomorrow,

I promise. How about you eat one of those gingerbread men in the bath? Special treat, okay?'

Claudia nodded eagerly, picking a yellow capeweed flower from the lawn. *Why did Angie let all these weeds creep into the lawn? They'll be lucky getting their bond back,* Rosa tutted.

'What a big daisy. Let's put it into a vase,' said Rosa, taking Claudia's sticky little hand.

Her heart swelled. It had been years since her children had needed her, truly needed her. Rob and Max were all grown up now, living their own lives, but she had known there would come a day when her nurturing skills would become indispensable again. When Rob and Angie moved to Port Fairview, she'd have more of this in her life. More purpose, more sweetness, more family. The thought made her feel good, as if the role of nurturer was nudging its way out of retirement.

She pulled her phone from her back pocket and messaged Angie, wishing them a safe drive. The phone trilled before she'd reached the front door.

That's a quick reply for Angie, she thought, unlocking the phone. But Rosa's breath caught as she saw who the reply was from.

Max?

Six

Angie's phone pinged as they drove out of town. She grabbed it, hoping the real estate agent was confirming their meeting. Her smile faltered when she saw it was from Rosa.

'We've been gone less than ten minutes and your mum's already sending me messages. Do you think she's misplaced your number?' Her dry comment was met with silence.

Rob's warm hand settled on hers. Just like his wild partying had stopped after he became a father, his rough hands had softened after two years of mining work.

'She's just excited. We haven't given her much to work with over the years, have we?'

Angie saw another yellow road sign flick past the windscreen, warning motorists to watch out for koalas, and winced at the sight of a recent victim.

'More dead koalas on the roadside than kangaroos down here,' she grimaced, averting her eyes from the roadkill as she messaged Rosa back. 'Sticking to the highway this time, are we?'

Rob had the good grace to look sheepish. 'Those back roads will be crawling with roos this time of night,' he said. 'And yeah, no need to sneak in the back way now that you've met the neighbours.'

Renovation discussions made the miles fly past and soon the ocean was in sight. The sun was waltzing with the horizon as they turned onto Enderby Lane. The bottlebrushes flanking the roadside glowed iridescent red in the golden light, and the last of Angie's ambivalence faded as they pulled into the driveway.

She looked at Rob. 'Home sweet home.'

'It's going to be the making of us, Ange, I can tell.'

He leaned across the handbrake to deliver a slow and sensual kiss that ignited a warmth deep inside her. She threaded her hands through the waves of black hair at the nape of his neck, pulling him to her.

A horn tooted behind them. Angie broke away, breathless and blushing.

The real estate agent stepped out of his ute. 'All yours, folks. Power's reconnected, as promised,' he said, pressing a set of keys into Rob's hand. He gave Angie a wink. 'I'll leave you young lovebirds to it.'

They grabbed the first lot of boxes from the back seat of the hatchback and carried them to the old shed beside the cottage.

Rob bowed dramatically. 'Your boudoir awaits, madam.'

They stepped inside.

'Gah! It stinks.' Angie covered her mouth and nose with a sleeve and patted her pocket to check her asthma puffer was there.

Rob set his boxes down beside the makeshift sink. He opened the windows and turned the taps on. Water spluttered indignantly before the stream of brown water cleared.

'An air-out will do it the world of good. And we'll have Diana's caravan in here soon. It's not like we're putting mattresses on the concrete floor.'

Angie opened the door to the tiny bathroom. A cheap shower base, decorated with mouse poo, sat crudely on the raw concrete. A mess of white paper overflowed from the bucket beside the toilet. Mice skittered in search of an exit.

Add mouse traps to the shopping list.

Rob spun her around and planted a kiss on the end of her still-wrinkled nose but Angie squirmed, unable to stand the musty, mousy smell any longer. Grabbing Rob's hand, she pulled him outside. She looped her fingers around Rob's waist and leaned against him.

'She'll be the perfect bike shed when we've finished the house. We'll whip it into shape easily enough, plonk the caravan inside and then we'll move onto the main game,' Rob said. They turned to both look at their cottage.

'Damn right we will, Rob Jones. Just watch us.'

Angie woke to the sounds of the rolling and crashing Southern Ocean and the river lapping against fishing boats. She rolled over, reaching for Rob, but found his side of the bed empty. She slipped into a plush 'Riverside Retreat' robe and wandered out onto the apartment balcony. Port Fairview's streetlights twinkled on the river in the pre-dawn and seagulls preened their wings on the boardwalk. Rob looked up from the cane chair, his grin wolfish.

'Morning. How did you sleep?' Rob pulled a chair out for her.

'Good, though I liked the bit *before* we got to sleep better . . .' She glanced at the trail of clothes on the apartment floor.

Rob's gentle hand snaked under the belt of her robe.

'You planning an encore? Thought I wore you out last night,' said Angie, her smile matching his.

He rose and pulled her up from her chair. 'Better move inside. With my luck someone I know will spot us from across the river. But I've got plans for you, lovely. Long as *you're* not too worn out?'

She drew the curtains, let her bathrobe fall to the floor beside last night's clothes and reached for Rob. If this wasn't the best way to celebrate being new homeowners, she didn't know what was.

Seven

Angie slapped the masking-tape dispenser over the side of the cardboard box, yanking the tool backwards so that the tape pulled off with a satisfying screech. She added the box to the shoulder-high wall of cardboard—their lives almost completely packed into boxes.

Angie paused in front of the fan and pulled her sweaty singlet from her chest before stuffing random items into another box.

Her sister Penny sat cross-legged on the kitchen floor, smiling despite hours of helping pack.

'You're a machine, Penny. Aren't you sick of it yet?'

Penny continued emptying the kitchen cupboards. 'I thought the whole nesting thing was a joke, but it's so satisfying,' she said. 'Besides, you'll never get this house packed with all those phone calls. How much time do you normally dedicate to committee admin?'

Angie took another gulp of water and peered inside Penny's perfectly packed box. 'Too much. Anyway, who am I to get in the way of a pregnant lady and her nesting instincts?'

'True. And it'd be a crime to let you just toss your kitchen-ware into boxes, like you did with your wardrobe. Go ahead and shove your mismatched clothes into suitcases and donation bins, but I'm not letting you do the same to all these baking tins and cookbooks. I can't imagine you without a kitchen, and I'm tipping the second you get an oven and a sink in your new cottage, you'll be itching to bake. And then you'll be thanking your lucky stars your favourite sister packed these boxes sensibly.'

Angie glanced down at the jumbled box in her arms. Penny knew her too well.

'The reno shouldn't take too long, really. Replacing a few weatherboards, putting a new roof on, installing a few cabinets here and there. It'll be done in a jiffy,' said Angie, her expression nonchalant.

Rob's arms burned as he took the last few steps towards the shed door, grateful to be finally lowering the potted plant to the ground. Angie stuck her head around the corner, a mop bucket in one hand and dripping mop in the other. Her smile almost made up for his twinging back as she admired the wine half-barrels he'd shifted.

'The lilly pilly looks good there. Imagine how much better they'll look flanking the cottage doorway.'

Rob rubbed his back dramatically. 'You're shifting them next time,' he laughed. 'How's the floor looking? Ready for varnish?' He could almost taste the cold beer that would quench his thirst. Their temporary shed-home had come a long way in two weeks, transforming from a mouse-ridden tin shell to a liveable space. The walls were insulated and clad, there were windows, roller doors and a sliding door on the north side, and the floor looked clean enough to eat off. Only two coats of floor varnish stood between them and moving in.

Angie looked as hot as he felt, with a sheen of perspiration on every exposed centimetre of skin. 'Ready as it'll ever be. Promise we'll have a swim after we varnish? I'm roasting hot,' she said.

He smiled. He liked the look of her all hot and sweaty, her clothes clinging to the curves he'd fallen in love with. 'Damn right you're hot. Nearly giving me heatstroke, sexy lady.' He pinched her bum as he walked past.

She flashed him a cheeky grin before her attention shifted to the paddock behind him. Her face fell. Rob turned to see his father walking with an esky in one hand and a picnic basket in the other. His mum followed, carrying what looked to be an enormous stuffed cow. *What the . . . ?*

Claudia launched out of her paddling pool and raced across the yard in her bathers. She flung her arms around the black-and-white toy.

'Angie, Rob, look what I won in the silent auction at the Dairy Ladies' Luncheon. Not cheap, but I knew our little girl would love it. Isn't it adorable?'

Rob couldn't contain his laughter as he got a closer look at the synthetic monstrosity. 'How about that, Claud? Your first calf.'

Angie groaned, and whispered so only he could hear, 'We barely have room for clothes in there, let alone a life-sized calf.'

Rob's smile slipped. He hadn't even thought of that. He looked from his mum to his daughter, both equally pleased with the present. He didn't want to be the bad guy, but he was going to upset one of his three girls no matter what he did.

His father's next words surprised him. 'It can live at our place until you move in. Won't eat much,' said John.

'Well, I guess so . . .' said Rosa. She scooped the esky from John's hand and passed it to Angie. 'We didn't forget you two either. This hamper should feed you for the whole weekend. Our little welcoming present.'

'Thanks, Rosa, John,' said Angie, accepting the gift.

Rob gestured to the shed. 'We're all ready to move in. Want a quick squiz?'

John put a hand on Rosa's arm, halting her mid-step. 'Can't stay, nearly milking time. I'm sure you've done a good job of it,' he said.

Rob blinked. That had almost sounded like a compliment. It had been a long time since he'd received even the tiniest morsel of praise from his father.

Is he ill? About to announce he's dying of cancer?

John cleared his throat. 'That's the easy bit though, mind you. Real test is yet to come, then we'll see if you've got what it takes. And you'll want to be checking the paddocks before too long. No use letting that grass go to ruin when you could bale it into hay,' said John, nodding to the cottage and then the far paddock.

Rob exhaled. *And there it was.* Nothing like a backhanded compliment to set the planet back on its axis.

Rosa rushed to fill the silence that followed. 'You and Angie make a mighty fine team, and we're really proud already.'

Rob wrapped an arm around Angie's shoulder. Mum was right. They'd made a cracking start to their project and he'd make sure no one could doubt their ability by the end of this renovation.

Eight

The Port Fairview Fete was in full swing, and the food on the craft group's trestle table was disappearing rapidly. Rosa plucked a stray grey hair from the plate of biscuits. *Not mine, obviously*, she thought. Her hair wasn't naturally dark anymore, but regular trips to the hairdresser kept it the same shade of deep chocolate it had always been. She stood by the importance of keeping herself attractive. *Not like some of the other wives*, she thought, looking around the bustling Mechanics' Institute hall. Of all the clothing stuffed into her wardrobe, there was not a single pair of tracksuit pants or item of horrid skin-hugging activewear to be found. She glanced at her watch. Only another hour manning the bake stall, and she'd be home in time to finish spring-cleaning.

There were old toys from the depths of the rumpus room cupboards waiting to be unpacked and pushed back into service for the next generation's entertainment. It pleased her no end to know the little clothes and toys she'd made over thirty years ago would finally be useful again. John had said she was mad, but she'd seen his eyes soften at the clothesline full of miniature woollen jumpers Rob and Max had once worn.

Rosa hummed as she moved the cream cakes to the front. They were sitting on a block of ice, but they wouldn't last much longer in this sudden burst of spring heat.

'Earth to Rosa? I'll have both these plates, thanks,' said a loud voice.

She turned to see a fellow crafter balancing baked goods on top of her overflowing basket. 'I've already got three bottles of your passata and six packs of your homemade gnocchi ready for the silly season, Rosa. No such thing as being too organised, I say,' said Eileen, handing over the correct change.

'Couldn't agree more. I've been thinking about Christmas myself, much to John's amusement. Our men don't realise quite how much pre-planning is needed for a successful festive season, do they?' She hadn't meant for John to find the stockpile of little presents she'd started acquiring, ready for wrapping and stashing under the Christmas tree.

'It's only October,' he'd said this morning. 'Why on Earth are you thinking about Christmas? And just because Rob's home, doesn't mean we'll be getting one of those pine trees again. Darn pine needles take over the house. Stick with the old fake tree, like the last fifteen years.' But she knew he'd come around. It had been years since she'd bothered with a real Christmas tree, and the prospect of having family home this year made her want to pull out all the stops.

Rosa pursed her lips, trying to contain her happiness. Eileen wasn't going to sniff out this secret; she needed a poker face.

'Too right, Rosa. Oh, and add a couple of your knitted beanies for stocking stuffers. You know you pretty much run this fete, don't you?'

'It's the least I can do,' said Rosa. Up until now, providing craft, produce and preserves for the twice-yearly Port Fairview Fete had been the best panacea for her loneliness.

Mightn't have as much time for craft fetes and baking stalls next year. The thought made her smile.

'Rosa? You look like you're miles away again. Dreaming about holidays?'

'Gosh, Eileen, not this year. We've got far too much to do with Rob moving home. And, of course, I couldn't bear to leave little Claudia for a month. Not now she's next door,' said Rosa, fanning her face again.

'You think you're hot now? Your son and his wife will be sweltering this summer in a caravan inside a shed. Wouldn't catch *me* living in a shed or a van. Or in a van inside a shed, for that matter. Ivan's old cottage needs so much work. They're mad, if you ask me.'

I didn't.

'They're young. They'll cope,' Rosa said, straightening the yo-yo biscuits. She didn't bother to correct Eileen about Rob and Angie's marital status either. Why Rob hadn't made an honest woman out of Angie was beyond Rosa, but after the baby formula debacle, and then the christening conflict, she'd agreed not to offer her opinions on such matters.

'Well, I suppose if they can survive a renovation and summer in a tin shed, they can survive anything. What about your Max? Is he coming home too? They used to be tighter than two coats of paint, those twins. Such a shame they fell out.'

The ache in Rosa's heart was now almost as sharp as that in her back. She would love nothing more than for her boys to reconcile.

Some people in Port Fairview thought the rift between the brothers had come out of nowhere, but, if she were honest with herself, Rosa knew it had been brewing for years. One moment she had been dressing them in matching outfits, the next moment they were young adults with shared dreams and ambitions, and then it had all been wiped out by a bad decision. If only Max had been honest with Rob, if only John had stepped in before it was too late, things might have been different.

But she had a plan to make it right. Even though she wanted to shout her news across the crowded hall, Rosa held her tongue as Eileen waddled off to the next stall.

Angie lifted the final cardboard box from the trailer and carried it into the corner of John and Rosa's hay shed, trying not to think about the fresh mouse droppings on the boxes they'd stacked there yesterday.

'You sure this stuff is going to be okay in here while we renovate, Rob?' She wrinkled her nose, wiping her damp hands on her shorts.

'Not many options, Ange. They won't fit in the caravan, I'm not keen on triple-handling them by shifting them from room to room as we renovate each part of the cottage, and it's not like we can leave my motorbikes out here. They're way too valuable to leave in this old hay shed,' said Rob, unloading his armful of boxes. 'Anyway, it's only for a few months. Nothing's going to eat'—Rob paused and read the black writing on the side of the box—'springform tins, mini-muffin tins, recipe books or the last five years of baking magazines, right?'

Angie cocked an eyebrow. 'Sometimes I think those bikes mean more to you than I do,' she teased, stretching her arms above her head. 'And to think your new work ute will be outside in the salty sea air just so your old bikes can be locked up safe.'

Rob closed the distance between them with a long stride and cupped her chin. 'You, my girl, are worth more to me than anything. Now, let's get cracking before Brett drops around to replace the hot-water service,' he said, landing a kiss on her lips.

She gave a mock salute. 'Yes, sir!'

Rob held down the top strand of wire as she climbed back onto their side of the fence. They stood for a moment at the boundary. Blue skies and harsh sunlight highlighted the thin patches on the cottage's rusty red roof and cast the southern side of the house in full shadow.

'What about gardens, Rob? I can see a full bed of colour on the east side, near the old rose bushes, and veggie gardens in front of the shed.'

Rob snorted. 'Gardens? Those rotten weatherboards and rusty roof are the only things I'm thinking about now. Don't you have enough greenery with all those pot plants? Plus, the trenching and stuff will rip up the lawn. Hold off till the renos are over.'

Angie shrugged, sweeping her hair off her damp neck. 'Maybe just a few bits and pieces to make the property feel like home. We've missed the boat this year, but when winter comes, I'll prune all those fruit trees and plant some new ones. And obviously we'll get rid of that death trap.' She nodded to the freestanding brick chimney, the last remnant of the original soldier settlement house. The faded red brickwork and chunky bluestone lintel hovering above the fireplace cavity had probably been built the same time as the chimney inside their cottage. To its credit, the long, skinny structure had barely weathered, despite losing the surrounding walls and roof years ago.

'You can't be serious? It's a relic! Thought we'd make a feature of it. We could build a garden shed beside it maybe, or a fire pit?' Rob's tone was reverent.

A feature?

Angie narrowed her gaze. 'It's gotta go, Rob. What if it topples over on Claudia? It's almost as much of a hazard as that pond. The quicker we fence that, the better too.' She shoved her hands on her hips as she looked from the old chimney to the algae-choked water feature. 'Haven't you read the stats on drownings?'

Rob rolled his eyes but Angie continued to ruminate on the two hazards as they walked back to the yard. The chimney in the paddock may well be a historical piece, but they couldn't afford to be sentimental when safety was at stake. She only had to think back to her father's accident three years ago to know that life was a precious gift. The idea of Claudia buried beneath a pile of rubble or venturing into the pond was unthinkable.

'I like the chimney,' said Rob.

We'll see about that, she thought, casting her eyes back to the brick column one last time.

Nine

The small storage yard was the last stop on Rob and Brett's way out of town. Brett waited out front with his ute and loaded trailer while Rob collected the final piece of the puzzle—his 1964 Harley-Davidson Panhead with matching sidecar. There was a spring in his step as he paid up the final account and returned the keys.

Rob looked over his shoulder to make sure Brett wasn't watching, then pulled a small ring box from its hiding spot under the sidecar seat. He flicked the lid with a smile. Sunlight glinted off the diamond and pearl setting.

It'd been a gamble stashing the ring in the motorbike and leaving it at the storage shed, but he hadn't wanted to risk Angie finding it in his sock drawer when she packed. Rob tucked the box into his jacket. He set the choke and throttle, kick-started the bike and let it warm up before following Brett out of the storage yard, mentally farewelling the small town that had been their home for the last few years. He'd arrived in Eden Creek with little more than a backpack and a room at the pub, and he was leaving with a child, a girlfriend, eighteen months of fly-in fly-out work under his belt and the last trailer-load of their belongings.

He opened up the throttle as he left the town boundary, feeling the engine respond to his touch. His mine workmates had joked about how lucky he had been to escape the 'old ball and chain' of marriage, but he knew, more than anything, that he wanted to slip this ring onto Angie's finger when they were more settled.

Nothing clichéd about a Christmas proposal, he thought wryly.

Diana guided the caravan into the far corner of the shed.

'Back a little more. To the left, yep, a bit further.' Angie held up her hand and called out to her sister. 'Yep. That'll do.'

She slipped a log underneath the back wheels and stood back to admire the white- and yellow-striped van.

'Home sweet home, huh?' Diana swung down from the driver's seat, admiring her reverse parking. 'Pete can go eat his hat. I'm pretty much a professional caravan reverser now. Not even a dent this time. Now, are you sure you'll be okay in this van for so long? Will Rob be happy with it being in this side of the shed?'

Angie brushed away Diana's worries.

'It'll be fine. And if he's that fussed, he can shift it when he's back from this last trailer-load,' said Angie.

Angie opened the caravan door, eager for another peek inside her new temporary home. It had felt good to hand back the rental keys this morning, and when Rob returned with the final load this afternoon, they'd be officially moved in.

Diana grabbed her hand. 'Let's swim first. I feel bad heaping all the kids on Rosa, even though she insisted. It was almost like she was watching for our arrival.'

Angie laughed. She'd lay money on the fact Rosa had kept at least one eye on Enderby Lane while doing her crafting, gardening or baking this morning. 'Highly likely. But she means well.'

'You seem more chilled now about leaving Claudia with her? That'll be handy during the renos.'

'It's a work in progress. One minute I'm cool with it, the next I'm having flashbacks to finding that half-empty tin of formula.'

As well as ruining Angie's plan to exclusively breastfeed, the baby formula incident two years earlier had all but annihilated her relationship with Rosa and almost ruined things with her and Rob. Rosa's apologies, and her plea that formula would help Claudia sleep longer, hadn't cut the mustard, and although Rob couldn't fully understand Angie's furious reaction, he had eventually agreed Rosa had overstepped the mark.

Angie shivered, despite the heat of the afternoon, trying to shrug off the memories and adopt a grateful attitude. Rosa's help today had given them the breathing space to shift boxes and reverse the caravan into place without Diana's four boys and Claudia underfoot. *It's in the past now.*

Her phone pinged with a text message.

Brett's about to leave with final trailer-load of boxes, I'll follow him on the Harley. See you soon xx Rob

She shot back a quick reply, telling him to meet them at the beach. She loaded an extra beach towel into Diana's car, directed her sister to a secluded cove down the end of their road, and felt instantly cooler when the water came into view.

The sight at the beach made them both smile.

Rosa had Diana's boys and Claudia all linked by a chain of hands as they jumped the small waves. As if she'd heard them over the excited squeals of the children, Rosa turned, shading her eyes as she squinted back into the sun, and waved.

The McIntyre sisters waved back automatically.

'Rosa looks like an angel in disguise. Maybe we could clone her?'

Angie laughed. 'Careful what you wish for.'

'Look, if you don't want her send her up my way. C'mon, I've got to get into the water. Last one in's a rotten egg.'

Angie tucked the blankets into the side of the narrow caravan bunk. She nestled Claudia's well-loved toy dog under her arm and leaned in for one last kiss.

'Sleep tight, princess. We'll be right over there,' she said, pointing to the double bed at the opposite end of the van.

Claudia's eyes lit up, but she couldn't stifle the yawn creeping across her face. 'Daddy?' Claudia smiled, snuggling the stuffed dog.

'He'll be home soon', Angie said, looking at her watch. 'Any minute, in fact.'

The sea air is working its magic, Angie thought, as Claudia's eyes fluttered closed. The afternoon at the beach with Rosa, Diana and the kids had been glorious. No sandflies, no wind and twenty-eight heavenly degrees. Rob's afternoon hadn't panned out quite so well, with the trailer blowing a tyre on the highway between Eden Creek and Port Fairview. They'd be ready for a cold beer by the time they arrived home.

She slipped away from the bunk bed, sliding the little curtains across to keep the light out of Claudia's eyes.

Which drawer were the stubby holders in? The bare essentials were packed in beside Diana and Pete's caravan collection of cutlery and crockery. She quietly rifled through the tiny kitchenette cupboards, finding what she was after.

Three months of renovations will fly by. Soon we'll be in our new home and have as much storage space as we could ever need.

Rob crested the final hill before home and accelerated out of the tight bend that twisted towards Port Fairview. It wasn't one of his favourite corners—that honour belonged to a series of dipping, weaving bends out of Eden Creek. But it was the last, and he always made it count. Although it had been bittersweet to leave the circle of friends they'd made in Eden Creek, he felt a distinct sense of homecoming as he turned onto Enderby Lane.

The cottage was silhouetted against a full moon. He took the slippery gravel track slowly—it would take a few months of traversing this driveway at dawn, on wet wintry afternoons and during dusty dry days before he knew each bump of the path well enough to trust it at speed.

Rob removed his helmet and leather jacket. As well as the sound of the ocean, he could hear the burbling of Bottlebrush Creek in the paddocks to the south. He folded his gloves neatly, before turning to look at their cottage.

The rickety table and chairs sitting on the front verandah made him grin. Ange had obviously been given free rein with the hand-me-downs in his parents' hay shed. He wiped his jaw, wondering what else his mother had foisted on them.

Through the darkness he could hear contented dairy cows snickering, coughing and walking through the grass. As a teenager, he'd felt trapped by the twice-daily milking. Not one fibre in his body had wanted to spend a minute more than necessary in the herringbone-style dairy, attaching vacuumed cups to udders and being showered with cow crap morning and night. He knew his father lived and breathed the farming life, relishing his role in putting milk on the table for families all across Victoria and the simple pleasure of listening to the cows on a calm night. Rob had never shared the passion. Max hadn't minded it, though.

Max . . . Another memory slipped into his mind, like a shot of whisky down the throat. The two of them standing on this very same spot as teenagers, Max outlining his vision for an extension out the side of the kitchen, with floor-to-ceiling glass on the eastern wall to capture the morning sun; Rob throwing around ideas for the cladding, back when they were planning their first business venture.

Max the architect, Rob the builder.

Max building new houses, Rob bringing old ones back to life.

Back before things had spiralled out of control. Rob picked up his leather jacket, suddenly cold. *Max made his bed, now he can lie in it.*

Rob looked at the shed, where Ange and Claudia were sleeping in a borrowed caravan, waiting for him to come home and start transforming the cottage into their new family home.

It's our *dream. Damned if I'll let Max spoil this for me too.*

Brett pulled in with the trailer.

'Thanks mate, sorry it ran a bit later than planned,' said Rob.

'No sweat, Jonesy. It'll be nice to sneak in after witching-hour's over. Tessa normally lumps the bed, bath, book routine on me as soon as I walk in the door,' said Brett.

They worked together to unhook the trailer from Brett's ute. A curtain of stars twinkled at them from overhead, with the clear skies adding a nip to the air.

'No rain tonight, I'll unpack it tomorrow, and whack a new tyre on it before I drop it back. Can I get you a beer?'

'Nah, I'll hit the frog and toad. Catch you soon.'

Rob farewelled his friend with a wave and headed inside.

Angie blinked in the inky darkness, trying to identify the noise. *Did I fall asleep?* She fumbled for her phone, illuminating the caravan interior as the door swung open and a tall figure ducked in. A beat of panic gave way to recognition.

'Hey, Ange.'

Rob crawled across the bed. His cheeks were like ice, his lips raised goosebumps as they pressed against hers.

Angie giggled as his hands reached under the covers, barely biting back a shriek when his cool skin made contact.

'God you're cold.' She snuggled back under the quilt to regain some warmth. She could feel his smile against her lips.

He murmured into her mouth. 'Worth a shot. You're deliciously cosy. How's a bloke to warm himself up after a long ride without a heater?'

Angie put a finger to his lips, then cupped his hands near her mouth and blew on them. 'Shh, you'll wake Claudia. I can think of a good way to warm up if you take the chill off those icy fingers.'

'I like the way you think,' he whispered, rubbing his hands together to expedite the process. Angie sought his lips again and the next minute she was tugging his clothes off, eager for his body against hers. A sound came from the bunk bed. Rob tensed; Angie held her breath.

A little voice came from behind the curtain. 'Mummy.'

Angie laughed into Rob's chest, feeling his arm tuck around her, their romantic plan instantly quashed.

'Bugger.'

'Bugger indeed. We'll continue this later.' He landed a kiss on her cheek then eased off the bed to resettle Claudia.

'How's it feel to be a Port Fairview girl?' said Rob, returning to bed.

'I won't be a local for at least another thirty years, but it's good to know all our stuff's in the one place. How was the trip home?'

'Slow. We limped along to avoid another blow-out. But at least it was just a tyre, not an axle. Or my bike.'

Angie laughed. She'd had a soft spot for Rob's motorbikes ever since she'd rescued him from the side of the road. It had been more than three years ago, but her random act of kindness in helping a broken-down motorcyclist—albeit a handsome one—sometimes seemed like it had happened only yesterday. Passing the time together while Rob organised a bike trailer hadn't been a problem, although it had later seemed ironic that Claudia's conception came before the vintage bike parts had even arrived in the mail.

'Be good to have my family and my bikes all together again in one place.'

Angie rubbed her eyes. 'Is everything going to fit? Rosa said they needed the hay shed soon. Time to downsize?'

He grinned, knowing her jibe was half-hearted.

'We'll squeeze them in somewhere, don't you worry,' said Rob, snuggling in closer.

Ten

Angie looked away as Brett crouched beside the bathroom sink, checking the underside for drips. She'd heard all about plumbers' cracks, and had waxed many nether regions in her time at the salon, but there was still something confronting about the sight of the pale, hairy backside in front of her.

Rob caught her eye and stifled a laugh.

'Good as gold, mate. It's not quite the Hilton, but it'll get you through a few months,' said Brett, straightening up and wiping his hands on his jeans. 'You're a brave one, Ange. My missus wouldn't last two seconds in a set-up like this,' he said, gesturing to the makeshift bathroom he'd helped upgrade.

Angie hoisted Claudia higher on her hip. 'We're pretty tough, aren't we, Claud.'

Rob gave her a wink. 'Besides, with this plumber on the job, we'll smash through it in no time, right, Brett? Let us know how much we owe you, mate,' he said, walking out into the shed and leaning against the caravan.

'No hurry, Jonesy. I know you're good for it,' said Brett. 'What are you up to tonight? You guys should join us for dinner at the pub, have a few frothies. Tessa's dying to meet you, Ange.'

Angie smiled back warmly. They'd only met an hour ago, but she could see why he was Rob's closest friend. They shared the same easygoing nature, good humour and quick smile.

'Sounds good to me. I look forward to getting all the dirt on this guy. He's been pretty quiet about his teenage years,' said Angie.

Brett snorted, clapping a meaty hand on Rob's shoulder. 'If you want mud, you've shacked up with the wrong guy, Angie. *Max* is the wild child of the Jones clan; this guy's as clean as a whistle. But I'll try to rustle up a few skeletons for old times' sake.'

Rob frowned, shaking his head. 'Don't listen to a word of it, Ange.'

The edge to Rob's voice came as a surprise. She slipped a hand into the back pocket of his jeans. Meeting his old friends was a step in the right direction. But one day soon she'd need to get to the bottom of this rift between Rob, his father and the twin brother whose name he never even spoke aloud. And then they'd have a clean start in their new home.

'Credit card?' Rob held out his hand after he'd peeled the backing off the sticker.

Angie passed him the card and watched as he used it to smooth bubbles out of the black vinyl lettering. His tongue poked out the corner of his mouth as he worked, the picture of concentration. She stepped back to admire the overall result, reading aloud the signwriting on the side of Rob's new work ute.

'*Bottlebrush Building Company. Call for jobs big and small.* Looks pretty snazzy.'

Rob cocked his head left then right, fighting a nonchalant expression for all of a few seconds before his pride shone through. 'Not too shabby. Better than *Jonesy's Odd Jobs*, I suppose.'

Angie socked him lightly in the arm. 'It was never going to be an odd-jobs business. You're a builder through and through,' she said. 'We should celebrate.'

'What do you have in mind? We've got dinner at the pub in an hour.'

'I can think of a quick way to mark the momentous occasion of opening your own business,' she murmured, glancing towards the caravan. Rob dipped his head, the rough stubble scratching her face gently as his lips touched hers.

'I like the sound of this, especially after last night's false start. Lead the way.'

They strode hand in hand towards the shed, checking the pram parked under the cottage verandah. Claudia had slept through their washing, polishing and branding of Rob's new work ute, her little chest continuing to rise and fall in a steady rhythm under the blanket.

Angie crept away from the pram as Rob opened the shed door, both of them holding their breath as the hinges creaked. Angie suppressed a chuckle as they turned in unison to the pram.

'Not even a stir,' she whispered to Rob. They tiptoed across the shed, taking extra care to open the caravan door slowly, and set about celebrating their new beginning.

※

The Port Fairview Pub was a melting pot of residents and visitors, from fishermen in white gumboots who looked like they'd stepped straight off a crayfish trawler, to families eating in the open-plan dining room underneath a ceiling strung with craypots, dried starfish and seahorses.

Rob waved to a couple near the bar as he guided Angie through the crowd. It took them several minutes to cover the twenty metres, thanks to a string of hearty welcomes from old acquaintances delighted to have him back in town.

'I never knew you were the long-lost son of Port Fairview,' Angie said as they reached Brett and the smiling woman beside him.

Brett's wife dived past Angie's outstretched hand and drew her into a hug instead. 'I've been looking forward to meeting you, Angie! Rosa hasn't let the craft group hear the end of it, either, told us all about your award-winning cakes and scones. She's told us you're a shoo-in for the champion baker at next year's show.' Tessa laughed at Angie's stunned expression. 'Mothers-in-law, hey?'

'Thanks, Tessa, lovely to meet you too. Brett's told me all about your baking too, though I'm not going to be much of a partner in crime until the renovations are finished. There's no oven in the shed house or the caravan,' Angie said.

'I probably bake enough for the both of us anyway,' Tessa said with a giggle. Her cute earrings and the colourful dress wrapped around Tessa's voluptuous figure were like little bursts of happiness, and Angie warmed to her instantly. Tessa found them a table and upended a bag of Barbie dolls onto it. Claudia and Scarlett clamoured for the toys.

'Play nicely, Claud,' Angie said.

'Don't worry, there's more than enough for them to share,' said Tessa, pulling board books and an Etch A Sketch from another bag. 'That should keep them occupied for, oh, a minute or two.'

'She's had trouble keeping her teeth to herself, that's all,' said Angie, preparing to be greeted with the hypervigilance that usually accompanied this admission.

'They'll be fine. Our Scarlett isn't an angel, either.'

Angie relaxed into her chair, liking Brett's wife more and more with every minute.

She stole a look at Rob. He was leaning against the bar, head and shoulders taller than most of the other patrons, deep in conversation with an older gentleman. His hand gestures and facial expressions were animated.

That mouth.

Angie felt her face flush at the memory of their opportunistic encounter in the caravan while Claudia had napped that afternoon. Buying the cottage and having Rob living under the same roof was paying dividends for their love life.

A cough broke through Angie's thoughts and she blushed at the perceptive look on Tessa's face.

'Ah, young love. Rob's a sweetheart, isn't he? I remember he was the quiet one in high school—all the girls were drawn to his brother Max. Look who's laughing now, hey?'

'He's great. Rob, I mean, not Max. I don't actually know Rob's brother. He's been overseas since we met.' It was hard to know what to make of Rob's twin, but the more time she spent in Port Fairview, the more she wondered what Rob hadn't told her.

Tessa scanned the room and leaned in close so her hair curtained them from the room. 'They used to be thick as thieves, but Rob's not a forgive-and-forget type of guy, is he?'

'I don't know, I haven't really known him long enough to say,' admitted Angie, taking a sip from her cider. The Rob she knew was kind and gentle—she'd never seen another side of him. It was almost embarrassing to admit that they'd spent so little time together before their surprise pregnancy.

'Brett used to be friends with both of them, but . . . I don't like to gossip.' Tessa trailed off as the men joined them.

Angie glanced at the little girls, pleased they were playing nicely, then looked back at Tessa. 'So, Tessa, what do you do with yourself when you're not whipping up a storm in the kitchen?'

Tessa fiddled with her unusual necklace. 'Well, these days I'm mostly looking after Scarlett. But I've got a little craft business online, more of a hobby than anything but it keeps me busy enough.' She took a sip of her drink. 'Brett's folks own the dairy a couple of clicks past your new place, so we're often driving past. Your cottage is going to be beautiful when it's done.'

'Thanks. I know it needs a lot of work, but it was an easy one to fall in love with. It's been great for us already. Living in the same place, working on something together, has already brought us even closer together.'

'I can see! You can barely keep your eyes off him. Yeah, it'll be a good challenge. So much easier when there's a tradie in the house, too. My friend's renovating an apartment with her white-collar boyfriend and she says it's like a bad episode of *The Block*, except with more swearing and a hell of a lot of hammer throwing.'

Angie sipped her drink. 'Watch this space—there's plenty of time for hammer throwing.'

The conversation flowed as they ate and Angie was surprised to look around two hours later and discover they were the last customers in the dining room.

'We'd better get these little rug rats to bed,' said Rob, picking up a sleepy Claudia and carrying her out to the car. Brett followed with Scarlett while Angie and Tessa ambled behind, planning a playdate for their daughters.

'You know you'll have the cricket and footy clubs knocking on Rob's door and the CWA after you before long,' said Tessa.

Angie laughed. 'Between the new business, the house and his vintage motorbikes, Rob doesn't have time for any more hobbies. And as much as I loved all the volunteer stuff in Eden Creek, it was starting to get a bit crazy,' she said.

'You'll need to lay down the law, then. Don't say I didn't warn you.'

 ༽

Rob rolled over in bed, making the van sway. He still hadn't managed to set the stabiliser jacks to the perfect height and small movements rippled through the whole structure.

Angie stirred. 'What's the time?'

'4.35 a.m. Can't sleep either?' Rob said.

She snuggled in. 'Nah, too excited about the cottage. I'm itching to get in there with a crowbar.'

He laughed, pleased she was as excited as he was. 'Just don't go ripping any weatherboards off yet, cos you were right—I've got more building work coming my way than I know what to do with.'

Angie stretched. 'I really liked Tessa. She's a sweetie.'

Rob yawned and nodded. 'Had a feeling you two would gel.'

'She makes the coolest earrings. Did you see those dalmatian ones she was wearing?'

Rob absent-mindedly toyed with her hair. 'Can't say I noticed. You two looked pretty wrapped up in conversation all night.'

'She said something about you and Max.'

Rob rolled onto his back and stared at the ceiling. 'Nothing to tell. Max leaves a trail of destruction wherever he goes. He's better off in Spain, or Portugal, or wherever the hell he is.'

'Surely he's not all bad? Your mum showed me photos of the two of you together as kids. You looked inseparable when you were younger.'

'Just because we're twins, doesn't mean we're alike. Let's focus on you and me and Claud, and our little cottage.'

Rob turned toward the wall and tried to plan his week's work. But try as he might, the snatches of information about Max his mum had forced on him clawed their way to the forefront. Max had bounced from country to country—picking olives in Brazil, becoming a horseback trail guide in Patagonia, working at quarantine feedlots in Uruguay—never sticking at one job for long.

Max can be tango dancing in Timbuktu for all I care, he told himself. *I'm the one who's got the balls to take on the cottage, not him.*

Eleven

The air was brisk and salty. A flock of cawing seagulls streaked across the sky and settled in front of the fish-and-chip shop as Angie and Rob walked down Port Fairview's main street. Rob waved to the familiar faces of townsfolk he had grown up with, trying not to let his quick lunch break evaporate into catch-up conversations. *It feels good to be back in town,* he thought, nodding at an old primary-school teacher.

'Just like when I walk down the street in my hometown, Bridgefield. You know everyone and everyone knows you,' Angie murmured as they escaped from one of Rosa's friends selling raffle tickets outside the post office.

Rob smiled at Angie. With her auburn curls tamed into a bun, her freckles unleashed without their normal veil of foundation and her curvy body tucked into a cream worker's shirt, she looked less like a beautician and more like a woman about to embark on a renovation project. It suited her down to the ground.

'I know. I think Claudia's lapping up the attention though,' he grinned, watching the little hand waving regally to passers-by from her pram. Rob's appetite surged as he held open the door, the smell of food frying engulfing him.

'Hey, Jonesy. Good to see you back, mate—you've timed it perfectly for the start of cricket season.' The man behind the counter moved quickly to wrap the mound of steaming chips.

'Not this season. Brett's already tried to rope me in for this weekend's match against Cavendish. Too much to do on the home front this year. Maybe next season,' Rob said.

'Fair enough. I'm guessing this is your lunch, then?' The man handed over the paper parcel. '$15 will cover it today.'

Angie looked up from her wallet in surprise. 'For two pieces of flake, chips and potato cakes? I like the sound of these Port Fairview prices!'

'Consider it a welcome-home special. And if you change your mind about cricket . . .'

'You'll be the first to know,' said Rob.

It's been a long time between overs, thought Rob. But it felt good to be in demand. Angie didn't seem opposed to becoming a cricket widow next summer, either.

They ate lunch on the riverbank, the hot treat disappearing quickly. He checked his watch, before kissing Angie and Claudia on the cheek and heading off for the afternoon's work.

'See you at home tonight. Love you two,' he said.

A strong south-westerly had picked up by the time Angie and Claudia returned to their car. Seagulls flapped valiantly against the breeze, takeaway coffee cups tumbled across the bustling main street and shopkeepers pulled their sale racks inside before clothes and bric-a-brac were blown across the footpath. Angie spotted the preschool by the town green, its brightly painted facade exactly how Rob had described it.

'Come on, Claud. Let's get you signed up.'

They strode through the bright foyer. The Wiggles' greatest hits blared through the double doors, and judging by the raucous noise, the afternoon crazies were in full swing. In the office, a woman was leaning over the unattended front counter. There was a dark-haired child by her side, and a newborn strapped to her chest—when she turned, Angie felt all three sets of bright blue eyes fix on her and Claudia.

'Any idea who's running this place?' the woman said, giving the bell another sharp shake and flicking her glossy black hair over her shoulders.

'Not a clue. Are you signing your little one up for next year too?'

'Yes, if someone was here to give us the paperwork. I'm Bobbi. I'd head in there and ask for it myself, but these two terrors have got horrid gastro, so I shouldn't really take them into the playroom. This is Jayden and the little one's Oscar.'

Angie took an involuntary step backwards and glanced at the woman's outfit: ivory jeans and a floaty white top. Angie didn't ever trust herself to wear white, let alone with a sick baby strapped to her chest. *She's either really foolish or really confident.* Angie snuck a quick glance at the woman's perfect nails, expertly straightened hair and toned physique. *Definitely the latter category.* Angie wondered what it would be like to be that comfortable in her own skin.

'I'm Angie and this is Claudia. So I guess she and Jayden will be in the same three-year-old preschool class next year.'

Bobbi flashed her a warm smile. 'How fabulous.'

They traded phone numbers while waiting for the preschool teacher, then walked back out together, chatting in the sunshine.

'Let's catch up before preschool starts. Or, if you fancy a running buddy, I'm about to start a couch-to-5k program.'

Angie felt a twinge of self-consciousness, as if she'd accidentally been picked to go in the sports team with all the popular girls, before they realised she was on the pudgy side and not particularly coordinated.

'Do I look like a runner?' she said.

Bobbi laughed and slipped a business card into Angie's hand. 'Gotta start somewhere. It's a great program for beginners, and even easier with a personal trainer at your side.' She looked Angie up and down.

Angie's face burned. *She probably thinks I'll never come.* 'I'll keep it in mind.'

'Trust me, I'll have you in a bikini by the end of summer. Your hubby won't know what hit him, and you'll come to love the buzz from a good run.'

Their budget wouldn't stretch to a gym membership any time soon, and personal trainers didn't come cheap either. Angie quickly grasped the excuse. 'We're renovating, so it's not a good time for extra expenses. Thanks anyway,' she said, lifting Claudia onto her hip.

Bobbi's arms were lean; there was not a scrap of fat on her body. They'd only just met, but Angie could tell the woman was the epitome of willpower. *She probably has more discipline in her little finger than I've got in my whole body.* Her admiration for Bobbi kicked up a notch.

'Well, running's the cheapest form of exercise going around. How about the first five weeks are on me, then we'll go from there. I want to build my business up, so you'll be doing me a favour.' She stuck out a hand.

Claudia reached out and they all laughed as she shook Bobbi's hand.

Angie remembered her pledge to try a healthier approach. *New town, new you, remember?*

'It's a deal,' said Bobbi.

Angie felt a mix of excitement and nerves as she and Claudia walked back to the car. New friends, new house project, Rob's business was taking off and a fitness plan had landed in her lap. Moving had been a good decision.

Twelve

Angie stretched her legs out, and switched the phone to her left hand to jot down prices on the notepad. Three sessions of walking and running with Bobbi this week and she was yet to 'love the burn', as Bobbi had so breezily predicted. But she'd stuck with it so far, which was two sessions more than any other fitness kick she'd attempted in the last decade.

Angie clicked the pen impatiently as the man on the phone continued his spiel about the digging machine they wanted to hire.

'Okay, well, that's a lot of money for a digger. I'll let Rob know and call back if we want to go ahead, thanks.'

She hung up the phone, her calf muscles protesting as she walked across the yard, trying to get her head around the upcoming expenses. She didn't have the budget spreadsheet in front of her, but she sensed they hadn't factored these figures into the early forecast. She shuddered, hoping Rob had a better idea.

Claudia looked up from the castle she was building in her new sandpit.

'Mum's got to make a few more phone calls, then we'll go see your new little friends Jayden and Oscar at the music classes, okay? Scarlett and Tessa will be there too,' Angie said.

Claudia nodded happily. Angie made the rest of the calls on her list and drove into town, satisfied she had all the information they needed about the new septic tank, and quotes lined up with three local glaziers. Hopefully, the glass costings would be more in line with what they'd expected than the machinery to clear the yard and trench in new garden taps.

Her phone rang as she pulled up at the Mechanics' Institute hall. Rob's photo sprang onto the screen.

'Hey, Ange. Saw your message about the digger. Brett might know someone who doesn't charge an arm and a leg?'

'You should have gone into machinery hire, not building. Sounds like a goldmine. I'll ask Tessa in a minute.'

She parked next to Bobbi's and Tessa's cars. It was strange to think her two new friends hadn't met before, considering they both had children of similar ages. They'd heard of one another but Angie was chuffed to think it had taken her, a complete newcomer, to bring them together. It was the closest thing she had to a mums' group and although it was only their second catch-up, she had a good feeling about her burgeoning friendship circle.

Music exploded out of the hall as she opened the door. Claudia ran to join the other kids, diving straight into the box of instruments.

'Hey Angie, how are your legs? I was telling Tessa how well you're doing. I've already noticed an improvement,' said Bobbi, yelling to be heard above the ear-splitting racket of tooting recorders, maracas and tambourines.

Angie waved a hand, not wanting to show how pleased she was by Bobbi's compliment. 'You flatterer.'

Claudia leaped up from the circle of toddlers, opened the lid of the dusty piano in the corner of the hall and started pounding on the ivory keys.

'I don't know why they call it a Rhythm and Rhyme class. There's not much of either, in my opinion. More like Death by Tunelessness,' Angie said.

'The kids seem to enjoy it though,' added Tessa.

Bobbi nodded towards the kitchenette. With a cheeky glance at the elderly music teacher, who was as patient as he was deaf, Angie, Tessa and Bobbi made their escape. Angie closed the door behind them, grateful for a sound barrier against the cacophony.

Bobbi pulled out an earplug. 'That's enough to send anyone around the bend.'

Tessa flicked the kettle on and started chopping fruit for the shared morning tea. She shot Angie a smile. 'Here, have a cream puff, you'll be fading away under Bobbi's regime.' Tessa pushed a container of choux pastry towards Angie. But just as she'd resisted Rosa's recent delivery of biscuits and coconut cake, Angie reached for an apple instead with a small shrug and a smile.

Tessa baulked in mock disbelief. 'Not sure we can be friends, Angie. I'm yet to see any hint of this amazing baking Rob's been bragging about, and now you're declining my cream puffs!'

'It's easier to quit sweets and baking without an oven, and a few months of hard training is exactly what I need to shake this extra baby weight,' said Angie. 'Mind you, if Brett doesn't have any contacts with discount diggers, I might be digging these trenches by hand. Have you guys heard how much a digger costs per day? Tell me you've got good contacts, Tessa.'

Bobbi jumped in before Tessa could offer any suggestions. 'Alex has a bobcat. He can drop it around on the weekend if you like. Send it home with a carton of boutique ale and he'll be happy.'

'You just happen to have a digger in your shed? Really? We can pay—I mean, I wasn't looking for a free ride, only something a little cheaper so we don't have to remortgage the house,' she joked.

But before Angie could protest any further, Bobbi airily waved off her objections and fired a quick text to her husband. Bobbi's phone beeped and Angie watched in amazement as Bobbi gave her a thumbs up. 'Sorted. Didn't you know he had a machinery business? He'll drop it off Saturday morning.'

Angie's eyes widened. She looked from Bobbi to Tessa incredulously. 'That's amazing!' she said, feeling a rush of gratitude for her new friends. *Bobbi sure knows how to get things happening, there's no doubt about it. I bet she doesn't let herself get roped into every committee in a fifty-kilometre radius.* She eyed Bobbi with newfound admiration. *Watch and learn, Angie, watch and learn.*

Tessa grabbed a cream puff, tucked her dark blonde hair behind her ears and walked back into the music class.

The hardware store's air conditioning wrapped itself around Rob's body like a long-lost girlfriend. He strode through the familiar aisles. The smell of rubber and plastic wafted over from the summer window display of steel-capped workboots and garden hoses. Not much had changed by way of décor or stock since Rob had started his first after-school job in the store's timber section. That job had paid for his first motorbike, bought his independence, and encouraged a love of woodworking.

An elderly man smiled at Rob from behind the counter. 'You're a sight for sore eyes, lad. Heard you'd started up a new business in town. I'm telling everyone I taught you everything you know.'

'Wally, nice to see you again,' Rob said, setting his notepad down on the worn counter. 'Real sorry to hear about Wanda. The place seems quiet without her.'

Wally dipped his head, pulling a pen from behind his ear. 'She was pushing seventy-five, Rob. And she didn't have an evening nip of whisky like me, so she was bound to go first.' His gruff voice, and the way he kept his eyes planted firmly on Rob's itemised list, suggested he was still coming to terms with the sudden loss.

'Those food baskets your mother brought around were much appreciated. And your father's been very helpful since Wanda passed. He took over the store when I went away to scatter the ashes. Not many people would volunteer to manage a hardware store and still milk twice a day.'

Rob frowned. He couldn't imagine his father standing behind the counter, directing people to screws and spare irrigation fittings, and supervising after-school employees on the saw bench to ensure they retained all ten fingers. Wally had been everything John Jones was not: patient, relaxed and sharp with numbers but never with his tongue.

'Mum didn't mention that,' he said, reaching for a plastic basket. 'Is it okay if we start up a business account? I've got a few jobs already, and I don't want to load up the debit card on business expenses.'

'Course it is. I've known you since you were in nappies.' Wally turned to the computer and began setting up a store account. 'And I don't see why your mum would make a fuss over it. There's a lot to be said for acting humble in an age where everyone broadcasts their good deeds across social media, expecting an award. I know you and your father don't always see eye to eye, but he's a hardworking man. Apple never falls far from the tree, either.

'We'll mark your cottage materials separately to your business, all right? Tell me which job to put beside each item and we'll keep it all straight,' said Wally.

Ange had been right—there was something inherently simple about setting up a small business in your hometown. Rob nodded, his eye landing on a hot-pink hammer and screwdriver set in the clearance bin. He placed the item on the counter. 'Add this to the "home" tab too, please.'

The older man smiled as he scanned the item. 'I *heard* you've got a good woman by your side these days. And I'm pleased to see you're having a crack at that cottage. I'm not blowing smoke up your bum, but you were always going to do a better job with it than your brother,' he said, handing Rob the tool set.

Rob fumbled with the package as the roar of the timber saw filled the store. Wally's comment and the smell of sawdust took him straight back to the brawl that had severed his and Max's bond. Did everyone in Port Fairview still compare him and Max?

He felt Wally's hand on his arm, gentler than the vice-like grip the old man had used to pull him off Max ten years ago. 'But no sense dragging up the past. I know that, you know that. You're a good man, Rob Jones, and mark my words, you'll do well. Now off you go and see what she says about her new hammer. I've got purple hammers ordered for Christmas if pink's not her cuppa tea. And don't be a stranger. I expect to see you in here weekly.'

Rob shrugged off sudden melancholy as he left the hardware store, pausing to drag the empty rubbish bins off the roadside and tuck them under the store verandah. *Why does it feel like*

Max is right here in Port Fairview, around every corner, when I know for a fact there are continents between us?

Rob wiped the sweat from his forehead and took another sip of water. It hadn't taken long to fill the large yellow skip bin with sheets of old plasterboard. Seeing the inside of the house stripped down to bare frames felt like progress.

Angie squirmed as he slung an arm over her shoulder. 'Ugh, you're even sweatier than me. I'm dreaming of a swim,' she said, shrugging him off.

Rob laughed. The sight of her all mussed up, with dirt smeared across her face and a sheen of sweat on her décolletage, stirred something inside him. 'I'm dreaming of helping my hot trade assistant out of those sweaty clothes and rewarding her for all this hard work,' he said, pulling Angie towards him by a belt loop. 'Skinny dipping sounds a lot more appealing than gutting the cottage bathroom.'

'Not sure Port Fairview is quite ready for that type of action,' grinned Angie, swatting his hand away. He hoisted the sledgehammer back over his shoulder and winked at her as he started towards the cottage.

Claudia toddled over with the fresh water bottle he'd asked her to fetch. 'Daddy?'

He bent down and kissed her cheek, her little giggle making his heart melt. This was what it was all about—working as a family to get stuff done.

A vehicle slowed on Enderby Lane and he looked up to see a ute and trailer pulling into their driveway. The bobcat on the trailer looked near new.

'I thought you told them we'd already booked something else,' he said quietly, studying the trailer and its contents. Borrowing machinery from a bloke he'd never even met didn't sit well. Bobbi's name had seemed to pop up every minute these last two weeks, but even so, Ange's new friend and personal trainer lending them a digger seemed excessively generous. What was in it for them?

'I tried, but Bobbi said she'd already sorted it,' said Angie. Her eyebrows had furrowed and he noticed her automatically smoothing her hair and standing up a little straighter. Who was she making a good impression for? Her new friend? Her new friend's husband? He tried to dislodge the stupid kernel of jealousy. *This is Ange, remember?*

The black dual-cab ute pulled to a stop in the driveway, not a speck of dust or dirt on it. Gravel crunched underneath the woman's sandals as she stepped out of the car. *So that's Bobbi,* thought Rob, blinking at her bright white jeans. He wasn't sure what he'd expected but she seemed more malnourished than the strong, determined woman Ange had made her out to be.

Looks like she'd blow away in a gust of wind.

A short man got out of the driver's side and strode across the driveway. Rob couldn't help getting a childish kick out of seeing his polished boat shoes immediately blanketed in dust and fresh lawn clippings.

The bloke's gold watch glinted as he stuck out a hand. His skin was cold, and soft for a man who apparently worked with heavy machinery. His darting eyes reminded Rob of a shifty salesman.

'Rob Jones.'

'Alex Richardson. Nice to meet you both. I've heard a lot about your girls in the last few weeks.' Claudia ran in Alex's direction, and Rob wondered what would happen if she coated his pale cream slacks with muddy handprints, but she continued to the ute's back door, waving to the dark-haired child in a booster seat.

'Nice to see Jayden's got a good eye for the ladies,' Alex said, smirking at the sight of Claudia and his son chatting away. Rob didn't share his amusement and was glad when Ange and Bobbi joined them.

Rob wiped his palms on his shirt before shaking Bobbi's hand. Her grip was firmer than her husband's, her gold bracelets jangling on skinny wrists.

Angie lit up as she talked to her friend. 'Sorry, we're all filthy! Thanks so much for loaning us the bobcat.'

Rob coughed uncomfortably as he turned back to Alex. Despite what Ange thought, he couldn't stomach borrowing such an expensive machine. 'What can we give you for the hire, mate?'

Another smirk appeared on the man's face. 'Save your money, buddy. You'll need it to repair *that* cottage. Swing me a box of beer when you return it, and we'll call it square.'

Rob fought the urge to defend the cottage.

The proof's in the pudding. Bobbi and Alex will be the first to get an invitation to our house-warming party when it's restored to its former glory. Then they'll see.

Rob shoved his hands in his pockets. He'd dealt with guys like this before. The desire to tell this guy to keep his digger rubbed against the need to keep Angie happy.

'Right . . . well . . . thanks. I'll get it back to you tonight.'

'Gotta help each other out, right? Port Fairview needs a new builder, and any friend of Bobbi's is a friend of mine.'

Alex pulled a wallet from his back pocket, holding it open long enough that they couldn't help but notice the thick wad of green notes within. He slid a business card out. 'Here's our address. You won't miss it—only place in Port Fairview with three storeys,' he said.

Three storeys? A house to suit his ego, Rob decided.

The sausage roll from lunch sat heavy in Rob's stomach as the Richardsons unhitched the trailer and left.

'Who's got the best contacts now, Rob Jones?' Angie did a little victory jig.

'Wouldn't trust him as far as I could throw him. Is he always so generous?'

Angie ran a hand over the bobcat tracks. 'Don't look a gift horse in the mouth. It'd take us days to clear all the shrubs around the house by hand.'

Rob's jaw clenched. He didn't know why Alex bugged him so much, but he knew it would be the first and last time he'd be forced into accepting something for nothing.

Thirteen

Rob eased the tractor to a stop and stretched in his seat. He'd been working a digger yesterday and a hay mower today, and was pleased to find both vehicles had handled well under his control.

He opened the cab door and admired his afternoon's work. Unlike the dairy paddocks, where he knew each dip, low stump and soft spot, he'd been cautious working this one. Had Ivan, the previous owner, known his property would be sold before hay season? What had Ivan been planning to do with a shed full of hay from his retirement home, anyway? It didn't make much sense, but Rob certainly wasn't going to let it rot in the ground.

Little pieces of straw settled on his skin as he climbed down from the tractor, each step bringing him closer to the sweet, ripe-smelling grass that would soon be turned into square bales. He whirled around at the sound of his father's voice.

'Just like riding a bike.' John nodded towards the neat rows of mowed grass in Rob's paddock. Rob raised an eyebrow, steeling himself for the inevitable follow-up—perhaps that he hadn't mown right into the corners, or the mower's cutting bar hadn't been set at the optimal distance from the ground.

He looked back at his father, surprised, when nothing followed. Had John Jones mellowed in his old age? 'Not likely I'd forget after all those years of driving this thing. Still okay if I borrow the baler next week?' asked Rob, watching his father assess a piece of cut grass. 'I'll only need a quarter of these bales, you're welcome to the rest.' The greenish stem splintered easily between John's fingers—almost ready for baling.

John nodded curtly. 'Your mother's invited you for dinner tonight. Got three kilos of pork defrosting on the sink already.'

Rob wondered what it would take for his father to phrase it as if *he* wanted their company too. Hell to freeze over?

John shot a look at the cottage. 'Saw you had some sort of digger there yesterday. Brett lent you one, did he?'

'Ange's friend. You know the Richardsons?'

John nodded slowly. 'Bit different, that bloke. Heard a few people have had run-ins with him.'

For the first time in ages, Rob agreed with his father. He scratched at the dirt with his boot, not liking the feeling one little bit. 'Yeah, that's the impression I got too. I'll let Ange know about dinner. She'll love a break from cooking.'

Angie unhooked her bra as soon as she walked into the shed. The mid-November heatwave had turned the cottage into a sauna, but at least the plaster was all out now. *Shower, cider and early to bed,* she thought, nudging Claudia towards the bathroom.

Rob loped into the shed half an hour later, whistling with the good humour of someone who had spent the day in an air-conditioned tractor cab.

'Good news, Mum's cooked a roast.'

Angie looked down at her nighty and cold cider. Small talk and a hot meal were the last thing on her mind. 'We're in a salad-and-PJs mood, aren't we, Claud. Next weekend?'

Rob shrugged, surprised. 'This from a girl who drove 200 kilometres north last weekend for her nephew's birthday? I thought you missed the Sunday roasts.'

I miss my *family's Sunday roasts.* As soon as the thought sprang into her head, Angie felt ashamed. She studied Rob's face. It would be easier to go than explain how she missed her family, not just the meals. *Just accept the hospitality.*

Claudia set upon the nibbles platter like a starved dog as soon as they arrived at the Jones's farmhouse.

'Aren't they feeding you?' said John, ruffling her curls.

Rosa hugged them enthusiastically and turned the ceiling fan up a notch, spreading porky aromas throughout the house.

Soft jazz played on the stereo and ice cubes clinked against glasses as Rosa set the table. She lifted the bottle of soft drink and beamed at Claudia. 'Another fizzy drink, poppet?'

Claudia nodded eagerly. Angie shot a look at Rob.

'Just water will be fine, thanks, Rosa. A third creaming soda and she'll be tearing the house down,' said Angie, moving the photo album from her lap and reaching across for the water jug.

'Fizzy, Granny!'

'Mum's right, two glasses is enough, Claud. You won't eat your dinner,' said Rob, picking up the plastic tumbler and holding it as Angie lifted the water jug.

Angie felt like the fun police but Claudia had already been given free rein on the nibbles platter, so her appetite for meat and three veg was already shot. Judging by the trifle in the fridge, there would be more than enough sugar in the dessert too. *I've got to draw the line somewhere.*

Rosa's face fell but she slipped the soft drink back into the fridge and busied herself with serving up.

John sharpened the carving knife. 'Everyone having crackling?'

Everyone but Angie nodded. Crunchy pork skin was normally a favourite, but she knew the fatty, salty treat would go straight to her thighs.

'So, tell us about your cottage,' said Rosa, sitting down to eat. 'Have you got the extension permit back yet? I dropped it into conversation when I saw the mayor yesterday. He might give it a nudge in the right department.'

Rob rolled his eyes. 'Nothing like keeping a low profile, Mum. Thanks.'

'Least I can do, Rob. I'm just as excited as you are. What colours are you thinking, Angie? It always looked so fabulous with a fresh coat of yellow paint.'

'We've decided on duck-egg blue, like a greyish blue. With white trim.'

John cut his meat into neat little pieces.

Rosa's brow furrowed. 'Greyish blue? Sounds a little maudlin, doesn't it? Yellow's such a cheerful colour . . .' Rosa trailed off, her eyes tracking from the buttercup walls of the lounge room to the vintage lemonade posters either side of her rangehood and the matching yellow floral curtains.

Angie's fork hovered a centimetre from her mouth as all eyes turned to her. She lowered the mouthful, hoping Rob would pipe up, but he was shovelling in food as if he hadn't eaten in days.

'We think it'll look good, but who knows? Maybe we'll buy a few sample pots in different shades and see how they go.'

'I'm sure it will be lovely, whatever you decide,' said Rosa, placing another shard of pork crackling beside Claudia's untouched beans.

'Lot of work to be done before you need to worry about picking paint,' said John.

Angie noticed Rob pause before slowly resuming his chewing.

'Oh hush, John. They're on their way and that's the main thing. Maybe we'll be able to do dinner together every Sunday,' she said brightly.

Angie pushed the carrots and corn around her plate, but before she could work out how to tactfully decline a weekly dinner arrangement, Rosa continued.

'And what about Christmas? We always have a fresh turkey from Mr Huppatz, but we could live on the edge and get some fresh crayfish if you'd rather? Whack a tablecloth over a few card tables and we could invite your family too, Angie. And you can come to mass with me if you like? John never bothers, but it's such a lovely tradition, don't you think?'

Angie sucked in a quick breath. *Is it suddenly hot in here?* Rosa's excitement and attempts to make her feel welcome were having the opposite effect. She hadn't discussed it with Rob yet, but she'd assumed they'd do something at the cottage with her sisters and Dad. Was she really so selfish that she hadn't yet thought to include John and Rosa in her plans? Angie grimaced into her roast potatoes, knowing it was true.

Rob's hand squeezed her knee gently. 'Steady on, Mum, we've only just moved in. Plenty of time to work something out.'

Angie nodded and drained her water in one big gulp, wishing for the millionth time her mum was still alive. Annabel had seen the good in everyone, and had always been quick with advice when her daughters asked for it. *What would Mum have suggested about how to live next door to my future in-laws without being in each other's pockets?*

Fourteen

The tradesmen worked as a team, removing heavy-duty jacks from around the house bearers and ferrying them back and forth to their trailer. Bit by bit, the base of the weatherboard house reappeared, floating upon its new foundations.

'That should pull her up. She'll be good for another fifty years on those new stumps,' said the head contractor, wiping his florid face. Angie poured him a glass of iced water and handed it over with a plate of morning tea.

'Thanks, Colin. We won't know that back room without a saggy corner,' she said.

He poured himself another drink before shovelling in a mouthful of chips. It wasn't quite the baked spread she normally offered guests, but the tradies weren't complaining.

'You'll be able to roll a marble on it, darl. Smart thinking to get this sorted first. It's a cardinal sin to forget about the bones of the building.'

Angie nodded; his sentiments mirrored Rob's exact words.

'The real test is making sure all the doors open and close properly.' Colin fished his ruler from a pocket as he strolled into the cottage. Angie followed, amused by the careful way he opened each door.

Satisfied with his inspection, Colin gestured to a window. 'Good as gold. Had any problems with those feral pigs in the scrub? Poll Dorset stud a few clicks down the road had loads of trouble a month ago.'

Angie laughed, looking at the forest along the back of their property, speckled with manna gums, and home to a healthy population of koalas, wallabies and kookaburras.

'Pigs? I'm more worried about snakes. I suppose we could set up some traps or something.' She thought of the roast Rosa had served up the week before. 'Fill the freezer with pork, perhaps.'

Colin stroked his moustache. 'It's no joke. Keep an eye out for the hunters too. Gung-ho shooters ripping across paddocks, leaving gates open, popping anything that moves,' he said, diving into the chip bowl again. A flurry of chips settled on the floorboards. His grim expression turned thoughtful. 'Slap a few "No trespassing" signs on your gates. That'd be a start.'

'Righto, Colin,' said Angie, biting back amusement.

Colin's brow furrowed as he studied her. 'These aren't cute and cuddly piggies, they're big hairy buggers armed with tusks that'll slice through leather. Keep an eye out if that creek behind your place runs dry. You don't want one in your backyard. Specially with your little tacker.' He gestured to the backyard, where the patchy lawn was already littered with Claudia's scooter, a basket of dolls and an upended tub of plastic farm animals. Angie's pulse raced, only easing when she spotted Claudia sitting underneath the mulberry tree, plucking leaves from the lower limbs.

She mustered up a breezy farewell for the tradesmen, but when their trailer rattled off along Enderby Lane, she turned back to the forest and tried not to imagine Colin's shooters or beasts lurking within.

A blast of spring rain chased away the previous week's hot spell. *There's one thing south-west Victoria does well, and that's rain,* thought Angie as she tugged on a cardigan. She rifled through the caravan cupboards, her stomach as empty as the biscuit jar she normally kept full. Her gaze caught on the recipe book in the bottom corner of the cupboard; the handwritten recipes and magazine clippings were useless without an oven. She didn't really need the recipes to make her favourites—the measurements for yo-yo biscuits, muesli-bar slice and carrot cake were imprinted on her brain—but the sight of her well-loved book prompted a jolt of hunger.

Angie paused at the water crackers, pushed aside the heaped pile of low-fat, sugar-free bliss balls Bobbi had recommended and sighed. Her loose waistband was a sure sign she'd started to strip excess fat, but how could one little recipe book be almost enough to lead her astray? She peered into the small cabinet once again, cursing Bobbi's suggestion to remove sweets, treats and temptations.

'Come on, Claudia, let's make a snack,' she said. Claudia raced out of the caravan. They crouched by the shed fridge, pulling out cucumbers, carrots and strawberries and stacking them on the bench.

Claudia clambered onto a stool, her disappointed expression reflecting Angie's. She probably hungered for something more along the lines of hot Milo and cake too.

'This will be yummy, Claud,' she said, raising her voice above the rain as her daughter crunched on carrot sticks. The grey clouds out the shed windows made the small space feel oppressive.

You're doing so well, don't spoil it now. New town, new you, she reminded herself, taking a cucumber stick. She channelled her inner Bobbi and conjured up an encouraging smile for Claudia's benefit. 'Jayden and Oscar love their veggies,' Angie said.

'Scarlett and me love cake,' said Claudia.

Angie burst out laughing. Tessa's pantry was as well stocked with home-baked goods as her own used to be, each Tupperware container filled with equal quantities of sugar and love.

Angie finished her snack before unloading the washing machine. The morning of wet weather would have spoiled the curing hay had Rob not stayed up till midnight baling it. It had also rendered the outdoor clothesline useless but there was no room to set up a clothes hoist in the shed.

Inspiration struck as she assessed Rob's motorbike collection. He'd squeezed seven vintage bikes into their makeshift living area so John and Rosa's hay shed could return to its original purpose—storing the freshly baled hay.

She slipped Rob's monogrammed work shirts onto coat-hangers and hung them from handlebars. Claudia giggled as she draped socks over foot pegs and clutch levers.

'Washing's sorted!' Angie wondered what Rob would say when he arrived home from work to find her bras stretched between his motorcycle mirrors.

Rain was belting down with such gusto that she didn't even hear the door open.

'Yoo hoo! Just me.' Water beaded off her mother-in-law's oilskin jacket and puddled on the concrete floor Angie had just mopped. 'Lovely weather for ducks out there. Hard to believe it was stinking hot two days ago,' Rosa said, shaking off her jacket.

Angie moved to put the kettle on. Like the swinging weather patterns of south-west Victoria, she was almost accustomed to Rob's mother unexpectedly dropping in now. 'Hi Rosa. Tea or coffee?'

Claudia flew across the room, aiming not for Rosa's outstretched arms but for the calico bag she carried. 'Cake, Granny? Pop coming too?'

Rosa laughed at Claudia's optimistic tone. 'He's out fixing a downpipe that came loose in the storm. Can't waste a drop of rainwater this time of year. Won't be enough to fill the dams or get the creek running again, but we'll take it. I'd murder a coffee, thanks Angie.'

Rosa pulled two large plastic containers from her carry bag. Angie looked on with a mixture of longing and irritation.

'Vanilla slice delivery. I know you're on some type of diet, but you've still got to eat, don't you?' Rosa eyed the cucumber and carrot sticks on the benchtop.

'It's a health kick, not a diet. Rob will be pleased, I'll bet. Vanilla slice is his—'

'Favourite, I know,' said Rosa, handing a square to Claudia, who almost knocked the veggie sticks off the benchtop in her hurry to grab it. 'Think she takes after her dad. There's plenty there for you too, Angie. Brought you milk too. Fresh from the vat this morning. I skimmed the cream off the top so it's healthier for you. Probably just as low-fat as shop-bought, but better. You need to keep your calcium up anyway. Don't want to pass on brittle bones to any future babies.'

Angie counted to three in her head as she placed a coffee in front of Rosa and wrapped her hands around her own mug. She wasn't sure if the gesture was to stop herself from taking a piece of slice or throttling Rosa, but either way, she clung to the mug like a lifebuoy.

'Thanks. It's supposed to rain all week?'

'Yep. Cats and dogs today, then lighter the rest of the week. The boys got the hay done in the nick of time, didn't they? It's so good of Rob to give us most of it. You sure you won't need it?'

'It's no use to us. You're the ones with cows to feed, and after all the help you've given us so far with moving and . . .' *Supplying us with an endless assortment of delicious baked goods.* 'Of course you should have the hay,' said Angie.

Rosa peered at her as if she were short-sighted before gazing around the room, suddenly silent. *That's odd*, thought Angie. Rosa was never lost for words. She thought back to the conversation she'd had with Rob months ago, before they'd purchased the property, and his suggestion of raising a few cattle of their own. She inhaled sharply, glancing out the window at the house that was already consuming every free moment. They didn't have time for cattle.

Rosa reached back into her calico bag, drawing out a stack of magazines and sitting them on the table. 'Found these in Rob's old bedroom. I know they're ancient, but there might be a few good articles in there for you.'

Angie leafed through the building magazines. The nineties décor and DIY mudbrick projects were good for a laugh, but she was less impressed by the extra motorbike magazines. The last thing Rob needed was more motorcycle eye-candy.

'How old was Rob when he started buying these? I can't believe you kept them all this—'

'All this time? Well, I couldn't bear to throw them out, like the old woollen jumpers I dropped off for Claudia. He saved his pocket money to buy these. I knew they'd come in handy one day.'

Angie glanced around the shed—at the bag of moth-eaten cardigans and pullovers Rosa had brought around last week, and the stack of magazines on the table. There was barely enough room to move in the shed as it was.

Where does Rosa expect us to keep them? At this rate, we won't have anywhere to eat breakfast.

Rosa pulled a piece of paper from her pocket and handed it to Angie. 'And this is a list of all the tradesmen we've used over the years, at the house and the dairy. We've worked out the hard way which ones are useless, so you won't need to make the same mistakes.'

Angie took the list and used a magnet to secure Rosa's tradesmen recommendations to the fridge. She knew it was a well-intentioned gesture, but it felt smothering, like Rosa wanted to micromanage everything.

'Thanks, Rosa, I'll show Rob.'

Rosa beamed at Angie, oblivious to her reservations. 'It's wonderful having you both here, Angie. And Claudia. Now all we need is Max home and everything will be perfect.'

Angie heard the note of hope in Rosa's voice. Even though she hadn't met Max, Angie knew enough to understand his return home would be far from perfect.

Fifteen

The ladder wobbled under Angie's hands as Rob climbed onto the roof. She stepped back and shielded her eyes against the sun to watch Brett balance on the ridge beam. Although they'd spent all morning working six metres off the ground, Angie still held her breath as the pair navigated the rusty tin.

He's a plumber. He probably does it every day, she told herself, catching Brett's eye.

'You look like Tessa. She's always scared I'll trip on my shoelaces and take a tumble,' he said.

'That's why he wears boots,' grinned Rob.

You still might trip on your baggy jeans, thought Angie, copping another eyeful of his backside as he crouched down and extended the tape measure. 'Aren't you supposed to use harnesses?'

'Nah, harnesses are for scaredy-cats. More of a nuisance than anything. Let go, Rob, we're almost done,' said Brett, writing down the final measurement.

'Wait up—leave the extra rope around the chimney for a sec. Ange, come check out the view from the roof ridge. You can see Lady Julia Percy Island from up here,' said Rob.

Angie shook her head.

'But he's got the rope up here, easy as pie.'

'You're joking, right? Anything higher than the gutter and there's no way I'm doing it.'

Rob looked confused. Angie felt her smile slip. Brett chuckled as he untied the rope from around the chimney.

'Such a sensitive soul, our Jonesy. What type of bloke forgets his girlfriend's scared of heights?' he said. 'You'll probably need to enter a reminder for your birthday into his phone too, just to be sure.'

'Yeah, yeah,' Rob laughed as he climbed to the ground, but Angie could see he'd been caught out. It wasn't that he'd forgotten—it was the fact they'd probably never discussed her fear of heights before.

Brett caught her eye as he scaled the roof, his sandy hair flopping down over his face. He suddenly yelled, 'Woah!'

Angie's breath caught as Brett stumbled, his arms stretching out for balance. She dashed to the edge of the cottage, knowing putting herself directly beneath a plummeting plumber was a completely daft idea, but unable to stop herself rushing towards him.

A cheeky look crossed Brett's face. 'Just joking, Ange. I've got the reflexes of a cat.'

Rob threw his head back and let out a roar of laughter.

Angie whacked his arm. 'It's not even funny.'

What if he really had fallen? It'd make the mums' group a bit awkward, wouldn't it? 'Sorry about your husband, Tessa. He was horsing around on our roof when he broke his neck.' She took two steps back and craned her neck to glare at Brett. 'I won't try to catch you next time.'

'No catching required, Ange, promise.' Brett climbed down and tied the ladder to the roof of his work van, then leaned against the side. 'I'll quote up all the roofing iron and gutters tomorrow, before I hit the frog and toad. Got leaking roofs all over Port Fairview to fix, thanks to last week's rain. But your tin should arrive quickly. If the rain stays away, we'll have her re-sheeted in no time. Which sparkies you using?'

Angie shot a look at Rob and replied in a dry tone, 'According to Rosa, we can only use Thompson Electrical. All the other electricians in town are useless, apparently.'

'Mum's only trying to help,' said Rob.

'If only they weren't the ones with a six-week wait,' Angie replied. 'You know most of the tradesmen in town, Brett. Anything wrong with Codrington Electricians?'

Brett held up his hands. 'I'm not getting in the middle of this. All I can say is there's a reason why you don't have to wait long to get the Codrington blokes around.'

Angie shrugged but couldn't help wondering if Rosa would back off and let them make their own decisions or if she was only warming up.

The alarm clock trilled on the bedside table. 4.30 a.m. Angie crawled out of bed, eyes bleary as she instinctively felt for exercise clothes laid out the night before, only for her fingertips to find stiff denim and a fleecy jumper instead of soft lycra. *Ugh, milking time.*

Rob flicked on the bedside light, sparking a wail from Claudia's bed. 'Sorry, little princess, we've got to get up.'

Every fibre in Angie's body rebelled against the notion of deliberately waking Claudia now that she was finally sleeping through. She'd fleetingly thought of asking Tessa or Bobbi to stay the night, or come around early, to avoid waking Claudia, but had discarded the idea just as quickly. Where would a babysitter sleep in the tiny caravan? And she didn't know anyone in Port Fairview well enough to ask those types of favours. *Yet.*

'Time to get dressed, honey. We'll go see the cows.'

'Granny and Pop milking?'

'We're milking today, Claud.' Angie helped Claudia into her clothes and gratefully accepted a cup of coffee from Rob, who looked equally tired. Getting up early for a run was one thing, but she sensed she was going to need a fully functioning brain to milk cows. Rob squeezed her hand.

'Two days, that's all. I know Mum said they were happy to call in a relief milker while they were away, but it seemed stupid seeing as we're right next door now.'

'Honestly, I don't mind. They've got enough to worry about with their friend's funeral. It's not like we'll be doing it often.'

'I'll get the cows in. See you there.'

The cows were waiting in the yard by the time Angie flicked the dairy lights on, plugged in the vat hose and fitted the filter the way John had shown her. She slipped on the pair of khaki overalls and the plastic apron John had left for her, trying to remember what else he'd explained the afternoon before. The cows shuffled into the stalls either side of her, angle-parked with their heads facing away, keen to have the milk suctioned from their swollen udders.

Angie began to fit the cups, cautiously at first, her hands darting in and out quickly to minimise the chances of getting kicked. A happy squeal came from the far end of the dairy. Angie looked up to see John's border collies, Mog and Patch, sitting on either side of Claudia's pram, daintily accepting pieces of peanut-butter toast. 'Careful with the dogs, Claudia,' she said, hosing down the concrete as she'd seen John do.

Rob passed Angie in the lowered milking pit. 'They're probably the best-trained dogs this side of Melbourne. She'll be fine. Should get her one of her own, really.'

'I think we've got enough on our plate. Watch out, that cow's about to—' Angie pulled Rob to the side as a cow emptied her bladder.

'See, I've lost my touch. You, on the other hand, look like you're getting the hang of it. Don't tell Dad, or he'll train you up as part of his succession plan.'

'Fat chance. I don't know much about cattle. Pretty sure your dad will be carted out of here in a coffin.'

Rob stroked a cow's flank. 'There's only so long they'll be able to manage a herd this size. Max was—' He stopped abruptly.

They worked in silence for a while, Angie hosing down the udders and Rob switching the cups.

'Hey, you didn't know much about building until a month ago, either, and look how well that's working out. We could get a small herd, start tiny and build up until we're cattle barons,' Rob finally said.

Angie opened her mouth to make another joke, but she stopped at the sight of his eager expression. She sprayed the next cow's udders, trying to decide if she was pleased or concerned about Rob's endless enthusiasm and boundless ideas. There was no doubt he was Rosa's son.

'I think we've got enough going on right now,' she hedged, hoping he'd forget all about it, like his latest suggestion to turn their freestanding chimney into a pizza oven.

The sun had been up for an hour by the time Rob patted the last of the milkers on the rump, sending them back down the laneway. They finished washing up the dairy yard. The conversation circled back to cattle as they checked the milkers had made it back to their paddock and shut the gate.

'Have you heard of Speckle Park cattle?'

Angie yawned and shook her head. Claudia mimicked her.

'They're the hottest new thing out of Canada. One of my mining mates told me about his brother's herd, reckons they're incredibly high yielding. They're pretty, with a gorgeous black-and-white-speckled coat, but I'm more interested in what lies beneath the hide. His brother got a 70 per cent carcass yield. Seventy per cent, Ange! Regular British breeds typically yield about 55 per cent. It's a goldmine.'

'Hold up, we were talking about *possibly* getting a few cows an hour ago. Now you're seriously considering starting a stud? I'm not sure we're ready to add livestock breeding to our to-do list, are we?' Angie was racking her brains trying to keep up with Rob's train of thought.

'You never know, Ange. You might love it,' he laughed, taking her hand and whistling as he lifted Claudia over the fence.

Angie yawned her way through the Rhythm and Rhyme class and the grocery store, then basked in the last minute of the car's air conditioning as she pulled off Enderby Lane and into their driveway. The new sign on their fence made her smile.

Bottlebrush Cottage.

Rob's tongue had poked out the corner of his mouth as he'd painted each letter, then coated the sign with so many layers of marine-grade varnish that Claudia spotted her reflection.

She unpacked the groceries into the shed fridge. Sweat dripped down her cleavage, the fridge providing only momentary respite from the otherwise sweltering space. Hot, then rainy, and now hot again. *Topsy-turvy weather.*

'It's like a sauna in here,' she groaned, switching on the pedestal fan as she made a green smoothie. Channelling her inner Bobbi, she downed a handful of almonds with brisk efficiency, focusing on the feel of her loose belt and not Rosa's latest delivery of slice. She moved the pile of freshly printed

Christmas cards to the outdoor setting. It was almost as hot outside the shed as inside, and slightly steamy after the recent rain, but at least the verandah offered shade from the belting sun and a tiny wisp of breeze.

Angie allowed herself a moment to study the cards, admiring their first proper family portrait. Claudia stood in between her and Rob, her head not quite reaching the top of the Bottlebrush Cottage sign. The morning sunshine cast a golden glow on the weatherboards behind them. The timer had captured a flock of yellow-tailed black cockatoos sweeping through the cloudless sky above them. Although the yard was cluttered with building supplies and the lawn was scarred by plumbing trenches, the cottage had a happy aura.

It wasn't magazine perfect, it wasn't even anywhere close to being habitable, but it was theirs.

Sixteen

Angie turned the radio down, listening to see if the noise she'd heard was just Claudia and her stack of blocks, or someone knocking on the door. The noise came again and she swung open the front door of the cottage to find a tiny lady on the front step. A bulging shopping bag dangled from each of her arms. Her hair was as white as her false teeth, and her razor-sharp gaze made Angie stand a little straighter.

'Can I help you?' Angie asked, wiping dusty hands against her shorts. The lady thrust the bags at Angie, then rebuttoned her cardigan.

'I'm Mrs Ellis, a friend of Rosa. Taught your Robert at primary school, so I did. Time to downsize my dahlia patch; half an acre is too much for an old duck like me. Pop them in the ground and you'll have cut flowers for months.'

Angie examined the brown, soil-encrusted tubers inside the bag. Green and white shoots poked out from some, looking more like sweet potatoes than anything floral.

'Thank you, but—'

'No need to thank me. But get them in the ground this week, mind, so they'll be ready for the dahlia show in March.'

Angie pursed her lips. What was she missing here? Was she supposed to know something about a flower show?

'It's our twenty-fifth anniversary this year, and, as secretary, you'll need the best stock for your entry.'

Angie's mouth gaped. *Secretary? When did that happen? And why is this lady talking as if it's a* fait accompli?

'I don't mean to be rude, but I think you've got the wrong end of the stick, Mrs Ellis. We'll be busy renovating—I don't have time for any committees.'

The old lady waved her hand dismissively. 'Young people these days ... too busy for reading, too busy for gardening. What's the world coming to? Rosa's told me all about your committee management skills. Said you'd be perfect for the job.' She clasped Angie's hands in her own and squeezed them with a strength belying her eighty-something years. 'Like I always say, "If you want something done, ask a busy woman." It's only a tiny role, really. Bright young lass like you will run rings around us oldies.'

Despite Angie's protests, Mrs Ellis wouldn't take no for answer.

Thanks a million, Rosa, thought Angie, dumping the bag of tubers on the ground. After hearing out Mrs Ellis's detailed instructions on how to plant, stake and tend to the water-hungry plants, she realised the secretarial role would be the least time-consuming part of the deal.

Country music filled the ute cabin as Rob turned away from the coast and headed inland. His phone vibrated on and off throughout the drive: new clients wanting quotes, suppliers trying to sell him tools and machinery worth more than a new roof, and a call from Angie he let go straight to voicemail.

'Don't want to spoil the surprise, do we?' he said, turning to Claudia in her car seat. She gave him a toothy grin in return and a thumbs up as the Grampians mountain range loomed on the horizon and they approached the turn-off for McIntyre Park Merino Stud. Instead of parking near the lavender hedge, where Ange always pulled up when they visited her family farm, Rob sought the shade and parked the work vehicle under a towering maple tree that had been planted by the late Annabel McIntyre.

Rob unfolded his long legs. Stretched, breathing in the sweet spring grasses and lingering smell of wool from the nearby shearing shed. The combination was distinctly Western District, so different to the salty, sandy scents of Port Fairview, and the hot dry desert of the West Australian mine.

He checked the crate of chickens on the ute tray as he walked past. Little red feathers poked out through the wire, the birds clucking and shuffling around as he walked to the passenger door. Rob leaned back in and unbuckled Claudia. He felt the press of paws on the back of his leg as he straightened. A young pup weaved in and out of his legs, its tail propelling its body sideways with each excited wag.

'Look, Claud! Your new puppy wants to say hello,' he said, holding out a hand. The kelpie sniffed at his hand. Rob crouched down quietly, keeping Claudia to one side as he settled the boisterous dog. 'You're a little beauty,' he crooned, ruffling her fur and pushing her down to sit. The pup obliged, ears pricked, and sat to attention. 'Gentle, Claud, she's a bit excited,' he said, guiding her hand over the pup's soft fur. The interaction between the two was priceless.

The farmhouse door creaked open and Rob looked up to see Angie's father standing on the top step. 'Nice-looking kelpie, Angus. Have you given her a name yet?'

'That's your job. Good to see you, mate. Snazzy ute you've got there.'

Rob turned to admire the sign-writing. He still got a buzz out of seeing his business name splashed across the side of the work ute. 'Yeah, not too shabby, thanks. Needs a wash though.'

Angus smiled and pointed to the farm vehicles parked under the carport, each coated with a thick layer of red grime. 'You've either got too much time on your hands, or too much water, if you're worried about a little dirt. Coming in for a cuppa? Penny and Tim are out drenching, they shouldn't be far off though.'

'Yep. Coming, Claud?' Rob scooped Claudia up into his arms and started towards the house. The pup jumped up, trying to nip her dangling feet.

She squealed, then laughed. 'My puppy,' she said, squirming until Rob set her back down.

'Careful with her, Claud. Don't let her bite you.' Rob watched the black-and-tan muzzle sniff at Claudia's hand, then lick it gently.

'I'll stay here, Daddy.'

'Grandpa and I will get a drink and we'll be outside in a minute, okay?' Rob kept an eye on the pair as he followed Angus inside, watching them through the window as the kettle boiled.

'I guess you've got a birthday party planned with all her little friends tomorrow? Has Angie already given the pup a name? Hope it isn't Scruffy or Rex. Never could quite come up with an original name when she was younger,' said Angus, wedging the tea canister between the bench and his waist so he could remove the lid one-handed. Rob bit back an automatic offer to help. It may have been years since the farm accident, but Angus still wore his independence like a badge of honour.

'Haven't actually mentioned the pup to her yet, or the chickens. It's a bit of an impromptu birthday present for Claud and I thought the chooks would be a nice surprise for Ange.'

Angus shot him a quick look. 'Good luck there, son. Angie's hated chickens since Randy the rooster attacked her when she was ten. They mess with her asthma too. Thought she would've mentioned it?'

Rob swallowed hard. He'd never asked the question. *What's not to like about chickens?* 'She loves free-range eggs for her baking, though she's barely had a chance to cook without an oven, so I just figured she'd love her own chickens. God, tell me she likes kelpies?'

Angus peered out the window. It was hard to tell who was having the most fun—Claudia or the puppy. The pup was nestled in her arms, lapping up the attention. Rob remembered Rosa's advice the previous week. *Mum was right, every kid needs a dog.*

'Angie's not too different to the little one out there. Loves a good sheep dog. Bit of training, and the pup'll be rounding up chickens in no time,' said Angus.

Rob let out a sigh of relief and held the back door open for Angus. Claudia rounded the corner, pup by her side, as they eased into the wicker chairs on the farmhouse verandah.

'How's the cottage coming along?'

Rob sipped his tea and studied the deep-blue mountain range stretching across the horizon. 'Pretty good. Foundations are rock solid again, footings are in for the extension and the roofing iron's arrived, ready to screw down as soon as the new wall frames are up. Humming along, really. How're things up here?'

Angus stared out at the golden paddocks. 'Dry as a bone, and it's not even proper summer yet. Already started feeding out, might have to de-stock if it keeps up. You got much grass in your paddocks? I'll send a truckload of woolly lawnmowers down your way if you need some help?'

Rob laughed. 'Sorry, you're too late. Dad extended his herd the minute we signed the papers, so most of our paddocks are full of Friesians. And hopefully cash crops and a few specialty-breed calves if all goes to plan.'

Angus nodded as Rob settled back in his chair and filled his future father-in-law in on everything he knew about Speckle Park cattle, his plans to start their own herd and the calves he'd paid a deposit for.

Angie almost felt like a Port Fairview local as she whizzed through the hardware store, knowing which aisles she needed for building supplies, plus the gardening items on her shopping list. A queue had formed behind her by the time Wally finished ringing up her purchases.

'Just on the home account, thanks, Wally. You'll be pleased the town is humming before school holidays even kick off?'

Wally's lined face creased into a smile as the electric doors slid open and another stream of customers poured in. 'Shaping up to be our best summer yet. Now, before I get silly-season fatigue and forget, Rosa was in here the other day, mentioned you were a fundraising guru. Can I tempt you to join the Tidy Towns committee? I know you've got your hands full with your little one and renos, but we need every cent if we're going to keep our title for the fourth consecutive year. Camperdown is champing at the bit to take our spot and Rosa said your bake sales are a cash bonanza.'

Did she now? What else has Rob told Rosa during their phone calls?

Angie thought of the kitchen benches back in their old rental, regularly laden with all manner of biscuits, cakes, muffins and slices for bake sales over the last few years, despite their temperamental oven. Their new cottage kitchen would be twice the size, but instead of filling her with joy, the idea of obligatory committee baking made her head pound.

'Can I get back to you?' Angie forced an apologetic smile, grabbed her trolley and almost took out a stand of camping chairs in her haste to leave. The queue surged forwards and she was grateful the store was busy. A lack of customers would have presented Wally with way too much time for persuasion.

'We'll talk about it next time,' Wally called after her.

Angie nodded and raced out the door, hoping festive fatigue would well and truly wipe the idea from the shopkeeper's memory.

Back home, she unloaded the car in a rush, hoping she'd have enough time to make Claudia's birthday treats before she and Rob returned home. *Next year I'll make her a whopping big cake,* Angie thought. But this year, it would be a fruit sculpture. She cut the fruit into perfect squares and threaded them onto skewers. Before she knew it, the watermelon was covered with spikes of multi-coloured fruit kebabs. She was pleased with the end result. The only thing left to do was make room in the fridge for the colourful centrepiece and ensure Claudia didn't see it until her party tomorrow. Angie was just about to transfer it to the fridge when a knock came at the shed door.

'Cooeee!' said Rosa. 'Special delivery for the birthday girl.'

Angie gasped at the pink monstrosity in Rosa's arms. It wasn't just a cake, it was a double-decker princess fairy castle cake decorated with every type of sweet imaginable. Rainbow sour-strap flags waved from turrets, musk sticks held up the drawbridge, marshmallows lined the roof, there were chocolate-chip windows and the whole thing floated on a cloud of fairy floss.

'Rob mentioned you were stuck for ideas, so I couldn't help myself. You don't mind, do you?'

Angie glanced at the healthy alternative she'd been happy with just two minutes ago, then back at the spectacular offering. It was the type of cake Claudia would remember when she was an adult, the kind Angie would have baked herself if she had an oven. There was no way she could turn it down, not after Rosa had gone to so much trouble. But somehow, even though she smiled and nodded, she couldn't shake the twinge of resentment.

Mum would have asked first. Lara, Diana and Penny wouldn't have assumed.

The optimism that had sustained Rob throughout the 400-kilometre round trip faded as he turned into Enderby Lane, and disappeared altogether when he saw the expression on Angie's face at their approach. She had a death grip on the garden hose, the watering forgotten as her eyes fixed on the crate of chickens.

'Please tell me you've brought those chooks for Brett, or your mother? God knows she needs them with all this baking she's doing. I don't do poultry.' Angie looked horrified. 'And a puppy?'

Rob stepped out of the ute, still struggling to think of a solution as he unbuckled Claudia. She wriggled out of his arms and climbed up the tyre and into the ute tray. The pup barked and licked Claudia. Feathers floated through the air as the chickens raced around their confined space.

He turned back to Angie, but her expression hadn't changed. 'I didn't know you were scared of chickens until after we'd collected them from Penshurst and I'm not sure the lady will give us a refund. I'm hoping you'll grow to love them? Claud loves them already. Think of all the double-yolkers they'll lay.'

Angie sighed. 'I'm not *scared* of chickens, they give me asthma! And I don't even have an oven, remember? Nor do we have a chicken coop. Unless you've knocked up a henhouse overnight?

'Mum thought . . .' Rob's heart sank as her face hardened.

'Oh God, of course your mother had something to do with this. Just like the Tidy Towns committee, the dahlia show and the whopping pink birthday cake. Why are you introducing a whole new level of work to our property? I don't have time to train a dog either!'

Rob watched Angie storm off. His boots felt heavy as he walked back to the ute. Even the sight of Claudia and the pup failed to lift his spirits.

'C'mon, Claud. You and me had better get these animals sorted while Mum . . .' He tried to think of a kid-friendly expression. 'While she cools off a bit.'

He looped a piece of bright blue baling twine through the dog's collar. She licked his cheek. He unclipped her from the chain, ruffled her soft fur and set her on the ground. *At least someone's happy with the situation.* Claudia grabbed the twine from his hands and dragged the puppy towards the sandpit, her laughter floating through the heat. *Make that two.*

The battery drill whirred to a sluggish halt as Rob sank the final screw into the sheet of burgundy tin. He wiped sweat from his eyes and stepped back to admire the chicken coop.

'How's that, Claud? Keep the chooks in and the foxes out for a few days?'

The final rays of sunshine reflected off the chook house and matching doghouse he'd whipped up with sheets of leftover roofing iron. Working with dark-coloured tin during a heatwave wasn't ideal, but neither, he guessed, was buying chickens for someone who didn't like poultry. He swore under his breath again. *How did you miss that one, Jones?*

'Very good, Daddy,' said Claudia, patting his leg and smiling up at him.

The old chimney stood like a monument in the middle of the new chook yard. He tapped the red-brick and mortar structure, satisfied the chook house he'd built on one side would solve Angie's concerns about its stability.

Claudia pushed the puppy off her lap and reached for the lightweight door he'd fashioned from chicken wire, tin and weatherboards. She swung it with glee, a huge smile on her face as she kneeled down to check the new set-up. He followed her into the weatherboard coop, grabbed a handful of straw and stuffed it into the roosting boxes now nestled against the side of the old brickwork.

'Chooky eggs?'

Rob nodded, feeling sweat dripping off the end of his nose. 'They'll lay in there when they're settled.' The puppy yipped from her kennel as they moved the chickens into their new home.

'Mummy see?'

Rob looked back at the cottage and shed, but Ange's little red hatchback still hadn't returned. If this was how she reacted to chickens and a puppy, how was she going to manage the next surprise he'd planned? *Too late now, Jones. You'd better suck it up. Maybe Mum will have some tips?* He recalled the way Angie's lips had compressed into a thin line at the mention of Rosa's recent 'help' and nixed the idea.

'C'mon, Claud. Let's take the pup for a swim. Mum might be at the beach.' He untied the pup from her kennel, lifted the dog onto the back of the ute, strapped Claudia into her seat and headed down the driveway.

Before pulling onto the main road, he noticed a bundle of envelopes sticking out of the mailbox. He quickly leafed through them. Two envelopes caught his attention. Rob's sweaty fingers slipped as he fumbled to open them. He winced at the figure on the bottom of the glazing quote. He'd hoped the first glazier had been way off the mark, but this was the second quote for windows, and it had just as many zeros on the bottom line. Unless both glaziers were incorrect, they needed to find an extra $20,000 on top of their allocated amount to double-glaze the cottage. Red tape jacked up the price of anything with a bushfire rating. A fresh torrent of sweat rolled down his back.

He looked at the empty spot where Ange's hatchback was normally parked. Today wasn't a good day to explain this one. He'd have to bide his time.

Even as the sun set, it still had bite. Angie waded into the ocean in her exercise shorts and singlet, letting it wash away the last traces of anger that had remained after her fast run. Saltwater merged with sweat as she ducked under a gentle wave then floated on her back.

Angie closed her eyes, trying to empty her mind of everything except the cawing seagulls and lapping water. But instead of letting go, her thoughts kept returning to her and Rosa. To her and Rob. Not so much the chickens, but what the gesture had unearthed.

A gaping big hole in their relationship.

An abyss of unknowns that divided them.

How was Rob to know each and every one of her likes and dislikes? They'd had three years and nine months together, and more than half that time he'd lived on the other side of the country. And only nine months of it had been without a child in their lives. Just like Bobbi had said earlier on their run, as she'd pushed Angie to go a little faster, there were bound to be gaps in their knowledge of each other.

Angie felt water rushing into her ears and flung her arms out wider to stay afloat. She'd expected their relationship to be threatened by big things, like whether or not to continue with their surprise pregnancy, or agreeing to disagree when it came to politics, or baptising their child just to keep the peace. But they'd weathered those storms and instead somehow skipped the conversations about hopes and dreams, fears and first loves, ambitions . . . and attitudes towards extended family.

Family . . . Angie squeezed her eyes shut as a wave of grief ran through her. Her mum had now been out of her life for longer than she'd been in it, but it was on days like these— moments of confusion, anger and frustration—that she felt the loss acutely.

Mum wouldn't be hovering at our door, dropping off food all the time. Mum wouldn't be signing me up for overwhelming volunteer duties when I've just managed to escape those shackles. Mum wouldn't make gigantic pink birthday cakes unless I'd asked her to.

She swam and floated, floated and swam until the sound of a car pulling onto the gravel car park interrupted the tranquillity. Angie kept her eyes closed. Whichever tourist had managed to find the secluded cove would leave as soon as they saw it wasn't patrolled by lifeguards.

Car doors slammed and a familiar voice called out, 'Mummy!'

Angie turned to see Claudia launch herself into the surf, fully dressed. In a split second, Angie's moping transformed into terror. Claudia bounded into the waves, not a hint of concern wrinkling her round face as she slipped beneath the surface. Angie threw herself through the water, only pausing for air and to scan the swirling water for a mop of curls. Another wave broke. Claudia popped up, coughing and spluttering. Angie reached her at the same time as Rob. She quickly snatched Claudia into her arms.

'It's okay, Mum's here,' she soothed as she carried the crying child to the shore.

Rob's arms wrapped around them both, his breathing just as ragged. 'By the time I'd untied the pup, she was gone.'

'That could have been . . . She nearly . . .' Angie sagged to her knees and flopped onto the sand. Claudia's bottom lip quivered. Angie sucked in a shaky breath.

'Claud, you can't just run into the waves,' said Rob.

'Dad's right, Claudia. You've got to wait for Dad and . . .' she paused as she looked at the puppy. It licked Claudia's face gently and rested its head on Angie's arm.

Angie sighed. Maybe she should just accept the puppy as the kind gesture Rob had intended it to be. 'You've got to wait for Dad and the puppy. What are we going to call it, anyway?'

'Baxter?'

Rob laughed. 'It's a girl, Claud. And your teddy is already called Baxter. Maybe Mum should name her?'

Angie softened. She didn't want Claudia to remember her third birthday as the one when her parents didn't talk to one another. Tomorrow's party was going to be big enough already and Rob's support would make a world of difference in the Rosa-wrangling stakes.

'Violet would be a nice name. But you two are handling the chickens, all right? And you can be on dog poo duty, too.'

Seventeen

Claudia's birthday party went off with barely a hitch, and the following afternoon they were back on the tools. Weatherboards creaked and groaned, hanging onto the hardwood frames as tightly as they could. Angie wriggled the crowbar deeper under the edge, levering it downwards until she felt the nail loosen and finally give in. She looked across triumphantly and was rewarded with a cheer from Rob.

'See, it's all in the angle of the dangle. We'll have most of the boards pulled off by Sunday arvo if we keep going at this pace,' he said. Multiple layers of paint flaked off the old timber as they added it to their growing bonfire pile. They worked side by side for the rest of the morning, a shoulder-high pile of old weatherboards amassing beside Claudia's sandpit.

'Still don't understand why we don't just replace the buggered boards instead of every darn one,' said Angie. 'Or offer them to a salvager.'

Rob laughed as he carried an armful of boards to the heap.

'Then you'll be chasing your tail replacing every second or third one, and the profile on the new ones won't match the old ones, or they'll be a bit thicker or thinner. And who the heck's going to want all of them anyway? Imagine scraping all that paint off. It'd take forever!' Rob pushed his sleeves up and nodded at Claudia in the sandpit, surrounded by her new toys.

'Party went well yesterday,' he said.

'Despite your Mum's brilliant party activities.'

Rob grinned. 'The kids *loved* the water pistols.'

'You weren't the one wearing white when they started aiming for us. It was like a wet T-shirt contest after half an hour, and that darn pony,' said Angie.

Rob mumbled under his breath. 'White's a ridiculous colour. Just because Bobbi wears it . . .'

This from a guy wearing paint-stained footy shorts and the shirt he repaired with a stapler last week, Angie thought.

She prised a particularly tight board from the frame and turned to look at the ruined rose bushes. 'If I'd known, I would've suggested the pony stay next door and then it could've munched on Rosa's garden while giving pony-rides.' She scanned the yard and caught Claudia helping herself to the bowl of dog food.

'Claud! Leave that for Violet. Oh, gross.' Angie groaned as Claudia offered the pup a handful of food and deftly slipped another piece into her mouth.

Rob guffawed, looking at his watch. 'Think Claud's right. It's after ten. Smoko time?'

Angie washed Claudia's hands in the shed bathroom and returned to find Rob staring into the fridge.

'Where's all the leftover party food? And the pantry's pretty bare too. Are we *all* on a diet?'

'I sent a plate home with everyone. Your mum's bringing cake and bikkies every other day. No chance of starving around here.'

Angie pulled a tub of cream cheese from the fridge, mashed it with tuna and sweet chilli sauce and passed it across the bench. 'It's not a diet. Here, whack this dip on a few Jatz crackers. I'll have an apple.' She reached for the fruit bowl, ignoring Rob's gaze.

'Just because Bobbi's wielding the whip, doesn't mean you have to roll over and take it. I haven't seen you eat anything tasty in ages. Things are pretty tough if Claud has to resort to dog food, right?' He laughed, loading a cracker with her tuna dip and handing it to Claudia. '*This* is healthy. Fish, dairy . . . chilli's a veggie.'

Angie took another bite of her apple, leafing through the pile of mail on the bench, determined not to overreact like when he'd brought the new animals home. She knew he meant well—there wasn't a hint of malice in his body—but as much as she'd appreciated his recent insistence that he liked her curves, she couldn't help feeling a spike of irritation. It was fine for Rob—he could eat sweet treats without gaining a kilo—but she only had to *look* at a tray of lamingtons and they appeared on her hips the next morning. She was starting to feel good about her body for the first time in a long time. *Is that so hard to understand?*

'Bobbi's helping me be the best version of myself. So I can be a good role model for Claudia and . . .' She bit into her apple before she added the words 'her siblings'. Despite Rob's and Rosa's hints, she didn't want to add to their brood until they'd settled in. No ifs, buts or maybes.

She opened the glazier's envelope. 'Ughhh, this one's even more expensive than the last. I've got no idea how people afford ceiling-to-floor glazing, if this is the going rate for a few sheets of glass.'

Rob tapped the invoice. 'You know what they say. Quality doesn't cost . . . it pays. Least these ones will be Aussie-made, and if we've got any problems we'll be able to call up the local glazier, instead of dealing with some city schmuck. All my clients will be up in arms if word gets out we're spending most of our reno budget with out-of-town suppliers,' he said.

Angie rested her head on his shoulder and closed her eyes. He was right. Their building project was a hot topic every time she ventured into Port Fairview. From shopkeepers and Rob's old school friends to the postmistress and Rosa's craft cronies . . . everyone asked which tradies they were using, when they'd be finished and how it was all going. She just hoped their budget would stretch to accommodate the extra expenses before that particular topic became fodder for the rumour mill.

Angie rolled out of bed, shaking off dreams of gold-plated windows, diamond-encrusted chimneys and empty bank accounts. She crept though the shed by torchlight, collecting her running watch and keys before Claudia stirred again. Rob could deal with the next wake-up. The morning was fresh and dewy, in stark contrast to her grouchy mood. Angie forced herself to jog towards the hatchback and think about the new route Bobbi had planned for them, rather than the number of times she'd settled Claudia during the night.

She yawned as she drove past the Jones's dairy, lit up like a cruise ship in the pre-dawn sky. Angie was glad Rob hadn't followed in his parents' footsteps. It wasn't just the early mornings and the twice-daily commitment; she'd seen enough newspaper articles and *Landline* episodes to know dairy farming was a tough way to eke out a living. Between consumers wanting to pay rock-bottom prices for milk and big corporations that swallowed ma-and-pa operations for breakfast, the industry wasn't for the faint-hearted.

Bobbi was waiting by her mailbox, her glossy black ponytail swishing from side to side, when Angie arrived at her house.

She tapped her watch theatrically. 'Thought you were going to stand me up for a minute there. Trouble getting out of bed?'

Angie stifled another yawn as they set off towards the Port Fairview river. 'Spent more time out of bed than in it. Claudia was up all night. Helping at the dairy last week wasn't hard, but we've been paying for it ever since with Claudia's sleep. Or lack of sleep, more to the point.'

'Sounds like a great excuse to avoid future milking duties. How's your mother-in-law going, anyway? Or should I say "smother-in-law"? Still trying to sabotage your healthy-eating regime? She was force-feeding my boys cake at the party. No wonder Claudia had her choppers out—all that sugar sends them batty.'

'I know, I'm so sorry. Did she leave bite marks? I told Rosa not to bring anything, but she doesn't take no for an answer.' Angie almost stumbled as they transitioned from jogging to walking.

'You've gotta do something. Honestly! Maybe hang on to all her Tupperware, so she can't bring you anything else.'

'She means well, she's just a bit full on. Food deliveries are one thing, but the showing up unannounced is doing my head in. Claudia and I were dancing around the shed the other day, and next thing I know Rosa's waltzing in with a glazier—one of her friend's sons who was home for holidays. I don't know who was more mortified, me for singing into the end of a broom handle at the top of my lungs, or him for catching me in my nighty. And did I tell you about the committees knocking on my door? I guess I should be flattered, but I've got enough on my plate already.'

'You've got to set boundaries, Angie. Get Rob to speak to her.' Bobbi's wristwatch buzzed. 'Start running again.'

Angie picked up her pace. 'That's the problem. Rob already talks to her too much. It was her idea to buy Claudia a puppy and some chickens and if she's not dobbing me in to committees, she's corralling tradespeople and dropping hints about another grandchild.'

Angie was breathless from the effort, unlike Bobbi who still managed to run and talk with ease. A wheeze niggled in her chest and she slowed to take a few pumps from her asthma puffer.

'Ray Charles could see her meddling's coming between you and Rob. You shouldn't have to play second fiddle to his mum. Only one thing for it. You need to tell her to back off.'

Angie tried to catch her breath as they turned and retraced their steps. It was easy for Bobbi to say, but Angie knew she'd rather do a five-minute sprint than confront Rosa. *What was it Diana always said? Sometimes you've got to put up or shut up.* They were making progress on the cottage and once they were living there, all these niggles would melt away.

Angie sank into the shed couch and felt her eyes fluttering shut. She had plenty to do today, but sneaking in a speedy power nap while Claudia slept was too hard to resist. She woke with a start to see Tessa through the shed window, a plastic bag swinging from one hand and a large box in her arms.

'Knock, knock,' said Tessa before Angie had a chance to open the door.

Angie held a finger to her mouth and mimed a sleeping baby. Tessa pointed back at the sedan that was still running and lowered her voice.

'Snap, Scarlett's out cold too. Thought you'd get some use out of this,' she said, handing the large box over.

Angie looked inside. A mini-oven. *Why didn't I think of that?*

'It's just a cheapo Kmart one, but it's yours to borrow as long as you like.' She handed over the bag. 'And we've got tomatoes coming out our ears. Sing out when you eat them all and I'll send Brett around with another lot.'

'Thanks, Tessa, you're a sweetheart.'

Tessa waved a hand. 'Don't mention it. Anyway, I wanted to come around and clap eyes on this new roof Brett's been telling me about. I was so busy yakking at the party that I forgot to look.' They both turned and admired it. 'And I hear the Tidy Towns committee's trying to draw you in their war against Camperdown.'

Angie groaned. 'I'm working hard to get out of that one. I hate to think what else Rosa's dobbed me in for.'

'Rosa knows everyone in the town, and then some. I'd say she's trying to help you integrate into Port Fairview, so you'll feel more at home.'

If that's help, I'd hate to see her sabotage tactics. Angie accepted the bag of tomatoes and tried to see the situation from her friend's perspective.

'Maybe you're right, Tessa. I hadn't thought of it like that,' she said, willing herself to share Tessa's optimism.

It's enthusiasm, Angie told herself as Tessa drove away. *Not meddling. Not interfering. Enthusiasm! And if Rosa's 'enthusiasm' is the toughest part of this whole renovation, then we're pretty darn lucky.* She wondered how many times she would need to say it before she started believing it.

Rosa blew the steam away from her face as she stirred the rich red sauce, thinking of Claudia with each swoop of the wooden spoon. *I'll teach her to cook this lasagne. Show her how to stir a little love into every saucepan,* she thought. Her cheeks were flushed not only from the December heat but from pleasure at the thought of summer at the beach with her beautiful granddaughter, delivering hot meals to Rob and

Angie, and slowly immersing herself in their lives. The way it should be. *Angie might have turned down the offer of Sunday night roasts, but she'll come around eventually.*

John arrived, and she called out a cheery hello as he scrubbed his hands before heaping his dairy clothes into the washing machine and stepping into the shower.

He'd come around soon too. Softly, softly, just like she'd handled the discussion on the farm's future.

She smoothed her dark hair into a bun, wanting to look nice for her husband, before starting to compile two lasagnes—a small one for them and a bigger one for Rob and Angie. Her eyes looked in the direction of the small granny-flat on the edge of their property and she felt a frisson of excitement as she remembered their imminent guest.

I'll be baking for Max soon too, she thought, gathering ingredients for a triple batch of his favourite lemon slice. It hadn't been easy convincing Max to trade Christmas in Portugal for Port Fairview, but he hadn't flat-out rejected her suggestion about running the farm or the money she'd sent him for a plane ticket home. *And soon we'll all be together.*

Rosa heard the shower turn off, and John appeared in the doorway. He padded across the kitchen towards her, completely naked. He wrapped his arms around her from behind and ran a hand along her thigh.

'You old nudist,' she said affectionately, swatting him away.

'Bloke should be able to wander around his house in the raw if he feels like it. Not like the cows are watching from the paddock.'

'No, but we have neighbours now, John. What if Angie drops in?'

John walked back to the bathroom and returned with a towel around his waist. 'I'm not changing my ways, Rosa. It's thirty-eight degrees out there, and you're steaming up the kitchen with a bake-up in mid-December. Crikey, woman, what do you expect? Besides, not everyone takes the liberty of dropping in on their neighbours unannounced. You'll want to be careful you don't wear out your welcome.'

Rosa turned to face him, pressing a chaste kiss onto his frown. He smelled like soap and her expensive volumising shampoo. 'At least pull on some shorts. I'll slip a cold beer into a stubby holder, and then I want to tell you all about my good idea while I make lemon slice.' She smiled at his grumbles, knowing that as long as he was listening he was persuadable.

He perched on the stool behind the island bench, taking a swig from the icy can in front of him. His steel-grey hair was neatly combed either side of a part so straight it wouldn't budge in hundred-kilometre winds. Like the wiry strands growing out of his ears, and the coarse ones he clipped from his nostrils when he thought she wasn't watching, John's hair was as stubborn as he was.

'Hit me with it. What's this big idea, then? Can't be much bigger than you cutting back at the dairy.'

Rosa set the lemon juicer aside, dabbed at the sweat on her cheeks with a tea towel and rubbed her lower back. The arthritis had finally given her something other than pain, in providing the perfect conversation opener to convince Max to return. It was going to be such a nice surprise for them all.

'Rob told me how he wants to breed some of those Canadian Speckle Park cows. You know, the ones we saw on *Landline* a few months ago?'

John nodded, his brow furrowing again.

'And I was thinking we could help out in some way.'

She watched him take a long drink, his eyes on the paddocks through the bay window. Rosa turned back to juicing lemons. Forcing an answer wouldn't aid her cause. This dance had to be played carefully, casually. She had sown a seed. Like her mother had once told her, in an Italian accent as thick as the sea fog that rolled in around 3 p.m., sometimes it's best to let him take the idea and roll it around in his head until he's convinced it's his own.

She poured the lemon juice into a bowl of icing sugar, stirring as she waited. Rob had only mentioned his cattle-breeding plans in passing, and he certainly hadn't asked for anything. But Rosa knew a few girls from the herd—only the best mothers, of course—would give Rob a distinct leg-up. She snuck a look at John as she poured sloppy icing over the biscuit bases, and sprinkled coconut on top. He was still looking out the window, his eyes far away. She wondered how he'd react when he saw Max.

Popping the slice containers into the fridge, she mixed herself a gin and tonic and sat down next to her husband.

'Guess we could offer them a few old girls to breed from,' said John, his brow still creased. 'The AI guy will be here for the next round of inseminating soon. Wonder if he's got any Speckle Park semen in stock? Just means we'll be a dozen Friesian calves down this year.'

Hook, line and sinker!

'Well, that certainly beats my Christmas present idea,' Rosa said, sipping delicately. 'But you're right, a few cross-bred calves *would* be the perfect kickstart for their new herd.' She slipped her hand over his, giving it a squeeze. He wasn't the most demonstrative man, never free and easy with his affections or compliments, but he was a good man. He just needed a little nudge sometimes, that was all. Soon she'd have them all together again and they could make amends.

Eighteen

Angie pulled on her lightly chewed Blundstones and chided herself for forgetting to bring them inside the night before. The tough leather had put up a valiant fight against the determined puppy's teeth, but moisture from the dewy lawn now seeped into her socks as she strode across to the cottage.

She dodged a stinky landmine as she walked, and knew she'd need to remind Rob about collecting the dog poo again. Angie called for Claudia, but again the only response was the warbling magpies and loud music from the electricians. Her impatience surged as she walked through the cottage, giving the sparkies a wave. She checked each room. No Claudia.

At least she's sticking to the rule about not wandering through the building site without me or Rob, conceded Angie. But it still didn't make her or the pup any easier to find. It was almost as if Claudia knew they needed to be in town at 10 a.m. and was determined to make them late.

'Claudia, we've got to go!' called Angie, straining to hear a small giggle, or anything that would give away her daughter's location. Her phone rang just as Violet gave a sharp yap. She answered the call and wedged the phone against her shoulder as she headed towards the chook house—of course Claudia would hide where Mum was least likely to search. She hoped it wasn't Mrs Ellis pointing out another typo in the dahlia show program or asking for an extra page on the website.

'G'day, Ed Nevins here. I've got a delivery for Rob Jones, should be there in an hour. You right to unload?'

Angie looked at the time on her phone, walking faster as she realised they were already late for their appointment. 'I'm headed into Port Fairview now, but I can juggle a few things and make it back in time. What's the delivery? I'm no weightlifter, but I'm happy to lend a hand.'

'A pallet of tiles. See you in an hour.'

Angie ended the call and in the next instant felt the ground disappear from beneath her feet. The phone flew from her hands and pain ripped through her left ankle. She landed on the grass with a jolt, millimetres from another foul dog poo.

'Ouch!' She pulled herself up and realised she had stepped into one of Violet's new holes in their previously flat lawn. 'For God's sake.'

Each step set off a fresh wave of pain and by the time she'd hobbled to the henhouse, she was in no mood for hide-and-seek. The chooks were running around the coop with Claudia and Violet hot on their tails.

'Claudia—*achoo!*—come out of the chook house *now* and bring—*achoo!*—Violet with you. Those chickens will never lay any eggs if you two keep playing in there. Quick! And watch out for dog poo.'

She grabbed Violet by the collar and clipped the dog's lead in place. Claudia followed dolefully, straw and feathers snagged in her blonde curls, and pouted the entire trip to the vet's surgery. Despite Claudia's protests, Angie kept the little girl buckled firmly in her seat when she hobbled inside with Violet and limped back to the car alone.

'Stop crying, Claud, we'll pick Violet up this afternoon,' said Angie. 'She just needs a little operation'—*with a very big price tag*, she thought, wondering when the dog would start endearing itself to her. Perhaps when Rob and Claudia started training Violet and cleaning up after her, or when she grew out of the shoe-chewing, chicken-chasing, jumping-up stage.

Claudia had nodded off to sleep in her car seat by the time Angie arrived back home. A delivery truck idled in the driveway and the rotund man leaning against the truck door sucked on a cigarette as if it contained life's elixir.

'What took you? You're me last customer before I head to Bali for Chrissy. Chop chop, missy.'

Angie coughed as she hobbled out of the car. Cigarette smoke irritated her asthma at the best of times, and she longed for a southerly breeze to disperse it. 'I rolled my ankle earlier, but I'll give it a go. How long does it normally take to unpack a pallet? Half an hour? How many boxes do we need to move?'

The truck driver let out a barking laugh, which quickly segued into a phlegmy cough. 'Now there's a good one. Ain't got all day to do it by hand. I thought you said you were right to unload?'

Angie looked at him blankly. 'I am. Well, I was before I fell over, but I'll soldier on regardless.'

His incredulous expression made her feel tiny. She thought of Bobbi and drew herself up a little taller. *Stop pussyfooting around the subject, just get on with it.* 'But how else would we unload it? You didn't expect me to have a forklift in my garage, did you?'

The driver scratched his balding head. 'That, or a front-end loader. When you said you were right to unload, and I saw your address was a rural property, I thought we were on the same page. I don't have time to trek back to Warrnambool and collect me forklift. Not missing me plane for a few tiles. I'll deliver it after New Year's.'

He started to heave his large body back into the truck cabin. Angie saw their holiday tiling plans slipping through her fingers. She wanted to be ready in case the tiler fitted them in early. 'Wait, don't go yet. We . . . ah . . .'

She looked over her shoulder at the tractor in the hay shed. John and Rosa wouldn't mind her borrowing it.

The guy glanced at her from the truck steps. 'I've got a plane to catch, missy. You either unload now, or you'll have to wait till mid-January.'

'I'll drive the tractor over and you can lift the pallet out.'

He shrugged, using the end of his cigarette to light another. 'No can do, I'm afraid. Your tractor, your risk. My insurance don't cover other people's machinery.'

Angie debated internally for a minute, dismissing the idea of calling Rob for back-up as the driver tapped his watch. She turned and moved as fast as her sore ankle would allow. Her hands quivered as she climbed into John's tractor cab, grateful it was a similar vintage and model to the one she'd learned to drive at McIntyre Park. She reversed out of the hay shed jerkily, keeping the machine in first gear until she was lined up with the back of the truck.

No big deal. Just slip the forks in, lift the pallet, and we're sorted.

Angie took a deep breath as she reached for the hydraulics lever and held it as she crept closer to the truck.

'Oi! Steady, you're only a couple of inches away from the left hinge. Back out and straighten up again.'

Angie slammed on the brakes when she saw how close the tractor forks had come to spearing a hole through the side of his truck.

Breathe, Angie, breathe.

She inched back, nearly wetting herself when a sharp screech came from beneath a back tyre. She immediately thought of Claudia as she threw on the handbrake and climbed down to see what she'd run over. The cigarette in the truck driver's mouth quivered as he pulled a rubber chicken out from beneath the tractor.

Violet's chew-toy. Angie cursed the dog again as she quickly checked on Claudia.

Still asleep.

She climbed back into the tractor. It took another three attempts to get the forks under the pallet. Her pulse went into freefall when she lifted the load and the tractor bucked under the weight of the tiles.

Oh God, don't drop them. Easy, easy. A little more.

Angie's shirt was drenched in sweat by the time the pallet touched down on the driveway. She limped across to sign the consignment note.

'I'll be sure to have a cold Bintang for ya, missy. Happy Christmas, eh?'

Angie sagged against the tractor tyre and thanked her lucky stars she hadn't had time to fret. And beneath the relief and gratitude that her inexpert handling hadn't annihilated a 5000-dollar pallet of tiles, she felt proud of herself.

The Port Fairview Pub was heaving with holiday-makers, and swags of tinsel and fairy lights added to the marine décor. Rob mopped up the last of his gravy and pushed aside his plate, nodding at Angie's barely touched meal. 'You going to eat that?' *Isn't she starving?*

Angie stopped pushing the battered fish around with her fork as he stole another chip. 'You can have it. I should've sent it back when it arrived battered and not grilled, and with chips instead of salad, but they'd probably have messed it up a second time anyway.'

Rob glanced at Bobbi's salad. *Rabbit food. Ange used to like fish and chips. She would've eaten it now if Bobbi wasn't watching her like a hawk.*

Brett looked up from his steak. 'Still two weeks until Christmas and the pub's already a madhouse. Gets worse every year.'

Rob tugged the plate towards him, nodding at the line of hungry customers flanking the bar. 'Understaffing's probably a tactic to sell more beer.'

'I'd make a complaint if it were my meal,' said Bobbi.

Brett shot Rob a look.

Bet she would, thought Rob, starting in on the fish before Angie followed Bobbi's suggestion. No matter how much Angie raved about that woman, he couldn't see the appeal.

'Tell them the tile pallet story, Ange. Brett and Tessa haven't heard it yet,' said Rob. Pride welled in his chest as she relayed the story to his friends. She'd already bowled him over with her work on the cottage, and now this. He loved how this project kept revealing new depths.

'Geez, that's impressive, Angie,' said Tessa. 'I can't even remember the last time I drove a tractor. God, imagine if they'd slipped off the end of the forks?'

Rob watched a proud flush spread across Angie's cheeks. *That's my girl.*

He glanced at her hand. In less than a week there'd be a pearl and glittering diamonds there—a sign of how much he loved her for everyone to see. 'Jack-of-all-trades, this one,' he said, resting a hand on her thigh.

'Small-business owner, kid wrangler, tireless volunteer . . . What a package. You'd better whack a ring on her finger before someone else snaps her up, Rob,' said Bobbi.

Rob nearly choked on a mouthful of fish. Jesus, last thing he wanted was someone to pre-empt his proposal.

'Yes, that'd be the smart move, Rob. She's the type of girl you want in charge of your business and budgets,' said Alex.

Rob felt an elbow in his ribs.

'That's exactly what I said,' laughed Angie, flashing him a 'told you so' grin. 'But no, someone's determined to handle all the bookwork himself.'

Rob felt everyone's eyes on him. He squirmed in his seat. *Do we really need to get into this here?* 'You handed it over happily,' he said. Between the dahlia society, the DIY reno and caring for Claudia, Ange had welcomed his suggestion to leave the budgeting to him.

'No use both of us losing sleep over the budget,' Rob shrugged. He wolfed down the rest of Angie's meal.

The women returned to their chat and Alex braved the queue at the bar.

'Haven't you told Angie why you're so funny about money, mate?' asked Brett.

Rob stopped chewing. 'Hasn't really come up.'

Brett let out a low whistle. 'Maaaate . . . you're game, keeping that under your belt.'

The fish sat like lead in his belly after that. Maybe he should tell her. *No*, he decided. *I'll show her instead. Just like I'll show Dad I can finish what I've started.*

I'll get my business humming and our renos sorted, and then she'll know I'm good with money. Not like Max.

Rob waited until Ange and Claudia were fast asleep before he snuck out of the van and crept across the yard. The torchlight bounced off the hay shed wall as he got closer, and Violet bounded in after him, her tail thumping on the dusty ground. He lifted the lid on the first plastic storage tub.

'Make yourself useful, pup. Catch some mice.'

He pushed the dog's nose away from the container of baking tins and towards the stacked hay. Judging from the mouse turd littering the tubs, there had to be hundreds of the buggers around.

Maybe we need a few cats too, he thought, clamping the torch between his teeth and unclipping another storage tub. Violet scrambled up the hay bales, barking loud enough to wake the dead. He hoped it wasn't loud enough to wake a dead-tired Angie, but he wasn't taking any chances. He pitched a silicone baking mitt in the pup's direction, groaning as it wedged on top of the highest bale. Retrieving it would be a job for another day.

'Put a sock in it, Violet!'

Rob picked up the pace, searching through the next three storage containers until he found what he'd come for. He flipped through the pages of the well-loved book, smiling as little clouds of flour and icing sugar puffed into the air. Violet came racing down the haystack, hot on the tail of a large rat. She knocked the book from his hands in her frenzied pursuit. It fell to the ground with a thud, and in the light of the torch beam, he saw a lined piece of paper flutter from between the pages. He shone the torch on the recipe, his worry replaced with triumph. *Gotcha.* Rob clipped the lid shut on the storage tub and headed across to his parents' place. *Ange is going to love this.*

The sun was high in the sky and scorching hot, and the corellas frustratingly chirpy, when Angie tried Rob's mobile phone for a second time. She jiggled Bobbi's son Oscar on her hip and grimaced at the building inspector when the call went straight to voicemail again.

'I'm so sorry. Rob said he'd be here.'

The man shifted his clipboard, pulled a pen from the top pocket of his neatly pressed uniform and walked towards the house. 'I've got another inspection in forty-five minutes, and the cement trucks there will be waiting for my sign-off. Surely you can show me around?'

She hesitated, balancing logic and practicality against self-doubt. 'Rob's the main builder. He knows all the nitty gritty. I'm just the lackey,' said Angie. What if he found a problem with the wall frames or they failed the inspection because she couldn't explain something adequately?

The building inspector drew his shaggy eyebrows together. 'Give yourself more credit'—he consulted his clipboard—'Angie. Your hands are covered in putty, those calluses are as big as any bloke's, and you're holding on to that set of plans like they're your child's birth certificate. I'm pretty sure you're as much a part of this build as he is.' He gestured to the cottage. 'I can come back after Christmas, but you've jumped the gun a bit putting the new weatherboards on before getting the framework inspection signed off, so we don't have any more time to lose.'

Angie scanned the road for Rob's work ute, or the trail of dust that usually preceded his arrival. Nothing. She hoped his tardiness was because he was working on the O'Connell's kitchen, and not because he was filling in for the pre-Christmas cricket match. She'd heard enough of Brett's pleading to know they were short of players, and from Rob's wistful tone when he'd declined, she was pretty sure he would've liked to. *Has Brett managed to convince him?*

Angie pushed the thought aside as she popped Oscar in the pram and wheeled it next to the sandpit so he could watch

Claudia and Jayden play. She led the inspector up the front stairs. 'Looks like you're stuck with me then,' she said, taking one last look at the lane before she pushed the door open. It swung freely on its refurbished hinges, lighter since she'd stripped off the multiple coats of thick dull paint.

'Nice door. Good to see people retaining the old leadlight panels too, instead of replacing them with all-new glass,' he said.

Angie smiled at the compliment, glad she'd pushed for black gloss paint instead of the bland ivory Rob had suggested. The bold colour looked smart against the grey undercoat, and she knew it would pop against the duck-egg blue top-coat.

Light flooded in through the new windows as they walked through the rooms, the mix of original hardwood frames contrasting with the green treated-pine framing in the kitchen extension. Angie loitered beside the building inspector, pointing out the slight variations they'd made to the original plans. Her heart hammered as he went quiet, thumbed through his notes and pulled out his tape measure.

Angie made an excuse about checking something and wandered into the kitchen, trying not to focus on how much she wanted today's inspection to go smoothly. *Needed* it to go smoothly, so they could stick to their schedule. She glanced around the shell of the room that would become the heart of their home.

Without the old cabinets cluttering the view, she could imagine it clearly. The dining table would go by the window, the island bench would be long enough to handle a full day's baking and there'd be enough cupboards to store her cake stands, platters, mixing bowls and oven trays. It was a blank canvas awaiting their brushstrokes, and today's inspection would pave the way for progress. They needed to make every day count.

The inspector jotted something on his clipboard, unclipped the form and passed it to her. 'I'll mail out the official report in the next few days.'

Angie scanned the sheet, barely able to make out his scribble.

'Not many inspections get full marks, but your project, young Angie, is almost faultless. A credit to you. A few more lengths of bracing along the kitchen wall frames and you'll be right. Keep up the good work.' Angie felt her confidence blossom as she scanned his brief recommendations.

I can do this. I am doing this.

She waved him off and turned to the sandpit. The pram was still there with Oscar happily sucking on a sandy spade, but there was no sign of the older two now. Angie did a slow 360, scanning the yard.

'Claud? Jayden?'

Panic set in as she hoisted Oscar onto her hip and scoured the usual spots, but they weren't in the mulberry tree or the chook pen either. Angie squirmed as she pulled a feather from her hair, hoping she hadn't caught some type of avian lice. Icky things.

A riot of laughter came from the shed, but Angie's relief evaporated when she stormed inside and entered the bathroom.

Her beauty products were upended in the shower. Moisturiser, cleanser, toner, foundation, eye shadow and shimmery blush were smeared across every tile in an abstract artwork.

'You little buggers,' she scolded, torn between laughing at their cheeky expressions and crying over the wasted beauty products worth more than the weekly grocery bill. She picked up the bottles. The containers were almost weightless.

'Granny painting. Claud painting,' said Claudia, brightly.

Angie cringed, remembering the foamy bath paints Rosa had bought for Claudia's birthday. They'd run out last night, and evidently Claudia had found herself a new alternative.

Rosa, Rosa, Rosa, thought Angie. She undressed the children and willed herself not to look at the empty bottles or dwell on the cost as she turned on the shower.

Diana's words echoed in her head: *It's when they're quiet that you should be most worried.*

I'll have to be smarter with the building supplies. Better to learn my lesson with moisturiser than construction adhesive.

Rob's elbow twanged as he passed Claudia the sticky tape, payback for every over he'd bowled the previous afternoon. The Fairview Seagulls may have won by seventy runs, but coming off the cricket field to seven missed phone calls and a lukewarm reaction from Ange had dampened any sense of celebration. Wheeling the Harley-Davidson out of the shed and going for a quick ride this morning hadn't earned him any brownie points either, but at least he and Claudia had managed to finish the last of their Christmas shopping and fit everything into the sidecar for the trip home.

'Mummy's going to like this one,' said Claudia, wrapping a colourful scarf for Angie. It was brighter than he would have chosen, but there had been no dissuading Claudia from the multi-coloured watermelon-and-pineapple print she'd spotted in the gift shop.

He added it to the pile underneath the table and thought about the surprises he had planned for tomorrow. Hopefully yesterday's cricket game wouldn't cast a pall on the occasion. Sweat trickled down his neck and he fumbled with the next present. Tomorrow couldn't come quickly enough.

Nineteen

Angie could see Brett and Tessa's home well before she turned into their driveway—Christmas lights dangled from the gutters, Santa Claus peeked out of the chimney top and a fibre-optic sleigh was mounted on the roof. Tinny carols played as she unloaded gift hampers from her hatchback and she had to walk sideways past a gigantic Christmas tree to make it into the house.

She found Bobbi and Tessa in the lounge. Bobbi's ivory blouse and red skirt were elegantly understated, while Tessa's green tinsel necklace, gold-and-red dress and candy-cane earrings were as festive as her décor. Angie smoothed down her new linen dress and whistled at the mass of gifts and platters on Tessa's coffee table.

'Wow, what a feast, Tessa! I thought it was just nibbles.'

Tessa stood, pulling Angie into a hug. 'I know, I did a little too much baking for tomorrow. Couldn't fit it all in the fridge. Hope you're hungry!'

Angie set her baskets down and popped a mini quiche into her mouth. 'Calories don't count at Christmas, right?'

She winked at Bobbi—this contradicted everything they'd discussed on their last run.

'Let's do presents. Here, you need some bubbles, too,' said Tessa. Angie accepted a glass of pink champagne while Tessa slid across a plate laden with tempting cupcakes, mini cheese-cakes and homemade baklava, and passed them each a gift.

Angie unwrapped hers, discovering the prettiest framed embroidery of a tree. Little scraps of brown fabric formed the trunk and myriad green stitches were the leaves, with tiny clusters of purple beads nestled in them. She ran her fingers over the different textures, traced the upraised stitching, and marvelled at the love heart on the tree trunk, with the letters *A+R* stitched inside.

'Like your mulberry tree. Probably better as a housewarming present but I didn't want to save it until then.'

'It's gorgeous, Tessa! You are so crafty.' Angie looked over to see the delicately embroidered *B* in Bobbi's frame.

'It's nothing really,' said Tessa, flushing.

'Very . . . country cottage craft,' said Bobbi. 'Maybe I should be saving my little scraps of fabric instead of throwing them in the bin.' Bobbi giggled as she sipped the champagne, then pulled two matching boxes from her leather tote. Even the packaging looked expensive. Angie opened the box. A pair of rose-gold earrings gleamed in the light.

Tessa's face flushed again as she pulled out an identical pair. 'These are beautiful, Bobbi. But they must have cost a fortune. My silly little craft piece doesn't quite measure up.'

One look at Tessa's red cheeks and Angie felt terrible. 'They're not silly craft pieces, Tessa,' she said, 'they're gorgeous works of art. Mine's going straight on the mantelpiece when we have one. And Bobbi's naughty for breaking the twenty-dollar rule.'

'Don't be silly, I was joking, Tessa. Your stitching is gorgeously rustic. Like the type of thing Anne and Diana would have given one another in *Anne of Green Gables*. Or in *Little House on the Prairie*. You really go nuts for that craft stuff, don't you?'

All three of them looked around the room, from the hand-embroidered advent calendar to the bunting made from recycled doilies. Tessa quietly unwound her tinsel necklace, tossed it on the floor and pushed it underneath the sofa with her feet.

Angie hefted the gift baskets up onto her lap, staring at the now-underwhelming collection of local produce. 'I stuck to the budget too. Hope you like jam and chutney!' Angie handed her gift baskets across to Tessa and Bobbi, desperate to cut through the tension.

Bobbi shot her a surprised look. 'I don't see any problem. You girls are worth more to me than money and Alex is raking it in with his new clients. Think of all the times you've babysat for me, Angie. Yesterday. This morning. A couple of times last week. And you, Tessa . . .' Bobbi paused, studying her hand-stitched gift. 'Well . . . it's . . . quirky.'

Angie looked from Tessa to Bobbi, willing the awkwardness to die a quick death. Bobbi's extravagance was like an accessory, as much a part of her as the Dior perfume she wore even when running, and the cool elegance she oozed, no matter what she was dressed for. Angie coveted Bobbi's self-confidence even more than she envied her friend's trim figure. She hoped the presents weren't a deliberate dig.

Judging by the way Tessa was shovelling handfuls of Cheezels into her mouth, it seemed Tessa had taken it that way.

Bobbi nodded, forcing a smile onto her face. 'There's love woven into these crafts. I'm sure they sell like hotcakes.'

Angie reached for the bottle of champagne and quickly topped up all three glasses, trying to skim over the moment. 'Oh, definitely. You've found a niche, Tessa. Can I commission one for Penny's new bub?'

Tessa reached for the earrings, getting cheesy orange crumbs all over the box, and fiddled with them before snapping the lid shut. 'Maybe,' she said, downing her glass of champagne and attacking the tray of sweets like it was her last meal.

Angie raised her glass. 'I'll drink to that. Here's to our mums' group. I'm proud to call you both friends. Merry Christmas!' The bubbles rushed to Angie's head as she sank back into the couch. *How am I going to smooth this one over?*

୧

When the magpies started their morning symphony outside the shed window the next morning, Angie flew into action, determined to retrieve the blue clam-shaped pool from its hiding place in the cottage kitchen and put it under the tree before Claudia woke.

Her head was a little fuzzy as she slipped out of the caravan. The paddling pool had escaped her mind when she'd curled into bed last night, slightly tipsy from the champagne Tessa had kept pouring.

She smiled at the twinkling fairy lights Rob had strung between his motorbike handlebars, the glittering tinsel draped around the gum sapling they'd plucked from the nearby scrub and the small collection of gifts huddled underneath.

Opening the shed door, she discovered Christmas morning had dawned bright and clear, with a hint of sea mist softening the landscape. Spiderwebs hung from long sprigs of grass, each little strand embellished with bauble-like beads of moisture, as if the spiders had stayed up late, putting the finishing touches on their own variety of festive decorations. Angie ducked under a dinner-plate-sized cobweb hanging from the verandah's iron lacework, and pushed the front door open.

The living room at the front of the house was flooded with soft morning light. *Next year we'll be waking up to Christmas in here.* She stood in the kitchen, picturing herself pulling croissants from the oven and baking up a storm with Claudia. The wall of glass stacker doors would give them unlimited views of the paddocks and state forest to the north. She smiled as she scooped up the paddling pool and pulled Rob's present from behind a pile of timber.

Rob rolled over, flinging his arm across the bed but instead of Angie, he found a warm space. *Where on Earth is she at this hour of the morning?* He rubbed his eyes and peered around the darkened caravan. Claudia's curtain was still pulled tightly across her bunk bed and there was no sign of Ange on the caravan's lounge. He smiled as he heard the shed door click closed.

Bingo. She must be putting the slow cookers on for lunch. Hot roast-beef rolls, cold chicken, barbecued squid and salads were a far cry from the roast turkey dinner his parents normally had, but the McIntyre family were like that. More flexible, willing to change tradition. *We could serve deep-fried tofu and corn chips, it wouldn't worry my family, as long as we're all together,* Ange had said when she'd first suggested hosting everyone for Christmas lunch.

He wondered if John and Rosa would fit in with the McIntyre clan. *As if I don't already have enough to think about today.* Rob relaxed his clenched jaw and forced his shoulders down from around his ears. Clearing the air last night with Ange when she'd returned from her mums' group Chrissy party had gone a long way to easing his nerves. The few glasses of bubbly under her belt had made her more receptive to his apology about the cricket, and paved the way for a little romance before the clock struck midnight.

He pulled on a pair of shorts and snuck out of the caravan. *It's time to get this great day underway.*

The shower was running when Angie slipped back into the shed. Setting the pool down by the Christmas tree, she nestled Rob's gift among the others and spun around as the bathroom door creaked open.

Her eyes traced the snail trail from Rob's belly button to where it disappeared into the waistband of his shorts. It was a sight she never failed to enjoy.

Rob wound his arms around her and she laid her cheek against his damp chest.

'Merry Christmas, beautiful,' he whispered into her ear.

'Merry Christmas.' She held him tight, tracing a trail along his smooth back. He pulled away, his green eyes twinkling as he studied her face.

'Your present won't fit under the tree, I'm afraid. But I'll have it for you after lunch,' he said.

'Thought we weren't doing presents?'

He pointed to the gift she had placed under the tree. Even with the wrapping and a gaudy bow, there was little disguising the fact it was a claw-hammer.

'You can't talk, Miss McIntyre.' Rob leaned closer. Angie kissed him, her hand cupping his freshly shaven jaw. The smell of his shaving cream and the lazy circles he was tracing on her neck were hypnotic.

It took all her resolve to step away. 'We'll have a deliriously excited three-year-old bursting out of the caravan door any second now. But I'll take a raincheck for tonight.'

'Deal,' said Rob, folding his arms behind his head and admiring the satin nightgown peeking out from underneath her bathrobe. 'A bloke could get used to this view, though.'

Angie smiled, pulling the robe back around her like a curtain. The exercise had started stripping the baby weight, but she still wasn't comfortable enough to parade around in a skimpy nighty in broad daylight. She kissed him chastely before padding across to the kettle.

'Time for coffee, Romeo. Then you can help me get those sides of beef in the slow cooker for lunch.' She smiled. *Rob's right. This is going to be our best Christmas yet.*

Rosa tucked the branch of gum leaves through the curtain rod and nodded to John.

'Up a little higher. More, more. Yep, stick the pin in,' she said.

He lifted the branch higher and fixed it in place, before climbing down from the stepladder and sinking into his recliner. 'Those the last of the decorations?'

Rosa looked around the farmhouse kitchen, her eyes critical as she assessed the red, white and green balloons in the corners of the room, the silver and burgundy wall-hanging she'd spent all November sewing, and the swags of eucalyptus over every curtain rod. She wanted it to be perfect for this evening, but it was still missing something.

'Needs a little pizzazz,' she said, tapping a finger to her lips.

John picked up the Sudoku puzzle book she'd given him that morning. 'Nobody cares about all the frills and fuss, Rosa. They're only coming for a light dinner and dessert. Sit down and do a puzzle with me,' he said.

Rosa lifted her chin. '*I* care, John. I want it to be perfect.'

She stalked outside. *Fairy lights would be just the thing,* she thought. The sound of laughter floated through the air and Rosa craned her neck towards the cottage.

She spotted Rob and a bearded man setting up gazebos and trestle tables, while Angie and one of the older sisters unloaded chairs from the back of a four-wheel drive. Lara or

Diana, she wasn't quite sure which one. Rosa hummed as she continued to the shed—she was delighted to be joining their lunch celebrations. It would be their first combined Christmas function with the McIntyre family. She'd met them all briefly at Claudia's christening, but it was hard to keep track of which sister was which, let alone the names of their husbands and children.

Rosa stretched up on tiptoe to grab the neatly labelled box of fairy lights from the shed shelf. *It'll be lovely getting to know Angie's family better,* she thought, carrying the lights inside. No matter how much she'd tried to welcome Angie into the fold, things remained stilted between them. *Still,* she reminded herself, *they're home now and that's the main thing. And hopefully tonight's little surprise will be a turning point for us all.*

Twenty

The smile didn't slip from Angie's face all morning, her excitement peaking as her family spilled from the convoy of cars. It felt like ages since she'd been home to McIntyre Park, and she hadn't realised just how much she'd missed Diana, Lara and Penny until they were all standing in her driveway, fussing over Claudia and gushing over the cottage.

Like Angie's sisters, Angus had loved the pre-lunch property tour and update on the renovations. They'd all oohed and ahhed, as if they too could see the potential in the old cottage. Having them all here was treat enough, but it seemed the neglected garden had given its own nod to the occasion. The pony-trimmed rose bushes had managed a few blooms, while the exuberant wisteria and jasmine perfumed their outdoor dining area.

Angus leaned back in his deckchair, loosened his belt and placed his Akubra back on his head. 'Best Christmas lunch I've had all year,' he said. His classic dad humour elicited groans around the table.

'It's the *only* Christmas lunch you've had all year, Dad,' said Angie, glowing under his praise nevertheless.

'And I mean it every year too, love. Top notch. But this one's been extra special,' he said, nodding at John and Rosa before gesturing to Rob and Angie's cottage. A mix of pride and delight washed over Angie.

'They've done us proud, haven't they, John,' Angus said.

All eyes turned to John, who took another sip of his beer and simply lifted his chin with a small smile. *No wonder Rob resents him. Even with an opener like that, getting a tiny morsel of praise from John is like getting blood from a stone*, Angie thought.

Rosa leaped in. 'They've done a marvellous job. We're extremely impressed,' she said.

'Who would have thought, after all those years sitting inside and eating a hot lunch on a sweltering summer's day, we could have been feasting on barbecued prawns and roast-beef rolls under a gazebo?' said Pete, wiping his beard with a green-and-red napkin.

The McIntyre sisters laughed as Diana elbowed her husband in the ribs. 'You sure you don't want to rephrase that, Pete?'

Pete grabbed his wife's hand and kissed it. 'Your Christmas lunch is always spectacular, darling. But you've got to admit, the cooler coastal temps make it a little more pleasant. Hard to believe the weather is this moderate, when just two hours north it's like a hot box.'

'The jury's in: I think we should do all future Chrissy lunches with a slow cooker and barbecue. The kids loved it,' Lara said, nodding to the collection of cousins, who were now taking turns to run through the sprinkler.

'Ditto,' said Penny, rising from her chair. Her dress stretched across her pregnant belly. 'Think I need to make some room before dessert, though,' she said, reaching for the empty plates.

She cleared her throat. 'Tim? You guys can get all the presents ready while we clean up here, right?'

Tim leaped to his feet, soon joined by Rob, Pete and Angus.

Angie hid a grin. *So, they bought Claud a new swing set for Christmas.* No wonder Angus and Lara had parked out on the road, hidden behind the thick stand of bottlebrush shrubs. She feigned obliviousness and busied herself collecting plates and cutlery from the trestle table.

Rosa also got up, gathering dishes from the table. Angie ducked her head to hide a tinge of disappointment. She knew it was selfish, but she'd been looking forward to five minutes alone with her sisters.

Diana gently ushered Rosa back to the deckchair. 'I'll take that, Rosa,' Diana said, easing the platter from Rosa's hand. 'You just put your feet up for a minute. No, no, we insist,' she said on her way to the kitchen, talking over Rosa's objections.

The four sisters worked like a well-oiled team: Angie washing, Penny and Diana drying and Lara handling leftovers. 'Go sit down, Penny, you're about to pop,' said Diana, swatting her away.

'I've got to stand or I'll never fit any dessert in,' said Penny. 'This baby loves the look of your croquembouche, Diana. Although it's not the same without your pav this year, Angie. I still don't know how you're coping without an oven. At least someone else will get a chance to win a ribbon in the show baking this year.'

Angie pulled another plate from the sudsy water. 'It's not too bad. I don't have much time for baking anyway, with these renovations. It's like a boot-camp weight-loss challenge, with a house as the main prize. And my friend Bobbi runs a tight ship. She knows when I'm slacking off on our runs and eating the wrong stuff,' she laughed. 'She's amazing. You'd love her, Lara.'

'We wouldn't fit a pav in here anyway,' said Lara, peering into the open refrigerator. 'If only Rob collected vintage fridges instead of motorbikes, we'd have a hope of fitting both the leftovers and the desserts. Some will have to go back in the eskies.' Lara reached down and opened the cooler boxes, restacking drinks to make way for the remaining salads.

'Can't hang fairy lights on fridges, though,' replied Angie, with a laugh. 'It's his thing. I can't stand in the way of a man and his motorcycles. And I have to admit, it is kind of fun riding in that one.' She pointed to the Harley-Davidson with the black-and-gold sidecar attached. 'Claudia loves it too.'

'Hmmm, it looks about as comfortable as living in a caravan.' Penny rocked her hips from side to side, one hand on top of her belly, the other underneath.

Even through the red fabric of Penny's dress, Angie could see the bulges as the baby kicked. Surprised by a sudden maternal urge, she dried her hands and cupped Penny's bump to feel the movements.

'It's an active little squirt. Won't be long till you're all in the birthing suite watching this little one make its grand debut,' said Penny.

'God, do you seriously still want us all in there, Pen? We won't be offended if you've changed your mind,' said Diana.

The dishwashing paused and Angie and Lara exchanged a look while they waited for her response. Penny didn't have an inkling of what she was in for, and as lovely as the invitation was, all three of them knew they'd be surplus to requirements—or, worse, they'd make Tim feel like he wasn't needed.

'Of course I want you all there. Mum's not here, so you three are the next best thing.'

Angie's sad smile was a mirror of her sisters'. Annabel had loved Christmas.

'Wherever she is, I bet she's looking down on us today and smiling,' said Diana.

Another thud fluttered through Penny's skin. 'Oh, I felt it move!' said Angie.

Diana and Lara stepped in and added their hands to the mix. The sombre mood vanished as the baby kicked again.

'You'll have another one of these on the way soon,' laughed Penny, rubbing her bump.

'Another baby? I've got enough trouble with a puppy and a three-year-old.' Angie smiled, studying the red peep-toe wedges she'd bought for her beauty salon opening a decade ago. 'Maybe when we've settled into the cottage.'

Lara snorted. 'You've changed your tune. Rosa will be sewing more baby blankets before you know it.'

Angie shot a look towards the door. The last thing she wanted was Rosa walking in and discovering herself the topic of conversation.

'Let's not get too carried away,' laughed Angie, returning to the sink. But as she scrubbed the knives and forks, she realised the idea of another baby wasn't half as terrifying as it had been three or four months ago.

Rob dried his palms on the seat of his khaki shorts, knowing they'd be sweaty again before he reached the end of the driveway. Violet danced around his legs and he wished he'd followed Angie's advice about chaining the puppy up during lunch. He was already nervous enough to fall over his own feet without any assistance.

'Relax, Jonesy,' said Tim, punching him lightly on the arm. 'What's not to love about a trailer load of polka-dotted calves? Angie will be rapt. Plus, they're a gift. She can't turn away a present, right?'

Diana's husband Pete nodded. 'Hope she likes cows more than she likes chickens, Rob. Three pure-bred calves must have cost a packet. You got a back-up plan?'

Tim and Pete burst into laughter.

'Give the guy a break,' said Angus, clapping Rob on the shoulder. 'He's already sweating like a pig.'

Rob followed his future brothers-in-law and father-in-law down the driveway. The calves he'd bought were one thing, but it was the pearl-and-diamond ring he planned to tie to the ribbon around the smallest calf's neck that was making him sweat.

He slipped a hand into his right pocket, toying with the loose ring as they walked along Enderby Lane. He'd spent the last two hours making sure it hadn't fallen out, distractedly answering questions as he showed their guests around the property and through the cottage. Perhaps a box-shaped bulge in his shorts would have been more comfortable than the fear of dropping it in between the rotten floorboards or into long grass. *Get to the trailer, secure the ribbon to the calf, secure the ring to the ribbon, and then hope like hell Ange says yes.* He picked up his pace. *God, I hope she likes it.*

'Got the bow, Pete?'

Pete nodded, lifting a carry bag. Although Rob had enlisted their help to deliver the trio of calves for Christmas, he hadn't told them about the proposal.

Rob's fingers trembled. He undid the latch on the trailer and climbed into the crate with the skittish animals. He wasn't sure who was more nervous, him or them, but he'd been around enough calves to know he needed to be calm and quiet or else they'd scatter. An expensive Canadian Speckle Park calf with a broken leg would *not* be a good omen.

He slipped a hand towards the biggest one's mouth, murmuring gently and crouching low. The calf sniffed him warily. Within moments, its little black-and-white mouth enveloped his hand, trying to suck milk from Rob's fingers. Tim slipped the red satin ribbon around the calf's neck and tied it in a bow.

'All good, Jonesy.'

Rob took a deep breath and reached into his pocket, trying to extract the ring while still crouching. 'Bugger, I can't get it. Can you reach into my pocket, mate? Right side.'

Tim gave him a puzzled look, but reached into his pocket as Rob straightened as much as he could without scaring the calf.

'Geez, that's a ring and a half,' Tim laughed, examining the pearl and diamonds. 'You're a dark horse, Rob. Explains why you burned the hell out of those prawns on the barbecue.'

Rob nodded tensely, swivelling around to face Pete and Angus behind him. 'You all right with me marrying Ange, Angus?'

A warm smile crossed Angus's tanned face. He gave a quick nod. 'Thought you'd never ask, son.'

Rob let out the breath he felt like he'd been holding for hours. 'Tie it onto the ribbon for me, eh, Tim?'

'Make it a double knot. Jonesy will have your guts for garters if that beauty slips off into the grass, never to be seen again. Or worse, if the other calves eat the ribbon,' joked Pete.

Rob's stomach lurched. He couldn't fathom the idea of losing the ring at this late stage, or sifting through piles of runny green calf poo to retrieve a ring worth more than a dozen purebred calves.

'Maybe you should bring Mohammed to the mountain, instead of us leading the calves into the yard,' said Angus.

Rob nodded gratefully. This was where Ange's practicality came from. The red-ribboned calf mooed, stamping its foot in frustration at the lack of milk.

'Make it quick, mate. These guys are getting cranky,' said Tim, using both hands like bottle stoppers to keep the bigger calves occupied. Pete jogged off, loping down the driveway. Rob felt the skin on the top of his knuckles rubbing painfully on the calf's bottom gum and swapped hands. He stroked its soft speckled fur. *This one will have to be called Pearly*, he decided, watching the ring bob up and down on the ribbon. Before long the children emerged from the driveway, whooping with delight at the sight on the trailer. *No going back now, Jonesy.* Sweat trickled down his chest. *What if she says no? Where the hell do we go from there?*

﹩

Angie hummed as she reset the trestle table for dessert, feeling content, with a belly full of food and her sisters, niece and nephews bustling around her.

'Aunty Angie, Aunty Angie! Come and see this!' Lara's daughter Evie called from the top of the driveway.

Angie set down the spoons and skirted around the pile of presents sitting in the shade, her curiosity piqued as another delighted cry came from the roadside.

'Ready for a surprise, love?' asked Angus, walking towards her and offering his hand. She took in his wide smile and allowed herself to be led towards the lane. *Do they need a hand dragging the swing set off the ute?*

They rounded the bottlebrush hedge to see a small crowd gathered around Angus's ute. Angie's breath caught in her throat.

A trio of the prettiest calves she'd ever seen were huddled on a trailer crate behind the ute, one with a red ribbon around its neck. She scooped Claudia up into her arms.

'Has Daddy got us some calves for Christmas?' she whispered, her ambivalence growing with each step. She wasn't sure they had the time or the money for such an expensive—albeit gorgeous—gift.

Her family stepped back, creating a path to the trailer. Rosa held out her arms for Claudia and Angie noticed a glistening in Rosa's eyes. *She's pretty excited about the new calves, considering she's surrounded by black-and-white cattle all day long. Was this Rosa's idea?*

'Merry Christmas, Ange. Come unwrap your present,' called Rob. Angie lifted her skirt, opened the gate to the trailer crate and ducked as she stepped up into it. She reached out to pat a tiny calf, whose black nose and mouth seemed attached to Rob's left hand.

'They're gorgeous, Rob.' Angie looked from the crowd to the optimism on Rob's face, and then back down at the calves. She coughed, trying to shift the gigantic 'but' that had formed on her lips. She also snuck a look at Penny, drew strength from her encouraging nod, and tried to forget about their overwhelming to-do list. *Accept them and work it out later*, she decided, kissing Rob. His delight reassured her she'd made the right decision.

'I think this one's sick of her ribbon,' said Rob, his voice hoarse, as the calf tossed its head.

Angie reached across to untie the ribbon and spotted the ring. She gasped, unable to stop a hand flying to her heart.

Rob dropped to one knee.

It took a few seconds before any words would come out of her mouth. *It's a ring. It's an engagement ring. It's a whopping great ring.*

'Is that what I think it is?'

Rob's reply was lost in the children's chatter. He cleared his throat and tried again. 'If it was, would you say yes?'

Giddy laughter rose in Angie's throat as she nodded. Rob pivoted around, still anchored to the calf by one hand, and took her left hand.

'Will you do me the honour of being my wife?'

Warmth flooded Angie's body as she nodded and leaned down to kiss him again.

'We can't hear you!' called Penny.

A chorus of laughter erupted around them as Angie raised her voice. 'Yes!'

As soon as the word left her lips, Angie realised her mistake. The calves responded to the sudden noise as if it was a gunshot. The ring-bearing calf shied away and careened into Angie. She felt a blinding pain in her ankle as she toppled onto Rob, looking up in time to watch the calf jump through the gate she'd forgotten to shut. Rob scrambled to close the crate before the other two escaped.

A flurry of quick instructions rose from the roadside crowd. Angie bit her lip and watched through the steel bars as their families tried to corral the skittish calf. She grimaced at Rob, her stricken expression matching his.

'Jesus, the ring alone's worth a small fortune,' Rob groaned.

The runaway calf let out a nervous bellow.

'Don't spook him, Harry. You either, Leo,' said Diana, tugging two of her sons closer to her side as they all took another step inwards to tighten the circle.

'Steady now,' said John, walking forwards cautiously. His hands were millimetres from the red ribbon when Claudia clapped.

'Shoo, shoo, cows!' she said, clapping again for good measure, just as Rosa had taught her when they were dealing with stubborn milkers.

The calf bolted, pushing its way through the human barrier and whizzing past the trailer in a flash of black and white. It was almost comical to see the procession after it: Rosa hopped the fence, jogging behind the shrubs on the roadside, while John, Tim, Lara, Pete and Diana calmly followed the animal down Enderby Lane.

Angie gave Rob a nervous look. She wasn't sure how much the ring had cost, or how she'd missed a ring-sized dent in their bank account, but she knew they probably couldn't afford to replace it if it slipped into the grass. 'Tell me you tied the knot tightly?'

'Hope so. The calf wasn't supposed to escape,' Rob said, opening the gate and holding it for her as they climbed out of the crate.

'Just had to add a little more excitement, right?' Penny's hand went to Angie's arm before returning to her belly. 'All we need is for my waters to break and we'll have a hat-trick.'

Angie swore. 'Don't you dare! They'd ambulance you to Ballarat if bub came this early.'

Rosa emerged from the hedge ahead of the calf.

'Go, Granny!' yelled Claudia, cheerfully oblivious to her role in the kerfuffle.

As Rosa quietly stood in the middle of the road, the calf slowed to a hesitant walk and then a stop. Rosa approached the calf quietly, and eventually slipped her hand through the red ribbon. She nodded back at them, letting them know the ring was safe. Angie let out the breath she'd been holding, Rob swore in relief and Claudia gave another little clap of excitement.

'Claud,' said Rob, tapping the end of her button nose, 'no more clapping around the calves, okay?'

Rosa's cheeks were flushed and her hair had escaped its neat braid by the time she brought the calf back to them. It barely protested as Tim lifted it back into the cattle crate and stood quietly as Rob untied the ribbon.

'Never a dull moment around here,' said Lara dryly.

Angie laughed with relief as Rob finally slipped the ring onto her finger. She stretched out her arm to admire the pearl's luminescence. *It's beautiful*, she thought, watching the way the diamonds flanking the pearl tossed beams of sunlight in different directions. She returned everyone's congratulatory hugs and heard the murmurs of cheerful banter start up again as they strolled back down the lane, glued to Rob's side.

'Love you, Rob.'

'Lucky. I was gonna look a right fool otherwise. It'll do the job, then?'

'The ring's gorgeous.'

'Bit like you. That calf's called Pearly, by the way,' Rob said, pulling her closer. She smiled as she slipped into his arms.

'What were you going to call her if I said no?'

Rob winked at her and squeezed her hand gently. 'Probably Esmerelda. Or maybe Gertrude.'

'Good thing I said yes, then.'

Rob pulled her into a tight embrace again, smelling like sweat and burned barbecue. 'Too right.'

Angie collapsed into the last remaining deckchair, too tired to carry it back to the shed. She flung an arm over her eyes, blocking out the late afternoon sun, and felt herself drifting off in a glow of champagne and happiness.

Rob's hands slipped over her shoulders, gently massaging the knots from running, renovating and Christmas-lunch hosting duties.

'Stick a fork in me, Rob, I'm done,' she said.

'Not a chance, my lady. I've got plans for you. Everyone's gone home, we don't need to head to Mum and Dad's for another two hours or so, and Claudia's zonked out in her pram. How about we sneak into the van and celebrate?'

His black hair tickled her neck as he dipped down to nuzzle her earlobe. Encouraged by her lazy smile and arched neck,

Rob trailed kisses along her jaw. He paused at her lips and kissed her so gently, it was sweet torture.

'Come on, Mrs Jones-to-be, I've got a very special gift in mind, but you're going to need to slip this off,' he said, running a fingertip along the neckline of her dress. She shivered, her tiredness replaced by desire. She allowed herself to be pulled from her chair, then grabbed the picnic rug spread out beside the sandpit and pointed to the cottage. 'Or we could christen our new home?'

Rob swept her up in his arms and carried her towards the cottage.

Twenty-one

Rosa stirred the custard, dividing her attention between the stovetop and the dinner table, trying to pick up the thread of the conversation as it continued without her.

Angie sat by the window, her curls almost aglow in the last of the Christmas sunshine. Claudia sat by her side, captivated by her new handmade doll. Rosa's heart swelled as she watched her granddaughter dressing and undressing the crocheted toy. *A new outfit each birthday and Christmas, and that little doll will keep her happy for years.*

Rosa smiled as she looked back at her son and husband flanking the southern end of the table. As always, they were seated in their favourite chairs. The place cards had been as unnecessary as the overabundance of food she'd served, but it made her happy to have everything perfect for such a special occasion.

The conversation wasn't exactly flowing, but it was a start. Rosa wished again that Max had been able to make it in time for dinner.

Rosa's eye fell on Angie again, watching her gaze tilt to her hand. She'd been doing it all throughout dinner, quietly looking at the stunning ring when she thought no one was watching.

Rosa rested the spoon against the side of the saucepan and lifted the lid from another bubbling pot. The scent of cinnamon and brandy enveloped her as she prodded the calico-wrapped pudding. It smelled about ready. *Will Angie recognise the recipe?* She hoped so.

Rosa turned off the gas knobs and wiped her hands on the checked apron. She could have asked the men to help—her back was begging her to sit down—but she was loath to interrupt them. She spread the dainty glass dessert bowls across the benchtop.

Angie appeared by her side, her ring twinkling under the kitchen downlights as she smoothed down the front of her skirt.

'Can I help, Rosa?'

'No, no, you've been rushing around all day. Let me do the honours, it's not often I have everyone here,' she said, bustling Angie back to the table. 'Besides, I need your expert opinion on this pudding, without any sneak peeks.'

John called across the kitchen. 'You could make Granny Jones's pud with your eyes closed. Can't see why it won't be delicious like every other year,' he said.

'Actually, smarty-pants, I've got a new recipe this year,' she replied. She laughed at his expression.

'Messing with tradition . . . If it ain't broke, don't fix it,' grumbled John.

'Keep your hair on, John Jones. You've had thirty-something years of that recipe. I thought a change was in order.'

Rosa turned her back to the table as she dished up, alternating spoons of the sultana-laden dessert with the thick custard. She wasn't sure how long Rob and John's truce would last, but at least they were being civil to each other.

Rob looked lighter, his happiness enveloping him like an aura as he stood up. 'Let me help, Mum.'

'No, you sit down,' she admonished.

Rob leaned over and kissed her powdered cheek. 'Thank you, Mum. For everything.'

She turned abruptly and flung open the freezer. 'Ice cream, I forgot the ice cream.' *Rob has no idea how much it means to have him and Angie home. One day he'll understand.* She shuffled icy packages of puff pastry, lifting and replacing T-bone steaks and diced beef as she pretended to search for the tub. 'It's in here somewhere,' she said, hoping her tears wouldn't be frozen on her face for all to see.

She turned back to the benchtop, took a breath and started scooping ice cream on top of the custard, then began ferrying the bowls to the table.

'Well, what are you all waiting for? Dig in before it goes cold,' she said, taking a seat herself and scooping up a spoonful. She lifted it to her mouth slowly, savouring her first bite. Nutmeg and walnuts, a gentle fragrant hint of cherry brandy . . . and the touch of curry powder gave it a certain richness she hadn't anticipated.

Rosa glanced at Rob. In unison, they both turned to Angie, watching a kaleidoscope of emotions cross her face: recognition, sorrow, happiness, gratitude. John and little Claudia continued to eat, oblivious. Rosa felt tears welling again.

'Is this . . . ?' Angie looked at Rob and then Rosa. Her voice wavered. 'Tastes just like . . .'

'Your mum's Christmas pudding? Yep,' said Rosa, quietly.

John paused, the spoon hovering halfway to his mouth as he looked at the three of them. 'Ah, right. Well, then.' He returned to his dessert.

'I found your recipe book so your mum could be part of this special day, too,' said Rob.

Rosa warmed with motherly pride. *My handsome boy with his kind heart.* 'Not that I knew quite how special it was going to be. That proposal was pretty exciting,' Rosa added.

'I'm so touched . . . you've made it such a special day. Thank you, Rob.' Tears slipped down Angie's cheek. 'And you too, Rosa.'

Rosa reached across the table, wiping away the tears on Angie's face as she'd once wiped away those of her own boys.

And to Rosa's surprise, John, who had never been much for public speeches or hoo-ha, as he called it, grabbed his water glass and tapped it with his spoon.

'It's high time Rob realised you were a keeper,' he said.

Rosa's breath caught in her throat. *Don't you dare ruin it, John*, she pleaded silently, nudging him in the ribs. Nothing was going to tear apart her family again. She wouldn't let it.

John cleared his throat. 'We're pleased you're a part of our family, Angie. Rob has exceptional taste.'

Rosa smiled. *He sure does.*

Angie made shooing noises as she ushered Rosa away from the sink.

'Sit down, Rosa, I insist. You've hardly stopped all after-noon. I bet your bones are aching after running to catch the calf,' she said, recalling how Rosa had winced when she'd eased herself up from the table. 'Spend time with your boys.' She opened the door into the lounge room and waited with her hands on her hips but instead Rosa strode past her to the back door and pulled on her boots.

'I'll be back in a minute,' said Rosa quietly, slipping into the dark night.

Angie rolled up her sleeves, wondering what chore Rosa could be doing this late on Christmas night. McIntyre Park Christmas dinners were usually followed by a few drinks on the back verandah, watching the sun sink down over the paddocks—no one did odd jobs outside while the rest of the family watched *National Lampoon's Christmas Vacation*.

A sleeping Claudia snuffled in Rob's arms as he made to get up. 'I'll help, Ange.'

Angie held up a hand, the luminous pearl catching her eye again. She smiled, feeling her cheekbones ache, and then adopted a sterner expression. 'Stay there, I can handle a few dishes. And besides, my mouth will crack if I smile or laugh any more today,' she said, closing the door behind her with a gentle click.

Angie stacked the bowls and plates into the dishwasher, then pulled on Rosa's washing-up gloves. *I'll have to invest in a pair of these*, she mused as she worked.

It was the first time she'd been alone all day and the peace was glorious. Rob's surprise proposal had sky-rocketed the emotions and energy of the day, aided and abetted by the extra intake of sweets from not one but two sit-down meals. She'd loved every minute of it but knew without a doubt that she'd be out for the count as soon as her head hit the pillow.

Mrs Jones. That'll take a while to get used to.

Another smile threatened, despite her aching jaw, and she quickly pressed her lips together. She'd finished the dishes and made a pot of tea when the back door opened. She turned, expecting Rosa, but instead the door was filled with a tall form. *Max?*

It was just like looking at Rob. The only photo she'd seen of him was the family portrait from the nineties, but the years since had only made their features even more alike.

Laughter erupted from the lounge room, no doubt Rob in hysterics at Chevy Chase's antics. She looked at Max.

'Guessing you're Angie? I'm Max,' he said, extending his hand.

Angie shook it woodenly. Rosa may have gathered all of her family together for the final hours of Christmas, but Angie knew tension was about to get a place-setting all of its own.

There was something about Clark Griswold sabotaging his family Christmas that never got old, and even though he'd watched the movie every Christmas, Rob found himself laughing in unison with his father. It was the only time of the year he willingly sat on the couch with his old man, probably the only time they ever laughed at something together.

'Ange, let the dishes drip-dry! You can't miss the cat-in-the-tree bit.' Rob moved Claudia onto the couch and bounded to the kitchen door, but his smile vanished as he opened it.

Just like looking into a mirror.

'What the hell's he doing here?' Rob's jovial mood vanished instantly. 'There's nothing left for you in this town, Max.'

'Merry Christmas to you too, bro.'

'Boys, please. It's Christmas!' Rosa pleaded, rushing into the kitchen after Max.

Rob fought down his anger. *How dare Max come and stuff up our special day? Who else knew he was coming* home? Ange's wide eyes and the thought of Claudia asleep in the lounge room were the only things keeping his clenched fists by his sides.

His mum looked gutted. *What did she expect? Back slaps and a polite recap of events since we last saw each other? Not friggin' likely.*

John appeared in the kitchen doorway. He and Max shook hands. 'Surprises all round today,' said John, walking back into the lounge room. 'Pull up a pew, Max.'

Rob's blood boiled and he stormed to the lounge room doorway. 'So, everything's forgotten, is it? He screws me over, nicks off instead of facing his problems, and we just welcome him back into the fold?'

'Steady on, Rob,' said John.

Rob stalked past his dad and scooped Claudia up. 'I'm not staying if he's here.'

Angie hesitated, looking between Rob, Max, John and Rosa. The Griswolds' comedy rolled on in the background. The canned laughter felt gravely out of place in the tense room.

'We're all adults here, Rob. Max,' said John.

Rob's head throbbed. Appearing immature was the least of his worries. Better than smashing a fist through a wall, or into Max's tanned face.

'C'mon, Ange,' Rob said, yanking open the door, relieved when she set down the tea towel and gave Rosa a quick farewell hug.

'Thanks for the pudding,' said Angie quietly and then followed Rob out the door.

He shifted Claudia's sleeping form to his other hip as he climbed over the fence. Angie lifted the top wire and ducked underneath, pulling the basket of presents through with her. Crickets and frogs sang their own Christmas carols down in the swampy end of the paddock, and a fox joined the chorus with an eerie cry from deep in the scrub.

'It was great day until five minutes ago,' she said, trying to match his long strides. A rabbit skittered out of the scrub, quivering at the sight of them, before racing across the grass.

Rob reached down and took her hand, running his thumb over her ring, still too angry to speak.

'Your mum went to a lot of trouble. I felt bad we hadn't made it for Christmas Day before. And that pudding. I never knew you were such a sentimental bloke, Rob Jones.'

'One of us has to be. I nearly lost it when Max waltzed in, expecting to play happy families,' said Rob. He struggled to keep the anger out of his voice. 'Gives me the shits that Mum didn't even warn us. How the hell did she think it was going to go?'

Angie opened the shed door and tiptoed towards the caravan. Transferring Claudia to her bunk bed was going to be tricky—the last thing they needed now was her waking up.

'So you had no idea he was coming?'

Rob ran a hand through his hair. 'Wouldn't have gone over there if I'd known. The quicker Max buggers back off to wherever he's been, the better.'

Twenty-two

Boxing Day dawned warm and sunny, a replica of the day before. Angie hoisted the plastic milk feeder over the fence, hooking the metal anchors over the gate so the teats pointed out like a triple-breasted wet-nurse.

'Steady on, you lot,' she yawned, pouring in the first bucket of warm milk. The calves headbutted the green contraption, their gummy mouths scrambling for a teat. Milk splashed out the sides.

'Welcome to feeding time at the zoo,' said Rob, tipping the next bucket into the trough. The first rays of sunshine turned the foam around the calves' mouths a golden hue, and warbling magpies accompanied the slurping noises as the calves guzzled their breakfast.

When the milk was finished, the biggest two calves continued to suck loudly.

'Oh no, you don't,' said Angie, slipping a hand into each mouth. 'Don't want a bellyful of air.'

Claudia wobbled precariously on the fence post as she patted their soft speckled coats. With both hands jammed in their mouths, Angie used her hips to brace Claudia, feeling like she was playing a game of Twister: left hand in one mouth, right foot away from the sloppy green poo, right hand in another mouth, left hip keeping Claudia from toppling to the ground. She watched Rob's face soften as he hoisted their giggling girl onto his shoulders.

Exhaustion was written in the dark circles under his eyes. They had both struggled to fall asleep. Angie had been surprised when Rob had knocked back their tried-and-true sleep remedy. That was a first. *Understandable*, she told herself after an hour of tossing and turning. Sex and a long-lost sibling didn't belong in the same headspace. Sleep, when it had finally claimed them, had been restless.

Angie hauled the feeding trough off the fence and hosed it down as Rob and Claudia stroked the calves. To ask or not to ask? Rob had shut down last time she'd queried him about Max, but now that he was here in person, their baggage would impact on her too. She switched the hose off and cleared her throat.

'So, what is Max's story?'

Rob's smile slipped away, replaced with a bitter look. 'He screwed me over years ago and I haven't wasted my time on him since.'

The calves drifted away from the fence. Angie rested a hand on his arm—she could almost feel the anger pulsing through him. Was this really how she wanted to spend the first day of the rest of their lives? Better to come back to it when he'd cooled down.

She tried another tack. 'Let's go for a ride—you, me and Claud in the sidecar. Have a stickybeak at those weatherboard houses you liked in Warrnambool, check out their finishings? Or we could work up a sweat painting weatherboards, then ride across to Yambuk and go on the giant slide.'

'Beach, beach, beach!' said Claudia, but Angie didn't miss Rob's quick glance across the paddock.

'Happy to be anywhere but here until he clears out. I'd get us on the first plane to Darwin if we didn't have the new calves to feed,' Rob said, clenching his jaw.

Or a house to renovate, thought Angie.

Rob tensed as footsteps sounded at the front of the cottage. *Max?* He set down his paintbrush.

'I'll go,' said Angie, climbing down from the small stepladder in her paint-splattered shirt.

Rob continued to paint, struggling to keep his strokes even as he worked out what he'd say if it was Max. He'd lain awake for hours, but he still didn't know how he was going to manage his brother.

Shame rippled through his anger. Like everyone else, Angie probably thought twins should get along. She and her sisters were tight. And as Bobbi had pointed out at the pub, Angie had proved she could run a business, and manage staff and all the financial complexities. *What will she think of me when she finds out the reason for my estrangement from Max?*

He slapped paint on the boards, not bothering to mop up the excess that dripped onto the path. *Max has made his bed, he can sleep in it. It's our cottage, and I'm going to prove I've got what it takes to fix it up. Damned if I'll let Max spoil this for me too.*

His brushstrokes steadied as he heard car doors slamming and several voices coming from the driveway. *Not Max then.*

He climbed down from the ladder, almost colliding with Claudia as she raced around the side of the cottage.

Two more children were hot on her heels, shrieking with delight at the sight of the mulberry tree. They scrambled up the branches like little monkeys.

Angie came around the corner, followed by a lady pushing a wheelchair. The man in the chair had aged immeasurably, but his big ears and gap-toothed smile were unmistakable. Rob rushed to greet his old neighbour and the woman who had babysat him when he was a boy.

'Merry Christmas, Ivan, Lisa! So great to see you.'

'You too, Rob, and so nice to meet your gorgeous fiancée. How about those kids!' She nodded to the children in the tree. 'I told my grandsons all about that tree, said it would be brimming with mulberries. They were my accomplices in jailbreaking Dad out of the old folks home today.'

Ivan nodded, his eyes darting around the property.

'Should've known you'd want to keep a keen eye on the project,' said Rob. Ivan didn't seem to hear, so Rob repeated himself, unsure whether he should crouch down or speak louder. In the end he did both, relieved when Ivan met his gaze.

'What type of autumn crop are you planning? You'll need to take some soil samples in the next month or so.'

Rob laughed.

'Once a farmer, always a farmer, right, Dad?' Lisa lowered her voice and leaned close to Rob. 'He's here one minute, in his own world the next. But he seemed to perk up when we drove down Enderby Lane. Recognised the cottage straightaway, even with the new paint job and the fancy new sign.'

They did a slow lap of the property, with Lisa marvelling at the progress as Angie and Rob filled them in on the renovations.

'You've done a top job so far. We'll come back next Christmas to see the finished product, won't we, Dad,' said Lisa. They all smiled, but Rob knew he wasn't the only one wondering if Ivan would see another Christmas. As if sensing his thoughts, Ivan fixed him with a stern look.

'Your mum didn't need to worry, Rob. I would've looked after you even if she hadn't put the extra sugar in my coffee,' he said, with a tap of his nose and a wink.

'Excuse me?' said Angie, her smile faltering.

Lisa shot them an apologetic look. 'I think we've tuckered him out. You don't even drink coffee, Dad.'

Rob felt Angie's hand in his as they waved Ivan and his family farewell.

'It's a bit of a sobering sight, isn't it? Ivan was always the fittest bloke for miles, ran rings around Dad even though he was twenty years older.'

'Wonder what Ivan meant about your mum.'

Rob shrugged. 'You heard Lisa, he's not running on all cylinders these days. Come on, let's finish painting that back wall. I'm almost ready for a swim.'

Rosa wiped her hands on her overalls, the khaki fabric absorbing the grime. She sprayed the cow's udder with iodine solution, making sure each teat was covered.

Patting the cow's black-and-white-splotched leg, she moved along to the next cow, waiting for the auto cup remover to do its job.

John moved behind her, gesturing to a speck of poo on her cheek. 'You're off with the pixies, love. Missed a bit.'

Rosa let him rub her face with the end of his handkerchief. 'Thanks,' she sighed, trying to dredge up the enthusiasm to move on to the next cow. It was the same every morning and night: the milking machines didn't wait for anyone. Dragging out the evening milking wouldn't make her life easier, nor help the cows impatient to be unloaded and back in their paddocks for the last rays of golden sunshine.

'She'll be right, love. Don't get your knickers in a knot over this blue. If Rob's not man enough to share a postcode with his brother, then I'll eat my hat,' John said over his shoulder. 'And remember what I said about meddling?'

Rosa bowed her head. 'I just wish Rob had given him a chance. Surely enough time has passed?'

John clicked his tongue from the end of the aisle. 'Just leave it be, Rosa. All good on your end?'

Rosa attached milking cups to the cows on the opposite side. 'All clear.' She was so distracted. The last thing she needed was an unmilked cow walking out. She rubbed her spine, wishing she'd remembered to slather Deep Heat on her back beforehand.

John opened the metal gate and patted the lead cow on the rump. 'C'mon, girls, out you go.'

Rosa walked along the pit to the opposite end of the dairy. With the press of a button, the feed troughs were refilled. They worked in tandem and in silence, John herding the fresh row of cows in and Rosa attaching the milking equipment on the other side.

'I haven't heard boo from Rob or Angie since Christmas, and now it's nearly New Year's. I'm babysitting our poppet tomorrow, so at least that's something. But I just wish Rob would give Max another shot. Don't you think there's something we can do, John? I've had a word with Max—he's happy to put it all behind them. He lost a lot of money too, not just Rob, remember.'

'Best thing we can do is leave them to it. Rob and Max are big boys, they don't need us fussing in their lives.' John checked the milk flow monitor and then checked his watch, whistling at the time. 'An extra set of hands will be handy for milking, but Max's got a lot to learn. Still takes him too long to feed the calves. He should have been back here ten minutes ago.'

Rosa rolled her eyes at John's back as he ushered in a fresh batch of cows. If only he was as good with people as he was with cattle. She pulled out a packet of Panadol and washed the tablets down with a glass of milk, warm from the vat. The arthritis wasn't helped by hours on the concrete floor. It was going to be up to her to sort this one out. A little nudge here and there and they'd soon be mending fences.

The caravan parks were overflowing with tourists, and Port Fairview seemed to be in full holiday swing, but Angie was determined to make the Christmas to New Year's break productive. *Outsourcing Claudia next door was a stroke of brilliance*, thought Angie as she surveyed her morning's progress. More weatherboards coated and the chance to plant the weeping cherry tree her sisters had given her for Christmas, in memory of their mum.

Violet danced on the end of her chain, her excited barks making the chickens rush to the opposite side of their new yard.

'Right, Violet. Time to collect Claudia. No chasing cows, okay?' She strapped on the leash and braced herself as the pup shot forwards.

Violet strained at the lead the whole way across the paddock, and by the time Angie had reached Rosa and John's fence, her arms felt like they'd been yanked from their sockets. The hot-pink roses lining the north wall of the dairy were in full bloom, reminding Angie of her mother's beautiful rose gardens at McIntyre Park.

Max wandered out of the calf shed. John's border collies ran alongside him, catching the drips from the empty milk buckets he carried. He nodded at the excited pup. 'Got your hands full?'

Violet yipped with excitement and scrambled to join the other dogs.

Angie gave a dry laugh. 'Not trained yet, so she's a bit mental.' Angie's arms twinged. 'Violet!' She yanked the pup back.

'Might want to keep her tied up for a bit, there's a mob of feral pigs on the move,' Max said. 'Bloke at the pub was talking about it last night, reckons there's a heap of them in the blue gum plantations and the reserves.'

Angie couldn't help scanning the scrub at the back of their property. 'The guy who did our new foundations said the same thing. Rob thought it was a crock of shit.'

Max laughed and continued walking. 'Good luck changing his mind, then. And tell Claud I've got a new calf for her to feed next time she's over, though she's going to need to come up with a better name than Princess Sparkles to impress Uncle Max.'

Angie watched him for a beat, examining the familiar stride. He walked like Rob, talked like Rob, looked like Rob. Was he really as bad as his brother made him out to be?

She tied Violet to the tank stand, well out of reach of the boot rack, and rapped on the screen door. 'Knock, knock,' she called, slipping her boots off.

'Come in,' called Rosa.

Angie went inside, expecting to see Claudia at the bench with a plate of sandwiches and evidence of a morning spent drawing, reading and baking. Seeing her huddled in the corner took Angie by surprise.

'Rough morning?'

Rosa stepped away from the oven with a tray of sausage rolls. 'We've had better.'

Angie spotted a red scratch along Rosa's cheek. 'Woah, what happened?'

'Tell Mummy, poppet.' Rosa's clipped voice worried Angie more than the scratch.

A sob came from the corner.

'There was a misunderstanding. Claudia thought it was a good idea to bite Granny when she didn't get what she wanted. It's happened a few times now. I didn't say anything because I thought we'd dealt with it, but today I bit her back. And that's when she scratched me. Hence the timeout and naughty corner.'

Angie's stomach plummeted. Claudia had never bitten an adult before. But she wasn't sure which piece of news alarmed her most: Claudia scratching and biting her grandmother or Rosa biting her back.

'You *bit* her . . . ? How on Earth is that supposed to teach her anything?'

Angie stepped back from the island bench, the rapport she'd begun to feel with Rosa crumbling like a top-heavy sandcastle. As much as she appreciated Rosa offering to take Claudia for a few hours, she couldn't condone this. *Wouldn't* condone this. 'Angie, really. I did the exact same thing to Rob and Max when they started biting and it cleared it up straightaway. She needs to understand how much it hurts.'

Angie shook her head, lost for words. 'Come on, Claudia. It's very naughty to bite people. Say sorry to Granny and we'll head home.' She scooped Claudia up and backed out of the farmhouse. Her pace matched her mood. *Who the hell bites a child?* She pulled the phone from her pocket and tried Rob's number. It went straight to voicemail. 'Rob, you won't believe this. Call me.'

Angie struggled to hold onto her temper as she strode to the cottage, yanking Violet's lead sharply when the dog veered towards the pile of discarded weatherboards.

Her phone buzzed in her hand. Lowering Claudia to the ground, she sat on the edge of the sandpit and answered Rob's call.

'Ange, what's up? Don't tell me the dahlia committee have added more jobs to your list?' Angie flinched. His mum's latest prank blew the demands of little old Mrs Ellis out of the water. And Rosa was the one who had landed her on the committee in the first place.

'Your mum bit Claudia! Apparently Claud's been biting again. Did you know?'

Angie dropped the dog's lead as she rubbed her neck. Violet bounded towards the woodpile by the sandpit. Her high-pitched barking amplified the beginning of a headache.

Angie wasn't sure what response she had expected, but it certainly hadn't been laughter. 'You think it's funny? Jesus, Rob, I'm fuming!'

'Mum loves telling the story of how she cured our biting. I'm surprised you haven't heard it before. Like when she caught me smoking, and she locked me in the wood shed and made me smoke the whole darn packet before I could come out. Sounds harsh, but it worked both times. Maybe you're overreacting?'

'*Overreacting*?' Angie sucked in an incredulous breath.

Violet's barking increased.

'You still there, Ange? What's the dog doing? Ange?'

Angie stood up and strode towards the woodpile. 'That dog has probably bailed up a rabbit or something. Maybe one of those feral pigs everyone's talking about.'

Rob groaned. 'Look, I've got to go. Don't let Mum bother you, Ange. She means well. And don't read too much into the wild pig stuff, either. The nutcases will be rolling out the Grampians mountain-lion conspiracy theories and the Tantanoola tiger legend if they think they'll get a rise out of someone.'

Angie shoved the phone into her back pocket, annoyed at the brush-off. She vented her frustration at the dog. 'Get out of it, Violet. Out!'

The dog wouldn't budge. Angie felt Claudia's hand slip into hers as she bent down to see what the pup had found in the woodpile. A coil of brown and yellow caught her eye. Angie leaped backwards.

'Snake!' She swept Claudia up and rushed her to the cottage verandah, grabbing the spade she kept by the back door. She ran back and thrust it into the woodpile. The snake reared up, surging forwards and striking at Violet. The dog sidestepped, narrowly avoiding the bite. Adrenaline kicked in and Angie brought the spade down again, slicing the reptile in half.

She dragged Violet away by the collar. Even though she knew the writhing reptile wasn't going anywhere, it was still deadly. Angie's knuckles were white as she clung to the spade. She thought of the snake biting, of Rosa biting, of Claudia biting, and she brought the spade down again and again and again until the creature's venomous fangs were still. Angie bit back a sob as she looked at the pieces of snake. She'd grown up with snakes, remembered Angus dashing for his gun whenever one slithered too close to the house, but never before had she killed one. She shrieked and dropped the garden tool when something brushed her hand.

Violet looked up at her, tail wagging. The pup licked her hand once again before wandering over to sniff at the dead snake. Angie sank to the ground as shame ripped through her. *Who's the barbarian now?*

୫

Rob pulled up beside the cottage and stretched as he emerged from the ute. It had been a long day on the tools. There was no sign of Angie or Claud, but Violet seemed happy to see him. He pulled the washing off the clothesline and took the basket inside before unclipping her from the kennel, then settled under the verandah with a cold beer. He chewed on his lip as he scrolled through the bank account. A familiar fear gripped him. Angie thought she had plenty to worry about with the biting, the dahlia society breathing down her neck and her newfound paranoia about snakes, but it was nothing like the fear of seeing their bank account sink closer and closer to the red.

At this rate, they'd soon be out of funds. He logged out of their shared account and opened the business account he'd set up for Bottlebrush Building Company. The O'Connells' marble benchtops had taken a huge chunk out of his account and the credit cards had also taken a hammering this month.

He closed the app, loosened the collar of his shirt and took a long swig. *Best keep that one to myself a little longer. Ange's got enough on her plate already.*

Her hatchback pulled into the driveway moments later, and Angie gave him the briefest wave before heading inside. *Still angry.* Claudia ran to him.

A shadow fell on the outdoor table and Rob turned to see his brother standing in his front yard.

Rob was hurt by Claudia's delighted response.

'Uncle Max!' she said, tossing aside the book she'd been showing him and racing to his brother's side. Just as she'd taken to her grandfather, Claudia was instantly smitten with her uncle. He looked down at the beer in his hand, feeling like knocking it back in one go.

Could this afternoon get any worse?

'Hey, Claudia. How's Baxter going?' said Max, picking up the stuffed dog and pretending to make it bark.

'Baxter's not a *real* dog, silly. He doesn't talk—'

'Build me a sandcastle, Claud,' Rob said, giving her a gentle push towards the sandpit. *Who the hell does Max think he is, waltzing in here and buddying up to my kid? Why couldn't he just piss off?*

Max ran a finger over the initials they'd carved into the outdoor table as young boys. The deep pocket-knife grooves had earned them a belting from John and a weekend spent scraping dried cow crap off the laneway and carrying it to their mother's rose garden.

'Tried to catch you a few times,' Max said.

Rob ripped off pieces of the beer label. 'Can't you take a hint? I don't want anything to do with you.' He looked at Max, wanting his words to wound, and was irritated when Max merely shrugged.

His brother nodded at the new timber cladding. 'Never thought you'd want to come back either, but here we both are. Remember the plans we had for this place? Ivan always said he'd give us first dibs when he put it up for sale.'

Rob was on his feet, his hands balled up by his sides. The chair clattered to the floor. 'That was pie-in-the-sky stuff. Don't stand here and pretend everything's fine. You lost that right when you lost all our money.' He shot a look at the sandpit and forced himself to lower his voice. The last thing he wanted was Claudia repeating his words.

'I messed up, okay? Can't we build a bridge?'

'A bridge? Fat chance.'

'Found a worm, Daddy!'

One look at Claudia's oblivious smile was enough to deflate Rob's rising anger. He unclenched his hands. 'You're not worth it, Max. You stick to your side of the fence and I'll stick to mine. Right?'

Max stepped back from the table. 'Everyone makes mistakes. It was an addiction. I lost everything, too. Being a dairy farmer isn't exactly my dream career, but there're worse ways to make a living. And from what Mum says, you're not interested.'

Rob sucked in a sharp breath. *Max is moving back permanently?* 'So, what, you're taking on the farm?' *Bloody hell, this just gets better and better.*

'Not yet, but Mum's days of milking are numbered. Haven't you noticed her hobbling around in the mornings? And Dad's no spring chicken either. I'll milk for a bit, maybe I'll be able to pay you back the rest of your money. Unless you've changed your mind about taking on the dairy?'

'Keep it. Just stay away from me and my girls.'

Rob thought back to their failed business venture. He'd given up on ever seeing the other half of that money years ago, but it still hurt.

He shoved his chair in and walked away, thinking about the sudden influx of bills. A cash injection would be pretty handy right about now, but he wouldn't hold his breath about getting the money back from Max. Not in this lifetime.

A restlessness chased Angie around the shed as she tidied up the next morning. Rob's recent tossing and turning had wreaked havoc on her sleep too. As much as she'd been annoyed to see him strap his helmet on and ride off, she hadn't missed his grumpy mood this morning.

She jumped as a knock rang out on the door.

John stood in the doorway, wearing one of the pairs of faded overalls perpetually hanging on Rosa's Hills hoist. He must have just finished the morning's milking. It was not often that she saw Rob's father outside the dairy in anything other than a neatly ironed shirt with his hair perfectly combed and parted. Now he looked softer, somehow.

'Rob just rode past the dairy like a bat out of hell. Everything okay?'

Angie nodded, surprised when John lingered. She couldn't remember ever talking to John alone before. Usually Rosa was there, filling in gaps in the conversation, or just speaking for them.

John nodded. 'Long as you're all okay. By the way, I've got those cows in ready for the AI guy tomorrow. They're in prime condition for insemination. Chap'll be here about midday, if you want to swing past and watch your new calves being made.'

Angie had forgotten all about the present John and Rosa had given them for Christmas. Letting them use their best breeding cows to build their own herd with a handful of Friesian–Speckle Park crossbreds was generous, and she'd planned to watch the artificial insemination take place, but was she ready to face Rosa yet?

The whole biting incident still made her blood boil, several days later. *I'd never bite my child. Mum would never have done something so drastic.*

A sleepy Claudia wandered down the caravan steps shortly after John left. Angie was midway through pouring milk into their bowls of Weet-Bix when there was another rap on the door and she jumped, slopping milk across the bench.

'Cooeee. Angie?'

Angie mopped up the mess as Rosa strode into the shed. *First one, then the other.*

Claudia climbed down from her stool, ran to the door and flung herself into Rosa's arms. *Well, she's obviously put the biting incident behind her.*

Rosa's face was creased with worry as she walked towards them. 'I've brought Violet back. She's been sniffing around the dairy again.'

'Again? I only let her off about ten minutes ago. I hope you gave her a good slap on the bum?'

'No, in fact, she was quite helpful in demolishing the last of the dinner scraps. But you might want to keep her chained up more often, till she knows not to stray. Walking her regularly might tucker her out too,' she said, fixing Angie with a helpful smile.

Angie forced herself to take a deep breath. If Rosa fed the pup each time she jumped the fence, Violet would only be there more often.

'We take her out for a walk most evenings. Rob's supposed to be training her, not me, but right now he's so furious about Max turning up unannounced that he's barely even sleeping.'

'Oh, Angie'—Rosa toyed with her necklace—'I've felt so wretched these last few days, you've got to believe me. But I couldn't tell you about Max coming home, in case you told Rob. I know my boys. Rob would have bundled you all into the car and spent Christmas somewhere else if he'd known Max would be there, and I couldn't bear upsetting your first Christmas here. I wanted it to be special,' said Rosa.

'Special? Rosa, it was a disaster! Christmas lunch and the proposal were great, even when the calf did a runner, and I loved the pudding, but it all turned to custard when Max walked in. You might have given Rob a little warning.' Angie took in Rosa's pained expression. The bags under her eyes suggested Rosa hadn't been sleeping well either. 'Look, why don't you sit down for a moment. I'll make us some tea,' she said.

Rosa pressed her palms into the kitchen benchtop as if for support as Angie boiled the kettle. 'I feel terrible about Christmas night, Angie. And about the biting, really, I do,' she said. She gratefully accepted a cup of tea, and sat down on the stool with a thump, as if the energy had drained right out of her. She looked out the window and folded her arms across her chest. When Rosa finally spoke, it was in an uncharacteristically quiet voice.

'Rob's always been my easy son. The one who got the best marks, who seemed to know when I needed a hug. Max was a great kid too, don't get me wrong, but when he and Rob had their falling out, things went downhill quicker than milk prices. Max wasn't good with money and before we knew it, their savings for their joint business venture had vanished.'

'They were in business together? And they went bust because of Max?' Angie massaged her temples, trying to absorb the information.

'They were *planning* a business together. It never got off the ground because . . .' Rosa sighed. 'Max took a gamble with their start-up money. First we knew about it was a debt collector knocking on the door. I wanted to try to fix it, but John refused to bail him out. Rob was devastated. He went his way—over to the mines—and we were so hopeful he'd come back home for good when he met you. And now he has. And Max left the country as soon as he'd cleared his gambling debts and repaid some of Rob's share. He's been wandering the planet trying to find happiness again, not that it's worked.'

Rosa gripped Angie's upper arm. Her gaze was pleading. 'Please, don't let my family fall apart again, Angie. They need to get over this hurdle, all three of them. My body's aching every night from the milking, and I'd love Max to take on the farm so we can think about retiring. Us women are good at smoothing things over. Life would be so much easier if they all got along, wouldn't it? Help me, please, Angie.'

Angie was freaked out by the intensity in Rosa's eyes. She had trouble imagining John handing over the reins of his beloved dairy, or how painful it must have been for Rob and Max to lose all their money, but judging from the fingers still gripping her arm, Rosa remembered it all too well. *Why the hell hasn't Rob mentioned any of this before?*

Twenty-three

The Dixie Chicks provided a soundtrack to Angie's painting that afternoon, but she couldn't stop herself from scanning the lane and resenting Rob's absence. She was desperate to talk to him, to quiz him about what Rosa had shared, but his phone continued to ring out. *Probably buried at the bottom of his motorbike saddlebags*, she thought.

She climbed down the stepladder and shuffled it a few metres across. Violet rushed over to greet her, and Angie patted her silky head.

'All good, Claud?'

Claudia waved from the paddling pool on the verandah, then went back to pouring water into her colourful collection of plastic containers.

Angie surveyed the yard for snakes once more before loading up her paintbrush and resuming painting. The top half of the weatherboards would just have to wait until Rob showed up.

Her singing was interrupted by a familiar voice and she turned to see Max striding across the lawn with an armful of Tupperware. He held up a hand, tattoos dancing across his bicep. Rob didn't have a drop of ink on his whole body, but from what Bobbi had said about Max's visits to the town gym, there were tatts all over Max's chest and back.

Claudia dashed up to him and wrapped her dripping arms around his leg. 'Uncle Max, can we go feed the calves?'

'Sorry, Claud, they're all done this morning. Soon though.' Max turned to Angie. 'Mum asked me to bring these around. Rob told her you're heading to a New Year's barbecue tomorrow and she thought they'd come in handy.'

Angie blew a curl from her eyes, trying hard to be grateful for Rosa's thoughtful gesture. 'We're all good, thanks anyway. I've already made a few things,' she lied. Rosa's baking gifts were undoubtedly well-intentioned, and her visit that morning had gone a long way to explaining Rob's attitude towards Max, but Angie still didn't feel right about the biting thing. And accepting all these baked goods would just pave the way for more.

Max shrugged, peeled the lid back and surveyed the items she was passing up. He slipped a quiche into his mouth and looked up at her. 'Waste not, want not. Rob around?'

'He's gone for a ride. It's not like we've got a house to paint or floorboards to lay or anything.'

A craving for the baked treats rolled through her. 'Claudia loves the water toys and the tool belt you gave her for Christmas.' Their gaze shifted to the paddling pool.

Max shrugged. 'It's nothing. We used to have a similar set when we were little. Kept us out of Dad's hair while he fixed the tractors.'

Angie climbed down from the ladder, remembering Rosa's plea for help. 'Can I get you a cup of tea? A beer? There's only water in the esky but plenty of beer in the shed.' Angie trailed off, aware she was babbling, as she struggled to work out the etiquette for how to act around an estranged brother-in-law-to-be. *How much money did they lose? Is there anything else I'm missing from the Rob–Max equation?*

Max shrugged, polishing off a second biscuit and another quiche before setting the Tupperware down.

Angie gestured to the cottage. 'I'm due for a break anyway. Want a tour?'

When he shrugged again and then nodded, Angie walked Max through the back door of the cottage and into the open living area.

'We've taken the kitchen out a few metres to the north-east, should get all the morning—'

'Sun,' they finished in unison.

Max looked at his boots but not before she saw a hint of a grin. 'Sorry. Less than a week around Mum and I'm already finishing other people's sentences.' He was quiet for the rest of the tour, running a hand along the dusty surfaces and opening a cupboard here and there. She wondered if he was remembering the house from his childhood visits.

The sunlight made them both blink when they returned outside. Max pointed to the bare weatherboards underneath the roofline.

'Want a hand with that?'

Before Angie could protest, Max had dipped her paintbrush in the tin and leaned the extension ladder against the wall. His light, even strokes had the highest weatherboard covered before she'd even found a second brush.

Do I stop him? Or invite him back tomorrow? If it had been Diana, Penny or Lara, it would be natural for them to lend a hand. Max's help made her miss her sisters even more. It was beginning to feel like they lived at opposite ends of the continent, instead of only 200 kilometres apart. Unsure, Angie settled on grabbing a second brush and working on the lower weatherboards.

An hour later, the wall was finished.

'Thanks, Max.'

'Too easy. I'll catch you around. Rob probably won't be happy to see me picking up the slack.'

Angie stared at his broad shoulders, so similar to Rob's, as he walked away, wishing Rob's point of view made more sense. *Max's not so bad,* she thought, rinsing out the brushes. She spotted the plastic containers Max had left in the shade and looked around before she peeled back the lid. *Just one piece of slice,* she told herself, *before I finish cleaning up.*

Rob parked his motorbike outside the hardware shop and pulled his phone from his leather jacket. Four missed calls from Angie while he'd been out riding with Brett.

I'll see her in five minutes anyway, he thought, quickly opening up the bank account app. It still wasn't looking great, but the payment for one of the smaller building jobs had cleared, so they'd be right for a little longer.

He swung around at a tap on his shoulder, coming face to face with Wally.

'I've called your name twice, Rob, but you're glued to your phone like a teenager. You buying something or do you plan on standing in my doorway all arvo letting the flies in?'

Rob gave the shopkeeper a sheepish smile as he shoved the phone back into his pocket and pulled out a wrinkled shopping list, trying to remember the reason he'd detoured into town after his ride.

'Don't mind me, Wally. I've . . .' *Got a lot on my mind.* Rob trailed off. The last thing he wanted was everyone in town knowing his business. 'I'll grab a few supplies and let you lock up.' Rob juggled the bike helmet as he worked down his shopping list. Lastly, he plucked a posy of native flowers from the bucket by the front counter and placed it next to the boxes of screws and a tube of chem-set glue.

Wally slapped a hand on the counter. 'What, you're planning on shoving a bunch of proteas and grevilleas down your jacket for the ride home?'

'It's only a few minutes to the cottage. Reckon it'll be worth it for the smile on Ange's face.'

Wally wrapped the bunch in yesterday's newspaper and clicked his tongue. 'Ah, the joys of young love. Knew you were a good bloke, Jonesy.'

Wally's comment niggled as he rode home. *A good bloke would swallow his pride and ask Ange for help, instead of trying to juggle the sums. A good bloke would be working on the house instead of blowing off steam on a bike ride. A good bloke wouldn't keep secrets . . .* The bunch of flowers prickled his chest through the light cotton work shirt, feeling remarkably similar to guilt.

Angie looked every inch the painter when he rolled down the driveway. She was gently hammering the lid back on the paint tin, and her wide-brimmed hat was speckled with paint, as were her shorts and singlet.

'Sexiest painter in Victoria, no doubt about it,' he said, pulling the bouquet of natives from underneath his jacket. 'Love you, Ange. Sorry for being such a misery guts.'

Rob kissed the surprised expression right off her lips.

'You're in a better mood,' she said.

'A few hours on the bike's good for that. Next time we'll all take the sidecar out, yeah?'

He leaned in, wondering whether now was the right time to mention the bookwork. Angie threaded her arms around his waist and rested her head against his chest. The closeness felt good.

The budget can wait.

Twenty-four

The Port Fairview playground was jam-packed with holiday-makers, and Angie had to scan the crowd to get a glimpse of Claudia and her little friends. She spotted them on the swing and settled back down on the picnic rug, lifting her skirt a little higher to soak up the glorious sunshine. An hour at the playground was just the thing to break up the long stretches of painting.

'Need anything for the barbecue tonight, Bobbi?' said Angie.

Bobbi adjusted her sun hat. 'All sorted. Just bring yourselves.'

'I'll bring nibbles and something for the kids,' said Tessa with a tight smile. They still hadn't cleared the air after the Christmas present fiasco, and Angie hoped tonight's barbecue would do the trick.

'I'd offer to bake something marvellous, but my caravan microwave isn't ideal and the mini-oven's only good for small things.'

Bobbi waved a hand, jewellery flashing in the sunlight. 'I'm sure Rosa would let you borrow her oven if you wanted to. Has she bitten any small children recently?'

Angie laughed. 'She called in a few days ago with an apology. And Max came with a peace offering yesterday.'

'Did he now? Was he stripped down to his footy shorts, showcasing his ripped body? Funny how the weights class attendance increased tenfold when Max started frequenting the gym. Is he home for long? Do you see him much?'

The fruit she'd been unpacking slipped from Angie's hand. She hadn't meant to mention that they had spent yesterday afternoon painting the cottage—or the fact she'd kept it from Rob—but somewhere between the swing set and the picnic rug, the admission had tumbled out.

'Home for good, apparently. Taking over the dairy. Luckily, he keeps to himself. Different to his mother in that respect.'

Bobbi laughed.

Tessa waved a slice of watermelon at them. 'Bet Rob's not thrilled about him coming around with armfuls of cakes?'

Angie grabbed another piece of fruit. Tessa's comment had echoed Lara's caution on the phone that morning: 'Don't let Max drive a wedge between you and Rob,' Lara had advised.

'I didn't mention it to Rob. When he's not working, he's out on his motorbike. We've hardly done a lick of work on the house together since putting up the weatherboards. He came home with flowers last night, so he's obviously feeling guilty about it.'

'You've got one twin bringing you flowers, and the other bringing baked goods. It's either a recipe for disaster or a seriously sinful romp . . .' Bobbi said.

Angie whacked her with a banana.

'Ouch! Steady on, Angie, I was joking.' Bobbi pouted and rubbed her arm.

'God, sorry, Bobbi, I'm not thinking straight.' Angie set down the banana and took a deep breath. *Maybe I'm the one with a guilty conscience.* She hadn't planned on keeping

Max's visit from Rob, but he hadn't mentioned a word about the cottage when he'd come home last night.

It won't happen again.

'Renovations are tricky, but you're doing a brilliant job. And you've got a wedding to plan soon. I'm so excited for you both,' said Tessa, shooting her a smile. Angie looked down at her ring, quickly scratching a smudge of blue paint off the pearl. It had been less than a week, but somehow it felt like months since she'd shared their engagement news. *Things will be smoother when we've moved in.*

Angie's phone vibrated on the picnic blanket.

'You going to answer? Might be Rob,' said Bobbi.

Angie gave her phone the side eye. 'Unknown number. It's either his mum, or Mrs Ellis from the dahlia club.'

Tessa laughed. 'It'd be easier to fake your own death than extricate yourself from the dahlia society.'

'I know, but they don't have anyone under the age of seventy on the committee. Still, I'll be resigning as soon as the anniversary show is done, trust me.'

The call rang out. Angie waited for the voicemail notification to pop up on the screen. She listened to the recording on speaker.

Mrs Ellis's crisp voice came down the line. 'Angela, we have the sponsorship committee meeting tonight. Kindly call me back with the whereabouts of your meeting minutes. I expected them yesterday. You *will* be at the sponsorship committee meeting, won't you?'

Angie sighed and deleted the voicemail.

Bobbi groaned. 'Are you really going to let her boss you around? What did her last slave die of? You can't be everything to everyone, you know, Angie. They'll survive without you, I promise.'

Tessa raised an eyebrow behind Bobbi's back, knowing Angie had been roped into watching Jayden and Oscar while Bobbi finished shopping for her New Year's Eve party.

'You say that, but in this case they literally wouldn't. No one else in the committee is under retirement age and they've got their twenty-fifth anniversary display in May. Easiest if I just get this over and done with.'

Angie hit redial as she walked away, bracing herself for the latest committee request.

Angie arrived home from the park to find Rob straddling the top of a ladder, holding the gutter level while Brett screwed it to the freshly painted fascia boards. The sight lifted a weight from her shoulders. *See, he's keen to keep moving forwards. Things are happening.*

'Brett, I thought you weren't back at work until after New Year's?'

'Jonesy thought we might as well whip up the gutters so we can catch the next downpour. They're tipping two inches tomorrow. With a roof this size, you'll almost fill those new water tanks.'

Angie smiled at Rob, softening. He looked happier than yesterday. 'Good thinking. I'll give you a hand.'

She changed into her work clothes, then ferried tools and packets of screws to the men as they worked their way around the house perimeter. The sun was low on the horizon by the time they pulled up stumps.

'What time are you heading to Bobbi and Alex's place tonight?' said Brett.

'Quick shower and we'll be ready,' said Rob. 'Not sure about that one though.' He nodded at Claudia. 'She might need some scrubbing.' Her blonde curls and milky-white skin were hidden under a coating of mud. As if she could feel their gaze, Claudia turned from her muddy puddle by the tap and cheerfully waved a small trowel. Angie headed over to start the clean-up process, keeping an ear on the men's banter as they packed up the tools. She didn't like the bitter edge that had started creeping into Rob's voice whenever he mentioned Bobbi's name.

'Bobbi will faint if Claudia brings that trowel to her place tonight and teaches their kids to dig dirt. From what I've heard, she's allergic to fun,' said Brett. Angie hesitated, waiting to hear Rob's response.

'I'm more worried about the food with Bobbi the health-freak in charge. Hopefully there'll be more than salad and tofu dip.'

Brett laughed. 'I'm hearing you. I'd rather stay at home than listen to Alex bang on about the new Lexus he's eyeing off. There's something about him, isn't there?'

Violet ran up to Angie, proudly presenting her with a filthy towel that had been white when Angie had hung it on the clothesline earlier.

'Gah, Violet!' She kneeled down and gently prised the fabric from the dog's teeth. Last week she would have yelled and chained her up immediately, but now she just sighed and resolved to hang the towels sideways next time, out of reach. She missed Rob's reply but caught Brett's laughter afterwards.

Angie turned and fixed Rob with a steely look. 'Bobbi's invited us into her home tonight, Rob. She's my friend. And Tessa's friend, too. You guys might want to keep that in mind.'

The year seemed determined to end on a high note, with the scent of neighbourhood barbecues and sound of soft music floating on the gentle breeze. The children weaved in and around the box hedge that screened the outdoor eating area from the kids' area in Bobbi's backyard. Angie turned to check on Claudia. There hadn't been any sign of biting at the playground earlier, and things had been smooth between the children for the last hour. *Maybe Rosa's tactic has actually worked?* Angie sighed and took another sip of champagne.

'Give me a look at your ring again, I've barely had a chance to admire it,' said Tessa. Angie fanned out her fingers.

'He's got good taste,' said Tessa. 'Brett said you've done so much on the house since he was there last. Are you thinking of a garden wedding?'

'Hell, no. Imagine adding that deadline to the mix!'

Bobbi breezed in with a grazing platter. 'Oh, don't talk weddings without me! You have to let me plan it,' said Bobbi.

Angie grabbed some cucumber sticks and stuffed baby capsicums, knowing she needed food before she consumed too much wine.

'Sit down with me, girls. These heels aren't made for standing,' said Bobbi, easing into a padded outdoor chair. She propped her lime-green stilettos on the coffee table and raised her glass again.

'I propose a toast, to the new Mrs Jones, to new friends and to the new year ahead.'

'Hear, hear!' added Tessa. 'May it feature many more barbecues, a wonderful wedding and harmonious renovations, Angie.'

Bobbi regaled them with a story about her interior designer and the new sofa she hadn't been able to resist, making Angie wonder if she'd ever have the same luxury of a bottomless budget. Whatever Alex did with his machinery, it was obviously profitable. *When's the last time I even checked our bank account?* The thought drifted away as their chatter moved to January holiday plans and recaps of their respective Christmas dinners.

'We're out of champagne.' Bobbi began to get up.

'No, you stay here. I'll get it,' said Angie, pushing herself up from the sumptuous chair.

'I'll come too, so I can have a stickybeak at your new lounge suite,' said Tessa.

They followed the bluestone path back to the house.

'Please tell me I'm not the only one who was drooling over Bobbi's old sofas and coffee table,' said Angie, bringing a sprig of jasmine to her nose and breathing in the fragrance.

'I know, right? I would have bought them for our house, if it wasn't a completely different floor plan,' laughed Tessa.

The men were standing around the sizzling barbecue and their conversation washed over Angie and Tessa as they approached the deck. Alex's voice rang over the top of the quiet laughter. 'Bobbi told me you've had all sorts of dramas over your way. Wild pig sightings, tiger snakes, biting grandmothers. It's just not your week, is it, Jonesy?'

Angie put a hand on Tessa's arm, using the raised garden bed screening to listen in, unobserved. Would Rob stick up for her or back Rosa again?

There was a pause, and then Rob said, 'Mum might be a bit full on, but she's only trying to help. Between you and me, it's a storm in a teacup.'

Alex's voice came next. 'Women, hey?'

Angie felt confused and humiliated, her cheeks burning as Rob laughed in response. *A storm in a teacup? Women? Is that really what he thinks?*

'You've gotta be kidding me . . .' said Angie.

'Alex is a jerk. Rob probably didn't mean it like that,' Tessa whispered.

Slogans for women's rights flashed through Angie's mind. 'Letting a comment like that slide is almost as bad as saying it himself though,' she said through gritted teeth. She stormed up the deck steps.

Brett was the first to notice them. His eyes flicked to Rob, then back to her.

Alex smiled at Angie as he nudged Rob. 'I always say, "Happy wife, happy life," eh, mate?'

Rob began to offer a quick apology, but Angie pushed past him. He followed her into Bobbi's house, not even stopping to slip off his shoes. 'Ange . . . that sounded worse out loud,' he said. Regret laced his words. She turned again and yanked open the first door she found.

'Isn't that the wine cellar?' he said.

Angie scowled at him before stepping inside and slamming the door behind her. Bottles of wine and cases of beer jiggled in protest, but she was too angry to admit she'd made a wrong turn. 'I think I've heard more than enough, Rob. Go back outside.' *The cellar is as good a place as any to nurse my wounded pride, isn't it?*

She sank down onto the steps, leaning against the door, surrounded by Coonawarra reds and boxes of boutique ales from the Otway Ranges. The handle rattled briefly, but Rob's footsteps soon retreated.

The cellar smelled musty, almost damp, and for a fleeting second she considered choosing something strong and squirrelling herself away between Bobbi's gazillion-thread-count sheets to drink a whole damn bottle by herself.

A storm in a teacup? Women?

It was absolutely crushing to be dismissed, even if the comment hadn't been meant for her ears. *How can I marry someone who thinks like that?*

A light knock came at the door, then Tessa's voice. 'Tucker's up. You right in there?'

Angie unfolded herself, grabbed the closest bottle and walked stiffly through the house, blinking away tears.

The rump steak, and rocket, pear and parmesan salad could have been sawdust for all Angie cared. She chewed each mouthful with short, deliberate movements, trying to focus on the number of chews on each side instead of the questions spinning through her mind. But as much as she tried to push aside the conversation, Alex's comment and Rob's laughter looped in her mind.

A raucous laugh erupted from the far end of the dining table, and Bobbi's voice rose as she tried to outdo her husband's joke. Bobbi would cause a scene if she heard Alex make a comment like that, Angie was sure of it. *Bobbi wouldn't sit through a dinner where everyone else around the table knew her husband had taken his mother's side over hers.*

A lump of steak lodged in her throat. She coughed, and looked around for a glass of water. A glass slipped into her hands. She gulped from it gratefully.

'You okay?' Rob's voice was gentle but cautious.

Angie bit back a sarcastic reply and glared at him. She scraped the remaining food to one side, set her cutlery down and pushed back her chair.

'I've got a headache. I'll take Claudia home, you can catch a ride with one of the boys, Rob,' she said, unable to meet anyone's eye. The last thing she could bear was another sympathetic look from Tessa, or a curious stare from the men, each trying to assess how much trouble Rob was in.

'More champagne!' called Bobbi. 'You can't leave yet!'

'And we haven't served dessert either. You're not going to stay for the fireworks?' asked Alex, draining his pale ale. Angie almost laughed. There'd be fireworks all right, but not at 10 p.m. and midnight as arranged by the local council. And she sure as hell wouldn't be standing on Bobbi and Alex's deck, gazing out at the ocean, when they went off.

'I'm calling it a night,' Angie said.

Rob stood up quietly, swinging the nappy bag over his shoulder. He turned towards the cubby house. She grabbed his arm.

'Don't leave on my behalf. You can still have a good night out.'

'Not happening. I'll grab Claudia,' said Rob.

Angie summoned up the brightest farewell smile she could manage and Bobbi walked her along the hall and down the front garden path. A drop of rain fell on Angie's shoulder, then another, and all of a sudden the sky dumped down rain.

'Happy New Year, Angie,' called Bobbi. Angie kept her eyes on the footpath as salty tears mixed with raindrops, not bothering to contradict her friend.

Heavy droplets of rain beat down on the shed's roof, the sound interspersed with cracks of thunder. Rob waited for the downpour to steady before he bothered speaking again.

His head ached with regret, and each fat raindrop on the tin drilled the mistake into his brain. Lightning illuminated the window over the sink and the rain finally let up.

Rob looked at Angie strangling her mug. Her shoulders were ramrod straight, and even her halo of red curls seemed to have their own strength and fury.

He swiped a hand across his stubbled jaw. 'For the tenth time, I'm sorry. You're right. I shouldn't have said it. I shouldn't have mentioned anything about Mum. I should have backed you up without a second thought, even if I did think it was a lot of fuss over nothing. But is this even about the biting? You said you were going to make more of an effort to relax around Mum, and then all of a sudden you're jumping down my throat again.'

'Don't put it on me, Rob. You could have said something like, "Here's a funny story, Alex. My mum's an interfering busybody who sticks her nose in other people's business and occasionally takes things too far, like biting my child. It upset Angie, so to keep the peace I'm backing her one hundred per cent." How about that?'

Rob winced as Angie spat out the words in a low tone. Yelling would be better. Yelling would indicate she'd momentarily lost her temper and things would calm down when she got it back under control. He raised his mug and took a sip. The bitter coffee tasted like it'd been brewed in a septic tank. *You're in the shit now, Jones.* He took another sip.

'It's a bit messed-up right now, but I *do* support you, Ange, and I shouldn't have said otherwise. But she's my mum. She loves us, she wants us to be happy and of course she wants what's best for Claudia.'

Angie glared at him.

'So it's Rosa's way versus Angie's way? Is her opinion more important to you than mine? And all this crap with Max. I'm stuck in the middle and I don't even know what's worse: you constantly taking your mum's side, or this cold war between you and your brother and your dad! I thought *my* family had its moments, but you lot are in a different stratosphere. Those feral pigs aren't a joke, either. And you didn't even tell me about the money you and Max lost.'

Rob hung his head. Less than a week ago, he'd felt like the luckiest guy in south-west Victoria. And now, if he wasn't careful, their relationship could slip between his fingers. If Max had taught him anything, it was the fragility of trust, and how swiftly ties could be severed.

'I'm sorry, Ange, you've gotta believe me.'

'You made me look like a fool, Rob, in front of all our friends. And the cottage . . .' She set her mug down. Liquid slopped everywhere. Normally she would reach for a cloth and wipe it before it left a ring, but the distraught woman in front of him barely noticed. It wrenched his heart to see her aching. She threw a scathing look out the window above the sink, towards the cottage.

'You don't even seem interested in our new home now. It's like you don't even care . . .'

He wanted to wrap his arms around her and smooth everything over, but the way she'd ripped her hand away earlier made her feelings perfectly clear. He'd have to try to talk it out. Or wait it out.

Angie shoved her feet into sandals. She needed to get out of the shed before the final tendrils of her self-control gave way. Rob reached out to her, anguish written across his face, but she shook his hand off with an icy flick of her shoulder.

The security light flickered on outside, highlighting sheets of heavy rain. She stalked across the lawn. *How could things go so pear-shaped in such a short time?* Rain streamed down her face as she sheltered under the cottage verandah.

A popping and crackling rang out and she looked up to see a burst of colour lighting up the night sky. Fireworks. She took a deep breath, pushing away memories of last New Year's Eve, when they'd driven to the coastal town of Beachport. The three of them had huddled on the grassy foreshore watching with delight as the fireworks were launched from what was apparently the second-longest jetty in South Australia. She and Rob had made a pledge there and then to make it a better year for their little family.

The verandah creaked and groaned as the wind picked up. Another firework burst, fizzing with a trail of glittering light. *Happy Damn New Year.*

Twenty-five

Angie whisked the milk powder furiously, setting the bucket to one side and grabbing another. She wasn't sure who she was angrier with: Rob for not backing her up; Claudia for fussing all night with hourly wake-ups; Rosa, for setting her on this path; or herself for getting so worked up about things she had so little control over. It'd be easier to herd cats than rein in Rosa's 'enthusiasm', she couldn't fast-track the renovations or rid the property of every dangerous animal, and she sure as hell couldn't force Rob to talk about his twin if he didn't want to.

Angie weighed the milk powder into the final bucket before adding warm water. She could already imagine her sisters' reactions. *We tried to warn you about moving in next door to your mother-in-law, Angie.* She whisked the milk vigorously.

She'd replayed the events of last night's party again and again as she tossed and turned, but it wasn't much clearer in the light of day.

Maybe I'm making a fuss about nothing.

It took two trips to lug the buckets down to the paddock. Snails crackled underfoot with a satisfying crunch as she trekked back and forth. It was harder without Rob by her side, she acknowledged grumpily. The calves stood at the fence, their glossy black noses pushing against the metal gate. A loud crack rang out through the calm morning. The calves jerked away from the gate, the whites of their eyes rolling towards the scrub. Angie looked around as another crack split the air. The bright blue sky, devoid of clouds, offered no answers. *Probably kids getting rid of their contraband fireworks before they roll up their swags, swallow their hangovers and head back home.*

The calves were skittish as they drank, startling when she reached down and rubbed their silky cheeks, one by one. Her father's words rang in her ears, the same words he'd delivered whenever she'd confided in him during high school, complaining about one sister or another. *There's naught funnier than folk.*

No, it wasn't that Rosa bit Claudia, or the fact that, maddeningly, her archaic technique seemed to have worked. It was Rob's brushing things aside, the way he'd laughed along with Alex last night instead of defending her, the same way as he'd brushed off her worries about the wild pigs as if her opinion hadn't mattered . . . That was the hardest pill to swallow.

The sound of air being sucked through the feeding teats interrupted her train of thought. She wrestled the plastic milk trough from the gate before the calves gave themselves a bellyache. *Get over it, Angie. There's too much at stake to dwell on this now,* she told herself.

Rob opened his eyes, then squeezed them shut again as the light prompted a pounding headache. Last night's unresolved argument felt no better after a broken sleep.

His phone beeped, a message from the cricket club about next week's match. He declined to play before he did something else stupid.

Coffee. I need coffee, and Panadol, before I can set this right.

Rob heaped two spoonfuls of Nescafé into his mug, following with two spoonfuls of sugar, and then milk almost halfway up the mug. It was a far cry from his usual white with one, but today he needed extra everything. He stalked around the shed, unwinding the Christmas lights from the motorbike handlebars, decommissioned for another eleven months. He paused, running a finger through the dust on the Harley–Davidson's tank. That was what he needed. Another ride to clear his head.

The kettle boiled and he made two strong coffees, wondering if Angie had calmed down yet. Knowing he'd been an idiot wasn't going to make the task of fixing it any easier. He heard a car door slam and tugged a pair of jeans on, groaning as he stepped outside and recognised their early-morning visitor.

Mrs Ellis looked just as scary standing in their driveway as she had in the schoolyard. Same crossed arms, same tatty cardigan, same just-sucked-on-a-lemon face.

Angie had jumped down his throat about not fronting Rosa. Maybe he should step in here?

I'll tell her Ange's got enough on her plate already, he decided.

'Mrs Ellis,' he said, feeling her beady eyes upon him.

'Robert.' She gave a brief nod, and then addressed Angie, who had walked across from the calf paddock. 'Apologies for the belated Christmas gift, Angela, but better late than never.'

Rob raised his eyebrows in a discreet 'Do you want me to get rid of her?' look. Angie shook her head and went to help her unload.

Mrs Ellis opened the door of her car and he saw it was crammed with plants. He didn't know much about dahlias, but those big green leaves looked thirsty and time-consuming. *God, just what we need.*

'Can you help me shift them over by the house, Rob? I'll get them in the ground after I've helped Mrs Ellis sort out a problem with these meeting minutes,' Angie said.

Rob realised she was now clasping the dreaded dahlia society notebook. *It's a bribe, not a present.* 'Do you even have time for all these flowers? You're falling into bed dead tired every night as it is.'

Mrs Ellis bristled as she stepped forwards and jabbed a finger into Rob's chest. 'Let the woman make up her own mind. She doesn't need a man telling her what to do.'

Rob almost laughed. *Tell her, Ange, tell her it's not like that.* But Angie only shrugged.

Angie flicked through her Instagram feed, hammering out the occasional *Like* with gritted teeth. She knew social media wasn't real life, but it felt like everyone else was having a picture-perfect holiday.

'I was only trying to help, Ange. I thought you were sick to death of the dahlia society,' said Rob, looking up from the motorbike he and Claudia were polishing.

Angie let out a measured breath and kept her eyes on the phone.

'And I know you're worried about those pigs, but do you really think they're going to come within cooee of here? Wild animals run in the opposite direction when they see someone. In hunting, you rarely get more than one chance—as soon as the first shot's off, they scatter.'

Angie drew herself up taller. 'Don't patronise me. I know what I heard. And Tessa said wild pigs had taken a few lambs at the Poll Dorset stud. Next thing we know they'll be bringing down calves and small children.' She shoved her phone into her pocket, all thoughts of apologising to Rob fading at the sight of his doubtful expression. She knew she'd veered towards the dramatic, but she didn't feel like being patronised. Not today.

'If there really was a feral pig problem, hunters would be crawling all over our paddocks. And then there'd be a police investigation. Honestly! Don't get all worked up about it. It's a beat-up by the local newspaper to sell a few more copies. They need all the front-page dramas they can get.'

'This is a becoming a habit, isn't it? What *else* am I getting worked up about, Rob? Any deadly reptiles I shouldn't bother about? Any other opinions you're keeping from me?' The volume of Angie's voice had risen with each sentence until she was shouting.

The hurt from yesterday had returned with a vengeance.

Settle down, Angie. No need to go full psycho on him.

She wanted to nestle into his embrace and at the same time she wanted to storm out on him. She stood as stiff as a board as he wrapped his arms around her. He smelled like sleep, he felt like warmth and safety, but she couldn't bring herself to soften.

'I said I'm sorry about Mum, and I wish the restumping guy hadn't got you so worked up about these pigs, but that's not the important thing. The important thing is that I love you and Claudia more than anything else. Look at those weatherboards through the window and imagine them all painted pale blue. Imagine us sitting in that kitchen, eating dinner as a family.'

'Duck-egg blue,' she corrected, the need to be accurate neatly dovetailing with her need to be contrary. He took her hand and pointed it towards the cottage again.

'Duck-egg blue, then. And Claudia is still going to love the swing set out the front and play with her dolls, hopefully with a little brother or sister by her side. Or maybe both.' Angie felt his thumb rubbing over her knuckles as he talked, feeling the furrows in her brow lessen with each sentence. 'And you and

I are going to make it happen. Because we're a good team, Ange McIntyre-soon-to-be-Jones.'

She let him tip her head back and plant a kiss on the tip of her nose.

'I want to finish our cottage, and plan our wedding, not argue over ridiculous incidents.'

Angie's eyes bolted open. She swore as she pushed him away.

'It's *not* ridiculous, Rob. That's the whole point! And if you can't understand why I'm upset, we've got bigger problems than I first thought.'

Twenty-six

Although she was still livid with Rob, Angie couldn't help pondering Rosa's entreaty to help smooth things over between the twins during the next few weeks. The last thing she wanted was to be piggy in the middle, or complicit in Rosa's manipulations, but maybe it made sense. They all had to live together somehow, and the distance between the Jones men was palpable every time they were in a room together—nothing like the close-knit bond she shared with Diana, Lara and Penny.

She wheeled a barrow load of gardening supplies across the lawn. The soil was loose and light under her trowel, the combination of a sandy loam and the New Year's rains making for easy digging.

'Next one, Claudia. The yellow punnet,' she called.

Claudia dipped her hands into the wheelbarrow, proudly pulling out a punnet full of petunias.

Angie planted them next to the cluster of annuals, then stood and stretched, admiring her handiwork. The garden beds were brimming with vegetable and flower seedlings. Neat rows of straw mulch nestled around each plant.

'There, Claud, two more garden beds finished,' she said, swiping the sweat on her forehead and taking the last sip of water from her drink bottle. Violet sniffed at the freshly turned earth, testing it with a paw.

'Don't you dare,' said Angie, nudging the pup away with her boot.

She turned at the sound of tyres crunching along the driveway.

'Daddy home, Daddy home!' Claudia called, racing to meet the white ute as it pulled up alongside the shed. Angie watched Rob unfold himself from the vehicle. She stood slowly, each muscle in her back and arms reminding her she had indeed spent the whole afternoon digging, levelling and planting out the new garden beds.

Grass tickled her ankles as she walked stiffly across the lawn. *Better add mowing to the to-do list.*

'Rob,' she said, leaning on the shovel. As much as she'd tried to get over the New Year's Eve argument, she hadn't been able to dismantle the icy barricade she'd erected two weeks ago. Each conversation was somehow tainted by a stiffness she hadn't felt before—the feeling she was treading on eggshells, or venturing into a trap of her own making. Gone were the warm hugs and kisses when he arrived home from work, and in their place was an awkwardness she didn't know how to overcome.

'Ange,' he said, lifting Claudia onto his shoulders. 'What have you two been up to today? Get all those weatherboards sorted?'

Angie glanced over at the side of the cottage she'd been meaning to paint. She looked back at the neat garden beds she'd dedicated her afternoon to instead. Rob followed her gaze, his eyes creasing in confusion. 'I thought we weren't starting any more gardens yet. We need the weatherboards finished more than we need flowers,' he said.

Angie knew he wasn't the type to coo over gardens, but she'd at least expected some type of recognition for her day's work. 'I've been painting weatherboards all week, Rob. And we could use a bit of colour around here, seeing the birthday pony ate all the roses. So Claudia and I grabbed a few things at the garden centre.'

'Don't like flowers, Daddy?' asked Claudia, her solemn face craning down as she wriggled on his shoulders to meet his eye.

Rob kicked at the dirt with his boots. 'I don't dislike flowers, but we needed to wait. No use planting a bunch of flowers if they're in the way of the new septic system or wood shed.'

'Did you have a crappy day at work or something?' As soon as the words came out of her mouth, she knew what could have been an olive branch had sounded too sharp, too snappy. *Good one, Angie, way to broker peace.*

Rob's face hardened, his eyes narrowing slightly. 'Nothing's wrong with work. Scored a new client today and finished the butler's pantry in the kitchen reno. Thought we could head out for tea at the pub, but . . .' He shrugged, his jaw tightening. 'Reckon I'll head out for a ride instead.'

Angie's shoulders dropped as he walked away. *Ask him about the kitchen he's working on, quiz him about the new client. Apologise.* But instead she watched him walk away, his back as stiff as hers felt. A stab of indignation ripped through her. *It's my house too. What about where I want things?*

'Hey, what about the verandah? Weren't we going to pull it down tonight?'

Rob paused, glancing back over his shoulder. 'I'll do it tomorrow,' he called, wrenching the shed door open.

The mood was still frosty the next day. Angie carried a bowl of chips and a jug of water into the cottage, hoping it might smooth the way.

Brett was crouched on the cement floor in the shell of their ensuite, the back of his jeans halfway down his backside as usual, as he threaded water pipes through the bare wall frames. She could hear Rob working on the opposite side of the house.

'Got it sorted, Brett? The tiler called to say he's right to start waterproofing, if we're ready?' said Angie.

He nodded, tossing a smile over his shoulder. 'All good, Angie. If you hadn't switched out the double sinks for a single, then we might have been a bit behind, but as it is we're set. Who wants to clean an extra sink anyway, right?'

'What? Wait, you're mixed up.' She pointed to the plans pinned to the hallway frames. 'See here. Double sink for the ensuite.' She tapped the laminated plans.

Brett stood, pulling his jeans up as he straightened. 'Rob canned the double sink last week. Said you were trying to cut costs.' His voice was apologetic. 'And it's a bit late now, we've got it almost all plumbed and the pipes are all covered.'

Angie inhaled sharply. Not once had Rob flagged a problem with the sinks.

She strode along the hallway and into the kitchen, careful not to brush up against the pink insulation batts stuffed into the skeletal wall cavities. Claudia, Jayden and Oscar looked up from the pile of nail boxes they were stacking.

'Mummy.' Claudia loped towards her.

Rob pushed the safety goggles to the top of his head. 'Hey Ange.' He took a handful of chips. 'Did you bring any of Mum's cake for smoko?'

Angie quickly brushed crumbs from her shirt. The cake had somehow disappeared between her third and fourth coffee of the morning. 'When did you decide to ditch the twin sinks? Least you could have done was consult me. Brett must think I'm an idiot.'

'I know you wanted the sinks, but we need to save time and money. I'm trying to claw back the timeline. We've waited ages for that tiler. Last thing we want to do is jump to the back of the queue because our plumbing wasn't shored up.'

First the glass stacker doors in the kitchen had been axed, now the ensuite sinks.

'The timelines wouldn't have been so tight if you hadn't been building chicken coops, riding motorbikes and playing cricket.'

Rob fiddled with the tape measure in his hand. Angie tried to remember what the plumbing shop assistant had said about returns and refunds. 'Will the plumbing store even take those twin sinks back?'

'Throw me a bone. It's not easy trying to project manage this place while working full time.'

'*You* were the one who demanded control of the budget. I can't even find the paperwork these days.'

'I've got it covered, Ange, trust me. We just need to economise where we can.'

Angie let out the breath she'd been holding. 'Let me know next time you decide to change the plans. It's my home too, Rob.'

Rob tugged on the throttle, throwing the motorbike into the curve. A rush of adrenaline whisked the worries and guilt to the back of his mind. He clung to the white line and leaned into the corner.

His old red Indian wasn't built for speed, but it could still pack a punch on the tighter bends around the back roads of Koroit, the only hilly area on the mostly flat south-west coast.

It had only been days but it felt like weeks since he'd been out on the open road, and the ride offered a much-needed release.

His new client Lilah was one of Bobbi's rich friends, whose endless pursuit of perfection was probably the driving factor behind her renovation. The bathroom she insisted on remodelling was structurally fine, but heck, who was he to turn away well-paying clients, even if he thought they were wasting their money?

It was one of the things he loved about Ange, the way she avoided the game of one-upmanship many women played. He believed her when she said they'd have their new kitchen for the next twenty years, not five or whenever the trends changed.

The visor on his full-face helmet steamed up as he let out a breath.

Ange.

He'd been a jerk on New Year's. He knew it. She knew it. What type of caveman spoke about his fiancée like that? He pulled his attention back to the road seconds before his front wheel headed towards the gravel shoulder.

Get off the road, Jones, before you drop this bike.

Rob lifted a glove off the handlebars and stuck his arm out to compensate for the faulty left indicator before pulling off the road. There was nobody else at the Tower Hill lookout, and he left the engine idling as he lowered the kickstand and climbed off the bike.

The dormant volcano was teaming with bird life. Birdsong rushed to his ears as he removed his helmet. Rob leaned against the tourist sign detailing the history of Koroit's craters, trying to get his head straight. If Ange hadn't jumped down his throat, he would have told her about the sinking feeling he got whenever he thought about their budget.

Maybe I need to lighten up, like Brett said. He pulled the helmet over his head, and gave the Indian a few revs before he climbed onto the wide-sprung motorbike seat. He depressed the foot clutch, pulled the gear change lever back into first and rode off, concentrating hard not to mix up the bike's unique left-hand controls. After basking in Ange's sunshine for so long, it felt cold to be thrust into her shade. Only problem was, he didn't exactly know how to fix things.

Angie fossicked through the tiny caravan pantry, cursing when a tub of honey spilled. She mopped up the sticky mess, cursing the cramped conditions.

On each trip from the cottage to the shed she passed the work ute Rob should have been driving instead of riding motorbikes, and it made her angrier and angrier. *And why is he making major reno decisions without me?*

Angie's elbow thumped against the kitchenette cabinet as she emptied a tin of baked beans into a saucepan and ignited the small gas cooktop. Sweat and dust were caked into the creases of her skin. She stirred the pot angrily.

Angie sifted through mail as Claudia slurped at her dinner.

'More mail today,' she said, slitting open a large green envelope. The sight of their new address—77 Enderby Lane—on the front lifted her mood a little, until she got to Mrs Ellis's copperplate writing. She groaned as she pulled out the handwritten minutes from the dahlia meeting she'd missed, setting it down beside her laptop, well out of the splatter range of Claudia's beans. *Another item for my evening to-do list. I'll be up until 3 a.m. at this rate.*

She thought of Rob's offer to fend off Mrs Ellis. Before New Year's Eve, she might have laughed with him and accepted help to bail out of the committee, but instead it had felt like a personal affront.

'Jayden coming, Mummy?'

'Not tonight, Claudia, but Bobbi will drop the boys around tomorrow. Sound good?'

Claudia nodded, chatting about her new friends all through her dinner.

'Daddy home, Mummy?'

Angie took the caravan steps two at a time.

'Soon, Claudia,' she said, gritting her teeth. 'Let's get you into the shower.'

Angie glared at the cluster of motorbikes as they walked to the bathroom, resenting the space and time they took up when they had barely enough of either.

Twenty-seven

Claudia's ears pricked up at the sound of a car coming up the driveway, and she threw down her spade, rushing towards the house.

'Jayden's here! Oscar's here!' she said, her gumboots splashing through the puddles left by last night's downpour.

Angie slipped off her gardening gloves and waved at Bobbi's car. Despite the clouds overhead, she still wanted to give the new plants a good soak before she took the children inside for morning tea.

'Come and check out the new garden,' she called, tipping her straw hat back for a better view. Bobbi picked her way through the backyard in her sandals, pushing Oscar in a pram better suited to paved city footpaths than country roads and rural acreages.

'Watch the boggy bit there, the gutters were overflowing last night. You'll lose a foot in it if you're not careful.'

Bobbi grimaced, holding her arms straight so the pram wheels didn't flick mud onto her pale-pink capri pants.

'This is why I leave the garden to Alex,' she said. 'There's not enough Napisan in my laundry cupboard to cope with all this mud. You're a beautician, how can you bear seeing your nails like that?'

Angie looked down at her short nails. The black line of dirt had become a regular feature despite her heavy-duty gardening gloves. She hadn't had time to miss the beauty salon. After seven years of ripping hair out of people, massaging away their worries and applying make-up, she was enjoying the change.

'Gotta be done. Landscaping certainly isn't in the budget, and I want to get things established. The quicker I plant these out, the quicker we'll have fresh flowers and veggies. Might even be enough for preserving.'

Bobbi laughed. 'I can picture you in the kitchen, bottling up chutneys and jams like a right Harriet Homemaker. Next thing you know, you'll be a card-carrying CWA member with an organic baking school and a brood of free-range children. Ugh. I couldn't think of anything worse.'

Angie wiped her hands on the back of her jeans. *What was with Bobbi today?* She hadn't heard that acerbic tone before—it was far from the usual encouragement and light-hearted banter that had urged her on for the last few months of their couch-to-5k program.

'Well, I'm enjoying seeing the garden and the cottage evolving.'

'Yes . . . all I'm saying is, don't go into town with those fingernails. It'll bite you in the bum when you try to set up your beauty salon next year. Alex always says you've got to be a walking advertisement for your own business. That's why he goes all-out for his clients. If they want tickets to the Boxing Day test match, he gets them. If they want to catch tuna, he arranges a fishing charter in Portland. You've got to spend money to make money.' She turned and watched Jayden playing tag with Claudia around a pile of old roofing tin.

'Which reminds me, what's up with Rob? I've left him messages about a building quote for my friend. I told her he'd give them a good deal,' she said, glancing back at the house.

Angie's patience faltered. Rob had already quoted for two of Bobbi's friends, and he was increasingly wary of mixing business with pleasure.

'He's under the pump but I'll remind him. What time are you coming back this afternoon? I've got an appointment of my own to get to.' It was a lie—she hadn't seen the inside of a hairdresser or beauty salon since she moved to Port Fairview, and the money she was about to spend on bathroom fittings would completely rule out luxuries like highlights and haircuts for a while to come. But Bobbi didn't need to know that. Her assumption that Angie had nothing better to do than babysit two extra children was starting to wear thin.

'I should be finished by two. I'd offer to have Claudia while you're out, but now you and Rosa are back on speaking terms . . .' As Bobbi trailed off, Angie realised her friend had never actually reciprocated babysitting. 'Oh, and Alex said he'll drop around the plaster-lifting thingamabob when you're all ready for it.'

Angie snapped out of her ungrateful funk. Bobbi and Alex had loaned them the bobcat to clear the yard in readiness for the restumping, Bobbi had sent business Rob's way and now she was offering the free use of a panel-lifter.

'I'm not sure, Bobbi. I'll have a chat to Rob. He thinks we'll hang the plaster without it,' she said, picking the dirt from around her cuticles. 'But thanks anyway.'

'Nonsense. It'll save you loads of time.'

Angie looked back at the cottage. She wanted to accept it. Rob was making decisions without her, maybe she could call the shots occasionally. Bobbi smiled, sensing she was wavering.

'Tell Rob I insist. The machine's only rusting away in the back of our shed. Let me know what you decide,' Bobbi said, passing the pram to Angie.

Angie peered down at the sleeping baby. Little Oscar was no trouble, happy to sit in a pram and watch the clouds float by between bottles. And Claudia and Jayden got along well, especially now the biting had stopped. As long as they had food in their bellies, free access to the swing set and enough blocks of wood to stack, sort and throw, they were a happy pair. Angie walked Bobbi back to her dual-cab ute, cringing when she caught sight of her reflection in the metallic black duco. Her hair was a frizz of curls, protesting against the humid morning, and her nose looked sunburned already. The extra-wide angle of the reflection wasn't particularly flattering either. She looked away quickly.

Bobbi leaned out the window as she backed down the driveway. 'And is there any chance you can have the boys next week too? My aunt is coming to town, and I promised to take her out for lunch. Jayden will help keep Claudia out of your hair while you play Earth Goddess.'

'I can't . . . I'm not . . .' Angie's attempts at an excuse fell flat as she thought of the panel-lifter. The least she could do was a little more babysitting.

'I guess so.'

I jinxed them, thought Angie, surveying the children's trail of destruction. Matchbox cars were strewn across the lawn, plastic containers from the caravan cupboards had been carried to the sandpit and the calf's milk buckets had needed to be rinsed twice to remove all traces of what Claudia called her 'magic potion' but smelled more like dog poo, mud, water and sawdust.

The calves called from the gate as Angie followed Bobbi's car out the driveway but she ignored their mooing. Right now she needed to be anywhere but here. The mess; the electricians' stereo blaring endless advertisements and Justin Bieber; the shed full of bikes reminding her of Rob frittering away his spare time—it was all too much.

Angie gave into her craving for takeaway food and then pulled into the beach carpark, far away from judging eyes such as Bobbi's. She unbuckled Claudia from her chair, set her on the picnic rug with a handful of chips and pulled a cider from the esky. With one hand wrapped around the cold glass, trickles of sweat running over her fingers, she dialled the phone number she knew off by heart.

Her father's cheerful greeting almost sent her into tears straightaway. She took a long swig of cider and listened to Angus's tale about a wayward ram. *Half an hour on the phone with Dad is as close to therapy as I'm going to get,* she thought, letting his words soothe her, one non-renovation, non-motorcycle, non-Rosa–related sentence at a time.

'You know those rams, they can't keep themselves to themselves. Some are so toey, they'd find a way through a brick wall.' She could hear the amusement in her father's voice as he spoke. 'I'm sure Rob's checked the fences for holes and whatnot, but perhaps you'll want to run a hot wire around your boundaries when you've got the second bunch of calves in there? They'll start pushing fences as they get older, especially if you've got a dozen calves or so, love. John got all those cows preg-tested yet?'

Angie nodded and passed Claudia another handful of chips. 'Yep.' The artificial insemination had gone smoothly, according to the AI technician who had pumped a high proportion of John's dairy cows full of premium bull semen. Most would be

Friesian calves, but a handful would be Speckle Park crosses to boost their little herd.

The line fell silent.

'Everything okay down there, love?'

Angie studied the yellow sand, the gentle waves lapping at the ocean's edge. Even the sight of the seagulls lined up for the half-eaten chips that Claudia doled out, one at a time, didn't prevent the tears welling.

'Fine. New roof is on, Rob's new business is going well, Claudia's singing the alphabet as she works beside me on the house, though she's picking up a few swear words from the tradies, and she and Bobbi's son Jayden spent more time bickering today than playing.'

Life is good, she tried telling herself. *I'm making things happen.* A small sob snuck through her tightly pursed lips. *We'll be in the house soon.*

'It doesn't sound fine, love. It's not the pup is it? You can send it back up here if you need.'

'Violet's fine, Dad.'

'Tell me if I'm wrong, but it sounds like you're sitting on a beautiful beach, crying into your potato cakes.'

Angie's nose started to tingle and she was grateful for the sunglasses that masked the emotion threatening to bubble over. Claudia clapped her hands, sending the seagulls flying. Violet ran off on a fruitless chase, barking.

'It's hard, Dad. Harder than I thought,' she whispered. Slowly but surely, the building site was morphing into a battleground.

'I know, love. But you're doing great. All couples have their tiffs, working so closely. Your mother, rest her soul, went almost a month without speaking to me during our bathroom renovation. She wanted the most ridiculous pink fittings, and I couldn't imagine morning ablutions on a darn Barbie doll toilet.' He laughed, a scratching coming down the line as his whiskers rubbed against the phone.

'But I love your pink ensuite, Dad.'

'It's grown on me over the last thirty years, but I swore black and blue I wouldn't have it at the time. Just like your mum got used to the floorboards I chose, instead of the terracotta tiles she wanted. It's give and take, love, and you'll look back in a year's time—or maybe ten, or maybe thirty—and wonder why you wasted your breath on little arguments. Chin up, love. Look at that snazzy ring and remind yourself that Rob loves you, and you love him, and it'll all be worth it when you've moved in. And Penny's baby will be here any day now. A few hours in the labour ward will be just the ticket to boost you out of this funk.'

The labour ward.

Angie did a mental facepalm. January, February and March had evaporated in a blur of renovations, babysitting and arguments, and she'd forgotten she'd soon be mopping Penny's forehead and bringing her whatever birth-expediting snacks she wanted during the labour. Of course she wanted to be there, but could it have come at a worse time?

Angie scooped out food for the calves, cursing as one of them nosed the bucket, sending a cascade of pellets down the leg of her jeans and into her boot. Rob hadn't been the only one tossing and turning overnight. She emptied her boot and put it back on, and then stroked Pearly's smooth ears, her mind drifting back to the argument about the panel-lifter that had kept them awake past midnight.

Rob hadn't wanted to accept Bobbi and Alex's generous delivery, but before she could nix the idea, Bobbi was pulling into their driveway with the panel-lifter on the back of a trailer.

The sun peeked out from behind the heavy clouds, casting golden sunshine across the yard, and she caught a glimpse of the panel-lifter through the cottage window. It had made plastering the ceilings so much quicker. Anything to help their budget was a good thing, surely? *Borrowing a few machines doesn't make us beholden to them, no matter what Rob says. And where the hell is the budget at, anyway?*

There wasn't going to be a perfect time to drill Rob on the reno budget—she'd just have to demand an update. Last thing they needed was for the project to stall because they couldn't afford to pay their tradies, or because she was too soft to challenge Rob's budgeting skills.

A small black van paused at the driveway, before turning towards the house. Angie smiled as she read the signwriting on the side of the vehicle. Top Notch Tiling. According to Rosa's list, the tiler wasn't the cheapest, but he was the best on the south-west coast. Three days of waterproofing, then they'd be right to finally start tiling the bathrooms.

She left the calves to their breakfast, wiped her palms on her work jeans and stuck out a hand. 'I'm Angie. Thanks for coming over, I'll show you where you'll be working.'

The tiler hesitated, then returned her handshake with a limp clasp. 'Your hubby here? I'll need to discuss a few things with him before I kick off,' said the man, his eyes scanning the property. 'No offence, darl, but I need a few technical details. I'd love a cuppa though, if you'd put the kettle on? There's a girl.'

Angie's face flamed with annoyance. *What era did this guy live in, the 1950s?* Ever since the frame inspection, she'd worked even harder to understand the ins and outs of the project and was confident she knew everything this tiler needed to know.

'Rob's getting our daughter breakfast. He'll join us soon, but in the meantime I can fill you in.' She strode ahead, shelving the offer to help him bring his tools inside. After Rob had kept her out of the loop with changes and budget overspends, the last thing she needed was a tiler treating her like chopped liver.

'Steady on, darl, don't get your knickers in a knot. Most of the women don't bother their pretty heads with the nitty gritty of a build. I assumed . . .'

Angie spun on her heel to face him again. There wasn't room on this building site for someone else intent on undermining her.

'I'm an equal partner on this build. If you've got a problem with that, tell me now.'

Twenty-eight

Rob strode out of the cottage and headed to the hay shed. A day in the paddock was already looking a lot more appealing than a day of laying floorboards with Angie. She'd been shirty for the last few weeks, bitten his head off about the panel-lifter, and now she was grumpy about the tiler. The bloke had barely been there a minute before she'd decided he was a chauvinist pig.

Though, he conceded as he reversed the old Fergie tractor out of the hay shed, it was kind of a relief to see her anger focused on someone other than him.

He looked at the paddocks north of the dairy. Max had commandeered the new tractor to get their father's paddocks ready for seeding. The new tractor would be quicker and more comfortable, but Rob sure as hell wasn't going to march next door and ask to borrow it. He'd given the place a wide berth since Christmas, and Max had only dropped around that one time.

The old Fergie's lumbering pace provided time for reflection as Rob cultivated the rich volcanic soil. He remembered being so eager to help as a youngster, fighting with Max for a turn on the dicky seat inside the tractor cab. He couldn't remember a single conversation, but there had been the hum of the machine, endless overs of cricket on the tractor stereo during harvest, the important job of scanning the flat horizon for hazards as John reaped the land. When had it come to an end?

He knew the cracks in his and Max's relationship had started to show well before their savings had been gambled away.

Rob stared at the dairy as he looped his way around the paddock. Did Dad ever wake up and wish he'd done things differently? Rob had vowed not to make the same mistakes when he'd discovered Angie was pregnant; he heaped praise on Claudia every time she achieved the slightest thing. She'd shot up an inch over the summer, and all of a sudden she was a little girl, not a baby or a toddler. What if he woke up one morning and she was sixteen years old, full of hormones and with no time for her old man? What if he failed to build a connection, buried himself so deep in his work and his own interests that she wanted nothing to do with him?

Everything will go back to normal when we finish the reno. Then we'll have more time as a family.

The money would sort itself out, as soon as the cheques started coming in and the cottage stopped sucking their money like quicksand. And a few high-yielding crops would pay dividends next summer.

I'll look at the accounts tonight, see what I can do to fix things. There was more than just pride on the line, and the drive to prove himself: he had Claudia and Ange counting on him. He couldn't stuff this up.

Angie's opinion of the tiler took a nosedive over the following days. 'It's like he missed the memo on women's rights,' she said, bracing the plaster sheet against the wall stud. The toe of her boot carried most of the weight. Rob stepped away to eye up the join.

'Little my way, Ange. Up a bit. Yep, that's it.' Rob pushed the plaster up against the frame, and screwed it in place. 'Don't let the tiler worry you. He's an old bloke, probably not used to working on building sites with women.'

Angie grabbed the edge of the next plaster sheet and helped Rob move it into the master bedroom. Music from the tiler's portable radio bounced off the hallway's fresh plaster. Normally, Angie tolerated the range of music the tradesmen brought to the house, but there was something about the old Broadway tunes, and the way the tiler whistled tunelessly to them, that set Angie's teeth on edge.

'It's enough to put you off musicals for life,' she groaned, rolling her eyes. 'I've got nothing against *Hello, Dolly!* or *Singing in the Rain* but honestly . . .'

'Don't suppose it's got more to do with the man than the music?'

'He's gone out of his way to avoid me since he arrived. He's a right Chatty Cathy when you're around, but when I ask him something, he grunts. And it would've been nice if you'd backed me up when I asked him about the edges and corners. I nearly socked him one when he told me not to fuss about it. Condescending old prat. Back me up next time, all right?'

'I'm sure it's nothing personal, Ange. He'll be out of our hair in a week. How 'bout I deal with him?' Rob turned his attention back to the plasterboard.

'No. That's giving him what he wants. It's the principle. My money is paying for these renovations as much as yours. He should treat us both the same.'

Rob fixed the plaster in place, sat down the screwdriver and wrapped an arm around her shoulder. 'You okay?'

'Fine.' She wriggled out from under his sticky embrace, awkward at the contact after such a hiatus. There was enough sweat and plaster dust on her skin already, anyway. 'I don't like being talked down to, or excluded from discussions about our home. And the budget thing is bugging me. I know you want to take care of it, but whatever you think you're protecting me from, it's not working.'

Rob fumbled with the tape measure. 'You've got enough on your plate, Ange. I said I'd handle it.'

Angie cocked her head to one side. *Pick your battles, Angie. If he says he's got it covered, trust him. This whole project is about bringing us together as a family, not pushing us apart.*

But she couldn't resist coming at it from a different tack. 'Are you worried I'm going to lose all our money, like Max? I *have* managed a business, remember?'

'Let me handle it.' He swiped his glistening brow. 'Please.'

'But if we're getting close to our limit, and your customers aren't paying their invoices, it becomes *our* problem. Say the word, and I'll go back to work. I'm sure that riverfront day spa will have me, or I could pick up a few shifts at the pub if we're desperate. Promise me you'll act on it if any clients haven't paid by the invoice due date, Rob. We're finally smashing through the renos. I don't want to lose momentum now.'

'We won't. This year was supposed to be a change: you finally at home with Claud, me finally working as my own boss. Hang in there, Ange, we'll make it work.'

Rob turned away and she swallowed the words on her lips. *I don't want to lose you, Rob Jones. I don't want to lose us!* She knew, deep down, that the longer the build dragged on, the deeper the cracks would run.

Twenty-nine

Angie felt an air of freedom as she drove towards the Grampians. On Tessa's advice, she was treating the baby shower as a mini-holiday. No babysitting, no kid wrangling, no plastering, no housework, no time to worry about Rob or Rosa. *Not a minute too soon*, she thought. The two-hour drive had been a breeze and before she knew it Angie was pulling into McIntyre Park. She wound down the car window and let the smell of home flood her senses.

Guests had come from all corners of Victoria to celebrate the occasion. The McIntyre farmhouse dining table, which had hosted hundreds of Sunday roasts and birthday parties, was today set up for Penny's baby shower. Little pink and blue cupcakes competed for space in a sea of presents, with a massive pink-and-blue balloon centrepiece from Penny's best friend Jade swaying every time someone opened the porch door. After weeks on the tools, it was nice to clear empty teacups and fill trays with chocolate slice and yo-yo biscuits instead.

Diana nudged the balloons out of the way as she restocked a platter with scones and homemade strawberry jam.

'Everyone will be rolling out of here if they keep eating at this rate,' said Lara, replenishing the cheese platter. She shot a pointed look at Diana. 'Lucky you've baked enough for an army.'

'Somebody's got to feed the masses,' said Diana, tucking an auburn curl behind her ears. 'With Angie's lack of an oven, your truck-driving course and Penny's swollen ankles, I'm plan A, B and C. And I love it!' she said with a smile.

Lara nodded to the cluster of children crowded around the trampoline in the backyard. 'I think the kids polished off more than the adults, though. Claud would have loved it. And I've lost count of the ladies who asked where your pavlovas and cakes were, Angie.'

Angie looked up from the fruit platter she had made. No matter how carefully she'd peeled mango and scooped out balls of melon, fruit didn't convey the same language of love as pineapple sponge, Peppermint Crisp–embellished pavlova or tangy lemon meringue pie.

'It felt weird walking into the party without an armful of cake tins and platters. But there's more than enough food here. Here's hoping we're moved into the new house by the time the next baby shower rolls around.'

Diana raised an eyebrow. 'You don't sound too sure.'

Angie shrugged as she straightened the pink and blue plates. 'It's going okay but it'd be nice to move in ahead of schedule. Claudia's basically nocturnal again, and Rob's distracted with work, getting the paddocks ready for sowing crops next week. And now there's Max. Since he showed up, Rob's been spending even less time on the build. Says it's because he wants to finish the kitchen upgrade he started before Christmas, but I know he's avoiding his brother. I feel like I'm the only one working on the cottage.'

'I'd tell Rob to build a bridge and get over it,' Lara said, slicing another piece of cake.

Angie's mouth watered. *Don't even think about it. You've already slipped up too many times with Rosa's baking.* Angie scooped up another platter and quickly shoved her sandals on to get away from temptation.

'Tried that. Didn't go down well. As much as I hate to say it, Rosa might be right about helping Rob and Max patch things up,' said Angie on her way out.

'What?' Diana spluttered as she followed her onto the back deck, where Penny's friends and neighbours were playing baby-shower games. The lush lawn and late flush of roses had proved the perfect setting for the celebration. Sounds of grazing sheep provided a backdrop to the chatter of guests and the squeaky trampoline, with enough cloud cover to keep them from being roasted by the late afternoon sun.

Angie heard Lara's voice over her shoulder as she fell in step and they began to circulate the yard with platters.

'You sure you want to be aiding and abetting a repeat offender? After all you've told us about Rosa interfering, do you really want to join forces?'

'I know, but the friction between John, Rob and Max is quickly becoming my problem too. Especially if Max really does stick around. What if they just need a gentle push in the right direction? They are twins, after all,' said Angie.

Lara sighed. They moved through the generous crowd together, greeting neighbours, octogenarians from the local yoga club, farm wives, old high-school friends and local women who had frequented Angie's Eden Creek beauty salon.

'I'm like the meat in the sandwich,' Angie said when they next had some privacy. 'Rob's never going to finish the cottage if he's avoiding the place because of Max.'

'Sounds toxic. It'll eat him up like cancer, if that's the case,' said Lara, heading towards the kitchen to restock her tray.

Angie set down a platter and then ducked behind the table to collect a few wayward napkins. Penny wouldn't want rubbish floating across her paddocks.

Angie started straightening up when a hushed voice caught her attention. Something in the lady's gossipy tone made Angie stay put. She tried to identify the voice from the shoes. The leopard-print heels and pink jewel-studded sandals could have been anyone's, and she cursed herself for focusing on champagne top-ups and platters refills instead of footwear.

'Did you hear about Angie McIntyre? She's renovating some cottage by the coast.'

Angie's smile disappeared as a titter of laughter floated up. She recognised that voice. It was one of Penny's high-school chums, who'd greeted her with gushy air kisses.

'Sounds like a recipe for disaster. Isn't she the one who got pregnant after a one-night stand?'

'Lara's the type of girl who could rock a sledge hammer, but I can't see Angie sinking her teeth into something like that. Not terribly bright, that one. Not like her sisters.'

'No staying power either, judging by her figure. Remember how she was always Chunky Monkey at school?'

Angie's face burned.

Get up and wave your calluses in their faces. Ask them how many weatherboards they've stripped, sanded and repainted recently. Ask if they've been sweating their butts off running and renovating. Bobbi would tell them where to stick it. How dare they? But just like she'd always done, Angie shied away from the conflict, hovering behind the table, praying for the ground to swallow her up.

She hurried to the kitchen as soon as their voices trailed away. If Diana and Lara noticed her sudden interest in the dishes, they didn't mention it. The containers of extra sweets took a major hit as she cleaned the farmhouse kitchen.

Angie stewed over the comments on the drive home, each dissected sentence taking her pride down a notch. Shame had turned to anger by the time she pulled into the driveway that night.

The sight of Rob and Claudia snuggled into the bunk, reading a book, and the sound of Rob reading the character voices out loud failed to lift her spirits.

Using the last of her energy, Angie kissed Claudia goodnight before flopping back onto the bed, fully clothed.

'You've barely said a word since you got in, Ange. Those 5 a.m. workouts are hitting you hard, aren't they? And the baby shower. You probably didn't think you'd be heading to bed at the same time as your three-year-old on a Saturday night, hey?' Rob's voice was playful as he sat beside her. 'Come to the cottage for a cuppa? I'll show you what I've been working on today.'

Angie climbed under the sheets and tugged the quilt up to her chin. 'No, thanks.' She'd felt like throwing in the towel more than once, but the gossip she'd overheard today had cut to the core. *What if we don't finish it? What if everyone is expecting me to mess up, or pull out halfway through?*

Rob tucked the blankets around her, like he did with Claudia. 'Righto. Night, night.'

He closed the caravan door, pitching the room into complete darkness, before Angie's phone lit up with a message. She squinted against the glaring light.

Hey Angie, bet baby shower was a hit. Hope you wore your new floral dress—you've earned it. Still good for babysitting tmoz while I get my nails done? You're so awesome!
Xxx Bobbi

Angie squeezed her eyes shut, wondering exactly when she'd become Bobbi's number one free babysitter.

Thirty

Despite hectic days at work, the effort of getting the paddocks ready for sowing and the tension at home, Rob found himself falling asleep as soon as his head hit the pillow. His internal alarm clock roused him before six each morning, giving him a chance to check water troughs and run an eye over the property. *The crops should be good,* he thought, striding across to the orchard and tipping an inch of water out of the rain gauge. If the autumn break kept up, little shoots of wheat would be poking their heads out of the soil in the next week or so. And if the agronomist at Elders was as good as his word, the higher-quality seed would give them a good return on their investment, aiding their anaemic-looking bank account.

He let Violet off the chain and ruffled her fur.

'Get the ducks, girl,' he said, flicking a hand towards the pond. Violet rushed past the chook house, cleared the fence without breaking stride and launched herself into the water. The ducks scattered as she swam towards them, settling on the opposite side, then flying back when she closed in on them again. Rob watched, pleased he'd finally found a way to wear her out. She hadn't dug as many holes or torn half as many towels off the clothesline since he'd taught her to jump the pond fence.

Rob whistled sharply and Violet ran back to him, shaking pond water all over his jeans. He stroked her velvety ears and brushed a grass seed from her coat. The kelpie sat patiently beside the old chimney as he unlatched the chook-yard gate. Five warm eggs waited for him inside the chimney, and he pouched them in his shirt, scattered grains for the hens and dropped the eggs back to the shed as he planned the day's work. A few more big days and he should almost be finished on the Rosebrook client's carport.

Angie's hatchback pulled into view as he tugged on a fresh pair of jeans. Her ponytail was a snarl of curls, and sweat dripped down her running singlet, but still the sight of her made him smile.

'I'm off. Have a good day,' he said, leaning in through the driver's side window to kiss her cheek.

'Yep, you too. Remember to call Mr Kent about his invoice. It's been a month since you sent it out. And can you please grab bananas and toilet paper if you're driving past the supermarket on the way home?'

Rob exhaled quietly, trying to identify exactly when romance had nose-dived to the bottom of their agenda.

The tiler's van was parked in the driveway by the time Angie had finished breakfast and walked to the cottage. She grimaced at the tradesman's grating whistle and stuck her head around the corner of the ensuite. Despite the open window, her nose prickled at the strong ammonia-like scent of the waterproofing membrane. The tiler had covered every inch of the floor and shower enclosure with a thick blue paste.

'The rest of the tiles arrived too, so you'll be right to start tiling next week.' She said it as a statement, rather than a question, but her assertive posture was lost as she broke into a coughing fit.

The tiler took his time to look up at her. When he finally did, Angie gaped at the sight of a cigarette tucked into the corner of his mouth. *How dare he smoke in our home?*

'I thought I made it clear this was a no-smoking building site?' She coughed again, then sneezed. Her eyes watered as she glared at the tiler. The window hadn't been open to air the house out and make it easier for her to breathe, as Rob had suggested. The tiler had opened it to cover his sneaky cigarette, a direct contradiction of the site rules.

Her eyes watered again and she felt like stamping her foot. She wasn't upset, dammit, she was mad enough to spit chips. And if the tiler didn't wipe the smirk off his face, she'd whack him over the head with his toxic-smelling paint roller.

With a curse, Angie used one hand to shield her nose and mouth and the other to search for her asthma puffer.

'You'd better put that cigarette out, or . . .' Angie broke off as her throat constricted. She whirled away from the door, striding out of the room as his tuneless whistling picked up again. She coughed her way to the kitchen, her anger increasing when she found the water flask was empty.

Angie broke into a jog, darting down the hallway. Her anger turned to panic as she struggled for breath. She burst through the front door, and crouched by the garden tap, gulping in water and fresh air. The murky bore water felt like bliss to her overactive sinuses, easing the constriction inside her throat. *What the hell was that? An asthma attack? A panic attack?* A wave of light-headedness sent the weatherboards spinning violently in front of her eyes.

Angie crumpled to the ground as nausea struck. It felt like she was on a topsy-turvy carnival ride, with something squeezing her throat and scratching at her eyes for good measure. She spewed all over the flowers.

Angie averted her eyes from evidence of Rosa's chocolate cake and the muesli bar slice meant for Claudia. Had she really eaten so much yesterday? A few pieces with her morning cuppa, another few squares of slice for morning tea, a little sliver of cake before lunch. Angie looked away, the high-school nicknames taunting her. She ran the tap again, rinsing the acrid taste from her mouth, then hosed the garden bed.

What would Bobbi say? Running three times a week, only to gorge on the smorgasbord of baked goods Rosa insisted on delivering. Angie switched off the hose with a sharp twist of the wrist. Enough was enough. Her mother's words floated back into her head again. *You're stronger than you think, Angie-bee.*

I can't keep hiding under a pile of sweets and pastry, or I'll never finish this cottage, let alone fit through the front doorway or a wedding dress. She pulled at the waistband of her jeans, finally admitting to herself she knew why the deep indent from the constrictive elastic was still visible hours after she'd thrown her work clothes into the washer and slipped into her trackpants.

No more sneaking food instead of confronting issues. No more being walked over.

Determination fuelled her as she hoisted herself up. *Spinning's stopped. Breathing's better. And at least no one else saw me.* She looked up at the cottage. As much as she wanted to march back into the bathroom and give the tiler a piece of her mind, she wasn't going to risk reacting to the combination of cigarette smoke and waterproofing membrane again. Not without a puffer at least.

She looked down at her watch. If the last two days were any indication, the tiler would break at midday precisely, and sit in his van to eat lunch and read the newspaper. Angie sucked in a deep breath of fresh coastal air, set her jaw and shoved her hands onto her hips.

And when he does, I'll be waiting for him.

The tiler was on her mind all morning and the first thing she mentioned when Rob phoned.

'Be calm, don't barge in with guns blazing,' Rob's voice floated down the phone line, the sound cutting in and out over the roar of a drop saw.

Angie shifted the phone to her other ear as she chopped carrots and cucumbers into lengths. Operation Healthy Eating would restart today, as well as Operation Toughen Up.

'I'm not going to fly off the handle, Rob. I'm just going to be firm and remind him of the site rules.'

'Wait until I'm home and I'll have a word to him . . .'

Angie sucked in a quick breath. 'What . . . man to man? I've had enough of him. If he can't talk to me, I'll tell him to bugger off back to Timboon.'

Rob groaned down the phone line. 'You sound like Bobbi, not my Ange, that's all.'

'I've been a pushover. Maybe this is how I have to be, instead of always being the "yes" girl,' she said, chomping on a celery stick.

A strong cup of coffee and a salad went a long way to settling Angie's stomach, but the nerves came in waves as she pushed Claudia on the swing and waited for midday.

Angie reeled around at the sound of footsteps behind her, exhaling when she saw it was only Max. He held up a hand in greeting, his eyes scanning the yard.

'Uncle Max!' called Claudia.

'Rob's not here, if that's who you're looking for . . .'

'Came to see if you needed a hand.'

Angie pinched the bridge of her nose. 'Not really, unless you want to watch me shout at Victoria's most sexist tiler? He goes out of his way to give me the irrits.'

Max slipped his hands into his back pockets, rocking on his heels like Rob.

'The irrits, hey? Sounds serious. What did he do?'

'What didn't he do, more like it. Doesn't know how to work with women, doesn't follow orders unless they're a testosterone-issued directive, and he smokes inside my house. I'm working to find a new tiler, but they're all booked up months in advance. I'd finish the waterproofing myself, but the smell of it sends my sinuses and stomach into conniptions, especially when combined with cigarette smoke,' she said.

Angie twisted the lid on and off her water bottle as Max pushed Claudia. *Is he going to laugh at me, tell me I'm over-reacting, like Rob?*

'What a tool. Sounds like he's taking the mickey.'

Angie's shoulders sagged with relief. Finally, somebody understood.

'I've done a bit of tiling in my time, it's not hard. Want me to have a word with your tiler?'

'Higher, Uncle Max, higher! Jayden goes higher than this,' called Claudia, her legs pumping to gain momentum. Angie smoothed down her fresh shirt and glared at the cottage. The sun was high overhead, throwing the verandah into shadow, but there was no mistaking the thin, reedy whistle as her watch struck midday and the front door opened.

'I need to sort this guy out myself. You keep pushing the swing, I'll be back in a second.' Angie strode across the lawn, wringing her hands to stop them shaking as she approached the tiler's work van.

Thirty-one

Rob had thought it was cold outside, but after half an hour in Mr Kent's kitchen he had a new-found respect for polar bears. He picked a long strand of animal hair off the edge of his mug and stared at the clumpy milk floating in the coffee.

A game show blared on the TV and Rob raised his voice to be heard.

'As much as I appreciate the offer, Mr Kent, I'd prefer to be paid in cash. My fiancée will have my guts for garters if I bring any more animals home.'

The old farmer squinted at him, and Rob tried not to stare at the John Howard-esque eyebrows. 'It's a good deal, young Jones. A dozen goats is worth twice as much. Whack 'em in the freezer if you're not keen on pets. Goat stew, goat schnitzel, goat patties—endless possibilities. Only take you an hour to slaughter 'em, a day to bag 'em up and then you'll have 200 kilos of grass-fed, organic goat meat. They charge a fortune for it in Melbourne, you know. I'm pretty much doing you a favour with this deal,' Mr Kent said, hooking his fingers through his braces and rocking back in his chair.

Rob looked out the dirty window to the trailer-load of goats in Mr Kent's backyard, right next to the new stables he'd built two months before. The timber alone had added a sizeable sum to his already sky-high hardware store account. He couldn't unscrew it and return it to the store, and there was no way Wally would accept a trailer full of goats when his account was due. *Be firm, Jonesy. Contra deals will not pay the bills. You don't have time to scratch yourself, let alone butcher a dozen goats.*

Rob's phone trilled in his pocket and he stood up to leave.

'The best I can offer is paying in instalments. A hundred dollars a week, if that's all you can manage.' He gave the man a business card. 'My bank details are on the back, same as on the bottom of the invoice.' *The now-overdue invoice.* 'I have a family to feed, Mr Kent.'

The old man threw his hands in the air, his face creasing with delight.

'Exactly, son! Now you're getting my point! That's why I'm trading these goats instead of cash. They're all loaded up and ready to go. Tax Man can't take his cut out of that, can he?'

Rob's shoulders sank. *Why aren't these conversations going to plan? Am I going to have to ask future clients to sign contracts about actually paying before I take on jobs?*

Knitting needles clacked and laughter rang out in the town hall as Rosa cast on a new row of stitches.

'Rosa?'

She turned to the lady beside her.

'Did you hear about Dossie Thompson? They've packed her off to a nursing home. Got to the stage where she couldn't find her way out of a paper bag,' said Eileen.

Rosa winced. News like that seemed to be coming in thick and fast. That, along with every new funeral listing in the paper, reminded her of the big ticking clock in the sky.

'Poor Dossie. I've known her since primary school. Beats me how her children abandoned her,' Rosa said. 'You'll know I've lost my marbles if I start missing craft group or putting the eggs in the freezer and the puff pastry in the pantry. Bring John's rifle over and pretend it's a hunting accident, okay? Save everyone the trouble.'

Eileen's embroidery needle darted in and out of the fabric as she answered. 'Least you'll have your sons and daughter-in-law to mind you when you start going soft in the head. With all those baby clothes you've been knitting, plus all those hot meals and sweets you make, you'll be in the running for mother-of-the-year award,' said Eileen.

Rosa clutched the lemon-coloured blanket to her chest and let out a sigh. 'I doubt it. Things seem to run hot and cold. No matter how hard I try, I can't work out the best way to handle Angie. She's a good mother, and she'll make a good wife, but this cottage seems to be taking its toll. I might never get another grandchild at this rate.'

Rosa resumed knitting. She had to come up with a better plan of attack to bridge this gap between her and Angie. Rosa chewed her lip as she cast on another row. *The bridge between Rob and Angie is looking pretty rickety at the moment too. I need to think up something to help smooth that over as well. But what?*

'I also heard on the grapevine that your lovebirds had a visit from Ivan a few months back, before he really hit the skids.'

Rosa's eyebrows flew to her hairline. 'Ivan at the cottage? Rob didn't mention that.'

Eileen nodded. 'I took Dossie some sweets the other week. Had a good old chinwag with Ivan in the games room. Not that the games are anything special. Half of the residents were asleep and the other half needed a helper to stamp their bingo cards. If you ask me . . .'

Ivan? Oh God, surely he wouldn't say anything to Rob?

Rosa's needles clattered to the floor as she held up a hand. She'd sat through enough of her friend's rambling stories to know obscure details often took precedence over the important ones. 'Back up, Eileen. Did Ivan say anything else? About the'—she shrugged, adopting what she hoped was a casual tone—'cottage? How did he even get there?'

'His daughter took him when she was down for Chrissy. Probably the last outing he'll ever have, judging from his stroke damage. Least it was a nice one.'

Rosa picked up her needles again and resumed knitting. *Ivan mustn't have mentioned anything about my quiet contribution, or Rob would have said something by now.* The thought eased her racing heart. *I'll tell them when they're all settled into the cottage.*

Angie rapped on the tiler's work van. The tiler slowly rolled down his window. A cloud of cigarette smoke escaped from the vehicle.

Angie coughed. She stepped back, letting the air clear. The same old-fashioned music pumped out of his tinny car stereo, and his moustache bristled, a shred of cheese stuck to his top lip.

'Can't a bloke eat his sanga in peace?' He gestured to the half-eaten sandwich on his lap.

A cigarette smouldered in an ashtray. How anyone could eat in a fog of cigarette smoke was beyond her. No wonder he didn't wear a wedding ring.

Angie took a deep breath before stepping closer to the car window. She was glad he couldn't see how her hands betrayed her, quivering in her pockets. She thrust them deeper, trying to remember the words she'd practised in her head as she'd pushed Claudia on the swing.

'You've got to put that out. You might be happy enough to send yourself to an early grave, but not on this building site. Strictly no smoking. Not here. And especially not in the cottage, as I explained on the first day.'

He reached for the cigarette.

'Or what? You going to fire me?' He blew a plume of smoke in her direction. Angie hoped her stomach wouldn't fail her again. She held her ground and caught a glimpse of Claudia, waving at her from the swings. She owed it to Claudia, as well as herself, to stand up to this bloke.

Angie turned back to him, standing up straight. 'If you're not willing to follow site rules, then yes.'

He laughed again. 'You're not daft, are you girlie? You got another tiler lined up, have you? You fire me, and you'll be waiting months to get that dump tiled.'

Angie narrowed her eyes. *One step too far, buddy.*

'Consider yourself fired.' She watched his smug smile falter. A trail of ash dropped onto his shirt.

'Pig's bum. You owe me money for materials and . . . and labour!'

'I'll assess the bill when it comes through.' Her hands still shook in her pockets as she strode back to the swing set and scooped Claudia up into her arms. She threw a look over her shoulder. *Don't do it, Angie.* But she couldn't resist.

'And you know what? I wouldn't have you work on my cottage if you were the last tiler in Australia. Get off my property.'

When the sound of the car engine disappeared down Enderby Lane, she heard a slow clap. Angie turned to see Max applauding her.

'Nicely done,' he said.

She gave a shaky smile and then a curtsey.

'I've got good news and bad news, Rob,' said Angie, her teeth gritted as she scrolled through the online trade directory.

'Tell me you didn't. Tell me you left well enough alone and you've gone and spent another bucketload of cash on flowers, instead of what I think you're about to say.'

Angie nodded into the phone. 'Unfortunately, we have to find a new tiler and waterproofer. But on the plus side, it'll give our waterproofing membrane longer to cure before we put the tiles down, and we don't have to deal with a sexist pig.'

She heard Rob swear under his breath. 'Geez, Ange. We waited weeks to fit into his schedule, and now we're back to square one.'

'So what? He was an A-grade jerk. You weren't going to say anything to upset him, so I dealt with it. You're talking to the new, improved Angie McIntyre. Who wants to marry a pushover anyway?'

Rob sighed into the phone. 'Look, Ange. I'll agree he was a knob, but tilers aren't exactly thick on the ground around here. It's Port Fairview, not Melbourne.'

'I'm onto it, Rob.'

Rob sighed. 'Look, I gotta go. The delivery van is unloading my client's new fridge and I want to make sure the blokes don't scratch the floors or chip the marble bench on their way through. Last thing I need is another headache.'

Angie hung up the phone and sagged against the bench, her earlier bravado fading as fast as the afternoon sun. Rob's annoyance had taken the shine off her bold move. It felt good to take back the power, but now she wasn't sure whether it had been a good move or a ridiculous mistake.

Thirty-two

Penny's due date came and went with little fanfare and Angie still didn't have a replacement tiler by the time the induction was scheduled. Angie filled a suitcase with grey and white T-shirts, jeans and a set of pyjamas. It was hard to know what to pack for the labour ward when she was just a bystander.

She stole a look at Rob, who was apparently immersed in his motorbike magazine, and wondered how long he planned to keep up the silent treatment. Suitcase packed, she slipped into bed and rolled towards the caravan wall. Rob closed his magazine, and the small space plunged into darkness as he turned off the side light.

'Night.' He rolled onto his side. A draught settled between them.

'Night, Rob.' She listened to his breathing, felt the caravan jiggle as he fidgeted into a comfortable position. Her body ached, not only from the gruelling week of renovations, but from nights stubbornly sleeping on her left side, her body angled away from Rob. One-word sentences and stilted instructions punctuated their afternoons. Days passed without the comfort of his touch, the intimacy that smoothed everything over. *How long can we keep this up? At what stage will one of us say enough is enough?*

She spoke softly into the darkness. 'I don't have to go to the labour ward with Penny if you don't want.'

The caravan wobbled again as Rob flipped onto his back. 'You changed your mind?'

'She'll have Tim there. And Diana and Lara too. I haven't said anything to them yet. But now we need to find a new tiler, it feels like a bad time to leave.'

He rolled towards the side again, then the light flicked back on abruptly.

Angie threw an arm over her eyes, squinting in the sudden brightness. She felt, rather than saw, Rob sit up in bed. His voice was gruff.

'Say if you want to call the trip off, Ange, but don't make me the bad guy. Yes, I've got a million things I could be doing. The O'Connells' overhead cabinets are going in this week—if she hasn't called the supplier again and changed the order a third time—and I want to get the cottage sealed up before every possum, mouse and bird in the district moves in.' He sighed heavily. 'But it's not my call.'

Angie looked up at the man she loved. The strain of the past two weeks was written all over his face, from the purplish circles under his eyes to the week-old beard barely camouflaging a new scattering of spots on his chin.

'But maybe a night or two apart is exactly what we need . . .' Rob said.

She heard the catch in his voice and rolled towards him. He slid down to lie beside her and she snuggled into his chest, pressing her face against his crumpled T-shirt with its holes and paint stains.

'Maybe,' she said, her heart hurting as she admitted to herself that a small break might be the only thing to interrupt their downward spiral.

The next morning, Angie tossed her bags into the car and belted up. 'Are you sure you've got all you need, Rob? Don't hesitate to call if Claudia's missing me, or you need me home,' said Angie, craning her neck through the car window.

'We'll be fine, won't we, Claudia?' Rob's voice was curt as he stepped away from the hatchback.

Angie took another look at the cottage before she put the car into gear. The new Colorbond roof was a rich burgundy against the blue, cloudless sky, and the new garden beds had thrived in the autumn rain, making the cottage look lived in.

'Love you.'

'You too.'

Angie mulled over the chasm that had opened up in their relationship as she skirted the backstreets of Port Fairview and peeled east towards the Princes Highway. They weren't having the yelling, screaming, hammer-throwing spats from reality TV property shows, but they weren't the united, excited couple that had signed the contract to buy the cottage either.

Angie may have skipped her morning run with Bobbi, but she quickly realised an afternoon chasing wayward lambs around McIntyre Park was as good a workout as any.

'You're fading away to nothing, love,' said Angus, passing her the laundry handtowel.

Angie laughed. 'You need to get your eyes checked, Dad. Bobbi reckons I can still strip a few centimetres if I stick to her eating program and running schedule.'

Angus fixed her with a worried stare. 'Doesn't Rob like something to cuddle in the middle of the night? Look at your sisters, they look better with a bit of meat on their bones.'

They both turned and looked at Penny, who was pulling dessert from the fridge while Diana carved the roast lamb. Diana's body had softened with each child, and although Penny was carrying an extra fifteen or so kilograms of pregnancy fluid and baby weight, Angie had to admit she looked even more beautiful with a slight roundness to her face. Lara strode into the kitchen, her lean running physique testament to her daily miles.

'They've got your genes, Dad. I was lumped with Mum's curves. I know I'll never be Lara-slim, but I could at least get somewhere in the ballpark. It's a girl thing. You wouldn't understand.'

Angus looked at her in disbelief and made a point of cutting her an extra-large slice of lemon tart for dessert.

'Ten out of ten as always, Diana. Thank you,' Angie said, gathering up the empty dessert bowls. She stopped at Penny's chair and pointed to the barely touched tart. 'You hardly ate anything tonight, Pen. You should've been enjoying your last meal without a baby in your arms. Nervous?'

Penny rubbed her bulging belly. 'A bit. I'm glad you'll all be there,' she said, standing up and rocking her hips. Angie smiled. She'd made the right decision to come.

'Penny's baby. Little baby,' came an excited voice from the far end of the table. The McIntyres turned to watch Tim's brother Eddie press his ear against Penny's belly. Angie knew he would be the proudest uncle in Bridgefield when the new baby arrived.

Tim paused to nod emphatically. 'I think I'm more nervous, and I don't even have to do any pushing. What time's the induction again?' He made light work of Penny's uneaten dessert.

Lara downed the last of her wine and grabbed a tea towel. 'They'll do it first thing, then hopefully we'll have some action tomorrow afternoon. Might be a long wait though. I hope you've packed your sleeping masks and pillows, girls?'

Angus stretched out at the head of the table. 'Can't say I'll be sad to stay here and wait for the good news. We'll hold the fort for a few days while the ladies stake out the hospital, hey, Eddie?' Eddie gave Angus a thumbs up.

Diana's husband Pete scratched his beard and raised his beer. 'I'll drink to that. I'd rather watch our four boys alone for a month than step inside a labour ward again.'

Angie finished collecting the dishes from the table and shooed Penny out of the kitchen. 'Go get a good night's rest, Pen. It's going to be a big day tomorrow.'

And when Angie climbed into her old childhood bed, the cast-iron frame creaking as she slipped between the Holly Hobbie sheets, she fell asleep almost immediately, and dreamed of the new niece or nephew she'd soon be welcoming into the world.

Rob woke to a pounding on the caravan door. Claudia started crying, and by the time he'd pulled his jeans on, Rosa was leaning over Claud's bed with an apologetic look on her face.

'Sorry for the early wake-up, but you'd better brace yourself, Rob. You've had a few visitors overnight. One of your crops is stuffed.'

Rob tugged a T-shirt on and barely broke stride as he crossed the shed, pulled on his boots and jogged to the edge of the closest paddock. Even in the soft pre-dawn light, he could see it was one godawful mess.

Heavy blockout curtains hid the moonlight as Angie rolled over and checked her phone.

The bright display dazzled her eyes and she squinted at the list of notifications lined up on her screen. It was 6.07 a.m. and there were missed calls from Rob, Rosa and a number she didn't recognise.

She jabbed at the voicemail icon frantically. *Please don't let it be Claudia*, she thought.

Rob's voice came over the phone, his short sentences amplifying her worries. 'Been a bit of a problem, Ange. Claudia's fine but . . . call when you get up,' he said.

Next message. Rosa. 'Angie, I'm sure Rob will call anyway but you don't need to worry about the rest of the paddocks. I've been around and checked the calves and all the cows. They're all fine. Oops, I think Rob's trying to call me now. Hang on . . .' Angie heard the sound of Rosa muttering as she tried to juggle the two calls, then a dial tone.

Angie frowned. *What did Rob mean about a problem? Had the calves breached the fences and gotten onto the road? Had something bad happened to the pregnant cows?*

Angie perched on the windowsill to get reception as she called Rob. He answered on the first ring.

'What's happening?'

'Feral pigs. They came through and ripped up the best crop. Mum disturbed a mob of them when she got the cows in this morning. It's ruined,' he said, his voice thick with frustration.

Angie sank back against the curtains, the chill from the window seeping into her skin. 'Ruined?'

'The small crops are okay, but every bloody wisp of wheat in the main crop is upended, just as good as if I'd run the plough through it myself.'

Rob hung up the phone and reached for the coffee Rosa had made him. The scalding on his tongue was nothing compared to the anger building inside him.

'Stuff this, I'm going to go and find the little bastards,' he said, pushing away from the table.

'Sit down, Rob. Those pigs will have scattered through the forest by now,' said Rosa. He jogged to the work ute anyway.

He called over his shoulder as he reversed out the driveway. 'Imagine the money I'll lose if they do it to all the paddocks. This year has been bad enough without having to forfeit more crops, rehabilitate more paddocks and buy in feed. I'll grab my old gun.'

He stopped at his parents' house, going straight to the gun safe. The firearms were still kept under lock and key in the laundry, though Rob wasn't surprised to find the old combination code still worked.

He lifted his rifle from the cabinet, noting the gleaming stock and the polished barrels, and fossicked behind the spare boxes of laundry powder for the key to the ammunition. The smell of gun oil and the rattle of rifle shells accompanied him on his drive into the scrub. Rob crunched the gears and ignored the branches scraping against the ute's paintwork as he followed the narrow track through the bush.

Where there were pigs, there'd be hunters. And where there were hunters, there'd be blood-hungry dogs, ready to latch onto a calf if they didn't catch a pig. He thought of their calves, his niche investment plan, being jeopardised, just like their best crop.

Angie had been right. He thumped the steering wheel with his fist.

Why does everything I touch turn to dust? If he'd gone out and hunted the pigs when Angie had first raised the issue, or spent thousands on exclusion fencing, would that have deterred them?

A wattle sapling whipped at the front windscreen as he took a corner too sharply. He inched his foot off the accelerator. Losing a crop was bad enough. Smashing into a roo wouldn't bring it back.

Rob drew the ute to a stop, waiting in the car until he'd cooled down a little. He eased open the door, crouched quietly, and listened for snapping branches or rustling bushes. The skin on the back of his neck prickled. He spun around, looking behind him. A rabbit hopped out from behind a fallen eucalyptus limb. Rob let out a frustrated breath.

He scanned the forest floor for pig tracks and scat, finding only a sleepy koala climbing down a manna gum, wallabies congregating by the dozen, and more rabbits than he could poke a stick at. The dry creek bed offered no answers either, only a few crushed beer cans and an old campfire. *Hunters?*

Rob walked until the sun was high overhead and flies followed in his wake. The rifle felt familiar in his hands, but he didn't like being out in the scrub. It was too much of a reminder of the adventures he'd had with Max—the wood-cutting days and fox-hunting nights before things had turned sour.

He spotted a patch of flattened grass. He crept ahead, his breath catching in his throat as he glimpsed a sow lying beyond the clearing, a dozen or so piglets suckling from her swollen undercarriage. Bingo. He crouched and aimed, releasing the safety catch.

Almost.

Steady on.

He shifted his weight to brace for the recoil, snapping a twig under his heel.

The sow hit the ground running, her piglets disappearing into the heath before he could even fire off a shot.

He kicked at the dirt. He'd always been the better hunter, the one who brought down the deer and collected the most fox tails.

Not anymore.

He reinstalled the safety catch. Defeat followed him back to the ute.

At least I can tell Ange I tried.

Thirty-three

The sky above the Grampians was blue and cloudless as Angie whisked eggs for breakfast at McIntyre Park, but neither the postcard-perfect vista or the sunshiney forecast did much to lift her mood. Lara breezed through the back door of the family farmhouse, her steps light and expression perky. *She probably managed a ten-kilometre run before sunrise.*

'Hope you've had your coffee, girls. All ready to head to hospital, Pen?'

Penny raised her coffee cup. 'Already on my second one. Tim'll be in from the paddock in a minute, then we'll be right to head to Horsham. The hospital's all ready for me.'

Angie yawned.

'Rough night?' said Lara.

'I was right about the feral pigs. They ripped up the biggest crop Rob had planted.'

'Ouch! Bet he was thrilled about that.'

'Sounds like it. I won't know more till later.' Angie busied herself drying the mugs on the sink, hating herself for feeling the teensiest bit triumphant about having been right.

Rob thought about the pigs as he worked on the cottage that afternoon. He recalled a photo of him, Max and John taken when he was in late primary school, maybe early high school. It was one of the few snaps he remembered where his dad looked proud of him. John was properly smiling in the picture, with a hand on each son's shoulder, a row of dead foxes strung along a barbed-wire fence. He'd shot the most, more than double the number Max had hit, taking great pride in lining the mangy predators up so everyone on Enderby Lane would see. Their red pelts had swayed in the breeze for months before perishing in the sun.

A knock at the door brought him back to the present.

Rosa poked her head around the cottage door, her frame dwarfed by an armful of Tupperware containers. 'I've brought some more tucker. Thought you'd be hungry with Angie away. Where's my poppet?'

Rosa's baking was exactly what he needed.

'Thanks, Mum. You're a mind-reader. She's asleep in the pram. Crazy to think she'll sleep through me on the power tools but wake at the drop of a hat overnight.'

'Plastering looks all right.'

'Bit of a dog's breakfast. You'd think it would be easy to hang a sheet of plaster, but look at it.' He took the piece of orange cake Rosa held out, closing his eyes at her sympathetic grimace and focusing on the sweet orange flavour filling his mouth.

'You'll get better as you go.'

Rob laughed, reaching for another piece of cake. 'Couldn't get much worse.'

Rosa set two mugs of steaming coffee on a sawhorse. 'I sent Angie another message—Penny's almost about to start pushing.'

Rob held up a hand. He'd seen enough in the labour ward when Claudia arrived—he didn't need details.

'Can't think of anything worse than having all those people in the room when you're trying to give birth. It's not a spectator—'

'Sport,' said Rosa, nodding. 'I grabbed your mail on the way in. I hope you get as many remittance statements as you get window-fronted envelopes?'

She set the mail down on a box of screws. Rob felt a stab of guilt. He avoided his mother's gaze and toyed with a set square.

'Ange isn't happy about me handling the budget. And I haven't even told her about the latest round of reno invoices. Maybe she'll be in a better mood when she gets back tomorrow.' *Keep telling yourself that, mate. You're going to need more than a good mood to soften the blow. Just wait until she hears about the goats.*

'The roofing bill was higher than we expected, the windows went way over, and I've lost thousands on that crop. It feels like we're haemorrhaging money.'

Rosa hesitated, as if she was going to say something, but instead she restacked a pile of timber offcuts, lining them up so the cut edges were flush on one side. The silence stretched on.

Even though it was his mum sitting beside him, not his dad, Rob felt the weight of his father's expectations. *You've got to finish what you start. Don't get yourself too deep in the red. Do a job once, and do it well. If you want it done right, then do it yourself.* Rob played with his safety glasses.

Between Ange and Dad, I can barely put a foot right. The to-do list to make the house habitable dangled in his mind like a noose.

Dozens of extra opportunities to stuff up.

'Dad would probably love to see our budget, tell me all the ways I'm messing this up. It's like he's waiting for me to ask for help, or admit I've bitten off more than I can chew.'

Rosa reached for his hand. Her voice was soft.

'He loves you, Rob. We both do. And he's so proud of you, even if he can't find the words to say it. And you and Angie are a great match. Tell her about the budget. Share the load a little.'

'Yeah, it'd really cheese Dad off to have two sons who are failures, wouldn't it?'

Rosa flinched at the bitterness in his words. She draped an arm around his shoulder and pulled him into a hug.

Rob felt another pang of guilt as his mum's arm started to shake. *Top work, Jones. Upsetting both the women in your life. All you need now is for Claudia to chuck a tantrum and it'll be a trifecta.*

'I wish you'd put it all behind you, Rob. You've only got one brother, and one dad. I thought bringing you and Max home would be a chance for you all to mend fences.'

She looked away, engrossed in the sliver of mulberry tree visible through the cottage window.

'Never underestimate how much I love you boys, Rob. Most mothers will do whatever it takes to keep their kids safe and happy, even at their own expense. The least you can do is budge a little too. Has it served your father well, all the rigidity? All the stubbornness? He's never been very good at showing his love, but it doesn't mean he loves you any less,' she paused, folding and unfolding the hem of her shirt. 'You're more alike than you realise.'

Rosa's words hit him hard. He was *nothing* like his father. Claudia knew she was loved, he told her how proud he was when she sang the alphabet and practised her numbers.

She stood up and faced the window.

'Come and see me when you've worked out what's most important to you, Rob. But don't leave it too late, or you might find you've put all your eggs in the wrong basket.'

❦

'Not long to go now, Pen,' said Angie as another moan filled the labour ward. Lara walked back into the birthing suite, talking to the midwife and obstetrician as they swept in behind her.

'The contractions are still infrequent, but they seem to be hitting hard. She says she doesn't want any pain relief, but I'm hoping you can talk some sense into her,' said Lara, in full nurse mode. 'Otherwise it's going to be another loooong night.'

Angie blinked in disbelief. *Night?* The catnaps and quiet hours had all rolled into one after a while.

Angie's phone vibrated in her pocket and she gave Tim the wet flannel she'd been holding against Penny's forehead. 'I'll leave you guys to it for a minute, okay?' She fished her phone from her pocket and frowned as she realised how long Penny had been in labour.

Angie looked back at the people clustered around her sister and quietly stepped outside. The hallway lights were painfully bright after the dimly lit labour ward. She scrolled through the messages and emails. Rosa had sent a photo of Claudia baking, Rob had forwarded an invoice to her instead of his latest client and there was a message from an unknown number.

Bottlebrush Creek is bone dry, reckon that's why pigs were heading your direction. Rob found tyre tracks and an old camp site too, probably hunters, and a litter of piglets. Have put video cameras in the scrub, streaming to my laptop, and already caught this ripper of a vid. Not quite candid camera, but good for a laugh anyway. Max

Max? Rosa must have given him my number.

Diana came out of the room as Angie opened the video clip.

'Not sure what Max found in the scrub, but apparently it's funny,' Angie said, glancing up at her oldest sister, who looked like she was equally in need of some comic relief. 'Want to watch it?'

Diana nodded wearily, squeezing into the uncomfortable plastic seat beside her. Angie pressed play on her phone.

Leaves obscured the top of the image, as if it had been mounted to a tree in the forest, and the dappled sunlight made for poor visibility. A figure walked through the scrub, paused, then looked left and right, as if searching for someone or something.

Diana peered at the screen, trying to get a better look at the grainy image. 'A hunter? I can't see any pigs.'

'Looks like he's wearing a uniform.'

Angie raised an eyebrow and returned her attention to the video. The man was back in the picture, a lot closer to the camera now, and he was leaning up against the base of the tree, still looking left and right.

'Is he a ranger? Parks and Wildlife? Eww, he's doing a wee.' Angie recoiled from the phone. 'Seriously?'

Diana snorted with laughter and grabbed the phone. 'Look closely, he's not doing a wee.'

Angie studied the screen, her eyes widening as the uniformed man moved his hand in a steady rhythm. 'Whaaaat? Is that what I think it is?'

Diana's laughter doubled as the clip ended abruptly. 'He's having a grand old time. Not only are wild pigs and hunters roaming your property, but our taxpayer dollars are paying for someone to jack off in the forest.'

Angie let out a giggle. 'I'd better delete it.'

'Delete it? You should upload it to YouTube! You'll make a fortune.'

'Redtube more like it.'

Diana passed Angie's phone back, holding it for a second until Angie looked up at her. 'So Max is sending you messages now? Careful about how you play this whole twin thing, all right? It's nice he's trying to help, but Rob's the man you're marrying.'

Angie rubbed her eyes and sent Diana a weary smile. 'You're not serious, Diana? It isn't like that.' She spun the engagement ring around on her finger as she walked back into the labour ward. She was old enough to form her own opinions about someone, and just because Rob didn't like Max, it didn't mean she had to automatically hate him too.

Rob walked out of the cottage that afternoon to find his father climbing across the fence.

Just what I need: Dad, to rub it in a little deeper.

'Don't need to hear it, Dad. Whatever you reckon I could have done isn't going to help now.'

'Just having a gander. Hard to believe the pigs can do so much damage in such a short time. Had a field day in the backyard too.'

Rob turned back to the cottage, taking in the annihilated flowerbeds at the back of the yard, the snapped fruit trees and ruined veggie patch. The trampled seedlings, uprooted plants, trellises and stakes were just the icing on the cake. All Angie's hard work had been for nothing.

How did I miss that?

John shoved his hands into his overall pockets. 'Feral pigs are one thing but setting a bunch of piglets loose in the scrub should be a hanging offence. Maybe . . .'

Rob noticed his father's brow furrow. It wasn't like him to censor his thoughts. Had Rosa had a stern word with him too?

John cleared his throat. 'Maybe we should hunt the blighters down? I'm not much of a shot, not like you and Max, but it will be a nightmare if they keep returning.'

Rob tore his gaze away from the ruined crop and garden beds and studied his dad's pensive expression. Where was the sting in the tail, the part where John told him he could hold the spotlight while Max did all the shooting? He was surprised when none came.

'What are you thinking?'

'It's a full moon tonight. How 'bout we see if we can take a few down? Max has rigged up a few cameras. We'll soon have a handle on their movements,' said John.

He has? Rob had trouble hiding his shock but one look at his father's face confirmed it: *Is that optimism?* Rob shoved his hands in his pockets and shrugged. 'Righto.'

Max's video fell to the back of Angie's mind as she watched her sister deliver an indignant baby girl into the world. Elation filled the room, along with the glorious sounds of a newborn's cry. Penny beamed, clasping her daughter to her chest.

'She's perfect, Pen,' said Angie. 'All the little fingers, all the little toes.'

Little Lucy Patterson didn't look that much different to a newborn Claudia, though her niece's entry into the world had been more of a social event than Angie's experience in the labour ward. Rob and a midwife had been the only ones to witness Claudia's arrival, and it had felt like their first big triumph as a family. The surge of love she'd felt for both Claudia and Rob in the labour ward had run deeper than she'd ever imagined, cocooning them through those hazy first months of parenthood.

Angie, Lara and Diana bid the new parents farewell and started the trek back from the Horsham hospital to McIntyre Park.

Conversation was sparse, the sound of talkback radio just as the sisters drove. It was only fifty k's but Angie felt herself nodding off in the car, and her legs felt like lead as she dragged herself from Diana's four-wheel drive.

Angus waited on the front porch of the farmhouse, tossing a set of keys in his hand. 'Don't drive home yet, love. You need some sleep before you get behind the wheel of your little buzz-box. Cuppa first, then a nap, all right?'

Angie stifled a yawn as she trudged up the steps. *What's another few hours away in the scheme of things?* She shot off a quick message to Rob, with a promise she'd be home by nightfall, and allowed her father to walk her upstairs with a cup of tea. He flicked the bedside lamp on and drew the curtains.

'A quick kip will do you the world of good, love.' Just as he had when she was a little girl, Angus blew her a kiss and quietly closed the bedroom door behind him.

Thirty-four

Shiny cars towing boat trailers outnumbered local traffic two to one as Rob headed into Port Fairview. He pulled up at the hardware store and retrieved the shopping list from Claudia's chubby hands. After grabbing a trolley, they worked their way down the list, picking out tile glue and grout, until they had all the supplies to finish laying floorboards and make a start on the kitchen. At the last minute, Rob also added a bottle of gun oil to the trolley, keen to give his rifle a clean before the hunt.

Claudia stacked and restacked the bags of grout and boxes of hardware as they waited for the trio of fishermen in front to pay for their hooks and bait. 'Careful with them, Claud. Don't poke a hole in the bags. Wally doesn't want his floors dusted with grouting powder,' he said, smiling at his old mentor.

'Rob, good to see you again. Drove past your place other day, looks like you've got it shipshape. Ivan and Ida would be proud.'

Rob nodded. 'Ivan called in for a squiz over Christmas. Seemed happy enough.' He looked down to prise his debit card from his wallet.

'G'day, Miss Claudia. Helping Dad with that cottage of yours?'

Claudia nodded proudly as she stacked the products on the counter.

Wally whistled. 'Clever like your dad, I'll bet.' He scanned the gun oil. 'Shame about those pigs. You nailed the ferals yet?'

'Not yet, but I'll be having a red-hot crack tonight. Max's tracking them with cameras. You haven't heard anything about cowboy hunters around town, have you? I found a few rifle shells on the ground by Bottlebrush Creek.'

Wally chewed on his lip. 'Not a word. I'll keep my ear to the ground though.'

A hardware staffer squeezed in beside Wally and gestured to the kitchen. 'I'll take over if you like, Wal. Your coffee's waiting for you, with extra sugar just the way you like it. Go drink it while it's hot.'

'Be out in a tick. Can't leave my favourite customers in the lurch,' said Wally.

The woman's comment jogged something in Rob's brain. *Coffee? Sugar?* But before he could grasp it, the card machine beeped.

Rob glanced at Claudia, who was piling their purchases high, and then back to Wally. *What was it about coffee and sugar?*

'Sorry, mate, the card was declined. Must have pressed the wrong key, happens all the time,' said Wally, handing back the machine.

'I'll give it another go.'

Wally's face was creased with concern. 'Sorry, Rob, the card was declined again. I'd let you take the shopping, but your account's too far overdue.'

He twisted the computer screen around. Even though

Rob could see the bold red text at the top of the monitor, he struggled to comprehend what it meant.

Rob laughed, glancing at the queue behind him. 'Of course we have money, I've entered the wrong pin again. Let me try once more.' He thrust the card back over the counter.

Claudia stacked the boxes higher. Customers shuffled awkwardly in the line behind him as he pushed the code into the touchpad, focusing on entering each number firmly and in the correct order, as his mind raced to stay a step ahead of the situation. *Maybe I can leave my licence at the counter while I dash out and withdraw money from the cash machine?*

Claudia's tower tumbled. A box whacked his hand, and then spilled onto the floor, 500 galvanised bullet-head nails spinning in all directions. The rest of the boxes followed.

The credit card machine grunted quietly, confirming the card had indeed been declined, as the rest of the boxes and grout bags rained down on the checkout, the trolley and the floor.

Rosa popped the leftover lasagne in the microwave and set it for three minutes. She was still staring off into the paddock, smiling at the forest and the black-and-white cattle in the distance, when the microwave started beeping at her. Rosa jumped and pulled the steaming pasta out to divide into serves for lunch.

Having a quiet word to both John and Rob had been worthwhile, and, as an added perk, she'd get to babysit while they were out hunting tonight. *If I'd known those pigs would be the catalyst for getting John and Rob conversing in more than one-word sentences, I'd have released them into the forest myself.*

She caught sight of her smile in the window and clapped a hand over her mouth. *You'll be struck down thinking wicked thoughts like that, Rosa Jones.* She rubbed the gold cross on her necklace until she felt suitably repentant. Now to get Max on board.

'What do you mean there's no money in our account?' Rob asked the bank teller, cradling his wrist. The pain in his hand throbbed with his pulse, and he spun around at a sound behind him: Claudia had pulled home-loan brochures from the display racks and was shoving them down the front of her skirt.

'Leave it, Claudia! Come here!' he said, cringing as his voice echoed under the bank's cathedral ceilings. At least there was only one other customer at the branch. The fewer witnesses to this embarrassment, the better.

'I checked the accounts the other day. They were getting low, but there should be enough money left to pay for small things,' he said, his voice sharp.

The girl behind the glass partition tapped at her computer, a quizzical look on her face. 'Yes, I can see we've got it all set up as an owner–builder loan, and I see here we gave sign-off for the last stage in December, but it looks like you made a sizeable withdrawal earlier this month. And no deposits since then—aside from a few small incomings.'

Rob tugged Claudia away from the brochure stand, shaking his head as he tried to recall the big outlays that month. It had been tight, but he didn't think they'd veered into the red.

'I can't think of anything besides floorboards, but that wouldn't have been enough to clean us out. Does it . . . Is there any . . . Where did the large withdrawals go to?'

Realisation dawned on Rob even as he asked the question: he'd had to shuffle some money from the home account to the business account to pay for his newest client's kitchen cabinetry.

'Look, is there any chance I can get a short loan, or draw down from the home loan account to top up the everyday account?'

The bank teller gave him a sympathetic smile. 'I'm sorry, Rob, but because it's a joint account, I can't do anything without your partner's approval. Why don't you make an appointment and we can discuss it together? The bank manager will be back in the office at the end of the week.'

Rob swore and banged a fist on the counter, regretting it when a jolt of pain ran up his arm and the young female teller sprang away from the desk.

Claudia's little legs worked overtime to keep up as he barrelled across the parking lot. 'Wait, Daddy!'

Her words made him pause mid-stride.

Look at you, Jones. Bellowing like an idiot, scaring the young teller, and storming around without any thought for Claudia. He kneeled down and picked her up. *Can't you get anything right?*

He worked through the list of outstanding invoices as soon as he got home, but again, many of the calls went straight to voicemail.

'Hi Mrs O'Brien, checking you got the invoice for the porch extension I finished before Christmas? If you can please take care of that, I'd very much appreciate it. Thanks.'

He then called the suppliers who were yet to deliver products he'd been waiting on, to ask how they'd feel about a short payment extension.

Angie would be home tonight. *What am I even going to say to her?* By the time the sun had set, he was more than ready to load up his gun and head into the scrub. *Maybe Mum will have a good suggestion or two.*

Rob jogged to the sandpit. 'C'mon, Claud.'

Claudia bounced onto his back and he strode across to the dairy, relieved to see Rosa feeding the calves. It wasn't a conversation he wanted to have within his father's earshot.

'Hello, poppet. Hey, Rob,' said Rosa, smelling of milk and lavender as she leaned in to hug them both. 'Come to feed some calves?'

Rob lifted Claudia down and she hurried to the tiny animals, listing off their names as she patted each one.

'This one's Princess Sparkles, this one's Peppa, this one's Bob, this one's Hamburger, this one's Boris . . .'

Rob turned to Rosa, his voice low and urgent. 'Mum, I've ballsed up. Nobody's paying their invoices and the bank's put a freeze on our account. Credit card's maxed out too. It's a dog's breakfast. How can I even tell Ange?'

He pinched the bridge of his nose, knowing this news would be ten times harder to admit to Angie. There was no way around it—he was going to have to tell her as soon as she got back.

Rosa lifted a finger in the air and raised an eyebrow. 'Maybe . . . we could loan you some money, so you've got some breathing space to sort things out? Angie wouldn't need to know. It'd just be a quick loan until those invoices come through. No sense having money sitting in our account when you're in strife,' she said with a shrug.

Angie woke up refreshed in the late afternoon.

'It's all to do with the way you look at things. Rob's a good man. Trust him, love. Don't be so hard on one another,' Angus assured her. She started her car and headed for home, embracing the unexpected burst of optimism.

There must be something about a new baby arriving that boosts hormones and gives perspective, Angie mused, as the Grampians disappeared in her rear-view mirror. They'd finish renovating and move into the cottage, things would go back to normal and they'd start thinking about the future.

Angie smiled as she drove, and leaned over to turn the stereo up. Dad was right. *Glass half full or glass half empty? It's my decision.*

Rob loped across the paddock. His head was so full of money worries that he didn't register Max behind him until he was halfway over the fence that divided the two properties.

'Uncle Max,' said Claudia, wriggling off Rob's shoulders and jumping to the ground.

Rob put his hands on his hips. 'Come to toss your five cents in, have you?'

Max ran a hand through his thick black hair and screwed up his face. 'Eh? I've caught something on camera, but if you're gonna be a dick . . .'

Rob snorted. 'I don't have time for another candid-camera tosser.'

'This's a shitload better than that. Trust me.'

Rob shook his head. It'd been a long time since he'd trusted Max, but something about his brother's tone made him lean in. He shielded the screen with his hand, straining to see the grainy images.

'Changed the camera to night mode last night, and bugger me dead if I didn't catch this bastard. Look.'

'Jesus,' said Rob, watching as a sixties Land Cruiser ute drove into the shot. A short man jumped out of the ute, looking over his shoulder. With a stubby in one hand, he dragged a large dog crate across the tray and then unlatched the tailgate.

'If he's a hunter, where's his gun? And those dogs look too small to be pig-hunting dogs,' said Rob, studying the small shapes running around in the crate.

'Keep watching,' said Max.

But instead of dogs, two small piglets raced out of the crate and dived off the edge, disappearing into the scrub.

Rob swore and looked at his twin.

'They *are* being deliberately released.'

'Now we've gotta find the bastard behind it. Can't be too many FJ45 Cruiser utes in Port Fairview, right?'

Rob froze as he realised what Max had just said.

We.

He hesitated. He'd accept Brett's help; hell, he'd even consider accepting Alex Bloody Richardson's help if it meant fixing this problem and making it up to Angie; but Max? He thought about Rosa's plea. Could he really give his brother a second chance?

Thirty-five

Darkness had fallen by the time Angie arrived home. She jogged across the lawn, mosquitoes teeming around her legs. Violet barked a greeting from the kennel. The calves snickered but the shed was dark and the caravan empty.

She pulled a note from the caravan door.

Out hunting for pigs, Claud is with Mum. Will be a back in a few hours. x R

Hunting was good. Hunting was a sign he was taking the pigs seriously. She wondered if he was out with Brett and sent up a little prayer that they'd arrive home with all their extremities intact. It was too dark to walk, so she drove next door, almost mowing down Rosa's garden gnomes in her eagerness to collect Claudia. Would she ever get used to days away from her little girl?

Rosa packed them off with a few litres of fresh milk, and Claudia insisted on bringing home a handful of biscuits, even in her sleepy state. Claudia fell back into a deep sleep immediately, but Angie found it impossible to wind down. After an hour of tidying the shed, she forced herself into the shower and then snuggled into Rob's pillow, breathing in his smell. She'd missed him, missed the closeness they'd shared. Missed the sweet moments when all the stars aligned and Claudia fell asleep in the pram, allowing them to sneak in a little afternoon delight.

The cottage is supposed to bring us together, not tear us apart. I need to tell him I love him, remind him how good we are together. She thought of Rob kneeling by Claudia's bed, his hair sticking up like a cockatoo's crest as he finished the final page of *The Gruffalo*.

The cluckiness Angie had felt watching baby Lucy's arrival intensified as she thought of the good times they'd shared, the way Rob had cradled Claudia in his arms as a newborn, and never hesitated to give his little girl a shoulder ride, even though she could walk just fine. The way he had taught himself to plait, so he could help tame Claudia's curls of a morning.

I need to give him more of a chance.

Rob steadied his breathing as he sighted the rifle, not wanting to lose the pig as it ambled along the dry creek bed. There was nothing left of the heavy rainfalls that had fallen mid-summer, not even a puddle, and he felt almost sorry for the animals that relied on the water supply. The big boar stopped by the corn and apples Max had scattered there earlier and scratched itself like a dog before hoeing into the food.

Rob's finger hovered on the trigger and he worked hard to empty his mind of the shitty day. Shooting wasn't the occasion for contemplation. A lack of focus and a misfired shot would have that pig running for his life and the night ruined.

'Still got him in sight?' said Max, leaning over his shoulder.

'Course I've got him. But I can't get a clean shot when he's wriggling. He'll bugger off if he hears you, so shut up.'

Rob exhaled as he squeezed the trigger. *Bang*. The rifle reverberated through his shoulder. He squinted through the sight again, pleased he'd hit his mark. Max awaited his nod, then flicked on the torch, lighting their way to it.

'Nice one. Been practising?'

'Nope.'

'Dad'll be impressed.'

Rob gave a dry laugh. 'He'd never say I was good at anything. He was always banging on about your shooting instead. *Sight it up like Max, shoot us a buck like Max.*

'Pull the other one. Dad always talked about *you* and your aim. I'd be lucky to hit the side of a shed if I picked up a rifle now. Never could quite match you there.'

Rob shrugged off the comment and sent John a message. Within moments, their dad's ute appeared in the clearing.

The boar's legs were still twitching and a host of fleas, ticks and lice scattered for cover as the vehicle's headlights illuminated the dead animal.

'Clean shot's a good shot,' said John. 'Get him up in the back, don't want wild dogs moving in too.'

The beast was heavier than a full-grown sheep, and Rob's arms sang under the weight as he helped Max manoeuvre it onto the tray. John swung back into the driver's seat and the brothers resumed their spot on the back of the ute.

'Won't hear the end of that in the dairy tomorrow,' said Max. He put on a stern voice and tucked his chin into his chest, impersonating their father just as he'd done when they were younger. *'Mark my words, boy.'*

Rob didn't smile, but somehow the scowl he'd reserved for Max over the last decade softened.

'Took the video to the cop shop. Unless the hunters are trespassing on private land, or shooting your cows, they reckon it's a Parks and Wildlife issue, not police business,' said Max.

Rob scratched his stubbled jaw. 'Figured as much. I'll keep an eye out for that ute then.'

They drove to the opposite end of the scrub, where Max had scattered another bag of fruit and corn, but an hour's watch proved fruitless. No doubt every other pig in the forest would be on alert for the rest of the night.

The high of Rob's clean shot was washed away by dread when he returned to the cottage. The weatherboards were crisp under the moonlight, but each step closer reminded him of their finances. And the only thing more unbearable than telling Angie about it all was keeping it a secret from her.

Angie woke with a start when the caravan door opened. She smiled at the sight of Rob tiptoeing towards the bed and reached for him when he slipped between the sheets.

'I missed you.'

It felt good to be in his arms again, to breathe in his familiar scent. Her tiredness receded as he told her about the boar he'd shot and the latest footage Max had captured.

'Who was it?'

'Dunno, the footage isn't that clear, but at least we've got a pretty distinct ute to look for. And one less pig to worry about.'

'Hopefully the first of many, and we won't have this problem again,' she said.

Angie propped herself up on an elbow, and, with her heart beating double time, shared the idea that had rolled around in her head the whole drive home. 'I know things have been crazy here, but I've been thinking. We'll be in the cottage soon and all these little niggles will disappear when we move in, won't they? We could start thinking about another baby?'

She studied his face, but instead of the delight she'd anticipated, he looked away.

'Let's not rush into anything until we finish the cottage, okay, Ange? Let the dust settle.'

Angie's face fell. It felt off kilter to be championing the idea of a second child when Rob had always been the one to raise the topic. 'Do you mean wait, or not at all?'

Rob rolled onto his back and stared at the ceiling. 'I just think we've got enough to worry about now.'

He turned away but as they lay in the dark, she could sense sleep was just as elusive for him as it was for her.

Rob woke early, from nightmares full of bank managers hammering sale signs into their lawn and hunters stalking their calves. He wiped the sleep from his eyes and crept out of bed, determined to sort out the budget mess before he went to work for the day.

Sitting on the shed couch, he pulled the laptop onto his knee.

He felt like a jerk for fobbing Angie off last night, but even now, in the pre-dawn darkness, he still couldn't wrap his head around her sudden change of heart.

The laptop took an eternity to load, each whirring rotation of the cursor seeming to take twice as long as normal.

Rob pulled up the bank web page, and opened their account. *Thank god!* Rosa's transfer had cleared and there was money in the account to buy fuel and groceries. The minute the next client's payment came through, he'd be able to repay it back in full and Ange would be none the wiser. He shut down the laptop and went outside to feed the calves. *Things are going to be okay after all.*

Rob jumped into his ute and headed into town. His mind was so fixated on the day ahead that he almost didn't notice the Land Cruiser ute bunny-hopping out of the Port Fairview boat storage yards. He slowed to a crawl and whipped his head around to try to identify the driver, but a stream of oncoming fishing boats blocked his view. *Was it a woman?* He made a swift U-turn but by the time the convoy of fishing boats had passed, the ute was nowhere to be seen. *Bugger.* Rob whacked the steering wheel so hard it made his wrist ache. He picked up his phone.

Angie walked around the garden, unsure how to start resurrecting her ruined backyard. The pigs had decimated her veggie patch and made a right mess of her back garden. Barely a flower was left, and the bark-chip mulch was spread across the grass. The seedlings could all be replaced, but the damage to her weeping cherry tree hit hard.

She watered the trunk, hoping it'd be strong enough to recover.

Looking across the lawn, she eyeballed the pair of mischief-makers digging in the freshly turned soil. Jayden's white denim jeans and dinosaur shirt were covered in dirt. *Why did Bobbi dress him in good clothes, when she knew he and Claudia would be playing outside?*

Angie's phone buzzed in her pocket as she staked the cherry tree.

Penny's voice rang down the phone. 'You won't believe what Lucy did today, Ange. She smiled!' said Penny.

'It's wind, Pen. They don't smile for months yet.'

'Oh, you spoiltsport, that's what Lara said too.'

Angie wedged the phone between her ear and her shoulder as she listened to Penny's besotted descriptions of the milk pimples spreading across baby Lucy's nose.

'You there, Angie? What did Rob say about the garden getting wrecked?'

Angie shifted the hose to a nectarine tree. 'We're barely talking.'

'God, what's up with you two? I told you renovations are the death of all happy relationships. Only joking! What about his twin? Found any pigs yet? Diana told me about the video of the park ranger. I nearly burst my stitches, I laughed so hard.'

'Rob shot a pig a few nights ago, and he's been out most nights since.'

'Gah, I don't know how you do it, Angie-bee: the renos, the gardening, coping with Claudia when Rob's gone all day and now all night. I can barely get off the couch or do anything other than breastfeeding. I'm starting to understand how Rosa and John's cows feel.'

A sudden wail came from Oscar's pram. Angie rocked it, hoping to lull him back to sleep.

'Tell me that's not Bobbi's kids again?'

Angie jabbed the mute button and cooed into the pram.

'Don't think I can't tell you've put me on mute, Angie! There were cows mooing and the dog barking down the phone line a minute ago, now it's complete silence. Fess up!'

Angie sighed. It was no use trying to pull the wool over Penny's eyes. Her sister knew her better than anyone else.

'Maybe it is . . .' she hedged, after unmuting her phone. Oscar blinked back at her, his pale skin and wide blue eyes so similar to Bobbi's. There was no way he was going back to sleep.

'Remember when Diana tore strips off me for stretching myself too thin?' Penny's transition from an ambitious corporate career woman to a farm manager several years ago had been fraught with stress and unrealistic expectations until their oldest sister, Diana, had stepped in.

'And remember when I regurgitated the very same big-sister speech back at you in Eden Creek? Wasn't it one of the reasons you were so excited to move to Port Fairview? Less on your plate, more time for Claudia and Rob? So why are you bending over backwards to babysit someone else's kids?'

Angie rolled her eyes. 'This is different, Pen. We've got an agreement. Alex and Bobbi help us with machinery and we do a bit of babysitting.'

'You've had those children every single time I've phoned,' Penny protested. 'Last week you said you were cutting back.'

Angie jiggled the pram from side to side as Oscar fussed. The incoming call alert buzzed on her phone, and she pulled it away to see Bobbi's name on the screen.

'I've got to go, Pen. Don't worry about me. I'm big enough to juggle a few extra things.'

Rob wedged the phone between his ear and shoulder as he trawled the back streets of Port Fairview, peering down each driveway and side street.

'Whoever was driving the Cruiser ute didn't look that comfortable behind the wheel. They were bunny-hopping like an L-plater. I've covered the south side of town—any luck on Nob's Hill?'

'Nothing on Mayfair Street, Quinn Lane or Greene Court. And I've had a squiz down the roads off Bayliss Street, both north and south. I'll try Kingsley Drive. They can't have gone too far,' Max said.

'They've got more money than they know what to do with in that neighbourhood. An old FJ45 should stick out like a sore thumb,' said Rob.

A police car slid into view and Rob dropped the phone like a hot coal, feigning an ear scratch. The policeman, who happened to be the Fairview Seagulls' opening batsman, lifted a finger from the steering wheel to wave as he drove past. Rob breathed a sigh of relief and decided to pull over rather than push his luck. Max was mid-sentence, and Rob could hear the triumph in his voice.

'. . . some wanky joint with three storeys, sprinkler's doing overtime wetting down the footpath instead of the lawn. Cruiser's parked down the side. Bingo!'

'You've found it? Three storeys, you say?'

Max repeated his location. 'Parked beside a black dual-cab with a flat tyre.'

Rob punched the air. 'You little ripper. That smarmy little bastard.'

'You know this place?'

'Sure do. Now do you want to call Parks and Wildlife to dob him in, or shall I do the honours?'

Angie heard the shed door open, and paused midway through helping Claudia into her pyjamas.

'We're in here, Rob,' she called. 'Get your jim-jams on, Claud, then you can go see Dad.'

Claudia raced out of the bathroom as soon as her top was buttoned, but Angie hung back, wiping down the flimsy bathroom vanity. *We won't be having these poxy vanities or cabinets in the new house,* she thought.

Rob appeared in the doorway, barely visible through the bathroom fug, Claudia on his shoulders. *No cheap exhaust fans for the new bathroom either,* thought Angie, waving the steam away. She gave him a weary smile. Maybe they could smooth things over tonight.

'How was your day?' She straightened Claudia's towel on the drying rack and glanced at her watch before looking back at him.

'The good news is we're now the proud owners of a trailer-load of goats. The bad news is we're still no closer to finding a tiler. All the blokes I called are booked up for a month at least. But guess what—'

Angie tipped her head back and groaned. 'Goats? Seriously? Aren't they the Houdinis of the animal world? Why did you buy goats?'

'I didn't exactly buy them. Mr Kent forced them on me, but he's going to pay the other half of the invoice in instalments. Now, brace yours—'

Instalments? 'Ugh.' Angie buried her face in her hands. 'This isn't good news, Rob. We don't know anything about goats. You're too nice for your own good.'

'Says she who's been roped into doing all the legwork for the dahlia committee and full-time babysitting for Bobbi.'

'Give me a break.' Angie exhaled slowly, grappling with her patience. 'Anyway, *I've* found us a tiler.'

Rob managed a wan smile. 'Thank God for that. Local or Warrnambool?'

'Local. It's us.'

Rob raised a finger. 'I don't do tiling.'

'Because you can't or because you won't? Your dad told me what he said all those years ago. Said he was too harsh.'

'There was never an apology for that, or all the other times I disappointed him,' he said sharply.

'God, do you ever forgive and forget? From what I've seen of your dad, he's not the big bad monster you keep making him out to be. Maybe he could've hugged you more as a kid or something, and it probably wouldn't kill him to say something positive every now and then, but he's not all bad, Rob.'

She tossed the handtowel in the sink and set her hands on her hips.

'It's not my family, but you might find life a little easier without that chip on your shoulder, Rob. Do you know Max offered to help with the tiling? Maybe we should take him up on his offer.'

Rob's head pounded as he tucked Claudia into bed, reading the storybook like a robot as he fumed over their conversation. *Chip on my shoulder? Max working on my cottage?* Jealousy bubbled inside him. The anger he'd felt at Max returned with full force. *Bloody snake in the grass.*

Rob kissed Claudia goodnight, wheeled his '69 Triumph Bonneville out onto the driveway and tickled the bike's carbies. The engine came to life with a quick kick-start. Angie stood in the doorway of the shed, frustration and disappointment in the set of her crossed arms. 'Another ride?'

Rob nodded as he buckled his helmet, anger merging with shame.

Isn't this exactly what Dad does? Bury himself in paddock work whenever he and Mum argue? John Jones had a place for everything in his dairy, his house, his machinery sheds and his farm. *Heck, even his underwear drawer is probably squared away.* Heaven forbid that anything would ever be out of place in his father's neat, carefully ordered life, especially his emotions. But even realising this, Rob couldn't fight the urge to avoid more conflict. His news about the Cruiser ute and the pigs could wait. The way him and Ange were going, he'd say something really stupid and ruin everything. He needed space. He needed speed.

'Trust me, this is the better of two options,' he said, thundering along the driveway.

Memories of Rob's first and only tiling experience flashed through his mind as he urged the motorbike faster. He remembered cursing as tiles broke in his hands, and his father's exasperation as Rob had fumbled with the cutter, applying too much pressure or not enough, ruining expensive tiles at a rapid rate. For every tile Rob'd messed up, Max had cut three perfect ones. For every grout line he'd botched, Max had showcased precision spacing and accuracy.

No matter what he'd done as a boy or teenager, he'd never felt like it was enough to earn his father's approval, or match Max's accomplishments. Even after Max had gambled away their money and buggered off to Uruguay, he still seemed to retain John's favour. Rob hadn't expected their father to compensate him for the money Max had lost—it wasn't John's debt to settle—but a little more empathy for the way his dreams had been crushed in the process wouldn't have gone astray either.

And no matter how hard he twisted the throttle, he knew he couldn't outrun the past.

Thirty-six

The lawn around Port Fairview's old railway precinct was flush with excited youngsters and so many cheering parents that Angie almost expected some of them to break out the pompoms and cheerleader moves.

'Faster, faster! Come on, Jayden, put your arms into it, mate. Go, go, go!'

Bobbi clapped as her son blitzed the field at the Kinder Olympics, leaving Angie in little doubt that Bobbi had begun coaching him well ahead of the day.

'You do realise it's not the real Olympics,' said Angie, watching Claudia and Scarlett skip across the line hand in hand, almost a minute after Jayden had raced through.

'Start as you mean to go on, I say,' said Bobbi, telling Jayden he'd run faster if he kept his eyes focused on the finish line.

Angie headed over to congratulate the girls for trying their best. She followed the children to the next activity station, and then the next, until sports day was finished and the back of her neck was more than a little sunburned.

'Hey, Angie, wait up.'

She turned to see Tessa jogging across the grass in an oversized sundress. 'What's up Bobbi's nose today?'

'Don't know. I'm not in her good books because I skipped the last few runs,' said Angie.

'Reckon she's found her niche: Bossy Bobbi in her element.'

'Don't tell me you've heard Rob's little nickname? I'll throttle him, honest to god,' said Angie.

Tessa looked down at her sandals. 'If you're going to throttle someone, it should be me for starting the whole thing. It slipped out a few months ago, then Brett started using it. I felt terrible when I discovered Rob was calling her that too.'

'You? Tessa, I've never heard you breathe a bad word about anyone.'

Tessa's rosy complexion turned a deeper shade of pink. 'You've got to admit, she's a bit . . . hard to like. Everything's a competition. The way she's using you for free childcare. Trying to mould you into a poster-girl client.'

Angie laughed. 'It's already a circus with Claudia and they entertain each other mostly. And whether I liked it or not, I needed a wake-up call. Bobbi's made me healthier than I've ever been. As soon as I get back into the fitness training, I'll be smashing those runs.'

'I didn't mean . . . Look, I know things have been tough. Brett mentioned the whole finance thing last night. Renovations, hey? Probably doesn't sit easy letting Rosa help you out, either, after the whole biting incident. I won't tell anyone, promise. But I'm here if you want to talk.'

Angie's jaw tightened. Rosa may have nearly killed them with kindness and smothered them with baked goods, but she had nothing at all to do with their finances. *Did she?* Angie fussed with her water bottle so Tessa couldn't see her confusion.

'Look, I need to go, Rob'll be home from work soon.'

Or heading off on another motorbike ride.

She drove faster than usual through Port Fairview. *What does Rosa have to do with our budget and why am I the only one who doesn't know anything about it?* It was past Rob's normal knock-off time when Angie returned from the sports day but he was nowhere to be seen. The smell of coffee lingered in the shed and she spotted a note Blu-Tacked to the bathroom door.

Back late. Don't wait up. Love you x R

Angie tipped Rob's half-drunk mug of coffee down the drain and stripped off her sweaty shirt. A shower did little to improve her mood, and by the time she'd scrubbed herself pink, pulled on a clean pair of jeans and eaten an apple for afternoon tea she was still livid. *Rob's out riding, Rosa's been sticking her nose into our business* again *and I'm completely out of the loop.*

'Feeding time, Mum?' Claudia's question distracted Angie from her brooding. The calves bellowed at the gate, the goats bleated and Violet barked until Angie unclipped her from the kennel. Even the chickens started clucking as soon as she came near, demanding to be fed. Angie resisted the urge to clamp her hands over her ears and drown out the sound of their mounting responsibilities.

She filled a bucket with calf pellets and hesitated, checking the underside of her boots. Dog poo caked into the tread. She cursed Rob again and wondered whether she needed to feed the goats in the next paddock. Darn goats. *Not only are they not cash, they're now costing us money,* she grumbled, tossing a bale of hay over the fence.

Angie dialled Rob's number but the call rang out again. *For God's sake, what is he up to?*

'Play with calves, Mummy?'

Angie swung Claudia up for a piggyback. 'Not now, Claud. We're off to see Granny and Pop.'

Claudia clapped. Angie strode across the paddock, wishing she felt a hint of Claudia's excitement and optimism instead of dread with each step towards the dairy.

John and Rosa's conversation ground to a surprised halt as Angie walked in.

'Is everything okay? Not more pigs again?' Rosa rushed along the pit towards them, her eyes saucer-wide.

'I can't get in touch with Rob and I've got no idea what the hell's going on with our finances. But apparently you do, Rosa.'

John stopped working his way across the dairy and straightened up, uncertainty etched on his tanned face. 'I don't follow.' He turned to his wife.

Rosa wiped her hands on her overalls, not meeting Angie's eye as she sprayed the cows' udders. 'Angie, please,' she said, 'you're tired, you're obviously not sleeping well. How about we have a chat when Rob's back? Is he home tonight or are the boys heading out hunting again?'

Max strode into the dairy. He wore the same khaki overalls and plastic apron as his parents, and when he lifted a hand in greeting, she spotted her name at the top of the invoice he was holding.

'Hate to interrupt, but the stock agent left a delivery in the feed shed. As well as our stuff, there's a heap of drench and calf pellets, plus a few things for you and Rob. Beats me why they're on the same invoice though,' he said.

'Rosa?' John said, ushering a fresh run of cows onto the platform. His face looked calm, but Angie heard an edge in his careful voice.

'It's only a loan. Only a tiny little bridging loan until Rob's business accounts are straightened out.' Rosa began to work as she spoke, zigzagging back and forth across the dairy until the other row of cows was completely hooked up. Max pulled the gate open to release the row. Claudia followed John to the stairs, and pressed the button to dole out the next batch of grain.

Angie tried to get a grip on her anger before she spoke again. A fear of spooking the cows was the only thing stopping her from shouting across the dairy. 'Why did he tell you and not me? How much money? When?'

Rosa mumbled a figure, and for a moment Angie thought she was going to puke on the dairy floor.

John swore quietly. 'I thought you weren't going to meddle, Rosa.'

'I'm not meddling, I'm *helping*. Don't be upset, Angie. Rob wanted to tell you, he really did, but he worried it might be the straw that broke the camel's back. Especially with your friend and those—' Rosa's voice rang with apology but Angie cut over her.

'Just stop, Rosa.' *If Rob can't trust me—won't confide in me—then how will we ever make a home together?*

Her voice dropped dangerously low. 'So he ran over here and told you instead, Rosa? Great. Just great. Come on, Claudia, time to leave.' Angie held out her hand, her anger at Rosa intensifying as Claudia huddled closer to John. 'Claudia!'

The little girl tucked her chin and shook her head.

'We can bring her back aft—' Rosa fell silent after a sharp look from John.

'I want to stay with Granny and Pop. Princess Sparkles and Peppa calf will be missing me.'

Angie's stomach dropped.

Was *she* the thorn in everyone's side here? Rob, John, Rosa, Claudia, Max ... For all her ideals about nestling into this neighbourhood, about helping the Jones boys fix their rift, had it been *her* that didn't fit in all along? *Her* that didn't belong here?

Angie backed away. A silent sob rose through her body as she turned and ran from the dairy.

Thirty-seven

Angie flung open the shed door, making a beeline for the pile of stacker boxes, the closest thing they had to an office. She pulled every last piece of paperwork from the folders within but there were no bank statements or budget spreadsheets to be seen.

She wasn't sure who she was angriest with: Rob for messing up the budget, herself for trusting him, or Rosa for always waiting in the wings, so that Rob confided in his mother and not her.

She snapped open the laptop, stabbing the power button until the screen lit up. Angie gasped as she logged into their online banking. The account balance before J&R Jones' transfer had been even lower than she'd imagined. She leaned against the wall and slid down to the floorboards.

How did things go so very wrong? And where do we go from here?

The sound of laughter and a creaking swing filtered in from the backyard.

Which Jones was standing outside right now, pushing her daughter on the swing? Rosa, with an armful of cakes and an open wallet, trying to play happy families? John, who had looked as surprised as her about his wife's loan? Or Max, whose reputation for upsetting the applecart had just been one-upped?

Her heart ached knowing it wasn't Rob outside right now. She'd driven him so far away he hadn't even been able to share their deepest financial woes.

She glimpsed her reflection in the shed window. Her hair was like a bird's nest, the brown T-shirt she wore was one that Bobbi had ordered her to banish as soon as she'd lost weight, and the red splotches on her face had merged with her freckles. *You can't stick at anything long, can you, Angie McIntyre? Whether it's a relationship, a renovation or some stupid fitness program. What right do you even have to this beautiful cottage?*

Her lip trembled as she stared back at her reflection, seeing the teenage girl who let the schoolyard taunts erode her self-confidence, and then the adult who had gotten so close to being the mother, the wife, the woman she'd aspired to be. *So close.*

She exhaled shakily. Shielding her eyes from the sun, she walked outside.

'You right?' Max said, pushing Claudia on the swing.

Angie lifted one shoulder, clamping her lips shut so her voice couldn't betray her.

Max wrapped an arm around her, his scent so different from Rob's. She felt her body shake.

'It'll be okay,' he said gruffly, patting her back with one hand. His awkward sympathy made her cry even harder.

Claudia wrapped her arms around Angie's legs just as Rob's motorbike roared down Enderby Lane. 'All better, Mummy. Daddy home now,' said Claudia.

Angie pulled away from Max, not knowing whether to thank him or apologise.

She stalked toward Rob.

'Why didn't you tell me about your mum and the money?' she said.

Rob stiffened. 'I didn't know she'd given Ivan any extra money until this week, and I've fixed it all up now. I was going to explain.'

'*Ivan?* What the . . . ? I'm talking about the cash your mother put in our bank account. What do you mean she gave Ivan money?' Angie thought of the real estate agent accepting their low offer on the cottage without any hesitation. *What was it the old man had said about looking after Rob with the house?*

Angie gasped. 'My God.' *How could I have been so oblivious?* 'I'll strangle her. I'll . . . What else are you hiding from me?'

Claudia raced back to the sandpit. Max backed away. 'I'll be over at the dairy if you need me,' he said.

She could feel the tension rolling off Rob in waves, his expression so far from that of the carefree man she'd rescued from the side of the road with a broken-down bike, or the doting father.

'Jesus, Rob, why didn't you tell me?'

Rob kneeled down and picked up a builder's pencil from the driveway. The chunky wood had split almost in half, no doubt crushed under the wheel of a delivery van or tradesmen's ute. The wide lead was the only thing holding the two sides of timber together. Rob wiped the lead pencil back and forth across the palm of his hand.

'I wanted to tell you. Apparently it was supposed to be an early wedding present.'

Angie's eyes were glued to the lead pencil, captivated by the way it drew white lines, then red welts, on his calloused skin.

Her throat pinched. She swallowed hard. 'But we weren't even engaged then. She can't just throw money around like she's waving a magic wand, and mess in people's lives like that. Maybe we were kidding ourselves this would work . . .' Her voice trailed off, the reality setting in as she said it aloud. It shouldn't be this hard.

Angie knew she should be fighting for their relationship, telling Rob every reason they should stay together, but she stayed quiet. *Is it over?* That Rob was equally silent confirmed it.

Rob closed the distance between them with a step. His eyes pooled with tears. 'I thought I could get on top of the finances and fix this mess I'd gotten us into.'

Angie backed away. 'Bobbi told me we were playing with fire trying to do this together. I should have . . .'

She watched the builder's pencil fall from Rob's hand and onto the driveway. The two pieces of timber split on impact and the lead shattered into the bluestone gravel.

Rob kicked at the dirt. 'I mightn't know much, but I know she's not your friend.'

Angie shook her head, unable to fathom losing anything more in a single day. 'What are you talking about?'

Rob's words came thick and fast. 'Can't you see she's only using you as a babysitter and her very own fixer-upper, Ange? She wanted you to be her big success story, someone she could parade around as an example of her fine work. But she was never doing it for *you*, she was doing it for herself. Damned if you weren't happier with a mixing bowl in your hand. And don't get me started on her husband, always flashing his wealth about.'

Angie backed away. 'Don't point the finger at *my* friends. Not much use baking when you've got your mum next door though, is it? I wanted to fix this cottage for us—for you, me and Claudia—but I'd barely even hung the first load of washing on the line before your mum made me surplus to requirements. *My* mum would never have gotten between us like that.'

'At least she's trying to help, not sabotage us like Bobbi and Alex. He's behind those pigs in the scrub. He'll stop at nothing to keep his precious clients entertained.'

Angie threw her hands in the air. 'Seriously? Why the hell would Alex do that?' She noticed the old tractor over by the chook yard and her anger rose further. She cut over Rob's reply.

'And your dad's tractor has been here for weeks, just waiting to shift that pile of weatherboards. Claudia fell off it and nearly cracked her head the other day.'

She was shouting now, unable to stop the torrent of furious words. She felt Claudia tugging at her skirt.

'Mummy?'

Get a grip, Angie. You're scaring Claudia. But as much as she tried, she couldn't rein herself in.

'She's a . . .' Angie spluttered. 'A meddling old cow who stretches the truth to suit herself. I can see where you get it from.'

Rob stepped back as if he'd been punched. He'd spent the morning haggling over a price for his motorbike collection, then the afternoon tracking down the owner of the Land Cruiser ute Max had captured on camera, but the sting in Ange's words meant the cheque in his top pocket and uncovering Alex Richardson's illegal hunting sideline were too little too late. The money from selling his bikes might fund the rest of the build, and the evidence against Alex might earn the smug prick a whopper of a fine, but it wouldn't repair the trust he'd broken.

His thoughts latched onto possible solutions to the problems that had pushed their relationship off course, scanning and dismissing the ideas as quickly as they arrived. Ange deserved so much better than him, than a half-finished cottage and God knows how many more months living in the shed.

He thought of Max standing beside Angie earlier, giving her the emotional support *he* should have. The sudden realisation of his failings scared him to the core.

He kissed Claudia's forehead. She shouldn't be witnessing this. 'I can't . . . I can't do this anymore.'

Rob ducked past Angie and lurched to the shed. Craving cold, hard metal and horsepower as an escape was yet another weakness, but at this point what was one more cock-up?

He ripped his leather jacket off the coat rack.

'Oh, great idea, Rob, go run away on your bike again. Like that will solve anything,' said Angie, walking towards him.

He hesitated, one hand on the motorbike helmet. *Maybe it isn't too late.*

Rob exhaled slowly. 'Okay, I won't go.'

Angie shot him a scathing look and the force when she shoved him away surprised them both. He stumbled backwards, almost falling into the sidecar.

'Do whatever the hell you want, Rob.'

Claudia burst into tears.

I'm damned if I do, damned if I don't.

Shame made him shove the helmet down hard on his head, but the padding inside the helmet that silenced Claudia's crying only amplified the voice inside that ridiculed him for running away.

Rob's hands trembled as he buckled up the helmet strap, a difficult task with his painfully clenched jaw. He shrugged on his jacket, throwing a leg over the Harley-Davidson that was effectively already someone else's property.

You can't get anything right, can you, Jones? You stuffed up the house budget, you made a mess of the business accounts, you can't even grow a crop without it going pear-shaped, you've kept secrets and pushed Angie away. What type of man are you? Until you've fixed this mess, you don't deserve to answer to 'Dad'.

The old engine took several kicks to turn over, but the sound when it finally caught was a balm for his nerves. He went wide around Ange, unable to look at their daughter stretching her little arms towards him. He took the driveway recklessly and pulled out onto Enderby Lane. *Face it, Jones: you're a stuff-up. Being taken out by a stock truck would be the best outcome for everyone. They'd be better off without you.*

Thirty-eight

A chill settled over Angie as Rob tore off down the lane.

She squeezed Claudia a little closer. It was bad enough their daughter had seen them yelling at each other, but for her to go and shove him?

Silent shudders wracked her body as she pondered questions she didn't want to know the answers to. *Where is he going? When will he be back? Surely he'll come back? Is Alex really mixed up with the feral pigs? Imagine if the roles were reversed, and Rob had shoved me . . . would I go back to a partner like that?*

She heaved Claudia onto her hip and walked towards the garden, craving the comfort of the weeping cherry tree she'd planted in her mother's memory. The huge weeping cherry at McIntyre Park had always been her safe place, and even though the pigs had damaged the new one, it was still budding with fresh growth. Claudia wriggled down to the ground and Angie found herself following suit. Sprawled on the cool grass for a beat, she wondered if anything would be the same again.

How did we get to this?

'Cuppa tea, Mummy?'

Angie nodded as she blinked away tears and hauled herself up. She glared at the tractor as they walked back to the cottage, dodging the forks that seemed to clip her shins every time she walked by.

I'll darn well move the weatherboards myself then, seeing as I'm doing everything around here.

'Tractor ride, Mummy?'

'Not you, Claud. Stay with Violet.'

She made sure Claudia was sitting by the dog kennel before starting the tractor. The old Massey Ferguson clunked into gear and she dipped the forks under the pile of weatherboards. A rabbit dashed out from beneath the heap. Violet gave chase, clearing the pond fence in a seamless jump.

Stupid dog, huffed Angie. She swivelled to ensure Claudia hadn't followed her dog, and spotted Rosa dashing across the yard. *Just. Frigging. Perfect.*

Had Rosa heard their argument? Was she here to offer advice, or maybe some more cash? 'For God's sake,' Angie muttered under her breath. 'What's she after, the accounts so she can take over the whole place?'

Angie pushed her foot on the tractor accelerator, not trusting herself to speak to Rosa in this mood. She bit her bottom lip as she drove between the chook house and the ruined garden beds, ignoring Rosa's waving arms.

When will this woman stop meddling?

A screech sounded and Angie gasped as the forkful of weatherboards clipped the chimney.

As if in slow motion, the brick chimney wobbled one way, then the other, before crumbling like a stack of Jenga blocks.

Rosa's screams filled the air. Her legs and hips had been swallowed by the chimney rubble. Angie flew off the tractor and raced across to the pile of bricks, flinging pieces of the chimney over her shoulder to take the weight off Rosa's half-buried body. Angie heard sobbing behind her and a teary Claudia tried to slip into her arms.

'Stay there, Claud. I need to help Granny.'

She tossed the rubble across the chook yard, desperate to shift the pile. *So many bricks.* Claudia's wails escalated and the chickens rushed out through the broken fences.

It felt like an eternity until she could see all of Rosa's body again, and the sight of her pained face was enough to make Angie toss the last few bricks twice as fast. She pushed Rosa's long dark hair away from her face.

Angie murmured urgently. 'Rosa? Rosa, are you okay?'

Act fast, Angie. Hurry.

'Stay here, Claud. I'll get help.'

As if sensing her mother's distress, Claudia quickly complied with the order to stay with her granny until Angie returned.

Angie cast one last anxious look at the pair before racing across the paddock. A rustling came from the long grass in front of her. A feral pig? She darted to the left, landing heavily on one leg as a familiar black-and-tan head popped up. Violet took a few steps towards her, dragging her back leg, before collapsing.

Had she been hit by the bricks too? Angie's guilt compounded as she ran past the injured pup. *I'm coming back, Violet, I promise.*

Guilt, urgency, adrenaline, panic and pain fuelled her mad dash for help. Angie's breath came hard and fast as she clambered over the fence. Her skirt caught on the barbed wire. She tugged the fabric hard and with a rip was free to keep sprinting towards the dairy.

Max and John turned in surprise as she raced in.

She cried out to be heard over the sound of the radio and milking machinery.

'John . . . Rosa . . . help . . . hurry.'

Thirty-nine

Rob tossed tiny red rocks into the volcano crater, wishing it hadn't been dormant for the last 6500 years. Throwing himself into a seething mass of molten lava didn't sound any more appealing than being skittled by a stock truck, but at least Claudia would have a better story about why her father had bombed out of her life.

Claudia. He'd rather drink engine oil than miss another day with her, but he was no good to them. How had he messed up so badly?

Rob picked up a stick and ditched it into the void.

Man up, Jones. You can't give Ange and Claudia half of what they need.

He coughed, trying to unclog his throat, and his thoughts. Had he been so hell-bent on proving he could handle it all—the renos, the bookwork, the business—that he'd lost perspective?

What's more important, Jones? Getting a tick of approval from your dad—or at the very least proving him wrong about the cottage, showing Alex Richardson up as the scumbag he is, or making it up to Angie?

He turned at a noise in the bushes and saw a family of emus emerge from the scrub. The adult emu fixed him with her beady brown eyes, snapping her beak as the cream-and-brown-striped chicks skittered across the walking track.

It's a him, *not a her,* Rob corrected himself as the two-metre-tall bird steered his young in the opposite direction. Rob thought of Claudia, how he loved every inch of her, from her glittery gumboots and sharp choppers to her curly hair.

He watched the emu walk away, the sole carer for the brood of chicks, and knew he didn't want that for his family. If he didn't pull his head out of his arse and fix things, he realised he'd regret it with every day that dawned.

Forty

Rosa lay on her side, with a cut on her chin that wouldn't stop bleeding no matter how much pressure Angie applied. Gone were her enthusiasm, her quick smile, her determination, her vitality.

'What's taking the ambos so long? It's only five kilometres to the hospital. Surely it's not rush hour in Port Fairview?' said Angie.

John clutched his wife's hand. His brow furrowed as Rosa winced again.

'Should've driven her in myself. Woulda been quicker,' John said, scanning Enderby Lane again.

'We only just called, give them a second or two.' Max pulled the blanket up higher around his mother's shoulders.

'I'm fine,' whispered Rosa. Her eyes were still squeezed shut but she couldn't hide the pain in her voice. 'Don't get any blood on that blanket. I spent hours hand-quilting it.'

Angie stared numbly at the embroidered birds and sheep on the blanket that normally lived in Claudia's pram. Claudia must have pulled it over her grandmother when Angie went to fetch help. The pale fabrics against Rosa's wan complexion made her look more vulnerable.

'I'll soak the blanket, I promise,' said Angie, turning her attention to Claudia and Violet. The dog's hind leg was matted with blood, and Violet barely lifted her head from Claudia's lap when the little girl stroked her fur.

Stupid idiot. Look what you've done. Driven Rob away, nearly killed his mother, and his dog, and now you're crouched here, as useful as a stunned mullet.

But as much as she urged herself to do something productive, something to atone for her mistakes, Angie could only stay rooted to the spot until the ambulance crunched along the driveway gravel. The paramedics assessed Rosa swiftly and prepped her for transport.

'We'll see you at the hospital, Rosa,' said John, flinching at his wife's hoarse yell as she was bundled onto the stretcher.

'John! Come with me.'

'One extra's fine by us,' said the paramedic, 'long as you're happy to give up your seat if we're called to another accident between here and the hospital.'

John nodded, quickly unbuttoned his green overalls, wiped his workboots on the grass and climbed in beside the stretcher.

'Angie . . .' Rosa called out as the paramedic went to close the door. 'Rob's a good man, Angie. Go find him. Please.'

Angie watched the ambulance drive away. Only an hour ago she'd wanted to cut Rob's mother from her life and now she wanted to hold her close. Her brain struggled with a tangle of guilt and shock.

Max's voice cut into her turbid thoughts.

Angie stared blankly as Max repeated his question, gesturing to the dairy for added effect.

'I've got to finish milking. Are you all right to follow Dad in?'

She hesitated for a second, agreeing without meeting Max's eye, or glancing at the cottage that had been supposed to bring her and Rob together, not rip them apart.

'Hey, did Rob tell you about the pigs? Seems Alex was luring in new clients with under-the-table perks. Poaching and illegal hunts were just the tip of the iceberg. He's going to be slapped with a big fine.'

Her tears fell into Claudia's hair as she carried her to the car.

Rob *was* a good man. She knew it, of course she did, but where would they go from here? How was he going to react when he learned she'd put his mum in hospital?

She tried his phone. Straight to message bank.

Forty-one

The bundle of fur quivered on the front seat as Angie rounded the corner to the veterinary clinic. A ripe smell wafted across the small cab each time Violet half-heartedly wagged her tail.

Angie let out a sigh, relinquishing her grip on the steering wheel to stroke the pup. The gesture soothed them both and she kept her hand there until they arrived at the clinic. She strapped a lead onto the purple collar and held out a hand.

'Stay, Violet. I'll come round and lift—'

Violet jumped up and tried to hobble across the seat, making it half a step before she collapsed. Angie leaned in to pick her up, trying to avoid touching the bloodied tangle of fur.

'Let's get you seen to before you injure yourself further. Wait there, Claud, I'll be back in a minute.'

Angie carried the dog to the vet clinic, but instead of opening automatically, the doors remained steadfastly shut. Angie stepped back then squinted to read the messily handwritten sign through the tinted glass.

Angie looked at her watch. The vet was out, and she had no idea where to find the Warrnambool vet clinics. *Maybe Bobbi can watch Violet for a while, then take her in for me?*

Angie carried Violet back to the car and drove straight to Bobbi's house.

The sprinkler system had created a dark arc across the driveway, watering more of the asphalt than the perfectly manicured hedges and front lawn. Angie scooped up the dog and rapped on their door.

A combination of air fresheners and perfume rushed out onto the doorstep, as artificial as it was sweet, when Bobbi swung the large door open.

'God, what's that smell?' said Bobbi, wrinkling her nose.

'I need to get to the hospital. Can you please hang on to Violet for an hour and take her to the vet when they reopen?' She stretched her arms out, proffering the bundle of fur.

Bobbi took a step backwards, the green smoothie in her hand tilting dangerously close to her white singlet. 'I don't think . . .' Bobbi tapped a finger to her glossy lips. 'I don't do animals, Angie. I don't even let the boys *eat* in my car, let alone put a dog in there . . . I've got a flat tyre anyway and I'm not driving Alex's old rust bucket again. Bloody manual.'

Angie was so stunned she didn't reply.

'Your dress! All your hard work losing weight! You finally fit into it and now it's ruined.'

Angie tugged at the torn floral fabric, remembering that Bobbi had been the one who insisted she buy the extravagant item. Angie had liked how it skimmed over her curves, found a daintiness in the way the tiny pink and white flowers floated in the sea of green. But watching her friend worry about a dress instead of an injured animal made her feel like ripping the dress off and throwing it at Bobbi's manicured toes. Rob's words rang in her mind.

The pup whimpered.

'Are you really telling me you can't do this?'

Bobbi hesitated a moment before setting her glass down on a hall table, next to a framed family photograph. Angie had admired the photo before, taken when Oscar was a newborn; the ideal little family, the picture-perfect smiles, Jayden and Alex with freshly cut hair, all dressed in white. Clarity settled on Angie as she took in the perfect outfits, their wrinkle-free shirts and the soft photoshopped glow over the whole photo. She didn't need to get closer to know that Jayden looked like a cardboard cut-out, a far contrast from the way she normally saw him, splashing in muddy puddles with Claudia at the building site, the size of their smiles directly equivalent to the amount of dirt on their hands as they moulded mud pies together.

'Rob was around here earlier, ranting about those wild pigs. After all we've done for you guys, you couldn't even turn a blind eye to a little harmless fun for Alex's clients?'

Angie backed away.

'It wasn't harmless, it wrecked our best crop. God knows what damage a bunch of gung-ho shooters would've done. I *was* only a project for you, wasn't I? You're trying to fix *me* up, like we're fixing the cottage.' She spun on her heel, marching back to her car.

'God, Angie, I *am* your friend. Haven't I helped you crawl out from the brown and beige hole you were hiding in? Didn't I liberate you from those elastic-waisted jeans? Who texted you at 5 a.m. to remind you about our runs? I did it for *you*, Angie. Let's face it, you need someone to steer you in the right direction, or you'll spend your whole life getting dragged along in the current. With a bit of luck, the new and improved you will rub off on Claudia too, and she can bypass the awkward ugly-duckling stage you seem to have been stuck in for so long.'

The mention of Claudia was like a shot across the bow. Angie was tempted to upend the green smoothie over Bobbi's sleek hair. 'I was fine until you came into my life and insisted I needed fixing. Rob, Claudia and I were happy, content.'

Bobbi laughed sharply. 'Is *that* what you call it? You're like I used to be, Angie, you need someone to help you find your feet. And then, one day you'll pay it forward too.'

'I'm nothing like you,' Angie spluttered. 'I wouldn't presume to know what was best for my friends, or take them on as a *project*. I wouldn't try and bribe friends into covering up illegal activity. And I sure as hell wouldn't hesitate to help an injured animal.'

She turned and hurried back to the car.

Bobbi's voice called after her. 'Fine, go back to eating all those biscuits and cakes, and telling yourself you're setting a good example for your daughter. Turn your crappy old cottage into a dinky little—'

Angie spun around and held up a hand, cutting Bobbi off mid-sentence. 'Stop right there. Forget I even asked for help. You're not the person I thought you were.'

Forty-two

Rob threw the bike around corners, suddenly eager to get home, but his optimism faltered as he pulled into the driveway. Ange's car was gone, the shed was empty, and the caravan was empty too.

What do you expect, Jones? A hot lunch waiting on the table and a 'Welcome home' banner?

Rob plugged his lifeless phone into a charger and strode to the cottage, his mind fixed firmly on the job at hand. *Might not be able to put the apology part into play just yet, but I've sorted the money, I've cracked the feral pigs problem and I can start on the next step. Quicker I get this bathroom tiling underway, the quicker I'll be done with it.*

Rob forced himself to consider whether Angie had been right about his dad. Had John praised both him and Max equally, but never within their earshot? Max had made it sound like he'd been on the receiving end of John's criticisms too, instead of basking in a golden-child status like Rob remembered. *Did I blow it out of proportion?*

He mixed up a bucket of tile glue and thought about the way Max had helped him with the pigs, refining the video footage and scouring the scrub until they had enough evidence to nail Alex.

Haven't I just done the exact same thing as Max? Hidden the truth about money and then lied about it?

He measured and cut the first tile, swearing when it broke. He lined up a second one. *I didn't run all the way to South America, but still . . .*

He recalled the look Angie had given him when he'd ridden off.

Rob gritted his teeth and kept working. Only a quarter of the bathroom floor was tiled by the time he finished his bucket of glue, but at least it was a start. Apart from the memories it evoked, the gig wasn't quite as bad as he remembered.

What else had he forgotten over the years? And how could he expect Angie to accept his apologies when he was still too stubborn to accept Max's?

Angie drove distractedly. Bobbi's surprising rebuke, her own role in the chimney accident and Rob's sudden departure played on loop as she raced toward Warrnambool. At least Tessa had been more than willing to take the dog to the vet, and had given Angie a sympathetic hug and pep talk before she left Port Fairview.

Angie's phone vibrated on the passenger seat. She took her eye off the road to switch the call to speakerphone and nestled the phone in her bra. Last thing she needed was a fine for handling her phone while driving.

'Hey Angie, I just got your message. You okay? How's Rosa?' said Lara.

Angie flicked on her indicator and drove through the industrial estate towards Warrnambool's medical hub.

'I'm almost at the hospital.'

A motorcycle hurtled into Angie's rear-view mirror, the rider gaining on her as the bike weaved in and out of traffic.

Rob?

The bike screamed past—its speed, high-pitched engine and plastic fairings so different to Rob's vintage machines.

'How's Rob holding up?'

Angie's voice caught in her throat. 'We had an argument right before the accident, and he stormed out.' Angie let out a breath. 'I was so mad . . .'

Even though Lara was the least likely of her sisters to pry, Angie felt a sudden need to blurt out everything.

'I think we're done,' Angie said, the car jolting as she overshot the parking space and mounted the kerb.

'Maybe, maybe not. Do you really want it to be over?'

Angie leaned her forehead against the steering wheel. Lara's question sounded so simple, as if she could either overlook the gaping holes in their relationship or not.

'I don't see how we can come back from this. He didn't tell me about the money problems, didn't listen to me about the pigs or that damn chimney. You didn't see the way he looked at me, Lara. It was like . . . like he'd already made the break in his mind. Like I was already dead to him.'

'It's been a pressure cooker for you both though, hasn't it? His business, his brother, his mother, your dieting campaign, your friend Bobbi. I didn't see the way he looked at you today, but I saw how much he loved you at Christmas—it was like you accepting his quirky proposal made him the luckiest guy in the district.'

Tears pricked Angie's eyes. 'If Rob had listened to me from the start, the chimney wouldn't have come crashing down around us. What if it had been Claudia? What if the chimney had collapsed onto her? What if Rosa dies and it's all my fault?' Her voice dropped to a whisper as she twisted her engagement ring.

Lara's tone was unusually gentle when she answered. 'But it didn't collapse on Claudia. Rosa's a tough old duck. And I bet Rob will wish he'd listened to you too. I'm not a poster girl for happy relationships, God knows I haven't even thought about letting another man into my life since Sam, but I know you, Angie. And I think you need to work out how bad you want it. Is being right reason enough to walk away from everything you've created together? I can tell you've poured a lot of love, sweat and tears into that little cottage. If you ignore what I've said, that'll be completely fine too, because I'm your grumpy old sister, not a romance guru. But if it's any consolation, I think you two are good together, Ange.'

Angie signed off from the phone call, Lara's words resonating with each step she took towards the hospital.

Forty-three

Angie and Claudia rushed through the rabbit warren of hospital corridors, dodging visitors and doctors as they tracked down Rosa's room. Claudia launched herself into John's arms as soon as they found the right door, and Angie felt a renewed pang of guilt at the sight of Rosa.

Angie walked to her side, taking in the IV drip, the bandage around her head and the cords trailing out from under the sheets. Despite the dried blood and swelling across her face and upper arms, Rosa's expression was calm.

'Morphine's working a treat,' said John, clearing his throat. 'Doc found a pelvic fracture. Stable thankfully, or else they'd be airlifting her to Melbourne. The scan ruled out internal bleeding too, so she's had a lucky escape. Just the fracture, a broken leg and a few scratches.'

'A lucky escape?' Angie's words came out in a gasp. She squeezed her fingernails into her palm. 'I wish I'd never jumped on that tractor, wish I hadn't flown off the handle. You were almost killed, Rosa! I don't even know where Rob is to tell him, *what* to tell him . . .' Angie's breath caught in her throat. 'And I'm terrified it's too late.'

Rosa beckoned her closer. Angie felt the older woman clasp her fingers, even though the effort made Rosa wince. 'It's *never* too late, Angie. Not if you think you can make it work. John always tells me not to meddle, but I . . .' Rosa grimaced again. 'I thought I was helping.'

Angie squeezed her eyes closed before looking Rosa straight in the eye. 'I'm the one who should be apologising, Rosa. I'm so sorry.'

A nurse streamed into the room, flinging back the curtain that divided Rosa from the four other patients, her sense of purpose at odds with Angie's inertia.

What should I do? Rob was wrong to keep secrets. Rosa was wrong to interfere. But I was wrong too, holding Bobbi up on a pedestal, constantly comparing Rosa to Mum . . . and I'm the one who nearly killed somebody.

'How're your pain levels after that scan, Mrs Jones? Are you right for me to check your vitals?'

Angie tucked Claudia against her body as they watched the nurse clip a monitor onto Rosa's finger.

'Oxygen saturations and heart rate is on the improve, Mrs Jones. So, why were you dicing with a pile of bricks? The ambo said they toppled straight down on top of you. Lucky they didn't knock your head clean off your shoulders,' she said.

'Guess I just can't stay out of trouble,' Rosa said, with a small smile.

'Lucky it was a single fracture, not a double. A little bit of rest, a few days of analgesia and you'll be trotting around before you know it. Recovery will take a few months, but it's much better than multiple surgeries.'

Rosa's joke, and the nurse's sympathetic small talk, made Angie feel even worse.

This is my doing.

Angie smoothed Rosa's blankets.

John's brusque voice cut through the silence. 'A little birdie told me your interfering mother-in-law will be in hospital for a while, so maybe now's as good a time as ever to patch things up with Rob. I know he used to head up to Tower Hill for long hard thinks when he was in high school. Claudia can stay with us for a while if you want to go for a look?'

Angie nodded gratefully at John. She grabbed her keys; she had a chance to set things right.

Forty-four

Rob pulled the charging lead from his phone, staring at the multitude of missed calls and voicemail alerts.

Angie? Dad? Max ... Why was Max calling him, had he found more dirt on Alex Richardson?

He listened to the voicemails.

An accident.

The tractor.

The chimney.

Angie's garbled message played over in Rob's head as he raced around the back of the cottage, horrified to see a pile of rubble where the chimney and the chook house had once been. How had he missed that when he arrived home earlier?

Everything Angie had feared had come true. The pigs and now the chimney.

Rob averted his eyes as he ran past the cottage. Its perfect exterior seemed to mock him: he'd nearly pulled it off and then dropped the bundle at the last minute. He mightn't have been driving the tractor that brought the chimney down, but he was as responsible for his mum's broken bones as he was for his ruined relationship.

Forty-five

The drab grey walls and the stuffy air-conditioned rooms did little to ease Rob's pounding headache as he hovered by his mother's bedside. Rosa's arms were covered in cords and bandages, yet her voice was laden with concern for *him* as she spoke.

'Angie's out looking for you, Rob. Go find her. I'm fine here.'

'Fine? I wouldn't call a broken leg and a fractured pelvis fine. I made a mess of everything, Mum. I never thought the chimney would collapse, or believed the rumours about feral pigs. I thought I was doing the right thing insulating Angie from all the money stuff . . .'

Rob felt a hand on his shoulder and turned to see his dad standing beside him.

'No one expected you to have a crystal ball, son. Your mum's not going anywhere. So get out there, find Angie and settle this before it gets any worse. Sometimes words left unsaid can be just as harmful as things you wish you *hadn't* said.'

Rob scanned his father's weary face. He'd never heard him speak this way before. His mum had always been an open book, worrying about sibling rivalry, bending over backwards with helpfulness and enthusiasm, but not his dad.

The curtain divider fluttered open and Claudia rushed in, followed closely by Max.

'Daddy!'

His heart hitched as she flung herself into his arms. He swiped his eyes with the back of his hand, looking from Claudia to his mum, feeling the weight of his father's gaze and Max's proximity. Max always used to know what he was thinking, how he was feeling—could he feel it now?

Rob rose slowly then scooped Claudia onto his shoulders. 'Let's go find your mum, Claud.'

Max cleared his throat. 'I'll take her home if you don't want an audience? I brought Mum's car and the baby seat's still in the back '

Rob bit back the automatic rebuff—his instinct to scorn his brother's olive branch, as he'd done so many times before. He looked back at their mum, so fragile in the hospital bed. Her nod was tiny, but he knew what she was saying.

How can I ask Ange to forgive me if I can't do the same for Max?

Rob exhaled slowly and lowered Claudia to the ground.

'Thanks,' he mumbled, giving Max a nod, before realising the non-committal nod was one of his father's biggest cop-outs. Rob held out his hand. It felt like an eon passed as he waited for Max to shake it, but when he did, his brother's grip was strong, and Max's brief smile offered something Rob hadn't known he'd been seeking until then.

He kissed Rosa's forehead gently and almost gave his father another nod.

Bugger it. In for a penny, in for a pound, he thought, sticking out his hand.

His dad's handshake was strong, but his red-rimmed eyes were soft. 'Go get her, Rob.'

Forty-six

Rob flicked the kickstand down and leaped off the motorbike, his boots crunching on the gravel as he took the steps to the Tower Hill lookout two at a time.

Tourists clogged the uphill track, stopping to pose for photos with the spectacular wetlands. On this day of all days, the heritage-listed site seemed to be experiencing a flush of tourism. He weaved through the dawdling hikers and sightseers, breathless by the time he reached the top.

Blood thumped in Rob's ears as he scanned the site for Angie. *I'm too late.*

The disappointment was crushing. He lowered himself to a bench and rested his head in his hands, remembering the way they had parted. Of course it was over.

A cream-and-brown fuzz veered into his line of vision and he spotted one of the emu chicks marching across the path, looking as lost as he felt.

Another noise came from the bushes and Angie stepped out of the shrubs, twigs and wattle blossoms sticking to her dress and her hair. Her forehead was slick with sweat and there were dark patches on her flowery dress.

Blood? Sweat? His eyes flew over her, searching for any signs of injury, but all he could see was a rip in the fabric, exposing a pale but unscathed knee, and a small cut on her leg. He let out a quick breath. It was bad enough Rosa had been injured; he didn't know if his conscience could handle any more collateral damage.

He allowed himself another look at her face, finding not anger but relief in her bloodshot eyes.

'Cheeky emu chick wandered off. I was trying to shoo it back to the mother, but now she's gone off in a flap,' Angie said uncertainly, pulling a twig from her hair.

'It's actually the father. Emu fathers incubate the eggs and raise the chicks . . .' said Rob, trailing off.

Kookaburras sang in the trees as they watched the chick fossick in the dirt. A group of tourists came and went. All the while Rob steeled himself for a final goodbye. But instead, after a moment Angie sat down beside him.

He took a deep breath. 'You were right, you know. I should have listened to you, Ange, should have noticed the trajectory I set us on with the budgets. You were always so good at handling your salon accounts, I wanted to show you that I could be that guy too. I was so scared you'd drop me like a hot potato if you knew about the business Max and I lost before we'd even started it.' *Why did I ever think I could keep secrets in a town as small as Port Fairview?*

'And the chimney. You were right about the chimney and the pigs, too.'

Angie's arm was warm against his. The smile she gave him was weak, but in that moment, he knew the notion he could walk away from this woman was the stupidest idea he'd had all year.

He paused, trying to choose the words to set things right. 'Ange McIntyre, I love you more than anything in this world.

I know I've messed things up, but if you forgive me, I'll fix things, I swear.'

Angie kept her eyes on the water at the base of the crater as she spoke.

'I need to know you trust me, that you've got my back. I'm not perfect either, blind Freddy could see that, but it hurts being at the bottom of your priority list, somewhere below your mum and your motorbikes.'

Rob started to say something, then stopped. He cleared his throat, reaching into the top pocket of his jacket. He passed her the cheque he'd collected earlier.

Was it really just this morning? It feels like a week ago now.

'I've sold the bikes. There's a collector over in Linton who's been hassling me for years about buying them. Money should cover the rest of the renovations, and pay back Mum and Dad. And Brett said he'll take Violet, train her up and give us a bit of breathing space until we've got time for a dog. The goats can go on Gumtree. Hell, we can get rid of the calves and chickens if you want. I'm sorting this thing out with Max too.'

Rob held his breath as Angie pushed herself up from the seat, dusted the dirt off her backside and walked over to the lookout platform. He stood too, hanging back. Was it too little, too late? Sweat slicked the inside of his shirt, his jacket trapping the heat like a sauna. He stared at the volcano shell but instead saw the wasteland of his future.

You're a stuff-up, Jones. A failure.

The wind blew straight across from the Southern Ocean.

A plane flew overhead and a chorus of crickets and frogs erupted in the scrub below, but all Rob could hear was the silent weight of his relationship, teetering on a knife's edge.

Angie stared down into the volcano crater, grappling with her emotions. The wind had whipped up, and the sound of trucks on the highway below mingled with bird calls and rustling leaves.

Didn't you come here to apologise? Tell him you were wrong too. Lara's encouragement echoed in her ear.

But what if I change my mind again? What if I've already ruined it? She turned and took a step. Then another, blocking out the self-doubt telling her she wasn't good enough.

The closer she got to Rob, the harder she had to work to ignore her doubts. *I will stick this out. We are good together. We can make this work.*

Her phone vibrated in her pocket and Angie hesitated, hoping it would be the vet with news on Violet, or John with an update on Rosa.

'Angela, glad to catch you. The dahlia committee is holding an extra meeting—'

Angie's eyes locked with Rob's and she grimaced. 'Mrs Ellis, I'm in the middle of something. I'll call you back later.'

Mrs Ellis tutted down the phone line. 'But Angela, you need to come and fix this mess! The dahlia show is next week and I don't think—'

But instead of filling her with a sense of dread, the disapproving tone propelled Angie to do something she should have done months earlier. 'Not now, Mrs Ellis. I'm busy.'

She hung up the phone, feeling a weight lift from her shoulders, and walked towards Rob.

Forty-seven

'I'm so, so sorry for hurting your mum. If I could turn back the clock, I'd never have been so reckless . . . So . . . So stupid. It wasn't just you, Rob—I was wrong too. I thought if we could get the cottage renovated, that'd be it—we'd have the little family unit I'd always dreamed of, but it became easier to sink my energy into something I could control.'

Rob held his breath, not daring to interrupt. Angie's voice was soft and although Rob strained to hear over the birds and the breeze, her words gave him hope.

'The running, the diet, the new clothes. They were easy wins compared to getting the cottage finished, even though I fell off the bandwagon a few times. Bobbi seemed like the type of woman I could be if I knuckled down. Strong, fit, fearless.' Angie bowed her head. 'I went to see her. She didn't even try and deny the pig thing.'

He could see from her face how much it hurt her to tell him about her row with Bobbi. Part of him wanted to cheer; the other part wanted to draw Ange into his arms, tell her she shouldn't have had to put up with it in the first place.

'I'm sorry. I think we've both messed up. But . . .' She tripped over her words just as he had.

He stepped closer. 'I need to take the lion's share of the blame.'

She looked up, her eyes searching his, and he saw a hint of the McIntyre determination, the strength she didn't even seem to realise she had.

'No, I *need* to say this. I was wrong, too. I love you, Rob Jones. I can't imagine my life—our life—without you. Let's give it another crack. No third umpires for arguments, no secrets. And Violet can stay. Imagine all the snakes we'd get without her around.'

Relief rushed through his body and a smile twitched at his lips as he took in his beautiful fiancée.

The adult emu stalked back into the clearing, gathered up the wayward chick and hurried away again as another group of camera-wielding hikers appeared.

'You're a good dad, Rob. I might not say that enough, but it's true.'

She took a step closer, and he hugged her with all he had, scared by how close he'd come to losing it all.

Forty-eight

Angie kept one eye on the road ahead and one eye on Rob's motorbike in the rear-view mirror as they drove back home. Had she really almost lost sight of everything they'd been working toward?

She turned into Enderby Lane, drove past the bottlebrushes where Rosa had caught the ring-bearing calf and pulled into the driveway. She blinked away tears, focusing instead on the hand-painted sign Rob had made them, and their pretty little cottage beyond.

The motorbike rolled to a stop beside her. Angie stepped out of the car and into Rob's arms.

It's more than just building a house—we're building a life together, she thought as she laid her head against his chest, *and it's our story to write*. Not Bobbi's, not Rosa's, not Mum's. *Ours*.

'Head inside? I hate to ruin the moment, but I've got a mess of paperwork and accounts, and I'm hoping you might help me untangle it all.'

'Thought you'd never ask,' she said, standing on tiptoe to meet his kiss.

Rob showed her his makeshift accounting system, then left her to muddle through the paper trail as he fetched Claudia from next door. Angie felt like she'd barely made a dent on the paperwork, but when Rob walked back in with a sleeping Claudia in his arms, she had almost a page of notes.

Angie looked up from the computer as Rob set two mugs of tea on the table. She turned the laptop towards him as he sat down on the stool, and pointed to the spreadsheet she'd created.

'So, if we get in touch with all these clients, we should be able to ease the cash-block until everyone's paid their accounts. The hardware store will be the priority, but I think I've found a problem—you've paid for the O'Connells' marble benchtops twice.'

They spent the rest of the evening going over the business accounts together before drawing up a plan for the rest of the renovations, and when she fell into bed at midnight, it had never felt so good to have Rob lying beside her and Claudia snoring softly in her bunk.

'We're a good team, Ange. A really good team,' Rob said, pulling her tight. She fell asleep to the sound of Claudia's light snuffling, the roaring of the ocean, the arms of the man she loved wrapped around her and the knowledge that things would work out just fine.

Epilogue

Rob leaned against the milk vat, stripped off his green overalls and held out his hand for the other two pairs.

Max waved it away. 'My turn this week. You and Angie washed the overalls last week.'

John rolled his eyes and held out a hand. 'You're like a pair of old hens, clucking over the last piece of potato peel instead of grotty working dungas. I'll wash them, but don't think I'll be ironing them too,' said John, a hint of a smile on his face.

Rob stifled a yawn as he handed the overalls to his father. The 4.30 a.m. starts had taken some getting used to, but milking wasn't the chore he remembered from his teenage years.

'Gonna fry up some bacon and eggs if anyone's keen,' said John, as he closed the dairy door behind them.

Rob exchanged a look with Max, biting back a smirk. At least he had a valid prior appointment this morning. There were only so many rashers of charred bacon and rock-hard eggs a guy could stomach. John had picked up most of Rosa's jobs in her absence, but he was yet to nail cooking, no matter how many tips Rosa offered from her sickbed.

'Nah, I've got to be home to get Claud to preschool. Ange's got something on in town again. Probably more wedding stuff. But thanks anyway, Dad.'

He looked up as John shrugged. 'Maybe on the weekend then. Tell Claud I'll try not to burn hers this time.'

The border collies bounded over, with Violet hot on their heels.

All three of them leaned down and patted the dogs. Working together to fill Rosa's place was one thing, but for the first time in weeks, they weren't rushing away the second they'd stripped off their overalls.

It's time.

Rob took a deep breath, and nerves jangled his voice as he took a step closer to reconciliation.

'Might grab a hand from you on Saturday if either of you are free? Got all the stuff for the new chook shed but Ange breaks out in a rash every time she's within cooee of a feather.' Rob plucked a harlequin beetle off Rosa's pink David Austins as he waited for a reply. 'I can ask Brett if you're busy?'

John cleared his throat. 'Long as it's between nine and three, I can lend a hand.'

Max shoved his hands into his back pockets and rocked on his heels. 'Fine by me.'

Rob swung open the new gate he'd cut into the boundary fence. Angie was right, a gate was a better option than straddling the fence each and every time they walked between the two properties. He whistled the rest of the way home.

Angie pulled the ring tin out of the oven and sat it on Rosa's stovetop beside the tray of blueberry muffins. Claudia fidgeted on the stool beside her, itching to taste-test the goodies she'd help make.

'It's a bit hot now, Claud. But by the time we take Granny her tea in the sunroom, it should be perfect,' she said.

Claudia jumped down from her stool and fetched the small milk jug from the fridge. Angie set three muffins on the tray with a vase of pink roses and poured three cups of tea. She stirred the dairy-fresh milk with a knife so the cream dispersed evenly, adding extra to the littlest cup so that it was a child-friendly temperature, and popped paracetamol on a saucer beside a few slices of warm cake.

Claudia ran ahead, Baxter the stuffed dog under her arm, as she weaved through the kitchen, past the lounge room with its open fireplace and into the sunroom. Rosa set her craft project aside and patted the seat beside her.

'Careful of Granny's hip,' said Angie as Claudia rushed to Rosa's side.

'I'm tough as old boots, really. Takes a lot more than a few broken bones to keep me down for long,' said Rosa.

Angie nudged the embroidery out of the way and sat the tray on the coffee table. 'Don't tell John that, or he'll have you rounding up the cows and shifting irrigation pipes before you know it,' said Angie. She watched the woman's eyes track towards the dairy, a smile on her face.

'Couldn't have arranged it any better myself. With Max taking my place permanently, and Rob chipping in when he can, those boys *have* to get along. Who would've known I just needed to take myself out of action for a while to bring them closer together?

Rosa looked back at Angie. 'How's your special project coming along, Angie? Should I be buying you leathers for Christmas?'

Angie smiled. 'Operation Easyrider is done and dusted. It's been a learning curve to say the least, but the temporary licence is in my handbag, and it'll do the job until the official one arrives in the mail.'

Rosa beamed. 'Good, good. And what about you, poppet? How's your little cottage coming along?'

'My bedroom is all painted now, Granny. And I've got a big girl's bed,' said Claudia.

Angie updated Rosa on the house progress as she cut the cake. 'Recognise this recipe, Rosa? It's your coconut—'

'Cake. I'd be able to recognise this one blindfolded, Angie. Two cups of sugar, two cups of self-raising flour, two cups of milk and—' Rosa broke off, her eyes glinting as she tousled Claudia's hair. 'Can you remember the final ingredient, poppet? Two cups of . . . ?'

Angie sipped her tea as Claudia pondered the question.

'Coconut!' she said.

'You've got a little MasterChef on your hands there, Angie. By the time your kitchen's complete, she'll be able to bake that cake all by herself.'

Angie smiled and nodded. It had taken a few weeks to feel comfortable cooking in Rosa's kitchen, but now that her own ovens were in place, awaiting connection by the electricians, she realised she'd miss this. It wasn't the same as cooking in her mum's kitchen at McIntyre Park. It never would be; she'd been crazy to imagine that. She now understood there was no use trying to recreate the same bond between her and Rosa that she'd had with her own mum, or replicate the bond Rob and Rosa shared—but she had a feeling they were on the right track.

Rosa looked at her watch and tapped a finger to the side of her nose as she nodded at Angie. 'Don't you have to go into town and pick up the you-know-what?'

Angie's gaze went to the grandfather clock that had been passed down through the Jones family. It was almost 3 p.m.

She brushed the crumbs off her jeans and pressed a gentle kiss on Rosa's soft cheek. 'I do, thank you. Come on, Claudia, let's go pick up Dad's surprise,' she said.

Rob carried the bulging black rubbish bag across the yard and pushed it into the already overloaded garbage bin, trying to make it fit. He'd lost count of the number of times he'd swept the floors during the renovations, but knowing this would be the last rubbish bag full of building-related debris made him whistle as he walked back to the cottage. The duck-egg blue weatherboards looked almost slate grey after the recent sun showers and the purple irises Angie had planted in the front garden beds swayed softly in the breeze.

'Where do you want the table, Rob? Centre of the dining room or close to the window to catch more sunlight?'

Rob stepped aside to let Tim and Pete through. Lara and Diana marched past in convoy, a chair under each arm, and Rob's reply was cut off by Penny, who sat under the verandah, breastfeeding baby Lucy.

'I think Angie wanted it by the window so you've got easier access to those double doors,' Penny called. 'She can always shift it a little later if need be.'

He gave her a thumbs up, hoping his mum would manage to keep Angie occupied for as long as possible so the kitchen transformation would be complete by the time she returned. Angus strode past, a lamp in his hand, and then Max and John emerged from the hay shed, craning their necks at an awkward angle to see around the stacks of plastic storage containers they held.

'This is the last of the cooking stuff, son. I'll head over to the house and fetch Angie in a minute,' said John. Rob nodded at his father, taking one of his boxes and walking beside him across the lawn and into the cottage.

John paused at the verandah. 'I reckon you've done all right,' he said.

Rob smiled, knowing it was as close as he was likely to get to a glowing endorsement. They walked into the cottage together. Tessa stood on tiptoe, wiping the glass with a scrunched-up sheet of newspaper as Brett washed the north-facing window with a squeegee.

'Looking schmicko in here, guys. Thanks so much for helping out. I know it's not all finished yet, but I reckon this will make Ange's birthday pretty darn special,' Rob said.

Lara tossed him a shrewd look. 'It's not like you need wardrobes or painted doors to move in. She'll love it, trust me.'

A rough rumble sounded in the distance and Rob moved into the hallway, away from the happy chatter of friends and family moving furniture around and boxes of cutlery and crockery being unpacked into cupboards. The throaty sound grew louder and he headed for the front door, a smile almost splitting his heart in two at the sight in front of him.

An unmistakable swirl of red hair spilled from a motorbike helmet as his black-and-gold Harley-Davidson puttered along Enderby Lane. A little hand waved furiously from the sidecar.

So that was where Ange had been disappearing to so often. To get her motorbike licence?

How did she convince the collector to part ways with the rare motorcycle? Violet bounded up to the bike, her tail propelling her body as she greeted her owners. He could see the smile on Angie's face underneath the helmet visor. The two girls he loved most in the world, and the bike he thought he'd ridden for the final time, stood in front of the cottage that had almost torn them apart. He looked back to see the crowd amassed on the front verandah. Rob strode towards the bike, and took Angie's gloved hands in his, marvelling at the gutsy and gorgeous woman before him.

'Is there anything you can't do, Miss McIntyre?'

She grinned, and as he leaned down to kiss her, Rob knew he really was the luckiest guy in all of Port Fairview.

Angie tiptoed along the cottage hallway, relishing the feeling of freshly polished floorboards under her bare feet. She ran her fingers along the plaster, appreciating every hour that had gone into straightening, plastering and painting the walls.

She paused at Claudia's bedroom and gently pushed open the heavy timber door. Even in the dim glow of the night-light, the teddy bears and dolls looked quite at home lined up along the window seat, surrounded by unpacked boxes and a makeshift clothes rack.

Angie crept across the plush carpet and straightened Claudia's sheets. It had taken a lot of soaking and scrubbing, but she'd managed to remove Rosa's blood and the dirt from the patchwork blanket. Angie smiled as she watched the hand-embroidered animals rise and fall with each of Claudia's gentle breaths.

She pulled the door almost shut and slipped into the bathroom. Her reflection stared back at her as she stripped in front of the sparkling bathroom mirror.

Another year older, another year wiser. Isn't that how it goes?

Instead of glaring at her reflection for all of a second and then averting her gaze, Angie tried to see herself through Rob's eyes. Her conscience gave a snort of laughter, a negative internal voice quickly querying how many slices of Diana's carrot cake she'd eaten after the birthday dinner. *Ugh, this is useless,* Angie thought.

She was tempted to shower in the dark, but something inside her made her twist the light switch dimmer and look again. She saw the rounded hips that had carried a child, and let her fingers trace the faded red stripes covering much of her breasts and midriff. Angie smiled as she turned on the shower and her reflection softened in the steam.

You'll do, Angie McIntyre.

She hummed as she lathered her skin and scrubbed her face, wondering what Rob had planned for her final birthday surprise. Spending the first night inside their new cottage was reward enough, not to mention the top-of-the-line ovens he'd suprised her with in their beautiful new kitchen, but he had insisted her big day wasn't over yet. Spraying herself with the new perfume Lara had given her, Angie shrugged into the satin dressing gown from Penny and Diana, and fossicked in the cupboard for toothpaste.

Ah ha, she thought, pulling out a thin box. She laughed as she saw it was a ten-pack of pregnancy tests and hesitated before shoving it to the back of the drawer and locating the correct box. *Wait till tomorrow*, she told herself.

She walked to their bedroom, and pushed the unpainted door inwards. Candles flickered from the mantelpiece and the bedside tables. Rob lay in the middle of their linen bedspread, surrounded by dried rose petals. Music played on the stereo, not quite covering his gentle snores.

Angie grinned. *Who said romance was dead?*

She gently eased a framed photograph from underneath Rob's hand. The print was an enlargement of the family shot they'd taken for the Christmas cards, with the hand-painted sign and Bottlebrush Cottage in the background. She removed the purple ribbon and bow and sat it on the chest of drawers, next to a framed photo of all four McIntyre girls with Annabel. Just as she did every night, Angie lifted a finger to her lips and then touched it to her mother's image. Someday soon, when she and Rob had added a few more curly-haired youngsters to their tribe, she'd make sure she got a similar shot of them outside their handcrafted home.

Angie padded across the new carpet and closed the door, smiling at the garment bags that hung on the back. Hidden in plain sight behind Rob's only suit was a second garment bag, containing the most exquisite ivory lace dress and matching veil.

I'm going to knock his socks off next month, no doubt about it.

Acknowledgements

The biggest thanks of all must go to you, my fabulous readers, for picking up a copy of *Bottlebrush Creek* and spending time with the McIntyre family. I was blown away by the beautiful messages I received from *Wildflower Ridge* readers, so big hugs and virtual lemon meringue pies for everyone who read it and then took the time to leave a review, posted photos of it in the wild, spread the word and celebrated Penny's journey. I hope you have loved Angie's story just as much!

I started writing *Bottlebrush Creek* in early 2018 after finishing my first manuscript. At the time, we'd just moved into our owner-built home in country Victoria. The internal doors were unpainted, wardrobes were in the too-hard basket, and the dramas, frustrations and joys of our project were still fresh in my mind. Having lived and breathed owner–builder life for two and a half years, I knew the theme was ripe with potential. So, with my dad's advice to 'write what you know' echoing in my ears, I set to work throwing the kitchen sink at poor Angie McIntyre and shining a light on the challenges faced by many owner–builder couples. To all the other owner–builder ladies out there—this one's for you!

I also loved weaving a few personal snippets into the story. Two motorbikes in the book are based on beloved bikes from my dad's collection, the funny footage captured in the forest is similar to a real incident captured in a friend's paddock, the scene where Angie unloads a pallet of tiles is one hundred per cent memoir (although I've embellished the delivery driver), and I've pinched the name Enderby Lane from the South Australian town of Millicent and inserted it into a fictional town similar to beautiful Port Fairy. Aside from this, *Bottlebrush Creek* is a complete work of fiction and any errors are mine.

My name might be on the front cover of this book, but plenty of work went on behind the scenes. Thanks to Karena, Katrina, Tony and Heather for being super neighbours, always chatting books and offering up possible plot lines over the fence, Larissa Gardiner for being a dairy-farming goddess, Stu and Amy Silvester for answering my hobby-farm queries, Kate Griffith again for her nursing prowess, my dad for his motorbike tips and Alistair Harkness at Federation University for his insights into feral pig behaviour. And also a nod to my English teacher, Alistair Minty, for his steady guidance throughout high school, and the beautiful crew from Tantanoola Primary who supported my debut book release just like they supported me as a student.

It's been a pleasure working with my publisher Annette Barlow again, and her fantastic A&U team including Jenn, Samantha, Yvette, Aziza and Emma, cover designer extraordinaire Nada Backovic, and the clever marketing and publicity team. It tickles me pink to see the story in my head come to life in the hands of such a professional and polished team.

I've been lucky to find a vibrant writing community in Romance Writers of Australia, particularly Kaneana, Jayne, Suzie, Fiona, Alli, Rachael, Victoria and Cathryn. An extra special shout-out for early readers Amber and Lindy Sloan,

Pamela Linnell, Karen Nancarrow and Julie Linnell. Your faith in Angie and Rob's story is much appreciated.

Support from family, friends and neighbours has been incredibly humbling. Thanks for cheering me on, sharing my excitement, travelling to launches, buying books, urging friends/parents/siblings/children/colleagues to buy books, quizzing me on book-related progress, writing reviews, taking my books on holidays and helping steer my author dream in the right direction. I am eternally grateful!

Thanks to the librarians and booksellers who stock and recommend my novel, throw open their doors after hours in the middle of winter for book launches and make me feel like a real author by asking me to sign copies. Cheers to the book reviewers, bloggers, journalists, podcasters and Insta-friends flying the *Wildflower Ridge* and *Bottlebrush Creek* flags. The McIntyre family and I are thrilled to have you in our cheer squad.

My three bookworms, Charlie, Amelia and Elizabeth—thanks for keeping me accountable with encouraging notes, beautiful drawings that were way too pretty to be made into book covers, and minimal complaints about being dragged across the countryside for so many book talks.

Jason—thanks for every road trip spent nutting out plot holes, in-depth discussions about completely fictional scenarios, your endless supply of Aussie colloquialisms, teaching me that hard yakka is always worth it, and doing the very last read-through with me.

Mum and Dad—all kids want their parents to be proud of them, so thanks for encouraging me every step of the way. Readers—if you bumped into a beaming five-foot lady and a tall bearded chap in a cowboy hat at a bookstore last year, and then walked away with a copy of my book pressed into your hands, you met my proud folks.

I love connecting with readers, so please head over to my website www.mayalinnell.com for book tour details, news and snippets from my writer, baker, green-thumb life. Happy reading!

Much love,

Maya

Read on for the first chapter
of Maya Linnell's new novel,
Magpie's Bend.

Magpie's Bend

Lara McIntyre and journalist Toby Paxton are thrust
into the limelight when an accident puts the beating
heart of their community in jeopardy.

The small country town of Bridgefield can't
manage without their general store and post office,
but Lara can't stomach the idea of out-of-town buyers
running it into the ground either.

With the help of the close-knit community, they
rally together to try to save the shop. Featuring a
black-tie ball, a fun run, a magpie called Vegemite
and a snake-chasing kelpie called Basil, *Magpie's
Bend* is a story about rural lives, family, love and
letting go.

One

Lara McIntyre charged through the front door of the Bridgefield General Store and headed straight for the postcard display.

As a kid she'd delighted in the store's one-cent lollies; through her teen years she'd posted letters to her pen pals and ordered countless hot pies and cold drinks; and she had bought more bread, milk and newspapers than she could remember—but never before had she browsed the postcard range.

In fact, Lara decided, wiping the layer of dust from the panoramas of mountains, sheep-filled paddocks, the sun setting over Bridgefield Lake, it seemed like nobody had browsed the postcard range in decades.

She chose one featuring the Grampians Mountain Range and headed to the counter, certain the memento would put a smile on her daughter Evie's face when it arrived at her fancy city boarding school.

The pie warmer glowed and cricket commentary blared from the radio, but there was no sign of the town's postmistress or her wayward nephew who helped run the shop.

Lara craned her neck to see into the back room.

'Mrs Beggs?'

Lara called out again. It still felt a little odd to not be standing on the other side of the counter serving, as she had done all through her teens. 'Mrs Beggs?'

Nothing.

She sniffed, trying to identify the strange smell. *And what was that crackling noise?*

Lara felt a prickle of apprehension. She dumped her postcard and keyring on the counter and rushed into the shop's kitchen.

A well-worn novel lay on the tea-room table, next to a half-drunk mug of tea and an empty egg carton. Eggs jumped in the now-dry saucepan, not just hard boiled but burned beyond redemption. Lara switched off the stovetop and opened a window to disperse the acrid smell.

'Mrs Beggs? Winnie? Dallas?'

Sweeping into the cluttered storeroom, Lara kept her voice calm. She gulped when she spotted a black shoe beside a pile of boxes.

Her nursing instincts kicked in. She quickly assessed the situation.

If it wasn't for the arm twisted behind her, or the blood seeping from a wound on her cheek, Mrs Beggs could have been sleeping. She and Evie had both joked about being buried alive in Mrs Beggs' storeroom during their years at the shop, but the sight of those boxes resting awkwardly on the postmistress's chest wasn't the least bit funny.

Lara crouched down, gently trying to rouse her.

'Mrs Beggs, are you okay? Mrs Beggs?'

Toby Paxton whistled as he locked the newspaper building. The decrepit offices of the *Bridgefield Advertiser* were a far cry from *The Ballarat Daily*'s bustling newsroom, but there was a charm to the heritage-listed building. The small farming community had a similar allure, and the 5 p.m. knock-offs were a pretty good perk of the job too.

He pulled on his bike helmet and cycled to the general store, sniffing as he opened the large glass door. The old-fashioned doorbell jangled and the strange smell grew stronger.

Maybe the pie warmer's on the fritz?

Toby grabbed a lonely bottle of soy milk from the fridge, plus a handful of bananas, and placed them on the counter, eyeing a seemingly forgotten set of car keys.

'Hello?'

Normally the shopkeeper was eager to greet each customer, the potential for local gossip quickening her movements, but not today. Mrs Beggs was too wide to hide behind the rack of birthday cards or disappear between the shelves of over-priced groceries. Her assistant, Dallas, was nowhere to be seen either. Toby scanned the bright little general store, normally pumping with customers but now eerily quiet. *Something's burning . . .*

His thoughts were interrupted as a slender woman rushed out from the back of the store. Her hair was scraped up into a high ponytail and there was a symmetry to her features that would look striking in black and white. He couldn't quite make out the logo on her monogrammed shirt, but whoever she was, she didn't look like she was here to serve pies or hand over his mail.

'Hurry, I need a hand back here,' she called, retreating without waiting for an answer. Toby automatically reached into his camera bag, then hesitated.

You're not in the city anymore.

He pulled out the Nikon anyway.

Lara cleared the boxes and pressed a tea towel against the wound on the older woman's cheek.

'Mrs Beggs, Winnie, can you hear me? It's Lara. We're going to get you to hospital,' she said as footsteps clattered down the hallway. Lara spoke over her shoulder, firing out instructions to the customer buying fancy milk.

'Do you have a mobile? I've left mine in the car. Can you call an ambulance? And flick the door sign to closed. We don't need somebody running off with the till while she's crashed out here. And a blanket if you can find one,' said Lara, checking the pulse again.

Weaker than she would have liked.

'Hang in there, Mrs Beggs,' she said, her concern growing at the postmistress's vague murmurings.

'I've got a delivery coming, Annabel . . . Christmas specials . . . Down by the lake, I said.'

Lara swept the curls off Mrs Beggs' forehead and pushed a small step-ladder aside to give her more space.

'It's Lara McIntyre, not Annabel,' she said gently. 'And Christmas has been and gone, Mrs Beggs.' Whatever box had knocked Mrs Beggs down, it had done a good job of it. Annabel McIntyre had passed away almost twenty years ago, when Lara and her sisters were in high school. Although Lara had the same pale skin, straight teeth and glossy auburn-blonde hair, it was rare for anyone to mistake her for her mother, especially Mrs Beggs, who had been Annabel's best friend and a strong, warm presence in Lara's life as long as she could remember.

The man returned with a mobile. He crouched down beside her, draping a tablecloth over Mrs Beggs. In the midst of the chaos, Lara noticed the gap between his shoes and his trousers: one sock was blue and the other featured colourful cartoons.

'What's happened? Should we sit her up?'

What type of idiot is this guy? Lara spun around and fixed him with a withering glare, first noticing the camera slung around his neck, then the bicycle helmet he wore, and finally the deep black eyelashes that belonged on a jersey cow, not a man.

Of all the people to walk into the general store when she needed help, did it have to be a cyclist with no idea of first aid who couldn't even match his socks? Even Mrs Beggs' inept nephew, Dallas Ruggles, would be more helpful than this bloke.

She looked at him again, placing his face. The new journalist in town. 'Brilliant, the paparazzi's here. Call the ambulance already!'

She kept one eye on him and one on Mrs Beggs, wishing he would move a little faster. He toyed with the camera strap as he spoke with the emergency operator.

'We've got a woman injured at the Bridgefield General Store. Hmm, not sure. Hang on.' He turned back to Lara.

'Her condition?'

'Dropping in and out of consciousness. Deformed right shoulder, possibly dislocated or fractured. Pulse is weak, with an open wound to her cheek. I think she's been down for about ten minutes or so. Tell them I'm a nurse.'

He repeated the information, then added his own. 'We're in Bridgefield, western Victoria. Um . . .' He looked at Lara. 'Street number?' Then shook his head. 'It's the only shop in the main street. Stripy verandah. Old bluestone. Trust me, the ambos won't miss it.'

He bobbed his head. 'They're on their way,' he said, shoving the phone into his pocket.

Mrs Beggs groaned. 'I'm going to be sick.'

'Let's make you more comfortable,' said Lara, helping roll her onto her side. The arm dangled awkwardly. Lara couldn't leave it like that. 'This might hurt a bit,' she said, repositioning Mrs Beggs' arm and shoulder as carefully as she could.

Mrs Beggs' breathing accelerated, and she gave a sudden shudder before going limp.

'She all right?' Toby crouched down beside them.

'I think she'll be fine until the ambulance gets here, it's just the pain,' said Lara tersely.

Lara worked on autopilot, blocking out the cluttered room and the tall reporter. She splinted Mrs Beggs' arm to immobilise the shoulder, and dressed the wound on her cheek, all the while keeping an eye on her pulse and breathing. She was used to handling patients and emergencies, yet she still breathed a sigh of relief when the paramedics filed into the storeroom.

Lara followed as they stretchered Mrs Beggs out of the store. She was surprised to find the sun still high in the sky, and fluttered her shirt to get some air on her clammy skin. A crowd formed in the street, locals unashamedly jostling for a better view.

'You've done well, Mrs Beggs.' Lara gently squeezed the older woman's good hand before she was loaded into the ambulance.

A light touch on her shoulder made Lara jump. She whirled around.

It was the newspaper guy, camera still dangling around his neck, his bike helmet now sitting at a jaunty angle.

'You've done well too,' he said kindly. 'You saved her life in there.'

'Anyone with basic first-aid skills would have done exactly the same,' Lara said, dismissing the praise.

He stuck out a hand. His smile was lopsided, which added a boyish charm to his closely cropped hair and carefully pressed clothes.

No wonder Mrs Beggs was singing his praises the other week. Half of Bridgefield's divorcees probably had designs on him already.

'Toby Paxton.'

Lara shook his hand quickly but firmly.

'Lara McIntyre.'

'Pleased to meet you, Lara. I got some great photos of you in action.'

Lara's stomach dropped.

What?!? She spoke through gritted teeth. 'Delete them. Now. Every bloody one of them.'

Alarm flashed across his face as she reached for the camera. He covered the Nikon protectively.

'I wasn't going to put them in the paper or anything. Well, not unless you and Mrs Beggs give the all-clear. They're great pictures. Don't you even want to see them?'

Like hell she did. She knew firsthand that nothing good ever came from sneaky photography.

'Unless you fancy joining Mrs Beggs in the back of that ambulance, you'd better hit delete.'

A long run and a hot shower beckoned, but Lara stood her ground and waited as Toby fiddled with his camera.

'Done,' he said quietly, twisting the camera monitor to her.

She peered at the screen, still seething. *The cheek of him.*

At her terse nod, he loaded the Nikon into a padded bag and slung it over his shoulder. 'I'll see you around.'

Lara watched him cycle away, then scanned the crowd, her frown deepening as a familiar Hawaiian-shirted man made his way towards her.

Dallas Bloody Ruggles.

'Bit of action in the street, eh? What did I miss?'

The man's eagerness was almost as off-putting as the strong cologne and cheap button-up he wore.

'Your aunt's on her way to hospital, which you'd have noticed if you were actually at work.'

Dallas gaped. He whirled around to see the ambulance disappear around the corner.

'No way? What happened? Is she okay?'

She caught his guilty glance towards the pub.

Putting another flutter on, I'll bet.

Lara narrowed her eyes. 'I don't know. But I'm sure she would have appreciated your help.'

Dallas followed her into the general store.

'Guess I'll lock up, then?' he said, the note of uncertainty in his voice making it clear that he was not normally given such responsibility.

Lara collected her belongings as well as Mrs Beggs' handbag, and shrugged off the temptation to watch Dallas close up the shop for the night, just to be sure. It wasn't until she was halfway home that she realised she'd left Evie's postcard on the shop counter. And not only that, but for the first time in months, she'd spent two whole hours without dwelling on the Evie-shaped hole in her life.

Bridgefield Lake appeared, vast and glinting in the sunlight, as Toby crested the dusty hill. The Grampians Mountain Range was mirrored in the water, along with fluffy clouds that were more for show than actual rain-delivery purposes. Windmill Track wasn't the most direct route home—it would have taken him five minutes in the car as opposed to thirty-ish minutes on the bike—and the hill was a killer on the way up, but the view across the lake and paddocks was worth it.

The old windmill at the top of the track creaked and groaned as Toby stopped to catch his breath.

The view was postcard perfect compared to the old commute. The streets of Ballarat and Melbourne's laneways held their own appeal, but he didn't miss the traffic fumes or crazy drivers. The past two months in his new home had instead been filled with colour and sound and wildlife of one kind or another, which suited him just fine.

He coasted down the hill, finally arriving at the cottage he leased. The lawn he'd mowed the night before looked sharp, and he could see it had flourished after last month's Weed 'n' Feed.

Parking his bike in the small shed, Toby strolled inside, pleased he'd made the effort to do a quick whip around before he'd left for work that morning. He liked it neat and tidy. Especially on the weekends his daughter, Holly, came to stay.

She'll be here within the hour, he realised, looking at his watch. He stashed Holly's soy milk in the fridge, gently placed his camera bag on the table and started fixing dinner. Before long, a bowl of pizza dough was rising on the windowsill, pizza toppings were diced and he was pouring himself a glass of Coonawarra red.

As the one-man-band running the town's weekly newspaper, every workday was different. Today's articles had taken him to the cattle sales, the primary school, a new farm-gate business, and the town's newly resurfaced netball courts all ready for the upcoming season. He loved the broad scope of his work. Small-town news stories and country articles were a nice change from front-page fatalities, although today at the shop . . .

He sipped his wine. It had been the most action he'd seen since he arrived in Bridgefield.

Lara McIntyre. The name rang a bell. Same surname as the father and daughter at the saleyards that morning. The woman buying cattle had similar features, but her smile had been quick, and she'd happily posed for a picture. Lara, on the other hand, hadn't even glanced at the photos he'd taken before ordering him to delete them. *What was with that?*

Toby was googling recovery software, trying to work out whether he could retrieve the deleted pictures—*Just for a look, then I'll format the memory card*—when a small, sleek car inched down his driveway. He strode across the kitchen, taking the front steps two at a time.

'Dad!'

Holly jumped out of the car before it was properly parked. She launched herself into his arms the way she'd done as a little girl, smelling like vanilla body spray and chewing gum and feeling taller than when he'd hugged her last. He squeezed her tight, rocking her from side to side before straightening his arms to get a good look at her. She turned away, suddenly a fifteen-year-old again.

'Hey Lollypop, how's my girl?'

'Daaa-ad,' Holly always protested at the nickname, but he knew she secretly liked it. He kissed the top of her head and slung an arm around her shoulder.

'You'd better hope the wind doesn't change, Holly,' said Petra as she leaned out the car window. Toby waved to his ex-wife, trying not to be offended by the glare she reserved just for him.

What now? Knowing Petra, it could be anything, from the blue polo shirt he wore—identical to another eight in his wardrobe—to her longstanding disappointment that he dared to cope, quite well, in fact, without her. Or, quite possibly, it was something completely new.

'How's things?'

Petra's face clouded with irritation at his cheerful greeting. 'Fine.' Her forehead hadn't creased, her eyes hadn't wrinkled, but there was no mistaking her grouchy tone.

Toby folded his arms across his chest, resisting the urge to groan aloud. There was no good response to that one. He backed away to retrieve Holly's luggage from the boot, trying not to dwell on the rapidly changing contours of his ex-wife's face. Petra might be thrilled with her new, 'improved' image but it was a far cry from the natural look he'd once fallen in love with.

Petra stayed in the car. She blew a kiss to her daughter, then fixed Toby with another icy glare. 'Make sure she does her homework, and can you please talk some sense into her about clarinet lessons? She'll never get into the school orchestra if she doesn't practise.'

Toby spotted Holly discreetly pushing the instrument case back into the car boot, and only just managed to keep a straight face.

'Nice seeing you too, Petra. I'm grand, thanks for asking. You coming in or heading straight back to Ballarat?' They all knew the answer, but he wanted Holly to see at least one of them making an effort.

Standing together, father and daughter waved until the car disappeared out of sight. 'She won't be happy when she realises you "forgot" your clarinet,' Toby said wryly.